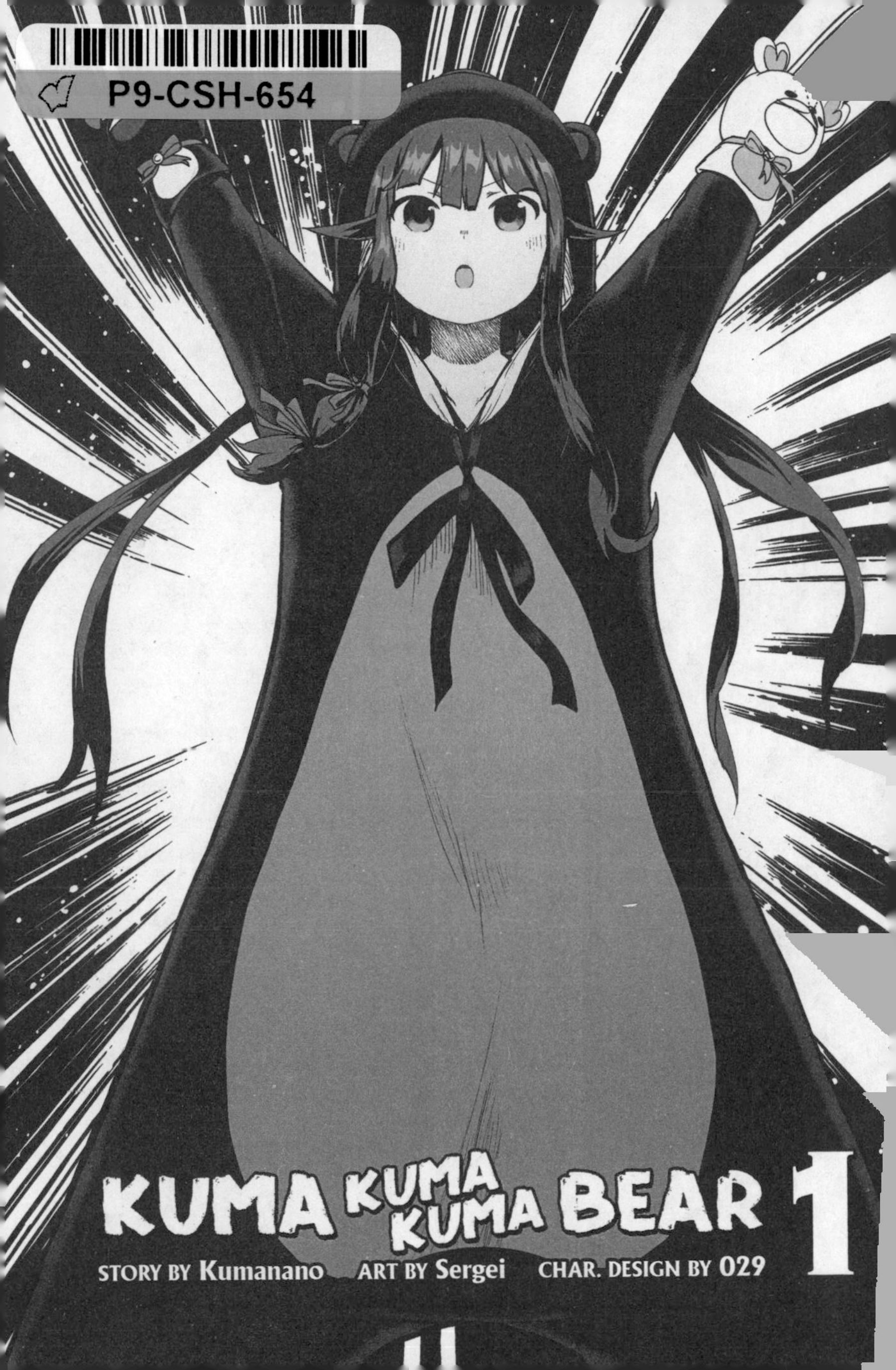

KUMA KUMA KUMA BEAR 1

STORY BY Kumanano ART BY Sergei CHAR. DESIGN BY 029

CONTENTS

Chapter 1 ·············· 3

Chapter 2 ·············· 17

Chapter 3 ·············· 35

Chapter 4 ·············· 52

Chapter 5 ·············· 67

Chapter 6 ·············· 83

Chapter 7 ·············· 99

Chapter 8 ·············· 115

Chapter 9 ·············· 131

Chapter 10 ·········· 147

Short Story: Yuna's Story ·································· 165

Bonus Manga ·· 170

KUMA KUMA KUMA BEAR
VOLUME. 1

Chapter 1

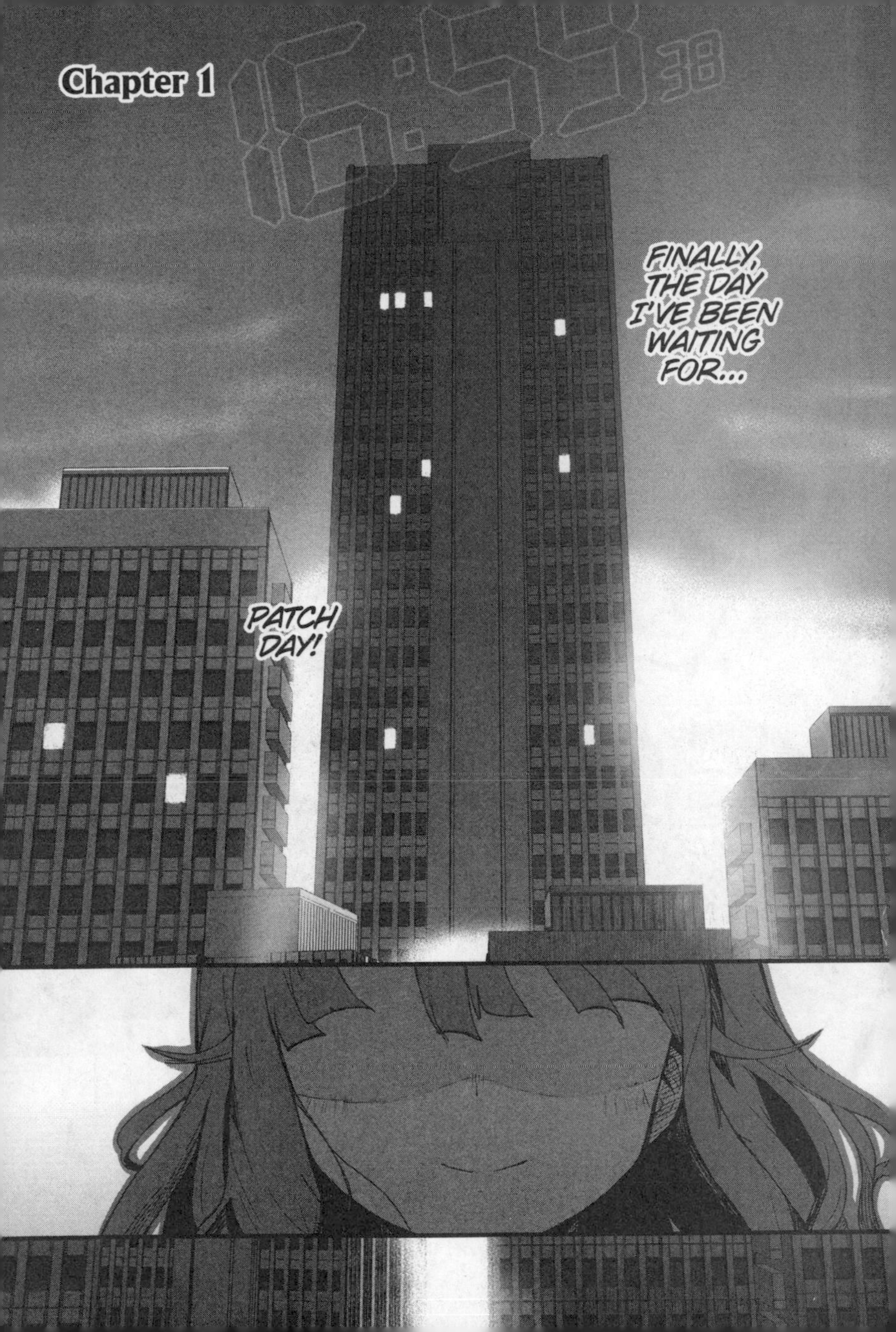
FINALLY, THE DAY I'VE BEEN WAITING FOR...
PATCH DAY!

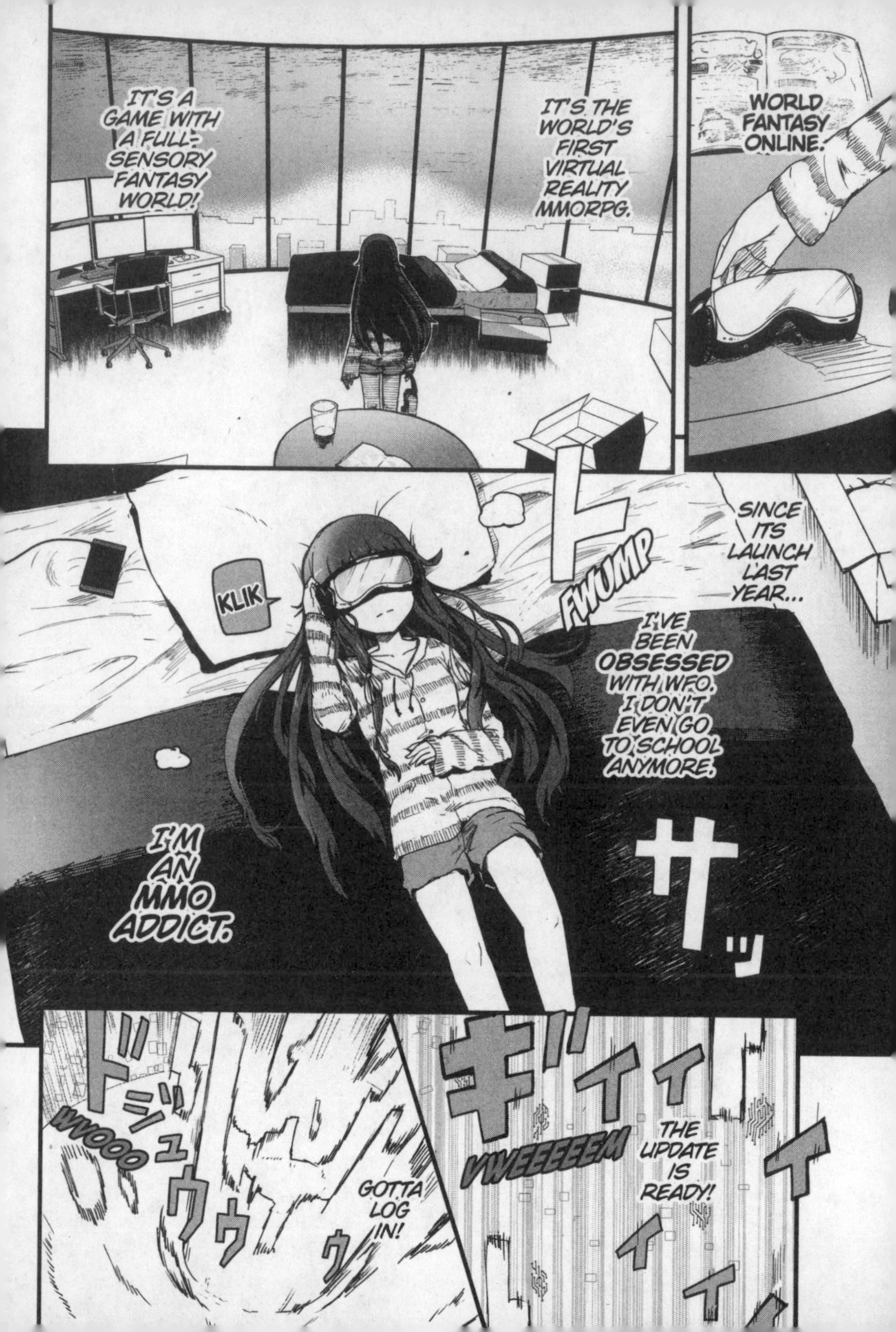
WORLD FANTASY ONLINE.
IT'S THE WORLD'S FIRST VIRTUAL REALITY MMORPG.
IT'S A GAME WITH A FULL-SENSORY FANTASY WORLD!
SINCE ITS LAUNCH LAST YEAR...
FWUMP
KLIK
I'VE BEEN OBSESSED WITH WFO. I DON'T EVEN GO TO SCHOOL ANYMORE.
I'M AN MMO ADDICT.
VWEEEEEM
THE UPDATE IS READY!
GOTTA LOG IN!
WVOOO

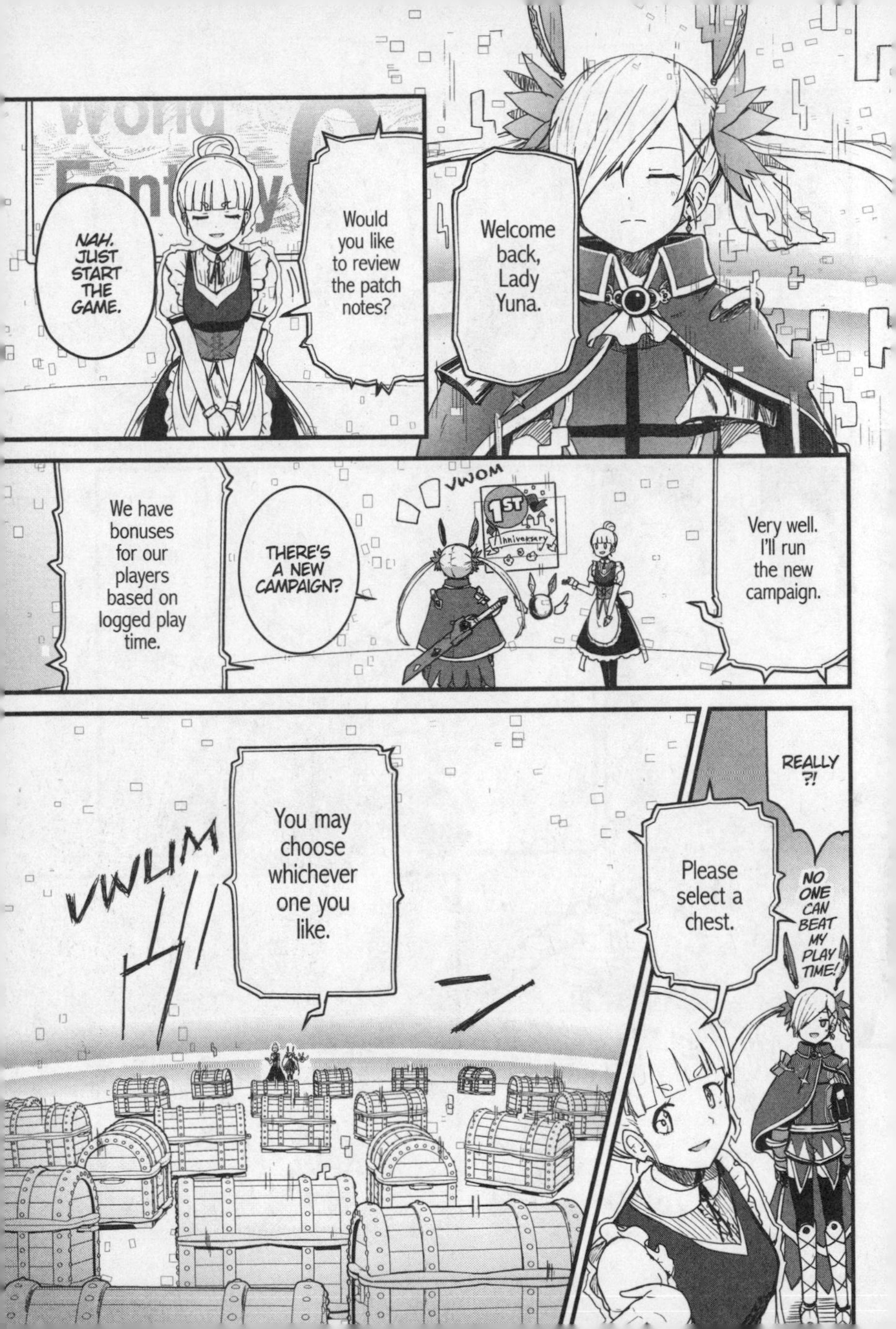
Welcome back, Lady Yuna.
Would you like to review the patch notes?
NAH. JUST START THE GAME.
Very well. I'll run the new campaign.
VWOM
1ST Anniversary
THERE'S A NEW CAMPAIGN?
We have bonuses for our players based on logged play time.
REALLY ?!
NO ONE CAN BEAT MY PLAY TIME!
Please select a chest.
You may choose whichever one you like.
VWUM

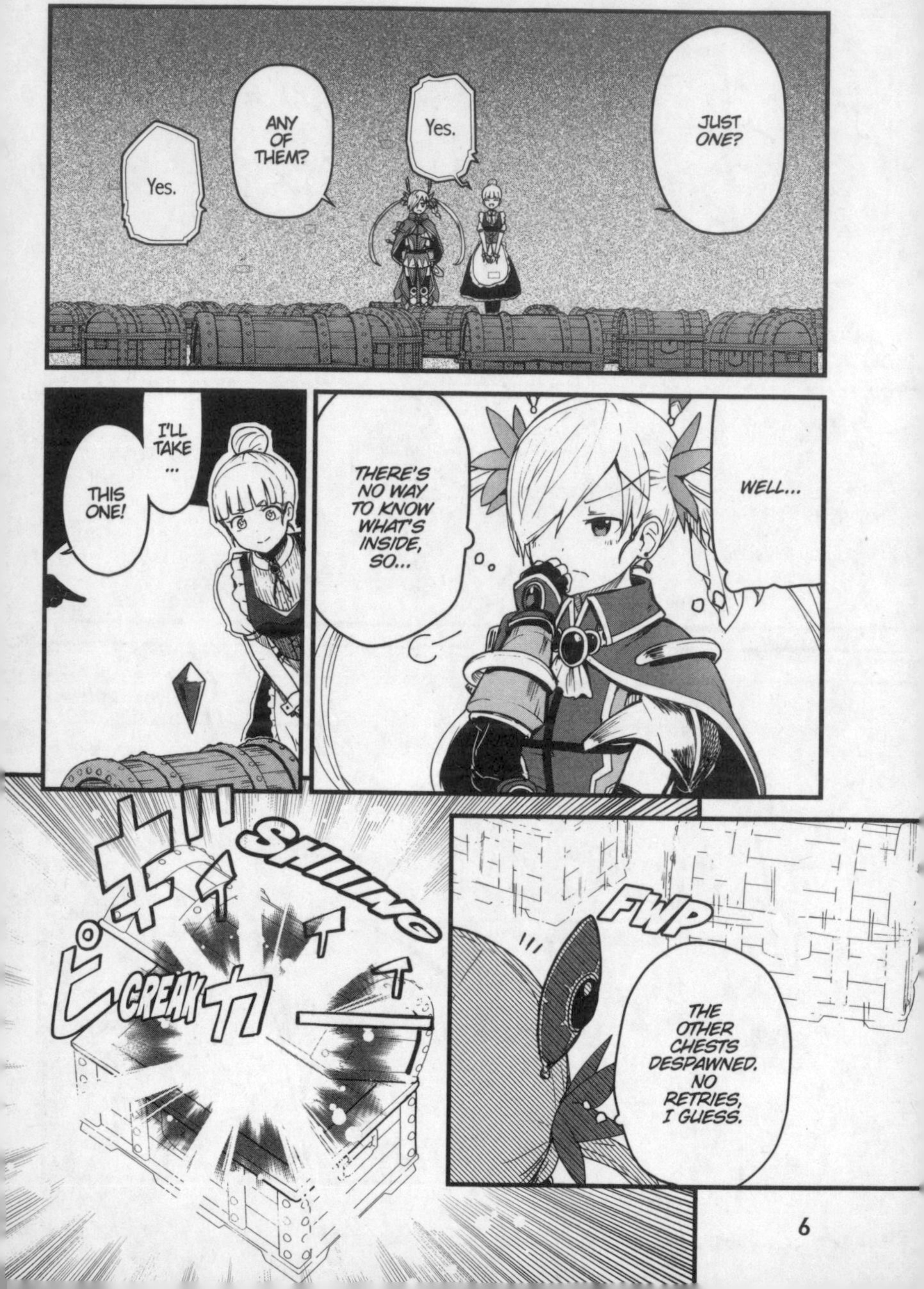
JUST ONE?
Yes.
ANY OF THEM?
Yes.
WELL...
THERE'S NO WAY TO KNOW WHAT'S INSIDE, SO...
I'LL TAKE ...
THIS ONE!
FWP
THE OTHER CHESTS DESPAWNED. NO RETRIES, I GUESS.
SHIIING
CREAK

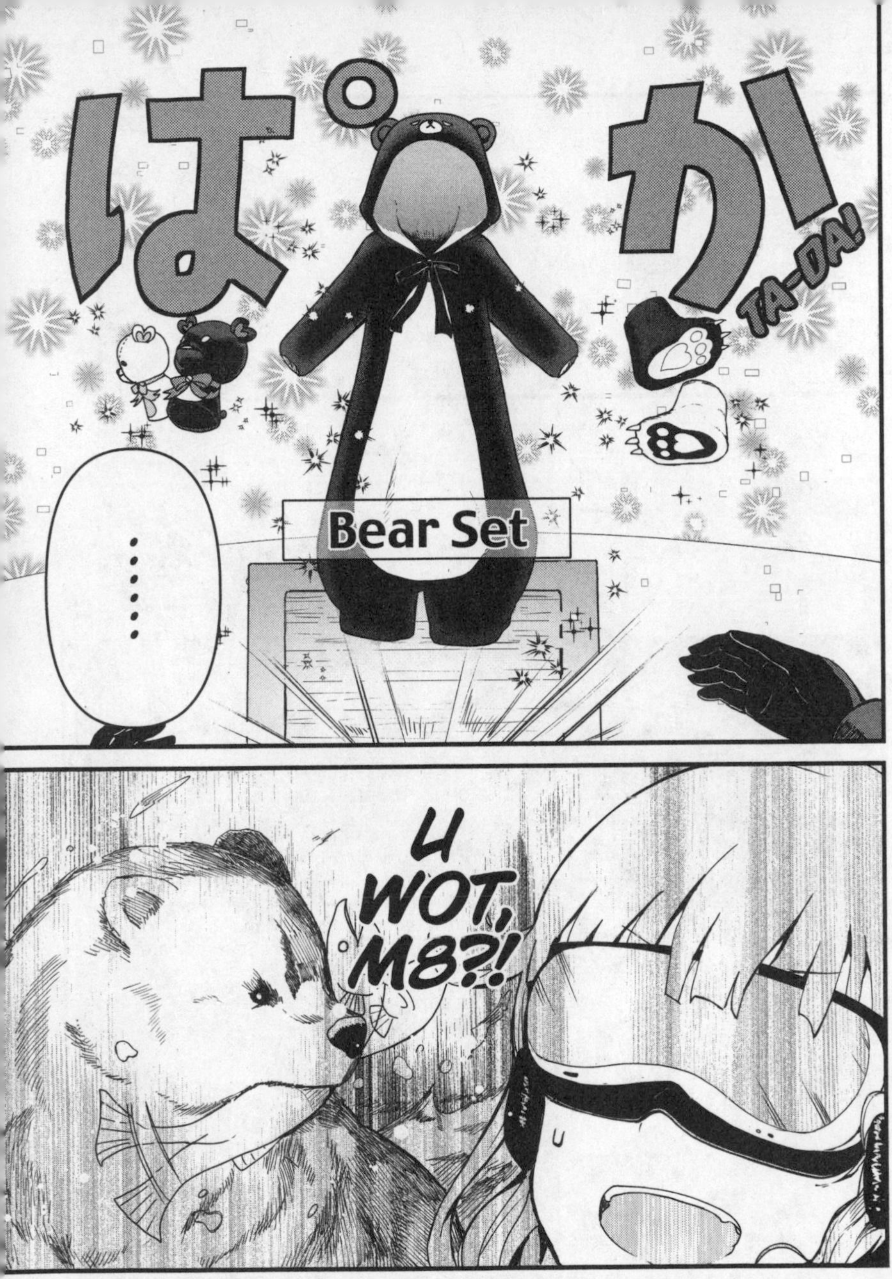
ぱか!
TA-DA!
Bear Set
......
U WOT, M8?!

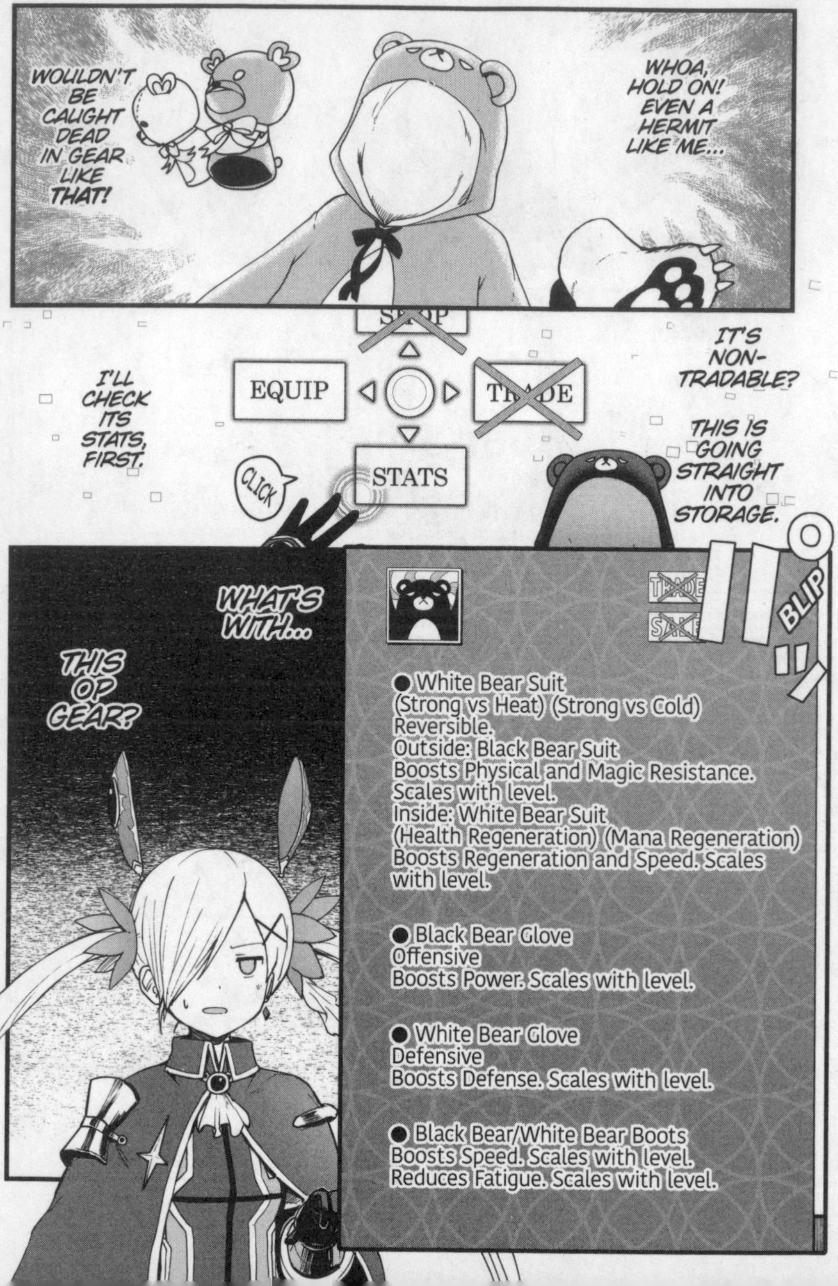
WHOA, HOLD ON! EVEN A HERMIT LIKE ME...
WOULDN'T BE CAUGHT DEAD IN GEAR LIKE THAT!
IT'S NON-TRADABLE?
THIS IS GOING STRAIGHT INTO STORAGE.
EQUIP
TRADE
STATS
I'LL CHECK ITS STATS, FIRST.
CLICK
BLIP
TRADE
SALE
● White Bear Suit
(Strong vs Heat) (Strong vs Cold)
Reversible.
Outside: Black Bear Suit
Boosts Physical and Magic Resistance.
Scales with level.
Inside: White Bear Suit
(Health Regeneration) (Mana Regeneration)
Boosts Regeneration and Speed. Scales with level.
● Black Bear Glove
Offensive
Boosts Power. Scales with level.
● White Bear Glove
Defensive
Boosts Defense. Scales with level.
● Black Bear/White Bear Boots
Boosts Speed. Scales with level.
Reduces Fatigue. Scales with level.
WHAT'S WITH...
THIS OP GEAR?

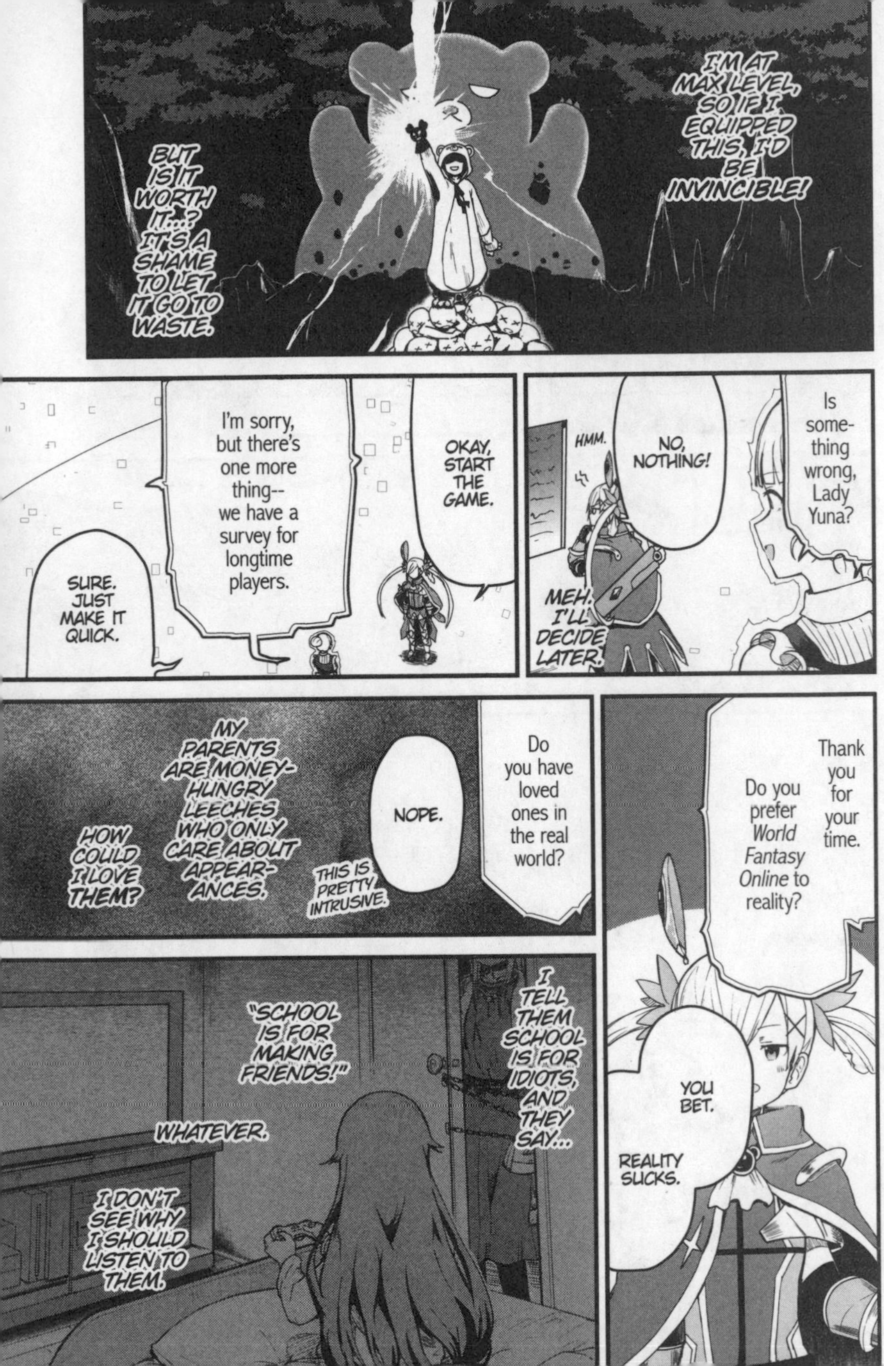
I'M AT MAX LEVEL, SO IF I EQUIPPED THIS, I'D BE INVINCIBLE!
BUT IS IT WORTH IT...? IT'S A SHAME TO LET IT GO TO WASTE.
Is something wrong, Lady Yuna?
NO, NOTHING!
HMM.
MEH. I'LL DECIDE LATER.
OKAY, START THE GAME.
I'm sorry, but there's one more thing-- we have a survey for longtime players.
SURE. JUST MAKE IT QUICK.
Thank you for your time.
Do you prefer *World Fantasy Online* to reality?
YOU BET.
REALITY SUCKS.
Do you have loved ones in the real world?
NOPE.
THIS IS PRETTY INTRUSIVE.
MY PARENTS ARE MONEY-HUNGRY LEECHES WHO ONLY CARE ABOUT APPEARANCES.
HOW COULD I LOVE THEM?
I TELL THEM SCHOOL IS FOR IDIOTS, AND THEY SAY...
"SCHOOL IS FOR MAKING FRIENDS!"
WHATEVER.
I DON'T SEE WHY I SHOULD LISTEN TO THEM.

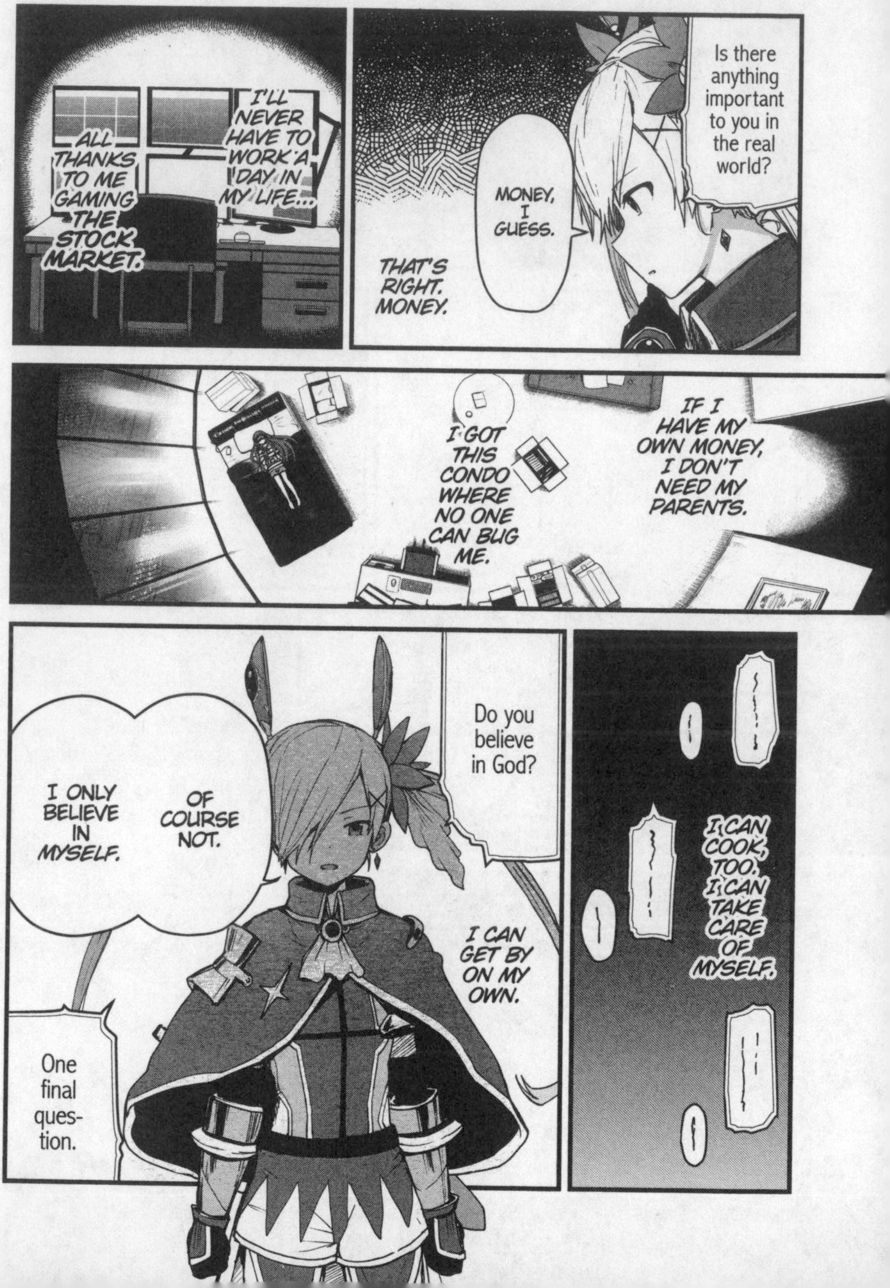
Is there anything important to you in the real world?
MONEY, I GUESS.
THAT'S RIGHT. MONEY.
I'LL NEVER HAVE TO WORK A DAY IN MY LIFE...
ALL THANKS TO ME GAMING THE STOCK MARKET.
IF I HAVE MY OWN MONEY, I DON'T NEED MY PARENTS.
I GOT THIS CONDO WHERE NO ONE CAN BUG ME.
I CAN COOK, TOO. I CAN TAKE CARE OF MYSELF.
Do you believe in God?
OF COURSE NOT.
I ONLY BELIEVE IN MYSELF.
I CAN GET BY ON MY OWN.
One final ques-tion.

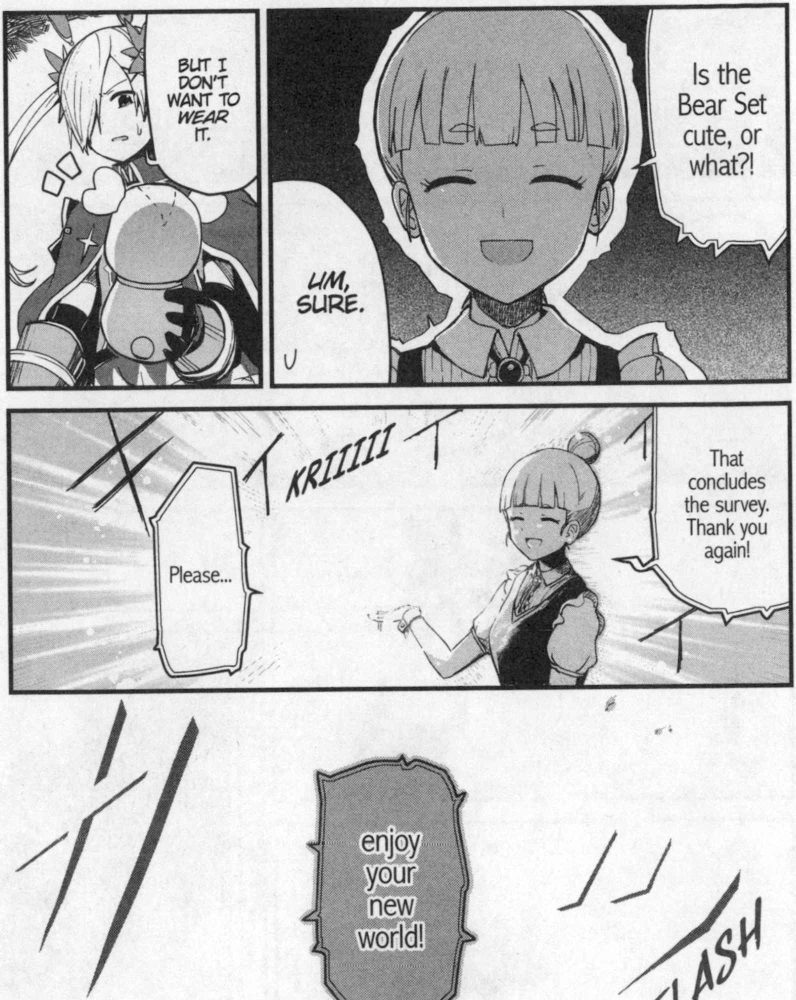
Is the Bear Set cute, or what?!
UM, SURE.
BUT I DON'T WANT TO WEAR IT.
That concludes the survey. Thank you again!
KRIIIIII
Please...
enjoy your new world!
FLASH

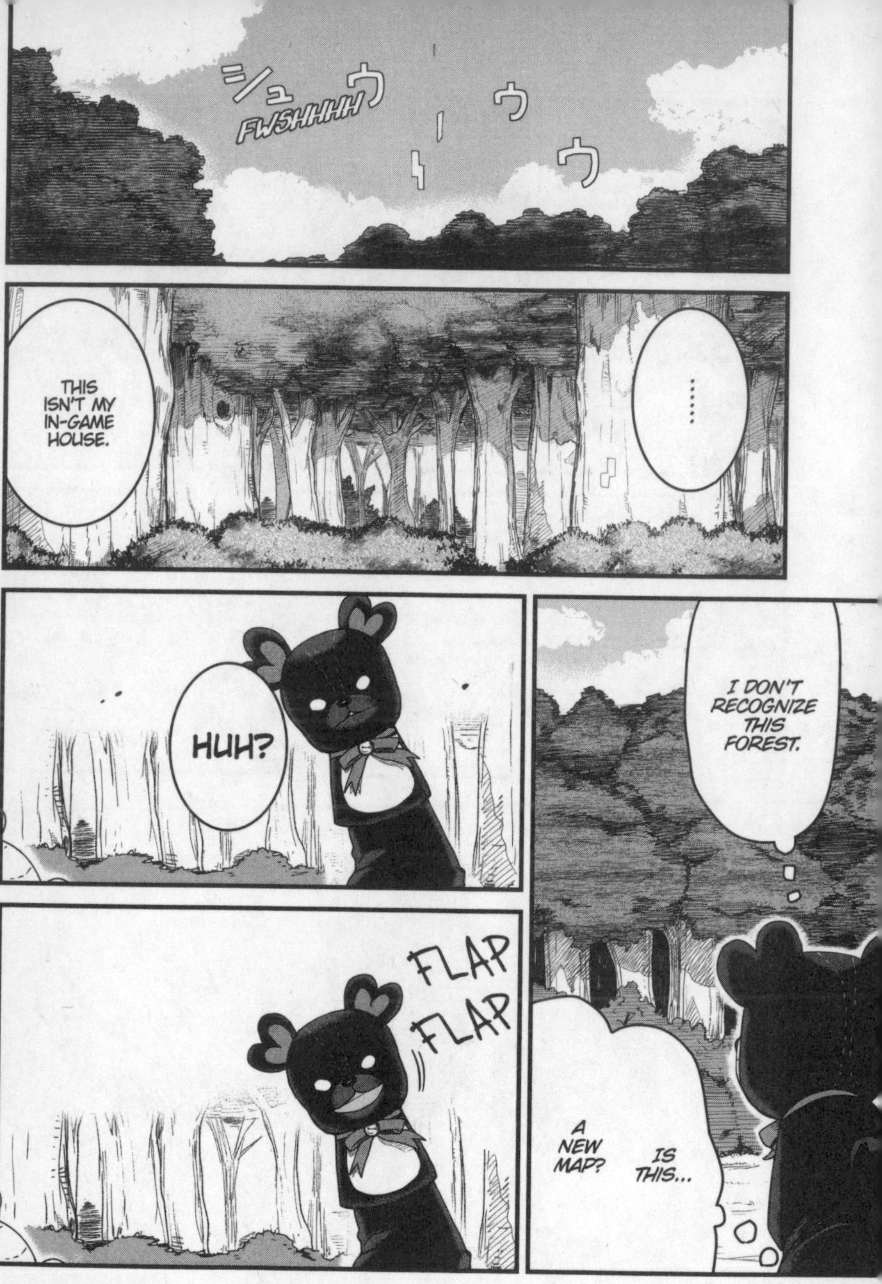
シュウウウ
FWSHHHH
……
THIS ISN'T MY IN-GAME HOUSE.
I DON'T RECOGNIZE THIS FOREST.
IS THIS...
A NEW MAP?
HUH?
FLAP FLAP

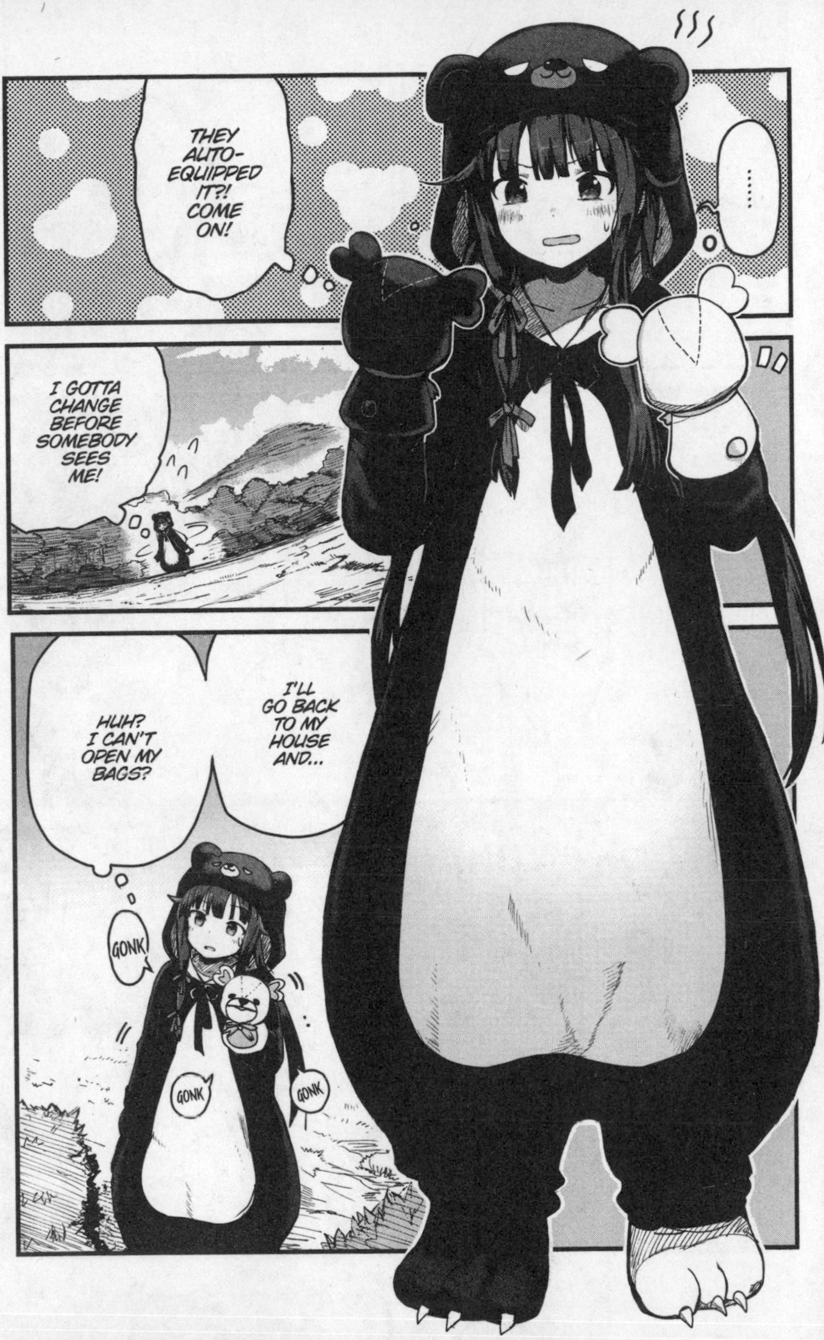
......
THEY AUTO-EQUIPPED IT?! COME ON!
I GOTTA CHANGE BEFORE SOMEBODY SEES ME!
I'LL GO BACK TO MY HOUSE AND...
HUH? I CAN'T OPEN MY BAGS?
GONK
GONK
GONK

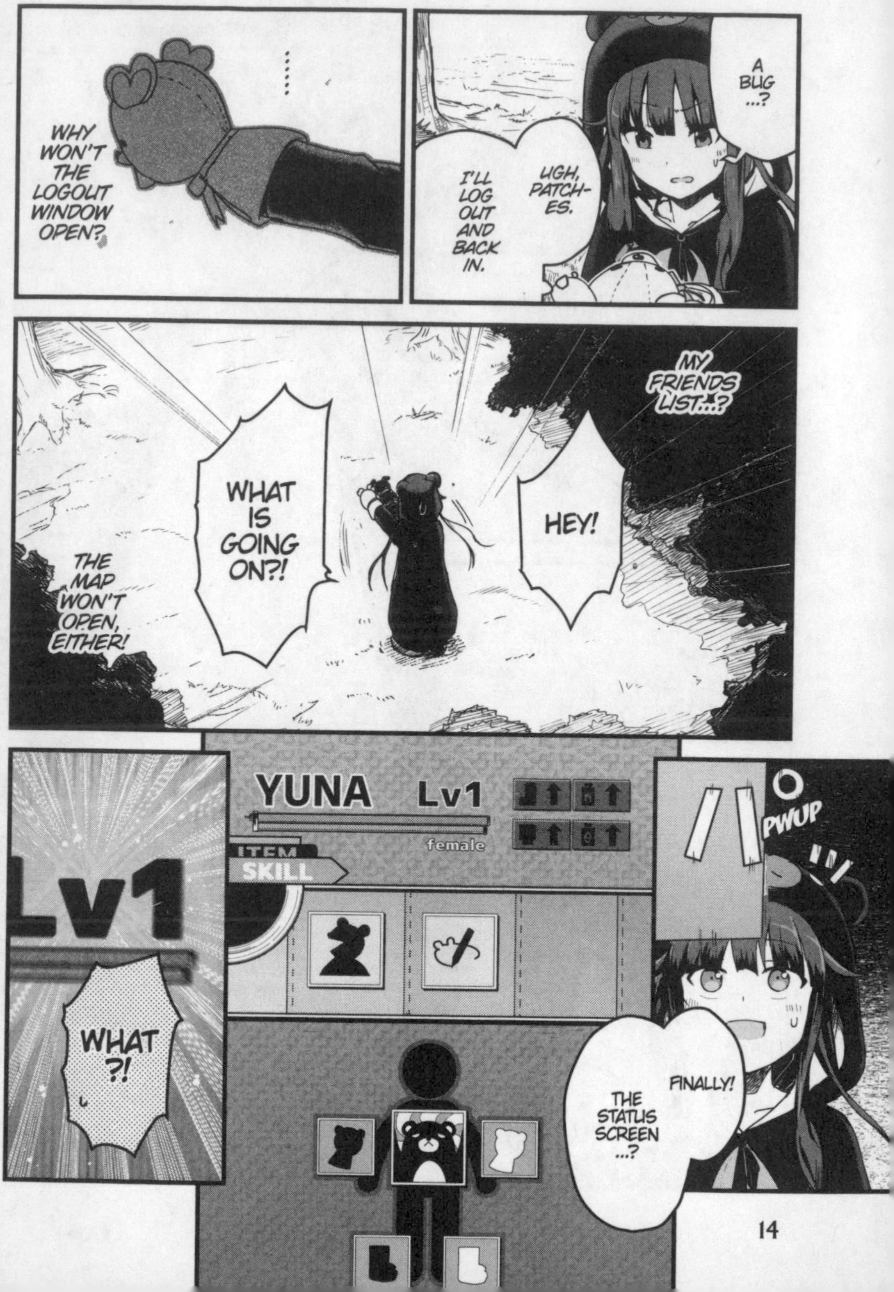
A BUG ...?
UGH, PATCHES.
I'LL LOG OUT AND BACK IN.
......
WHY WON'T THE LOGOUT WINDOW OPEN?
MY FRIENDS LIST...?
HEY!
WHAT IS GOING ON?!
THE MAP WON'T OPEN, EITHER!
PWUP
FINALLY!
THE STATUS SCREEN ...?
YUNA
Lv1
female
ITEM
SKILL
Lv1
WHAT ?!

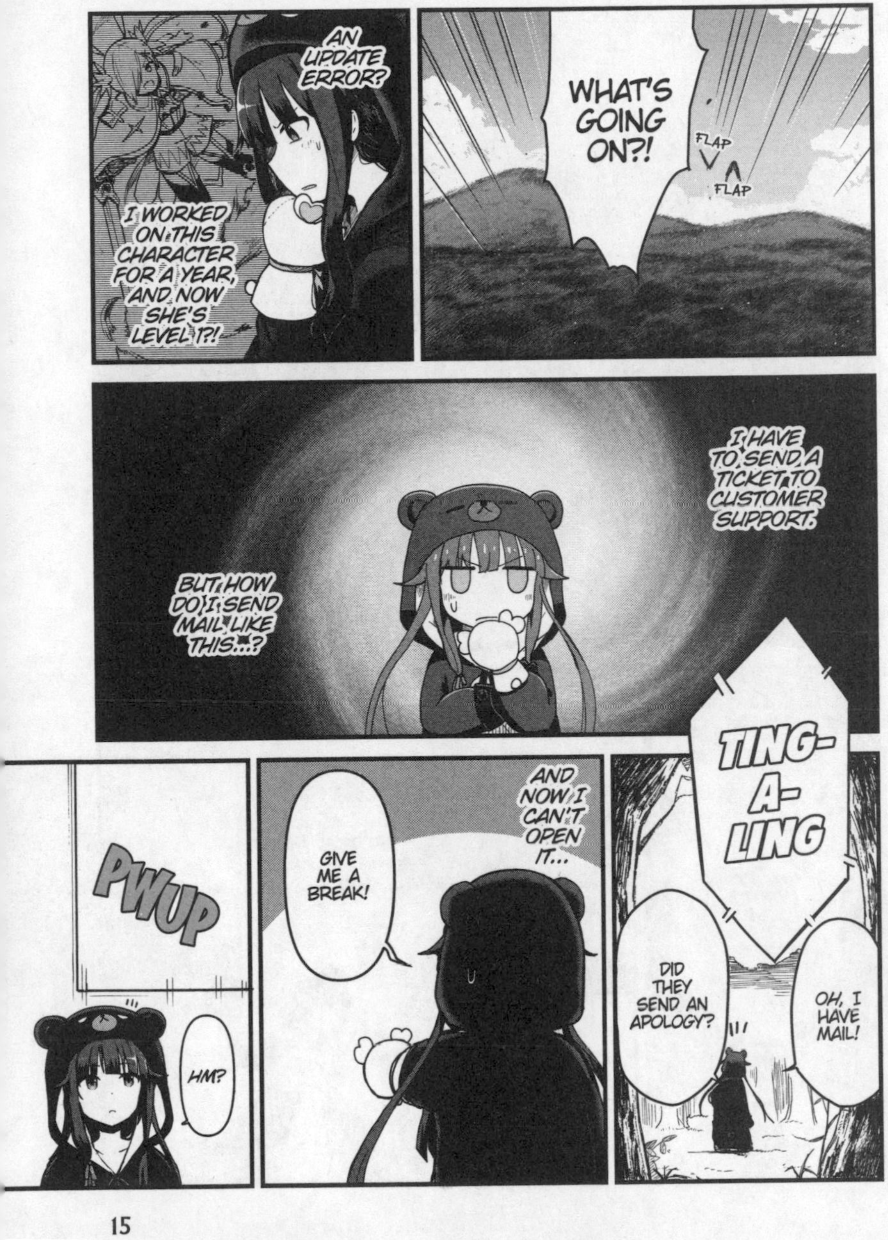
WHAT'S GOING ON?!
FLAP
FLAP
AN UPDATE ERROR?
I WORKED ON THIS CHARACTER FOR A YEAR, AND NOW SHE'S LEVEL 1?!
I HAVE TO SEND A TICKET TO CUSTOMER SUPPORT.
BUT HOW DO I SEND MAIL LIKE THIS...?
TING-A-LING
OH, I HAVE MAIL!
DID THEY SEND AN APOLOGY?
AND NOW I CAN'T OPEN IT...
GIVE ME A BREAK!
PWUP
HM?

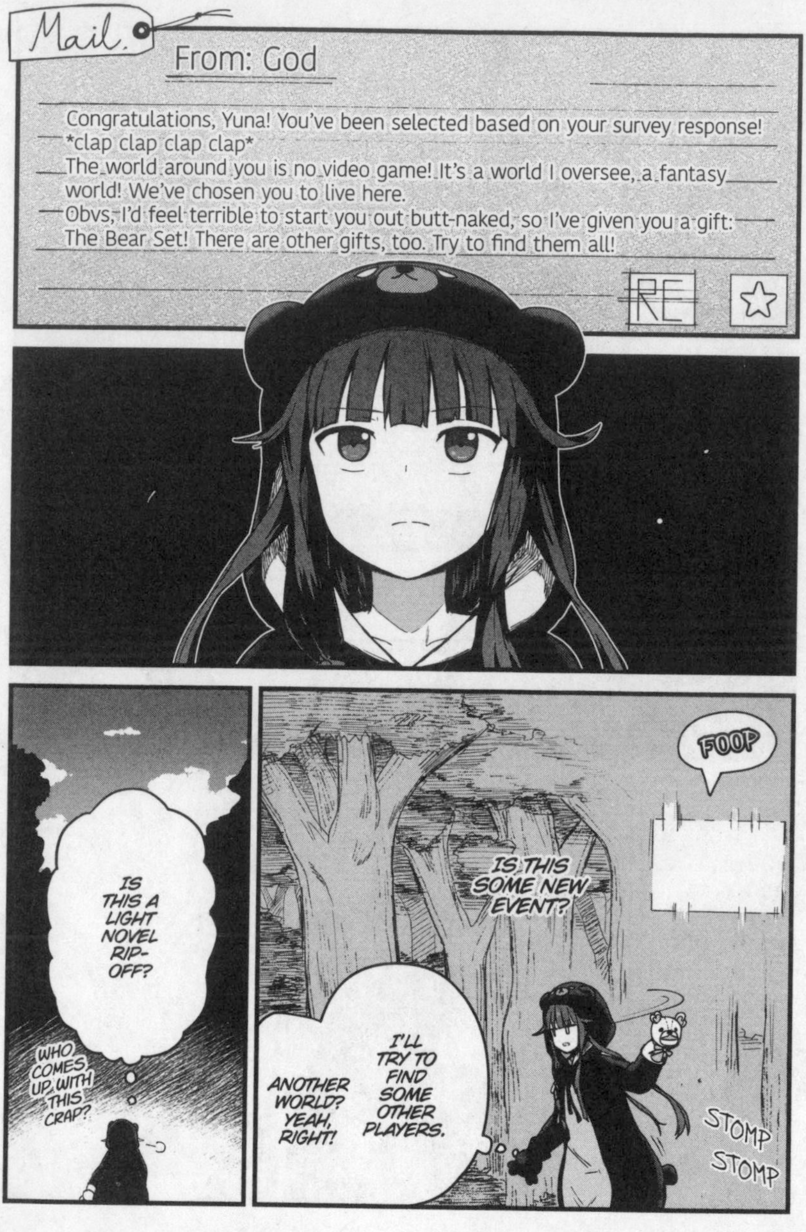
Mail.
From: God
Congratulations, Yuna! You've been selected based on your survey response!
clap clap clap clap
The world around you is no video game! It's a world I oversee, a fantasy world! We've chosen you to live here.
Obvs, I'd feel terrible to start you out butt-naked, so I've given you a gift: The Bear Set! There are other gifts, too. Try to find them all!
RE
FOOP
IS THIS SOME NEW EVENT?
I'LL TRY TO FIND SOME OTHER PLAYERS.
ANOTHER WORLD? YEAH, RIGHT!
STOMP STOMP
IS THIS A LIGHT NOVEL RIP-OFF?
WHO COMES UP WITH THIS CRAP?

Chapter 2

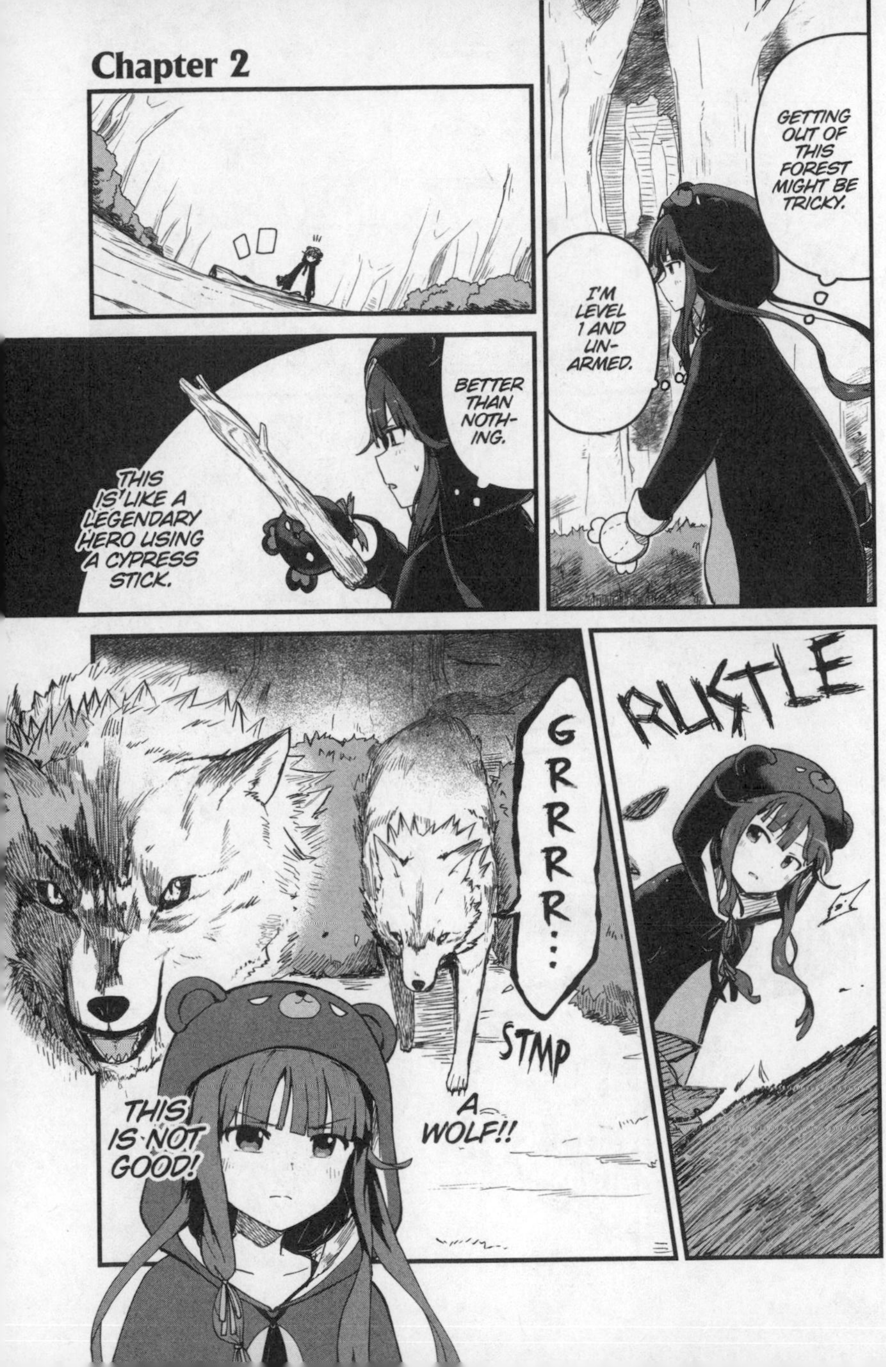
GETTING OUT OF THIS FOREST MIGHT BE TRICKY.
I'M LEVEL 1 AND UN-ARMED.
BETTER THAN NOTH-ING.
THIS IS LIKE A LEGENDARY HERO USING A CYPRESS STICK.
RUSTLE
GRRRR...
STMP
A WOLF!!
THIS IS NOT GOOD!

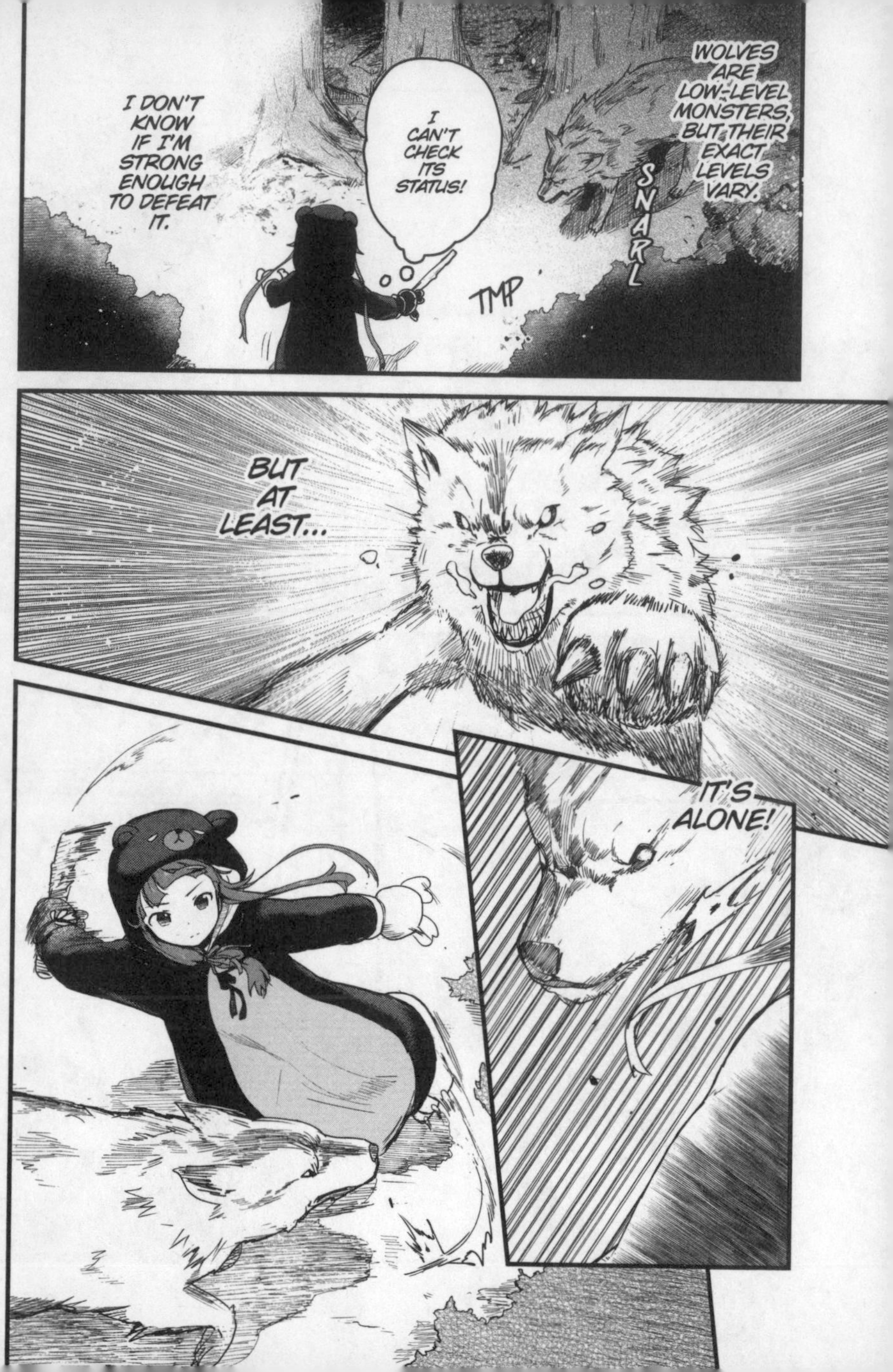
WOLVES ARE LOW-LEVEL MONSTERS, BUT THEIR EXACT LEVELS VARY.
SNARL
I CAN'T CHECK ITS STATUS!
TMP
I DON'T KNOW IF I'M STRONG ENOUGH TO DEFEAT IT.
BUT AT LEAST...
IT'S ALONE!

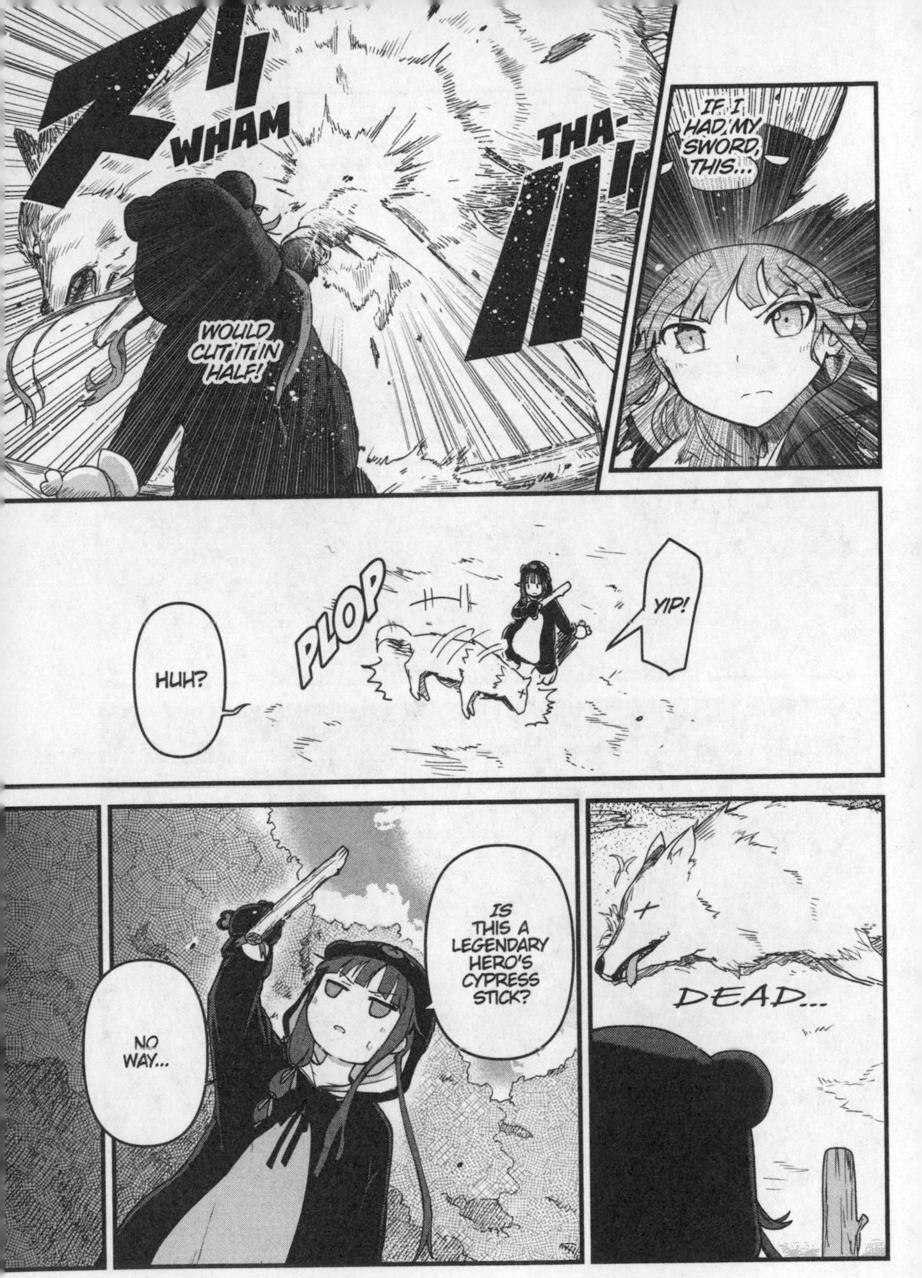
IF I HAD MY SWORD, THIS...
THA-
WHAM
WOULD CUT IT IN HALF!
YIP!
PLOP
HUH?
DEAD...
IS THIS A LEGENDARY HERO'S CYPRESS STICK?
NO WAY...

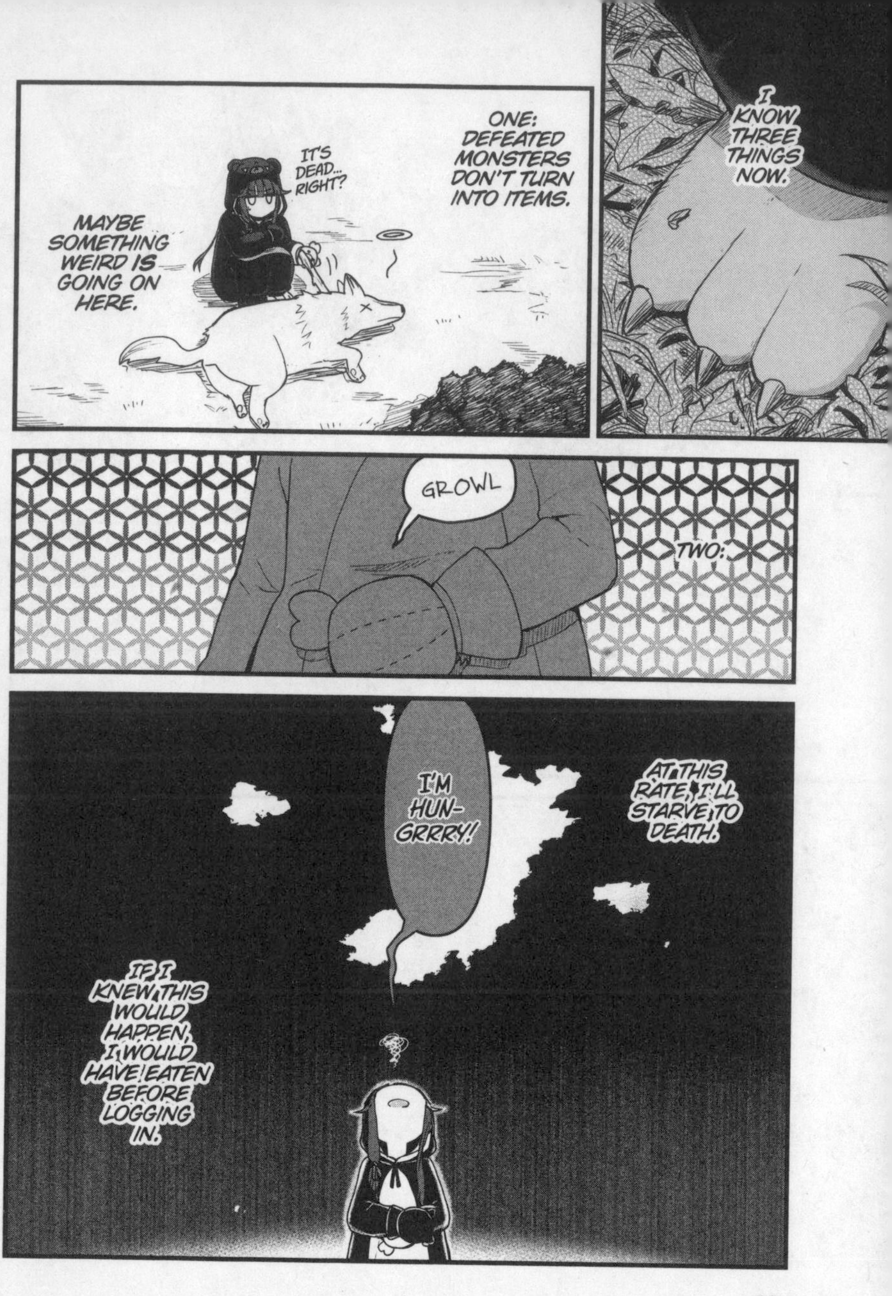
I KNOW THREE THINGS NOW.
ONE: DEFEATED MONSTERS DON'T TURN INTO ITEMS.
IT'S DEAD... RIGHT?
MAYBE SOMETHING WEIRD IS GOING ON HERE.
GROWL
TWO:
AT THIS RATE, I'LL STARVE TO DEATH.
I'M HUN-GRRRY!
IF I KNEW THIS WOULD HAPPEN, I WOULD HAVE EATEN BEFORE LOGGING IN.

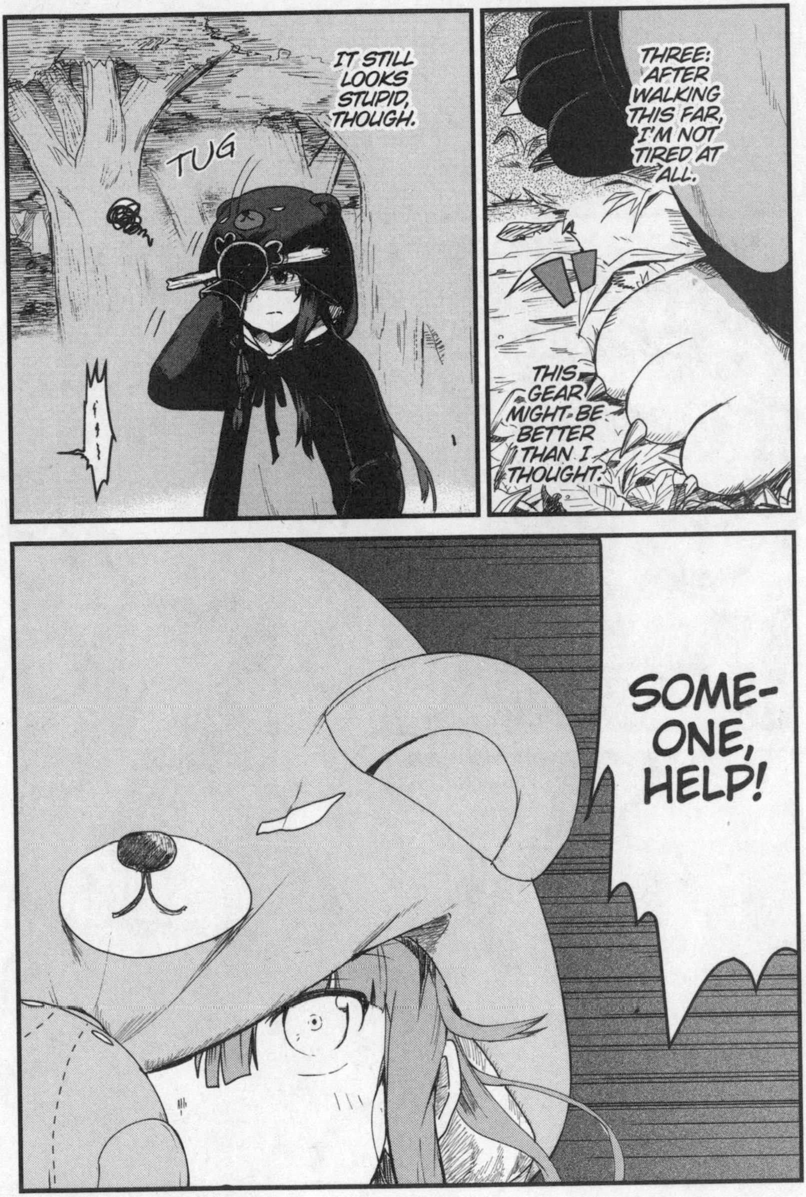
THREE: AFTER WALKING THIS FAR, I'M NOT TIRED AT ALL.
THIS GEAR MIGHT BE BETTER THAN I THOUGHT.
IT STILL LOOKS STUPID, THOUGH.
TUG
SOME-ONE, HELP!

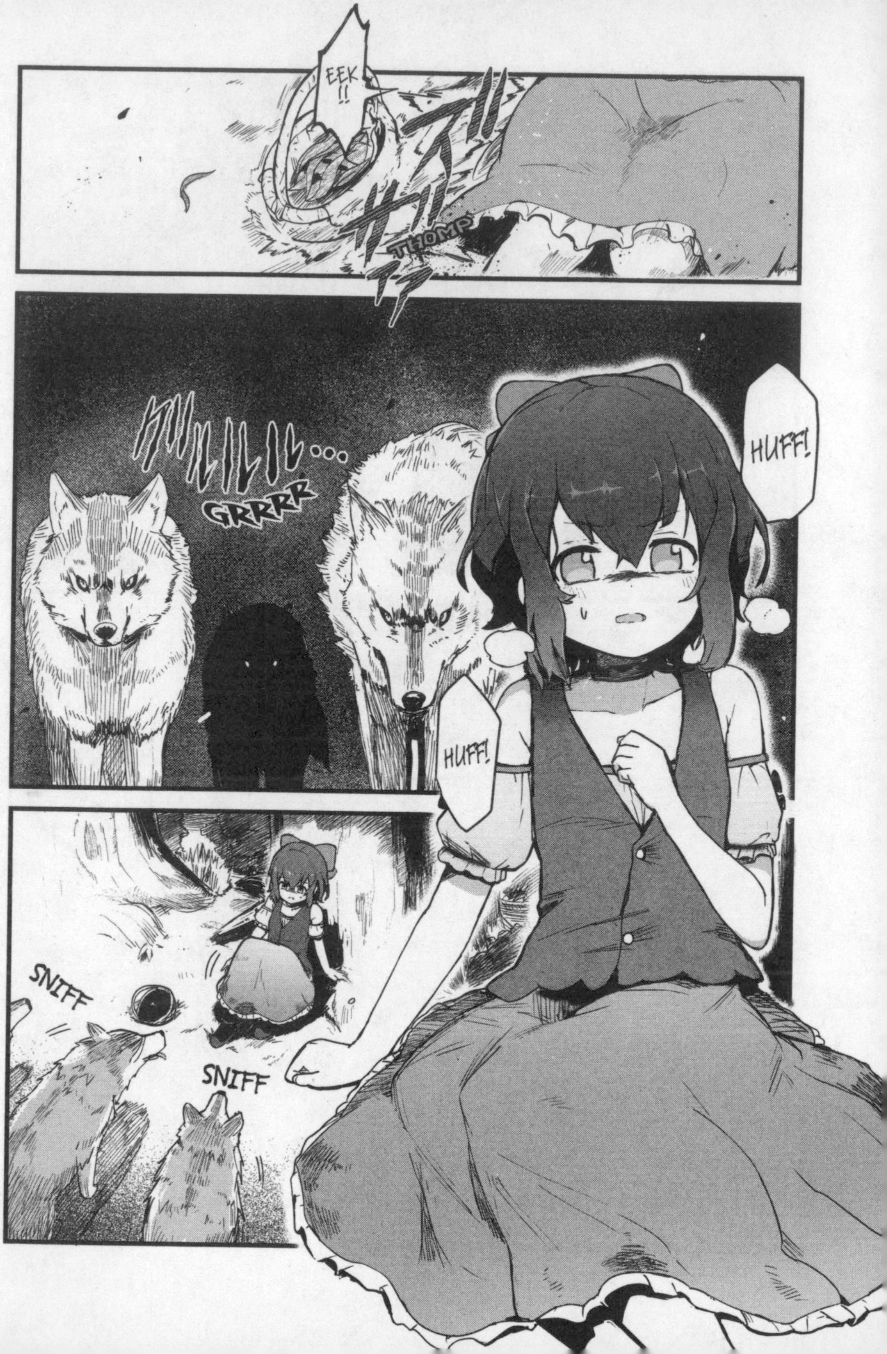
EEK!!
THOMP
HUFF!
GRRRR
HUFF!
SNIFF
SNIFF

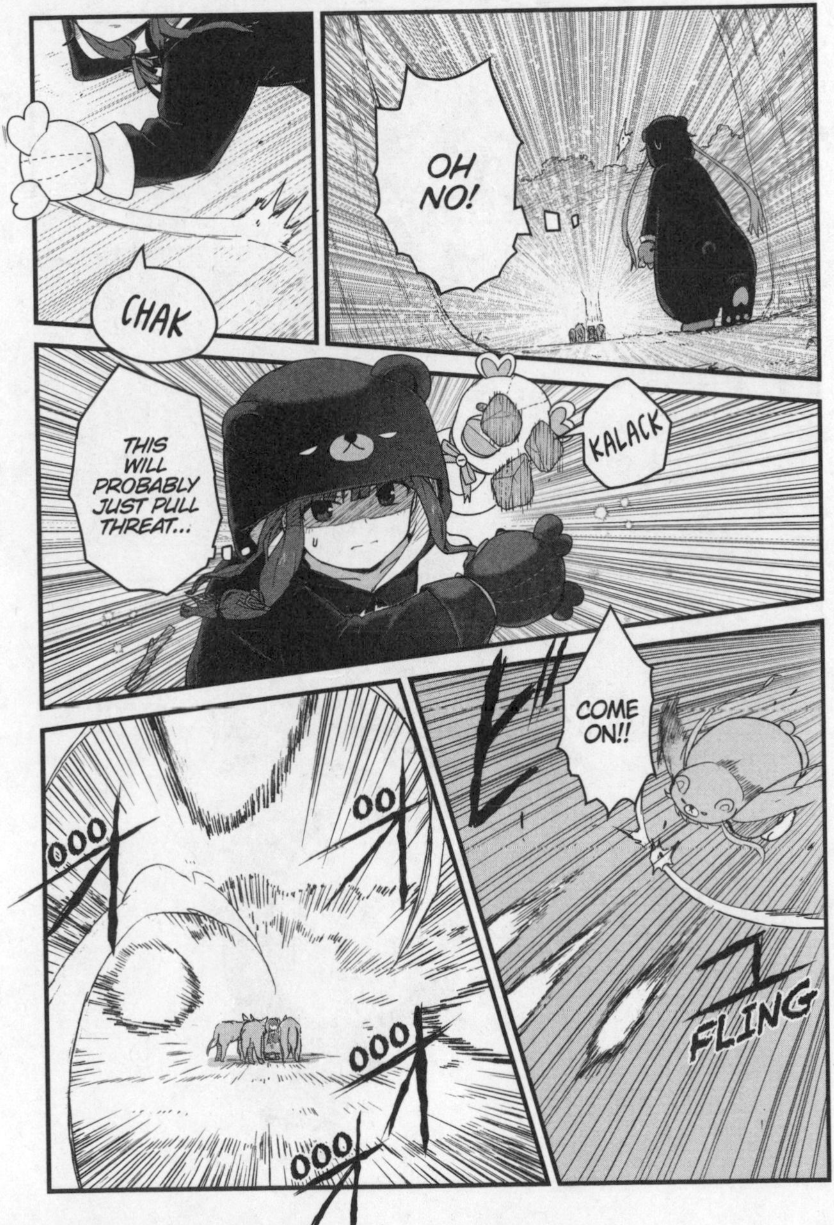
OH NO!
CHAK
KALACK
THIS WILL PROBABLY JUST PULL THREAT...
COME ON!!
FLING
OO
OOO
OOO
OOO

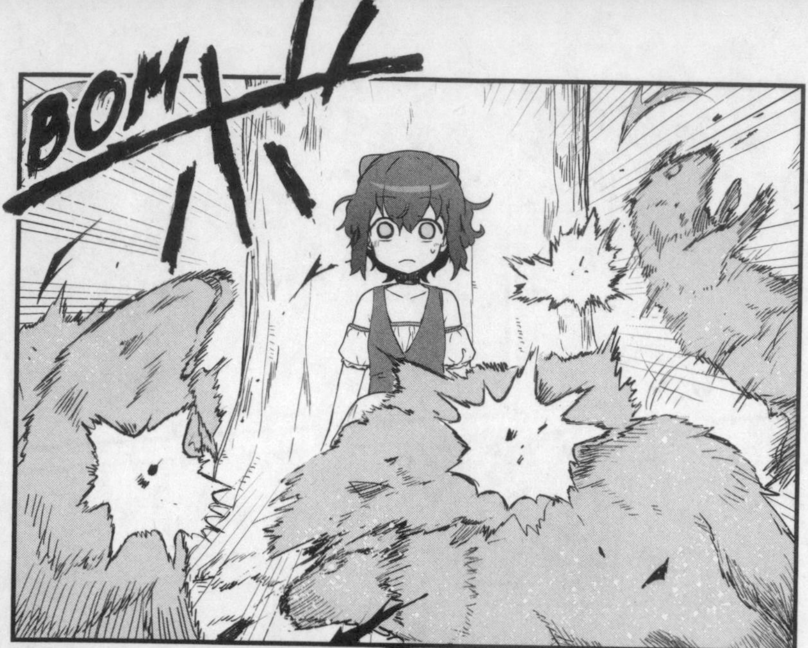
BOM

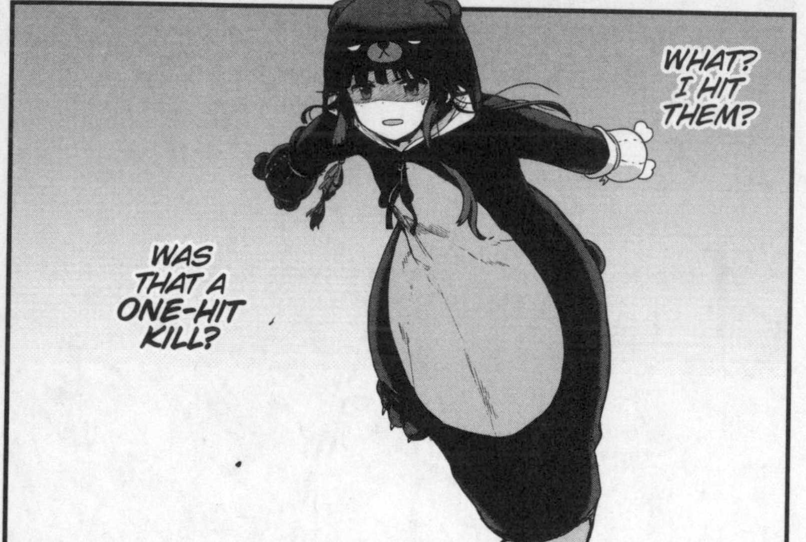
WHAT? I HIT THEM?
WAS THAT A ONE-HIT KILL?

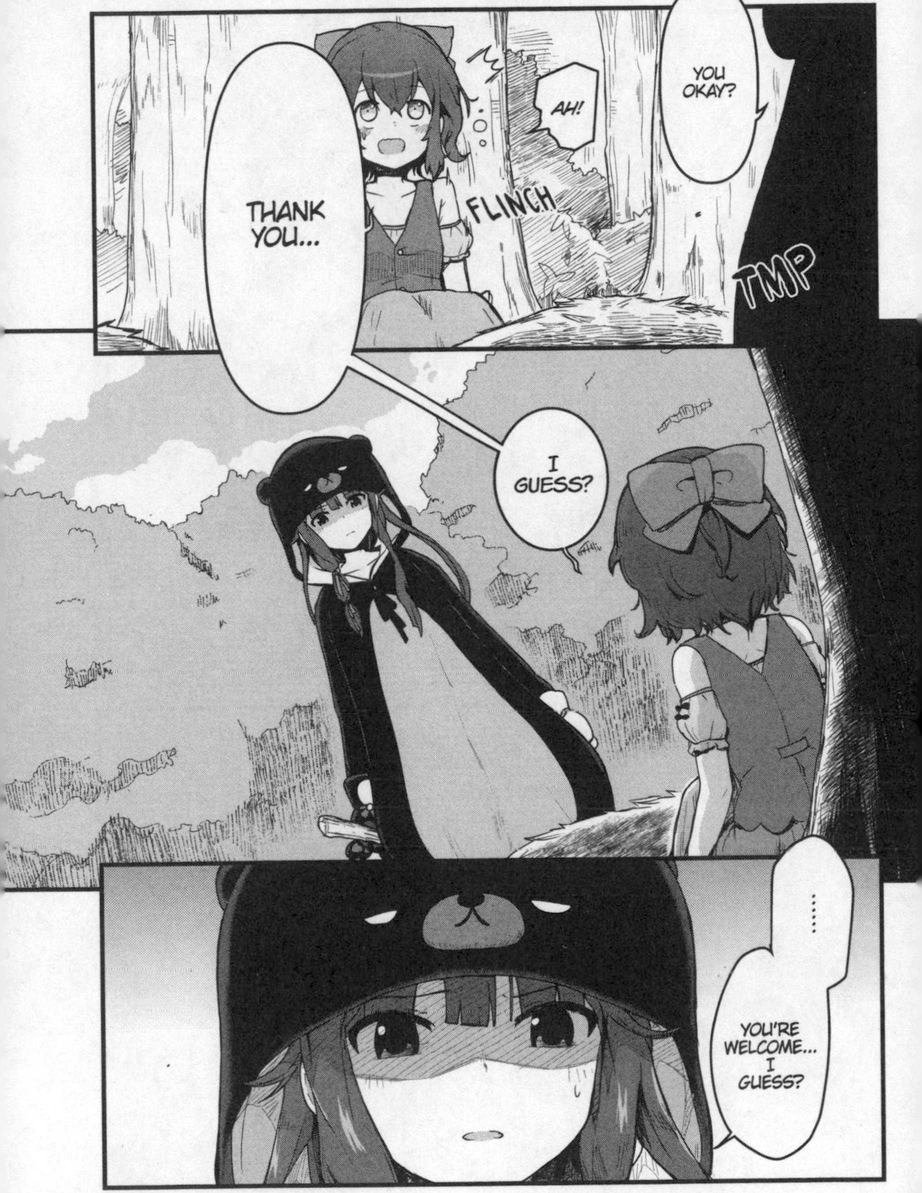
YOU OKAY?
AH!
TMP
FLINCH
THANK YOU...
I GUESS?
......
YOU'RE WELCOME... I GUESS?

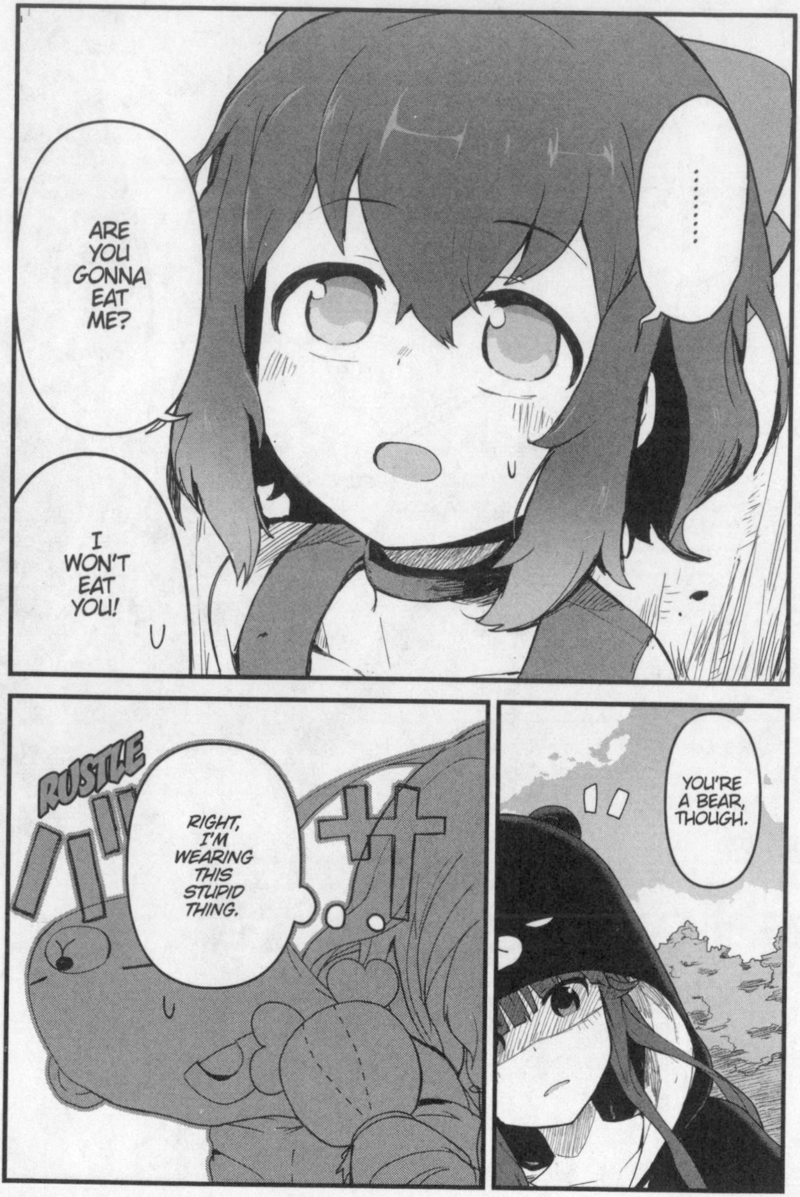
……
ARE YOU GONNA EAT ME?
I WON'T EAT YOU!
YOU'RE A BEAR, THOUGH.
RUSTLE
RIGHT, I'M WEARING THIS STUPID THING.

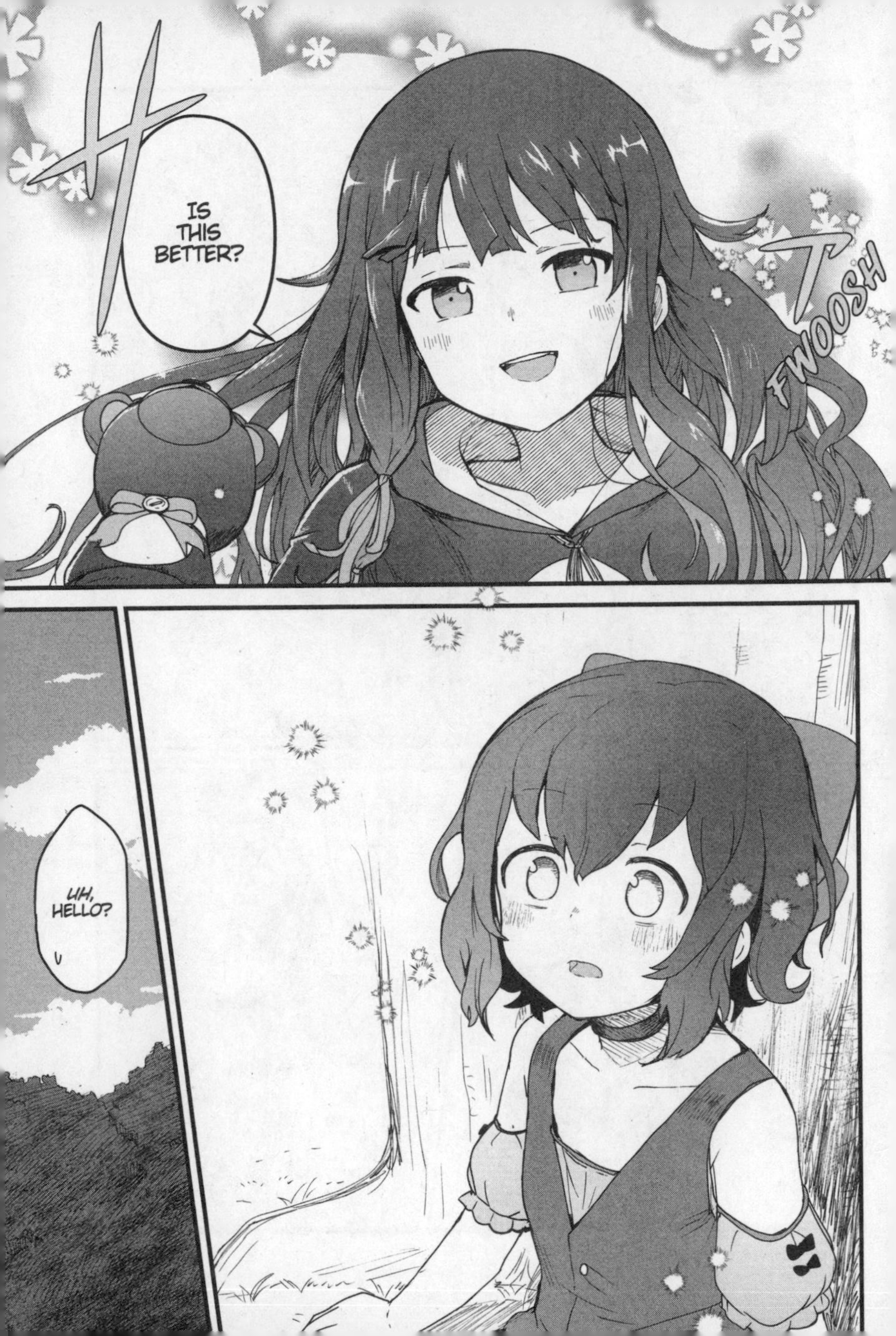
IS THIS BETTER?
FWOOSH
UH, HELLO?

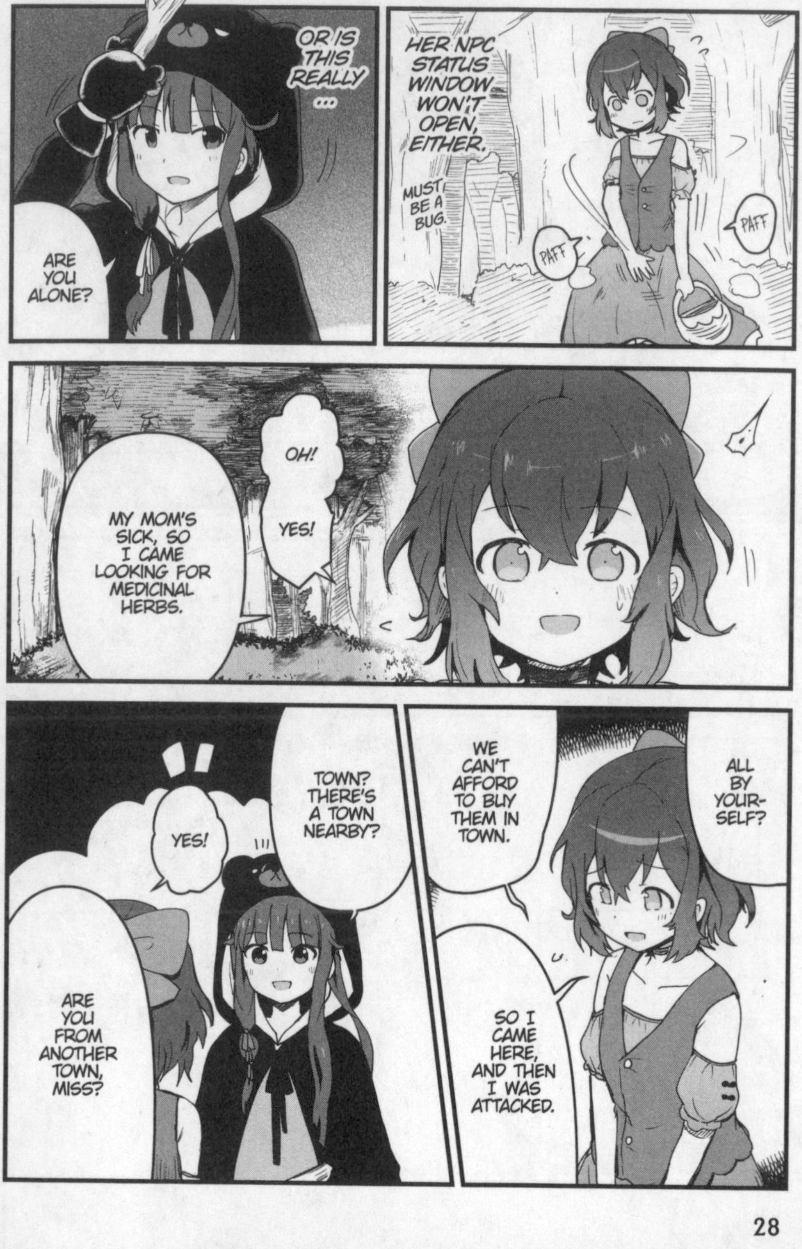
HER NPC STATUS WINDOW WON'T OPEN, EITHER.
MUST BE A BUG.
PAFF
PAFF
OR IS THIS REALLY ...
ARE YOU ALONE?
OH!
YES!
MY MOM'S SICK, SO I CAME LOOKING FOR MEDICINAL HERBS.
ALL BY YOURSELF?
WE CAN'T AFFORD TO BUY THEM IN TOWN.
SO I CAME HERE, AND THEN I WAS ATTACKED.
TOWN? THERE'S A TOWN NEARBY?
YES!
ARE YOU FROM ANOTHER TOWN, MISS?

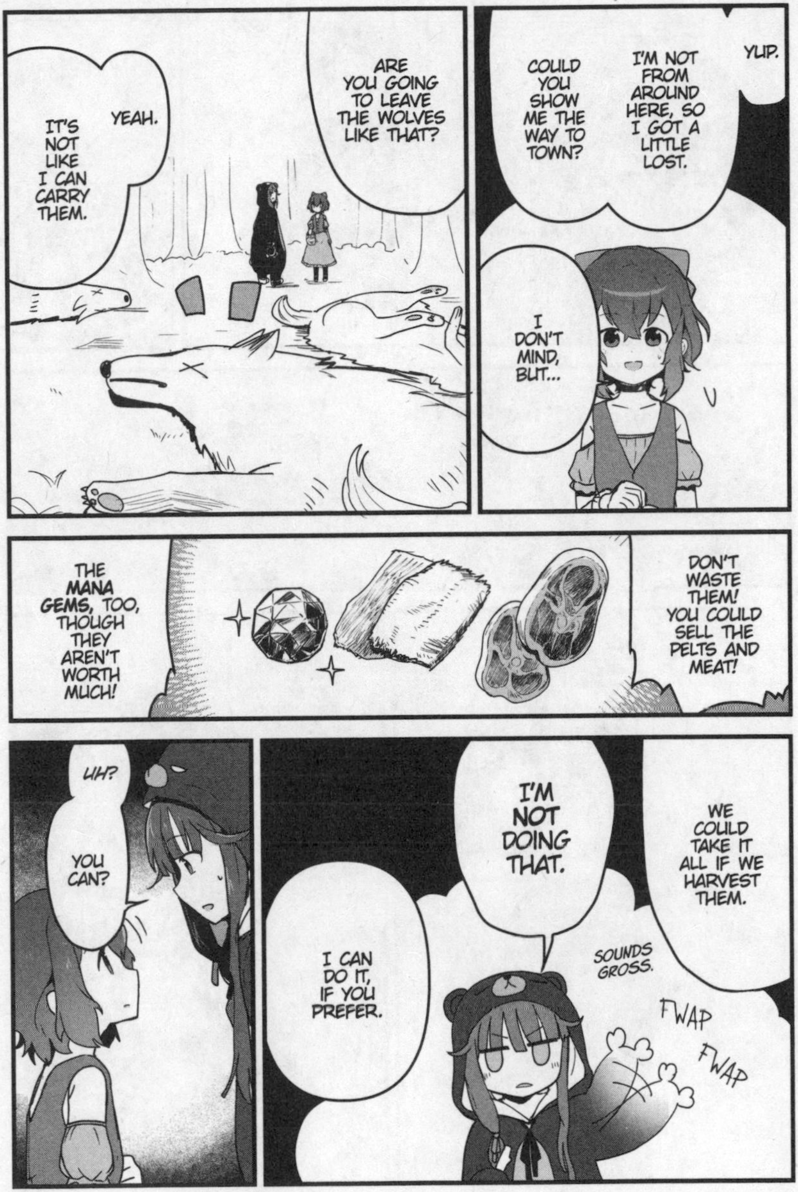
YUP.
I'M NOT FROM AROUND HERE, SO I GOT A LITTLE LOST.
COULD YOU SHOW ME THE WAY TO TOWN?
I DON'T MIND, BUT...
ARE YOU GOING TO LEAVE THE WOLVES LIKE THAT?
YEAH.
IT'S NOT LIKE I CAN CARRY THEM.
DON'T WASTE THEM! YOU COULD SELL THE PELTS AND MEAT!
THE MANA GEMS, TOO, THOUGH THEY AREN'T WORTH MUCH!
WE COULD TAKE IT ALL IF WE HARVEST THEM.
I'M NOT DOING THAT.
SOUNDS GROSS.
FWAP
FWAP
I CAN DO IT, IF YOU PREFER.
UH?
YOU CAN?

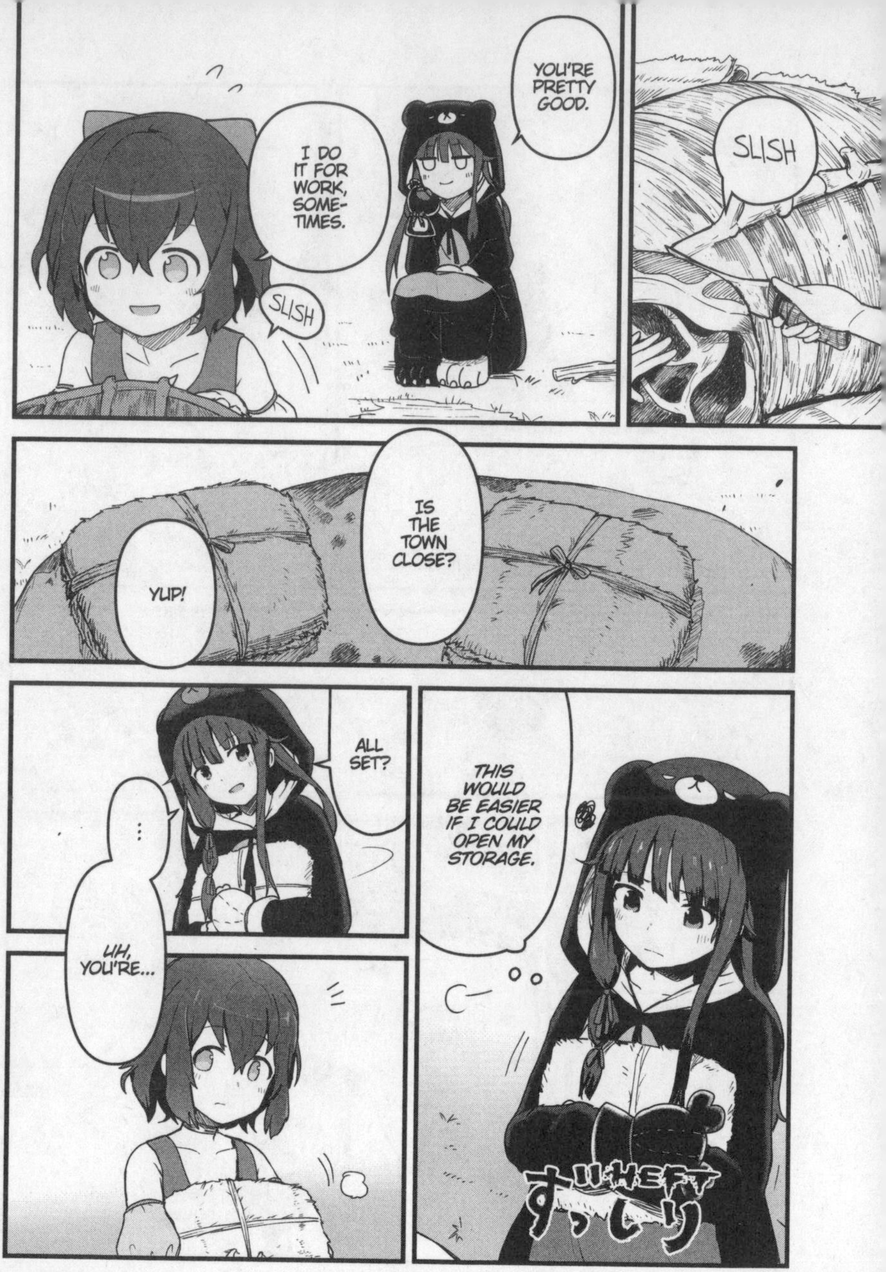
SLISH
YOU'RE PRETTY GOOD.
I DO IT FOR WORK, SOMETIMES.
SLISH
IS THE TOWN CLOSE?
YUP!
THIS WOULD BE EASIER IF I COULD OPEN MY STORAGE.
HEFT
ALL SET?
...
UH, YOU'RE...

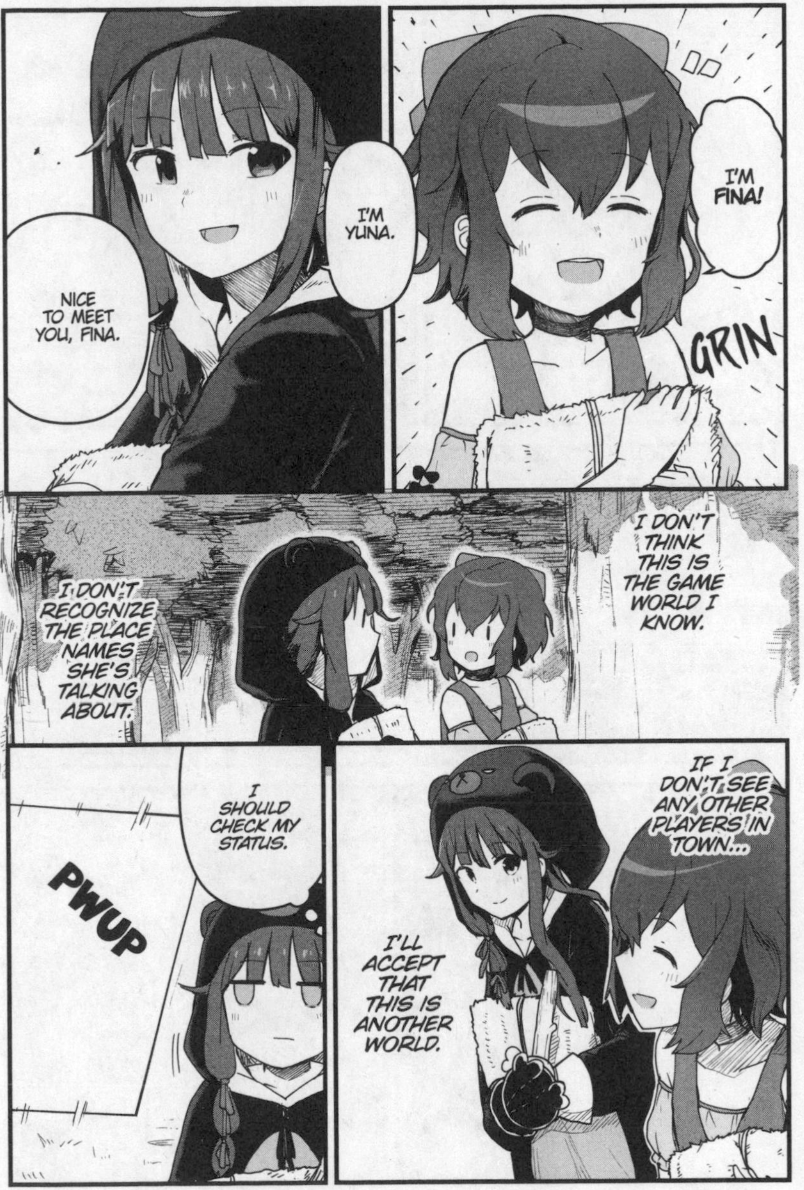
I'M FINA!
GRIN
I'M YUNA.
NICE TO MEET YOU, FINA.
I DON'T THINK THIS IS THE GAME WORLD I KNOW.
I DON'T RECOGNIZE THE PLACE NAMES SHE'S TALKING ABOUT.
IF I DON'T SEE ANY OTHER PLAYERS IN TOWN...
I'LL ACCEPT THAT THIS IS ANOTHER WORLD.
I SHOULD CHECK MY STATUS.
PWUP

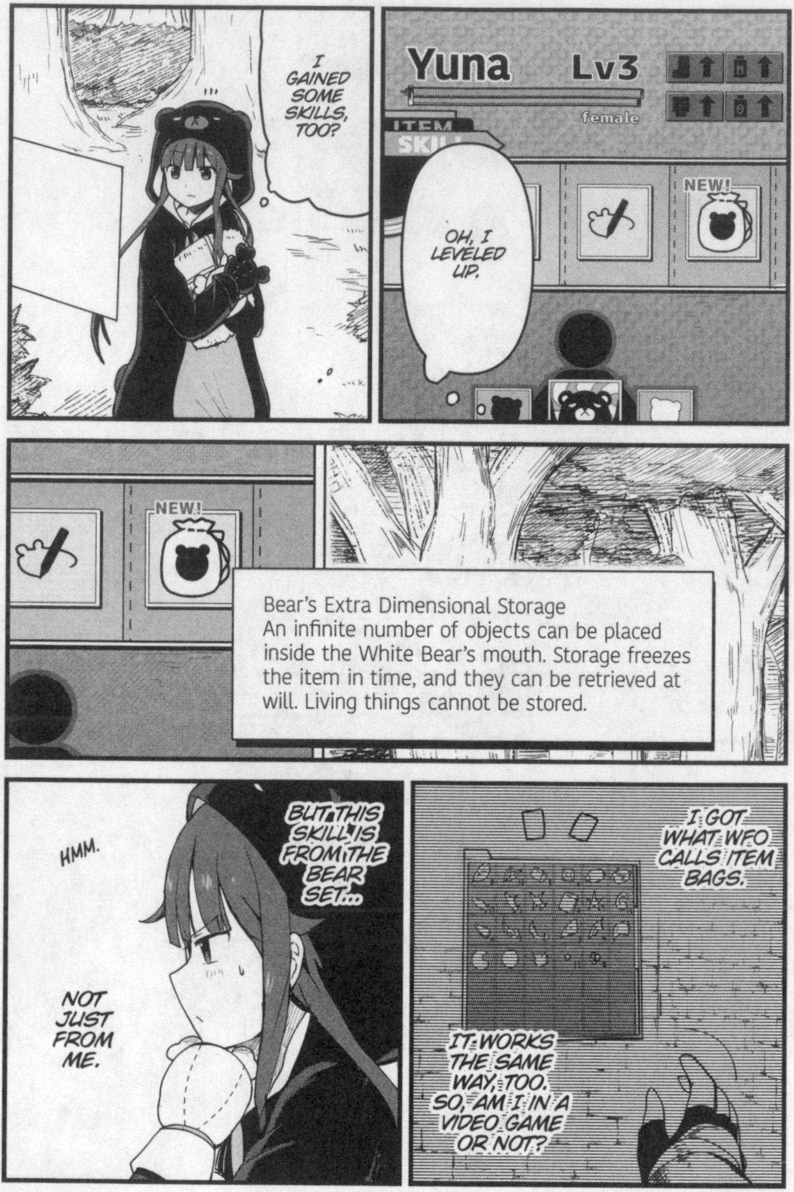
Yuna
Lv3
female
ITEM
NEW!
OH, I LEVELED UP.
I GAINED SOME SKILLS, TOO?
NEW!
Bear's Extra Dimensional Storage
An infinite number of objects can be placed inside the White Bear's mouth. Storage freezes the item in time, and they can be retrieved at will. Living things cannot be stored.
I GOT WHAT WFO CALLS ITEM BAGS.
IT WORKS THE SAME WAY, TOO. SO, AM I IN A VIDEO GAME OR NOT?
BUT THIS SKILL IS FROM THE BEAR SET...
HMM.
NOT JUST FROM ME.

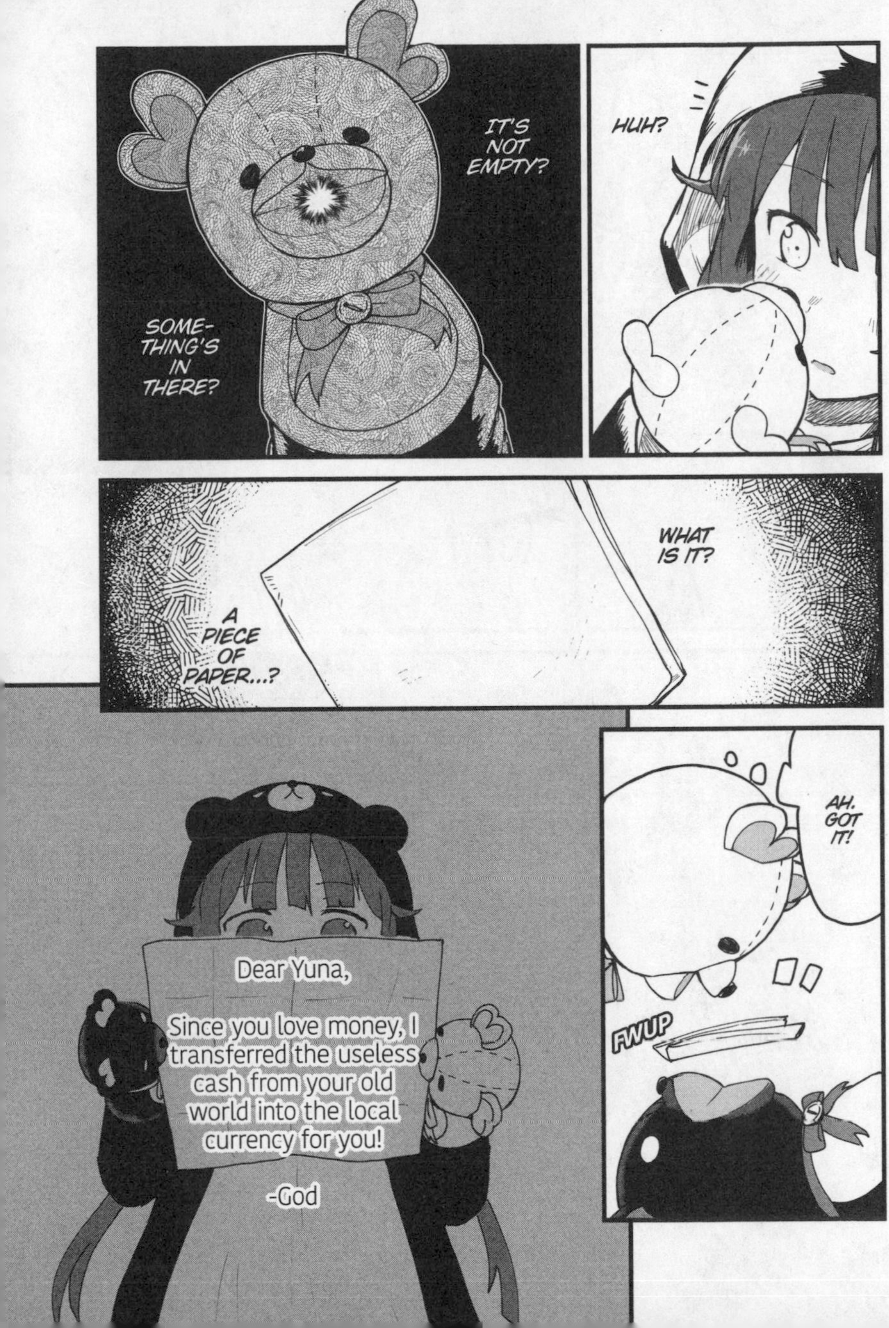
HUH?
IT'S NOT EMPTY?
SOME-THING'S IN THERE?
WHAT IS IT?
A PIECE OF PAPER...?
AH. GOT IT!
FWUP
Dear Yuna,
Since you love money, I transferred the useless cash from your old world into the local currency for you!
-God

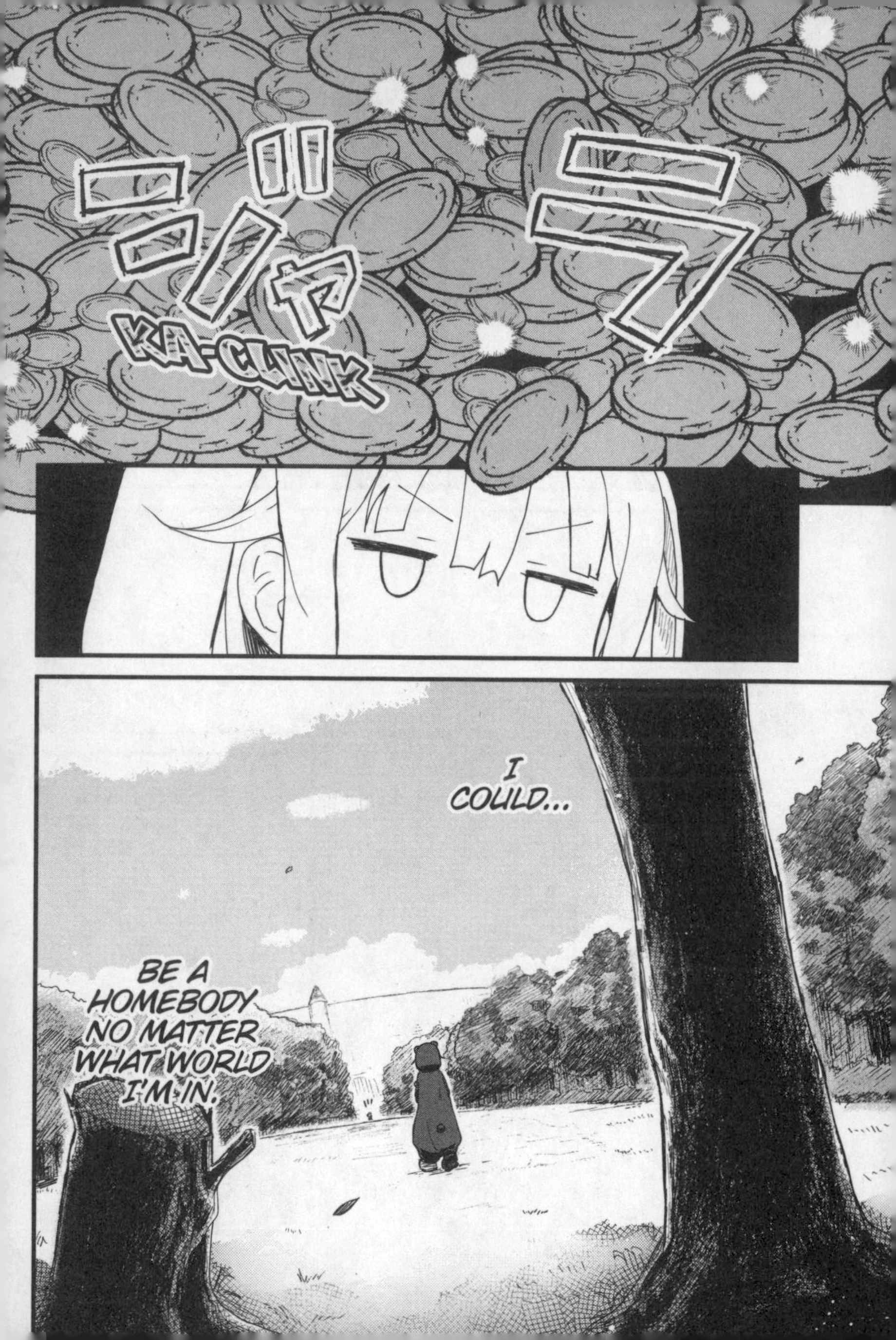
ジャラ
KA-CLINK
I COULD...
BE A HOMEBODY NO MATTER WHAT WORLD I'M IN.

Chapter 3

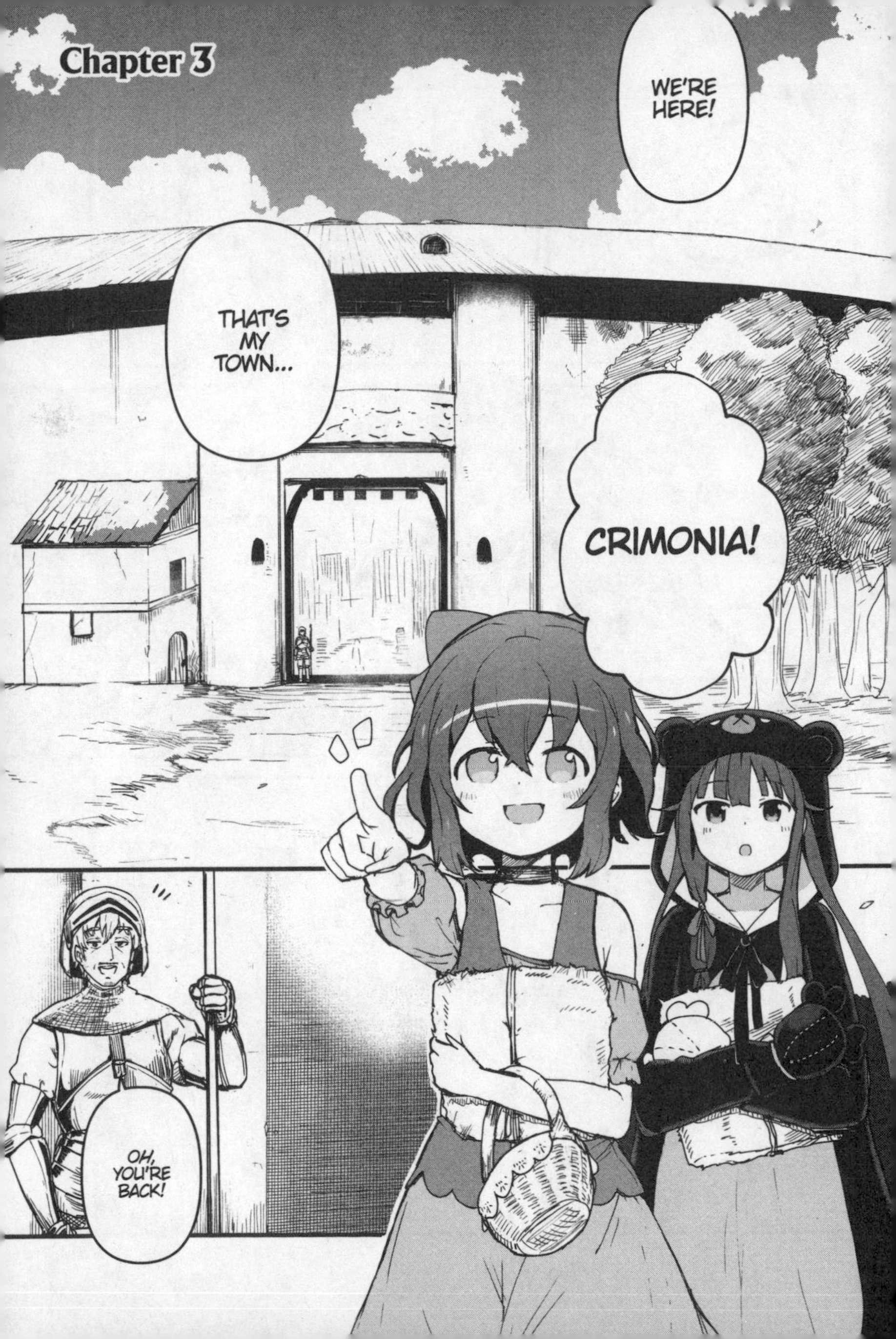
WE'RE HERE!
THAT'S MY TOWN...
CRIMONIA!
OH, YOU'RE BACK!

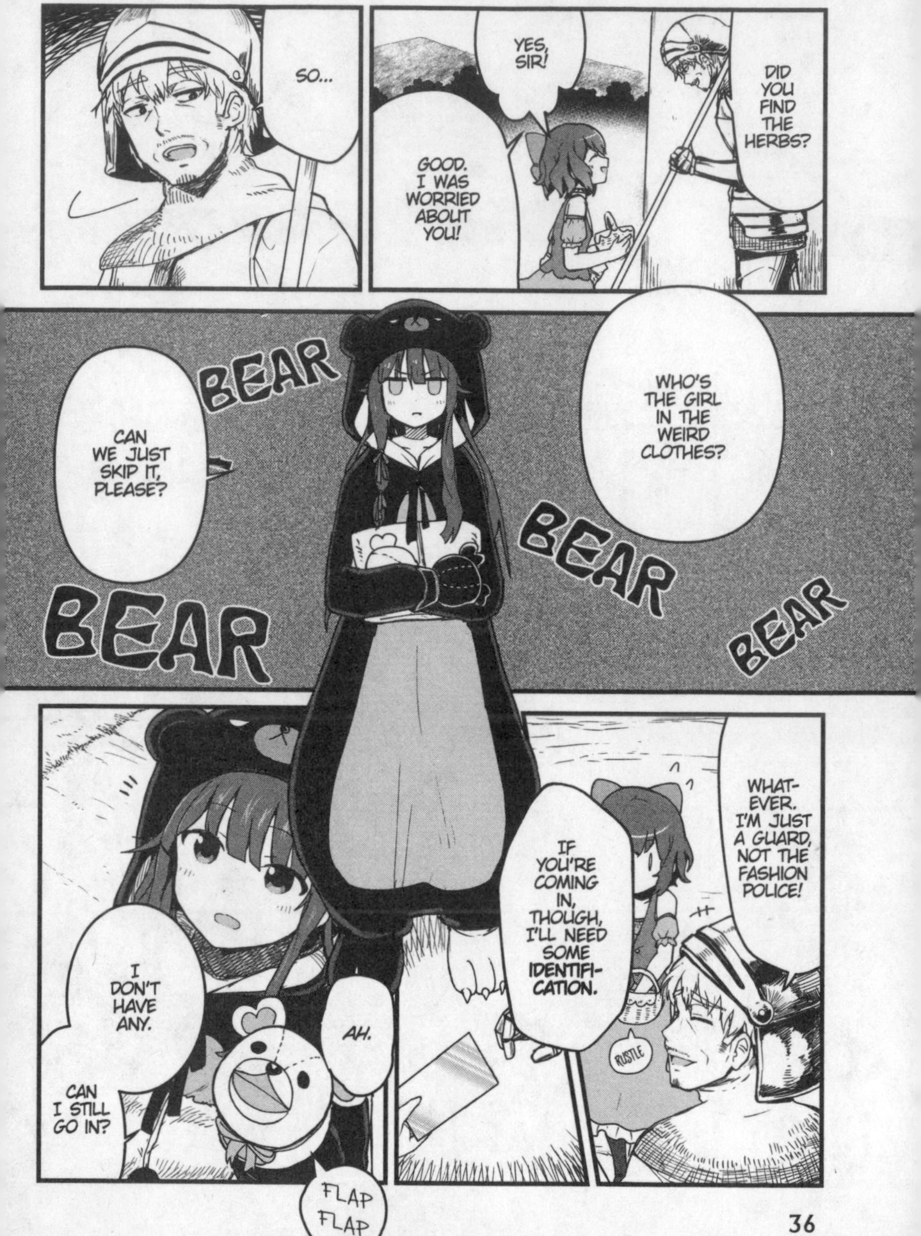
DID YOU FIND THE HERBS?
YES, SIR!
GOOD. I WAS WORRIED ABOUT YOU!
SO...
WHO'S THE GIRL IN THE WEIRD CLOTHES?
BEAR
BEAR
BEAR
BEAR
CAN WE JUST SKIP IT, PLEASE?
WHAT-EVER. I'M JUST A GUARD, NOT THE FASHION POLICE!
IF YOU'RE COMING IN, THOUGH, I'LL NEED SOME IDENTIFI-CATION.
RUSTLE
AH.
I DON'T HAVE ANY.
CAN I STILL GO IN?
FLAP FLAP

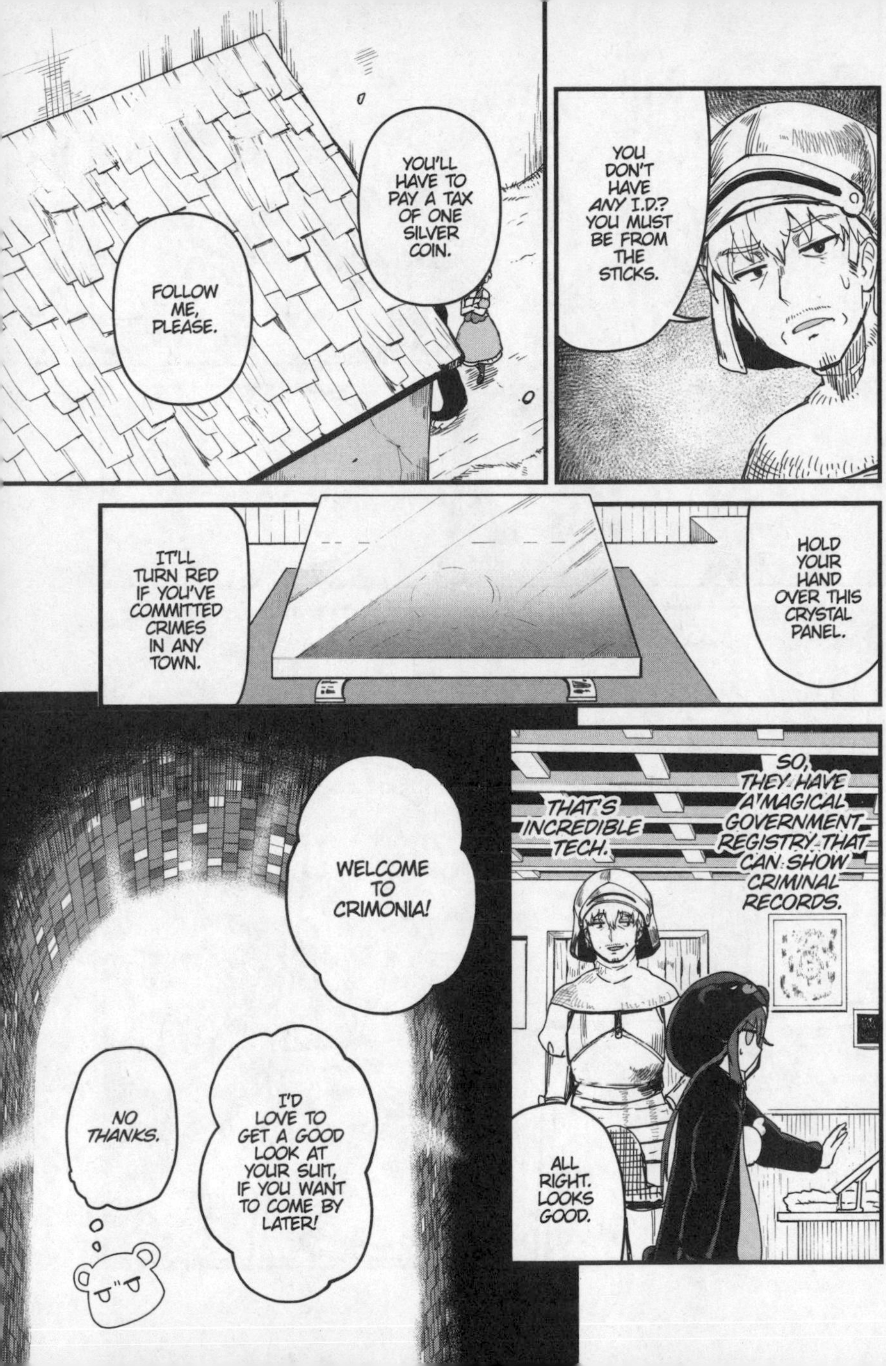
YOU DON'T HAVE ANY I.D.? YOU MUST BE FROM THE STICKS.
YOU'LL HAVE TO PAY A TAX OF ONE SILVER COIN.
FOLLOW ME, PLEASE.
HOLD YOUR HAND OVER THIS CRYSTAL PANEL.
IT'LL TURN RED IF YOU'VE COMMITTED CRIMES IN ANY TOWN.
SO, THEY HAVE A MAGICAL GOVERNMENT REGISTRY THAT CAN SHOW CRIMINAL RECORDS.
THAT'S INCREDIBLE TECH.
ALL RIGHT. LOOKS GOOD.
WELCOME TO CRIMONIA!
I'D LOVE TO GET A GOOD LOOK AT YOUR SUIT, IF YOU WANT TO COME BY LATER!
NO THANKS.

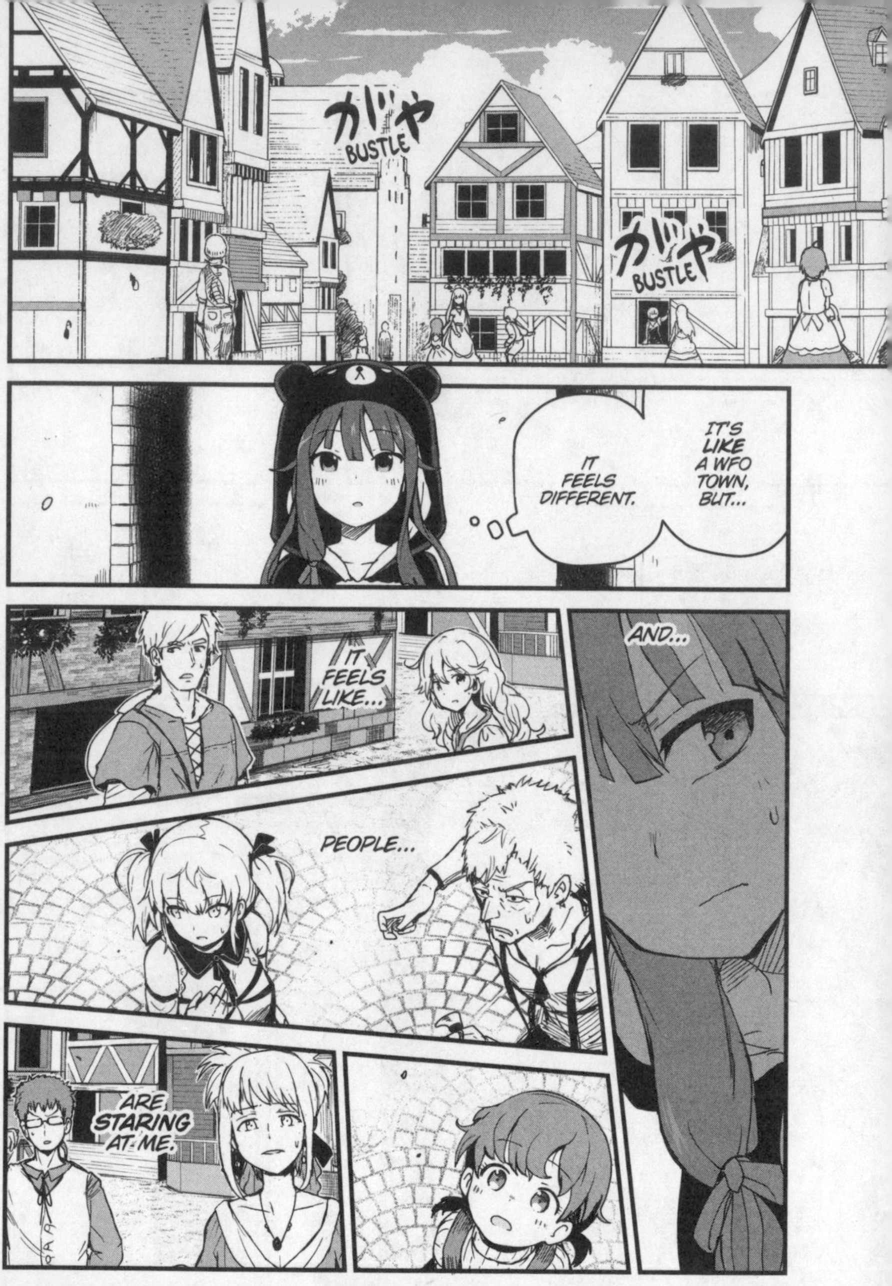

ガヤ
BUSTLE
ガヤ
BUSTLE
IT'S LIKE A WFO TOWN, BUT...
IT FEELS DIFFERENT.
AND...
IT FEELS LIKE...
PEOPLE...
ARE STARING AT ME.

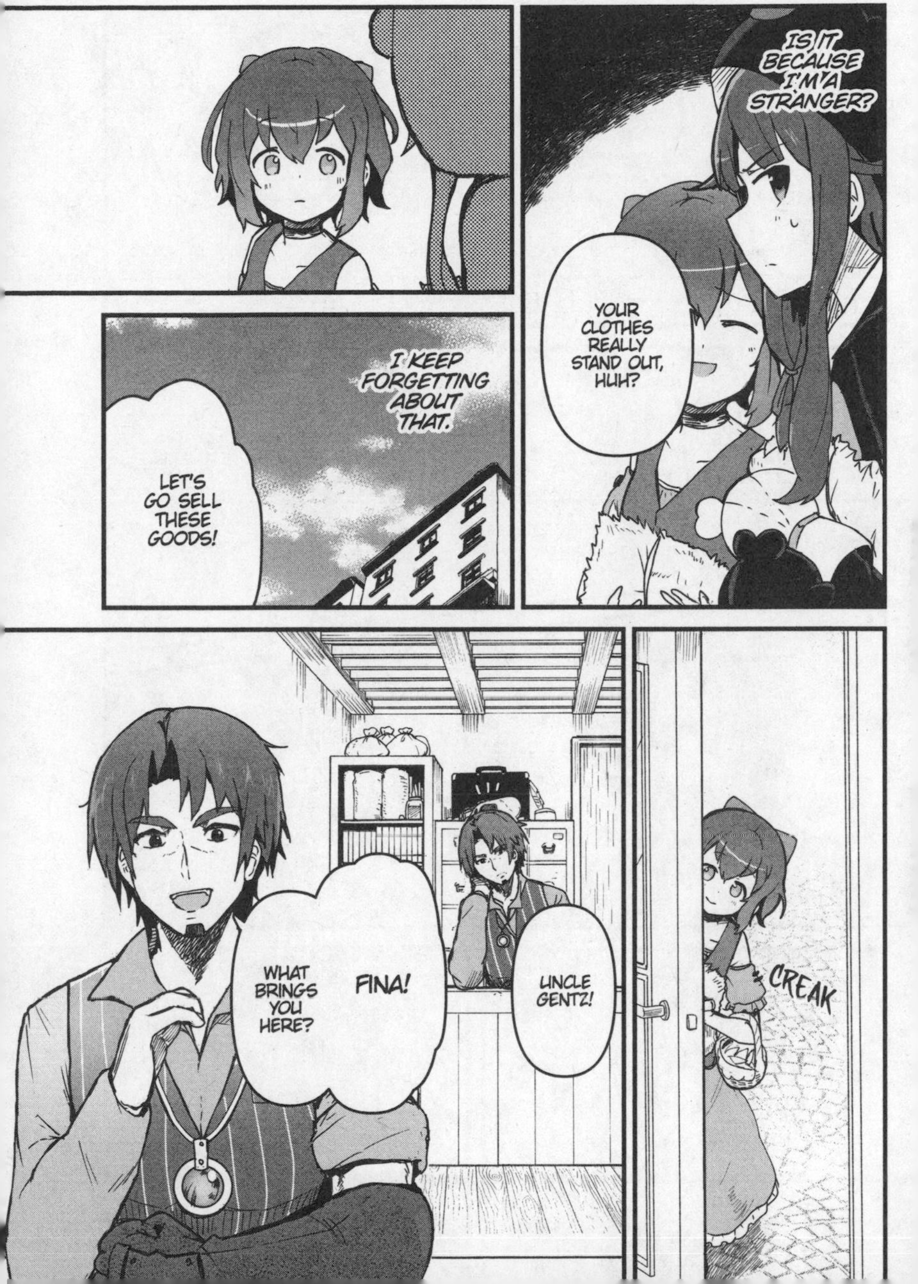
IS IT BECAUSE I'M A STRANGER?
YOUR CLOTHES REALLY STAND OUT, HUH?
I KEEP FORGETTING ABOUT THAT.
LET'S GO SELL THESE GOODS!
CREAK
UNCLE GENTZ!
FINA!
WHAT BRINGS YOU HERE?

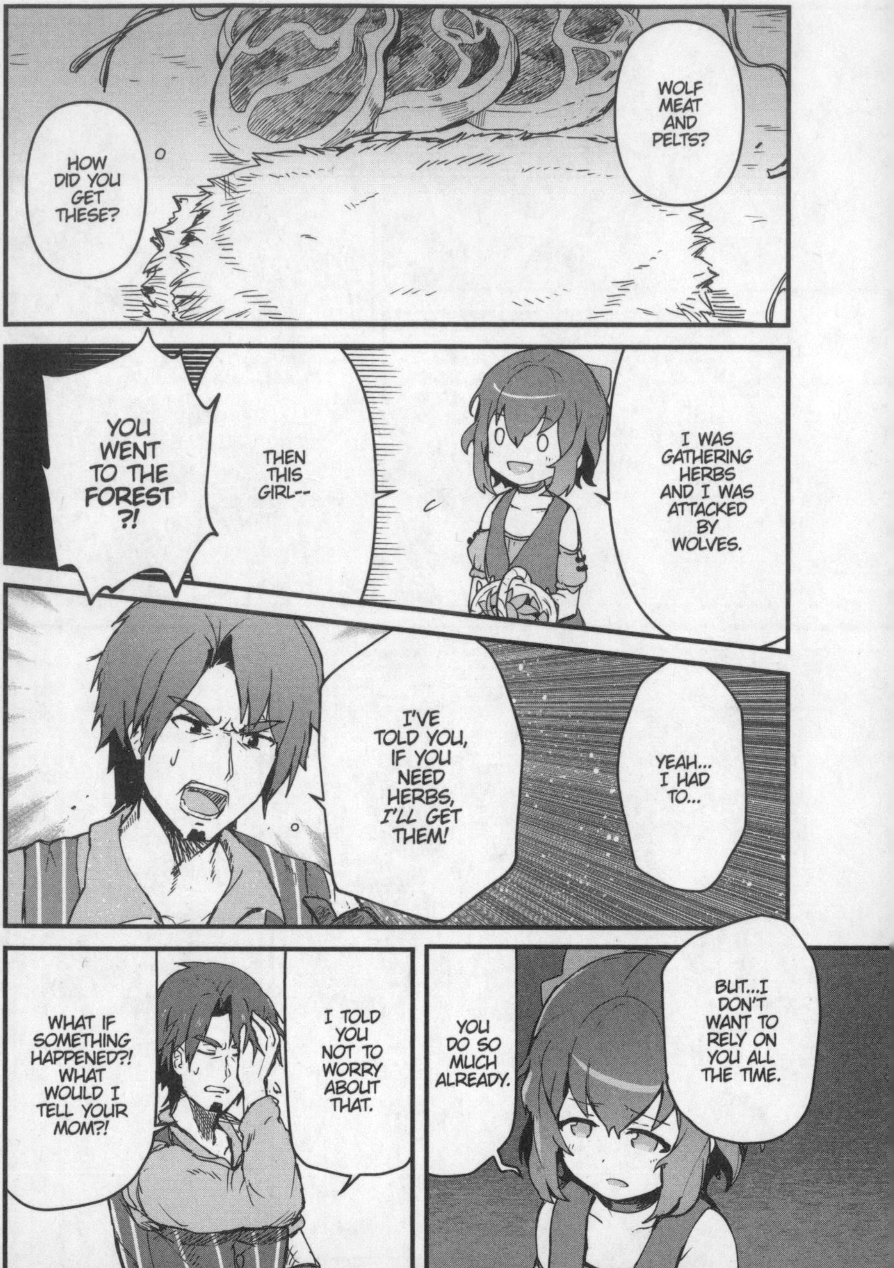
WOLF MEAT AND PELTS?
HOW DID YOU GET THESE?
I WAS GATHERING HERBS AND I WAS ATTACKED BY WOLVES.
THEN THIS GIRL--
YOU WENT TO THE FOREST?!
YEAH... I HAD TO...
I'VE TOLD YOU, IF YOU NEED HERBS, *I'LL* GET THEM!
BUT...I DON'T WANT TO RELY ON YOU ALL THE TIME.
YOU DO SO MUCH ALREADY.
I TOLD YOU NOT TO WORRY ABOUT THAT.
WHAT IF SOMETHING HAPPENED?! WHAT WOULD I TELL YOUR MOM?!

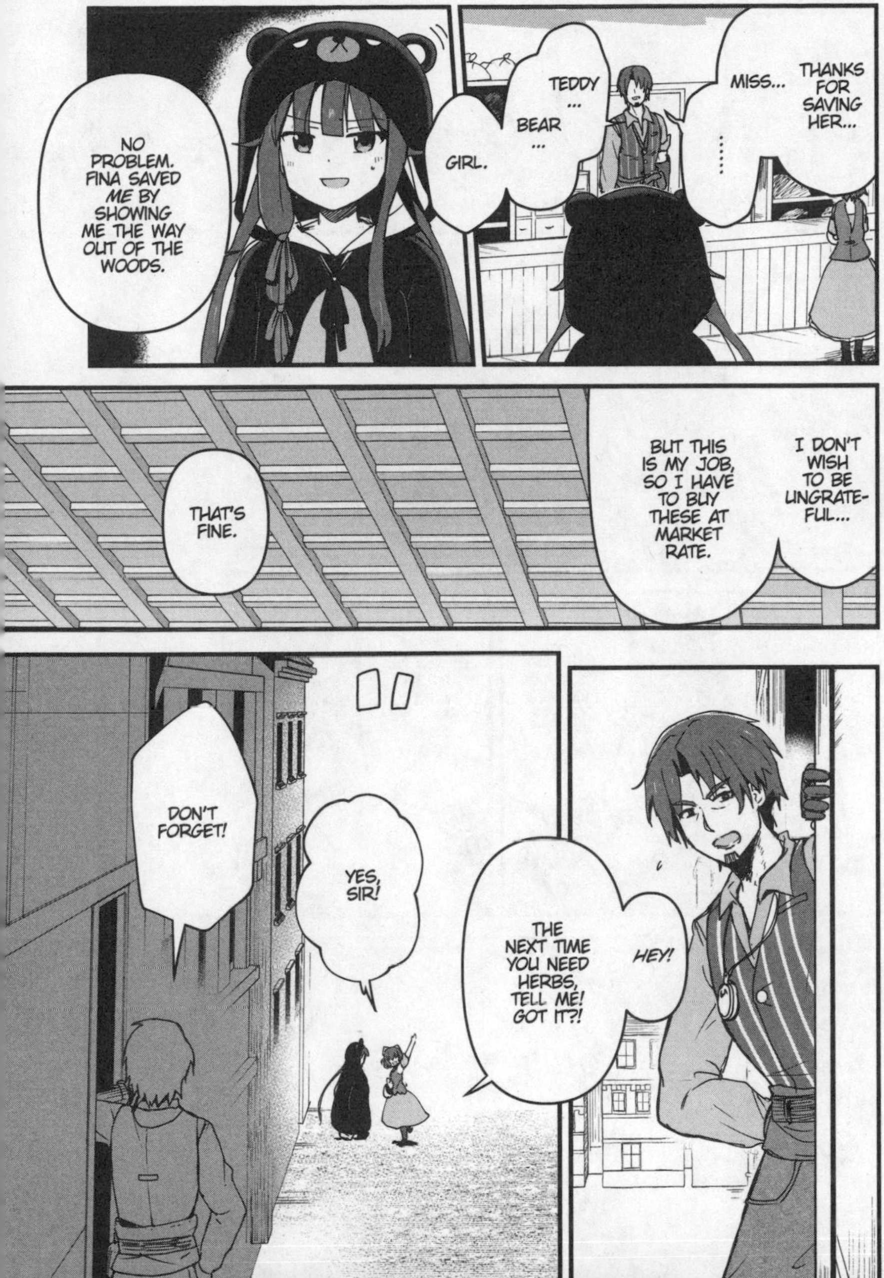
THANKS FOR SAVING HER...
MISS...
......
TEDDY ... BEAR ... GIRL.
NO PROBLEM. FINA SAVED ME BY SHOWING ME THE WAY OUT OF THE WOODS.
I DON'T WISH TO BE UNGRATEFUL...
BUT THIS IS MY JOB, SO I HAVE TO BUY THESE AT MARKET RATE.
THAT'S FINE.
HEY!
THE NEXT TIME YOU NEED HERBS, TELL ME! GOT IT?!
YES, SIR!
DON'T FORGET!

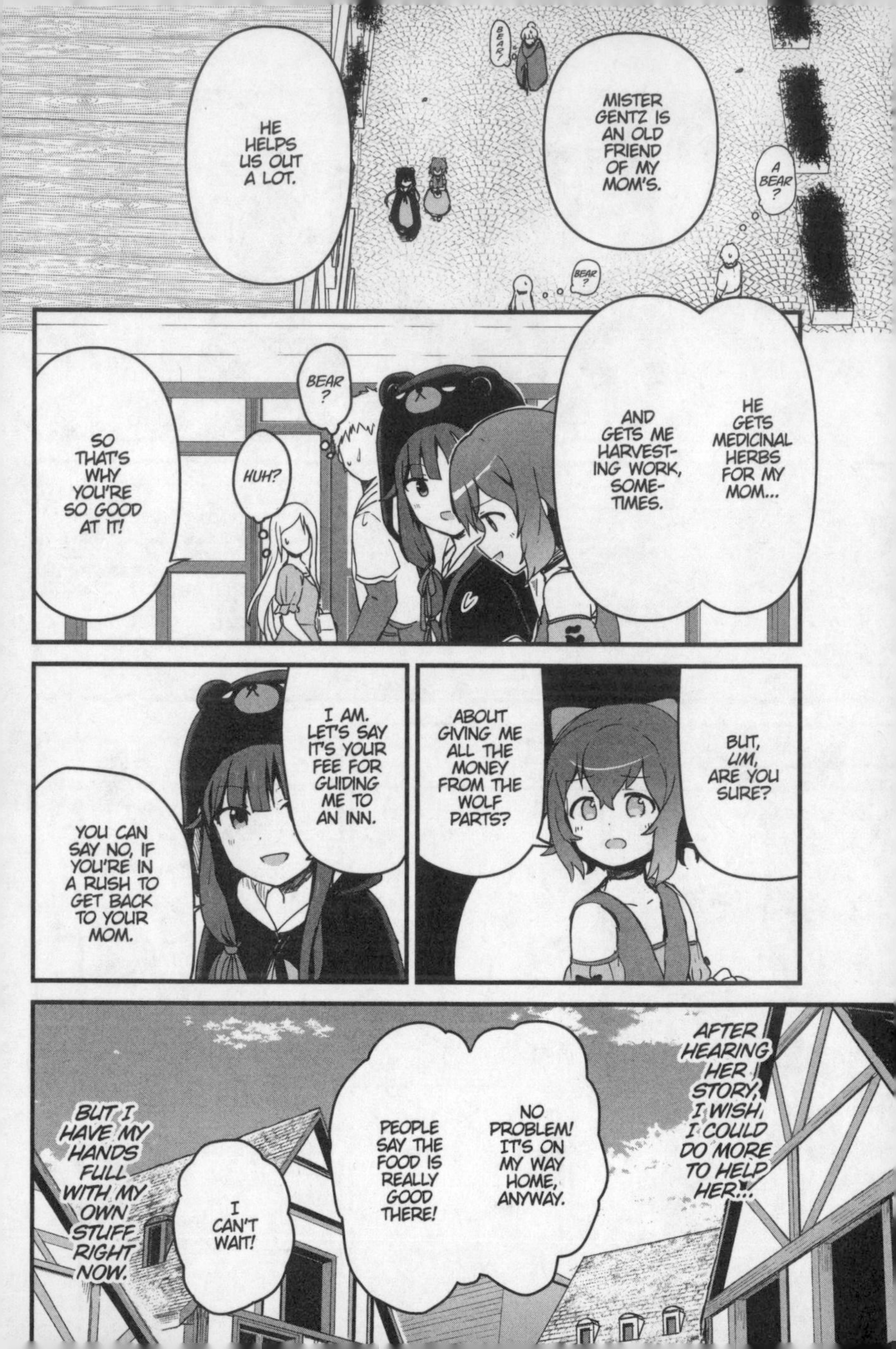
MISTER GENTZ IS AN OLD FRIEND OF MY MOM'S.
HE HELPS US OUT A LOT.
A BEAR?
BEAR?
BEAR?
HE GETS MEDICINAL HERBS FOR MY MOM...
AND GETS ME HARVESTING WORK, SOMETIMES.
BEAR?
HUH?
SO THAT'S WHY YOU'RE SO GOOD AT IT!
BUT, UM, ARE YOU SURE?
ABOUT GIVING ME ALL THE MONEY FROM THE WOLF PARTS?
I AM. LET'S SAY IT'S YOUR FEE FOR GUIDING ME TO AN INN.
YOU CAN SAY NO, IF YOU'RE IN A RUSH TO GET BACK TO YOUR MOM.
AFTER HEARING HER STORY, I WISH I COULD DO MORE TO HELP HER...
NO PROBLEM! IT'S ON MY WAY HOME, ANYWAY.
PEOPLE SAY THE FOOD IS REALLY GOOD THERE!
I CAN'T WAIT!
BUT I HAVE MY HANDS FULL WITH MY OWN STUFF RIGHT NOW.

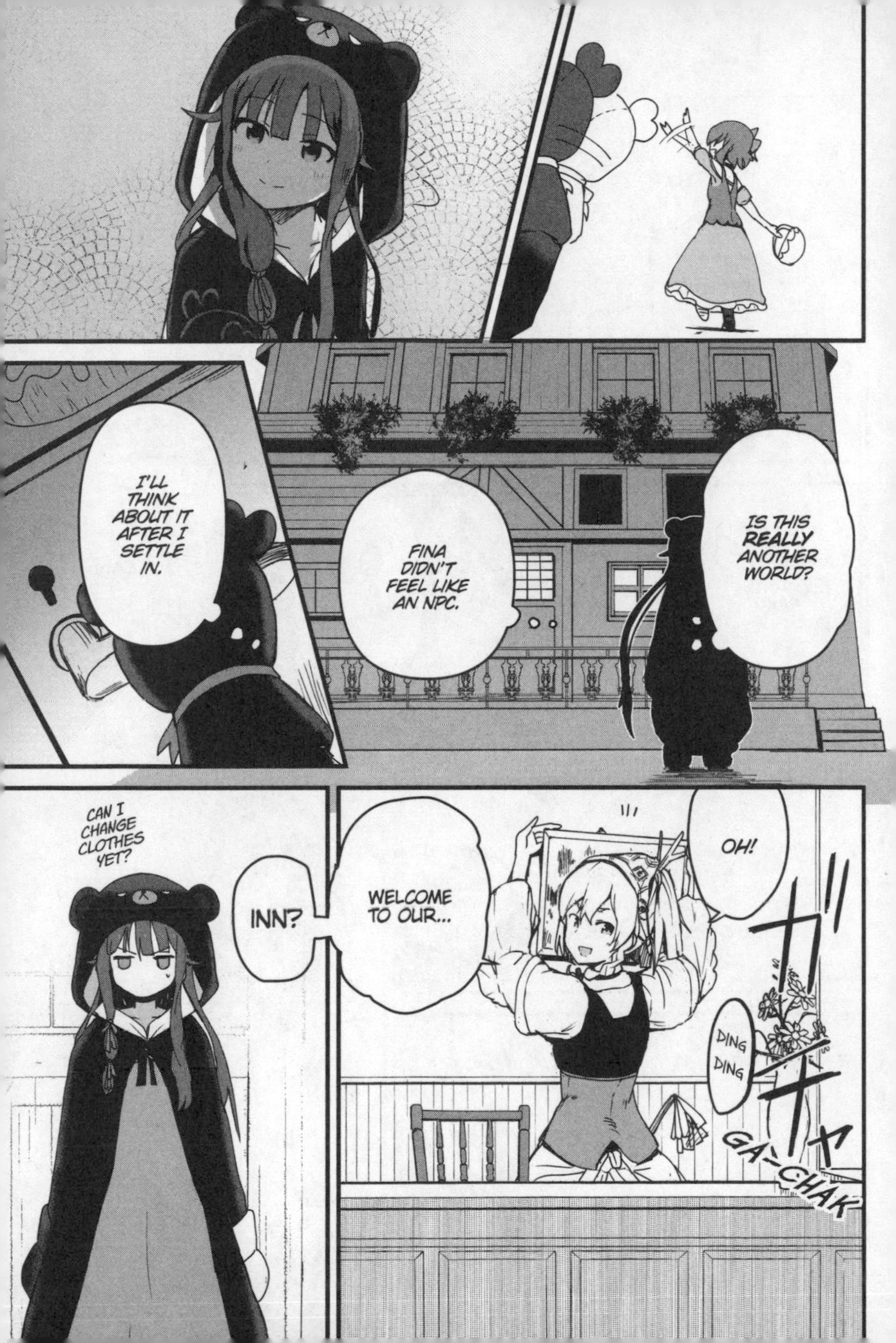
IS THIS REALLY ANOTHER WORLD?
FINA DIDN'T FEEL LIKE AN NPC.
I'LL THINK ABOUT IT AFTER I SETTLE IN.
OH!
GA-CHAK
DING DING
WELCOME TO OUR...
INN?
CAN I CHANGE CLOTHES YET?

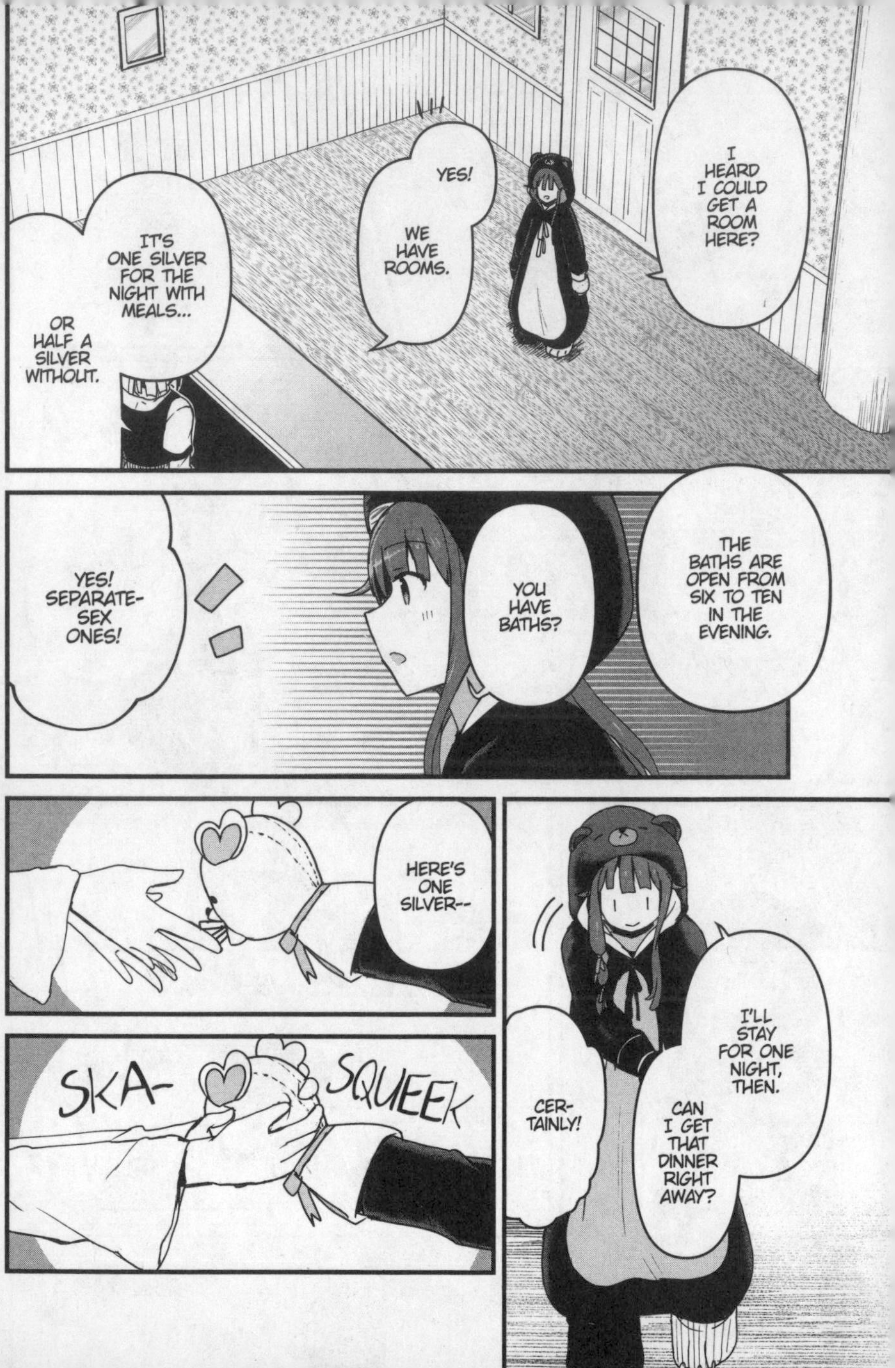
I HEARD I COULD GET A ROOM HERE?
YES!
WE HAVE ROOMS.
IT'S ONE SILVER FOR THE NIGHT WITH MEALS...
OR HALF A SILVER WITHOUT.
THE BATHS ARE OPEN FROM SIX TO TEN IN THE EVENING.
YOU HAVE BATHS?
YES! SEPARATE-SEX ONES!
I'LL STAY FOR ONE NIGHT, THEN.
CAN I GET THAT DINNER RIGHT AWAY?
CER-TAINLY!
HERE'S ONE SILVER--
SKA-
SQUEEK

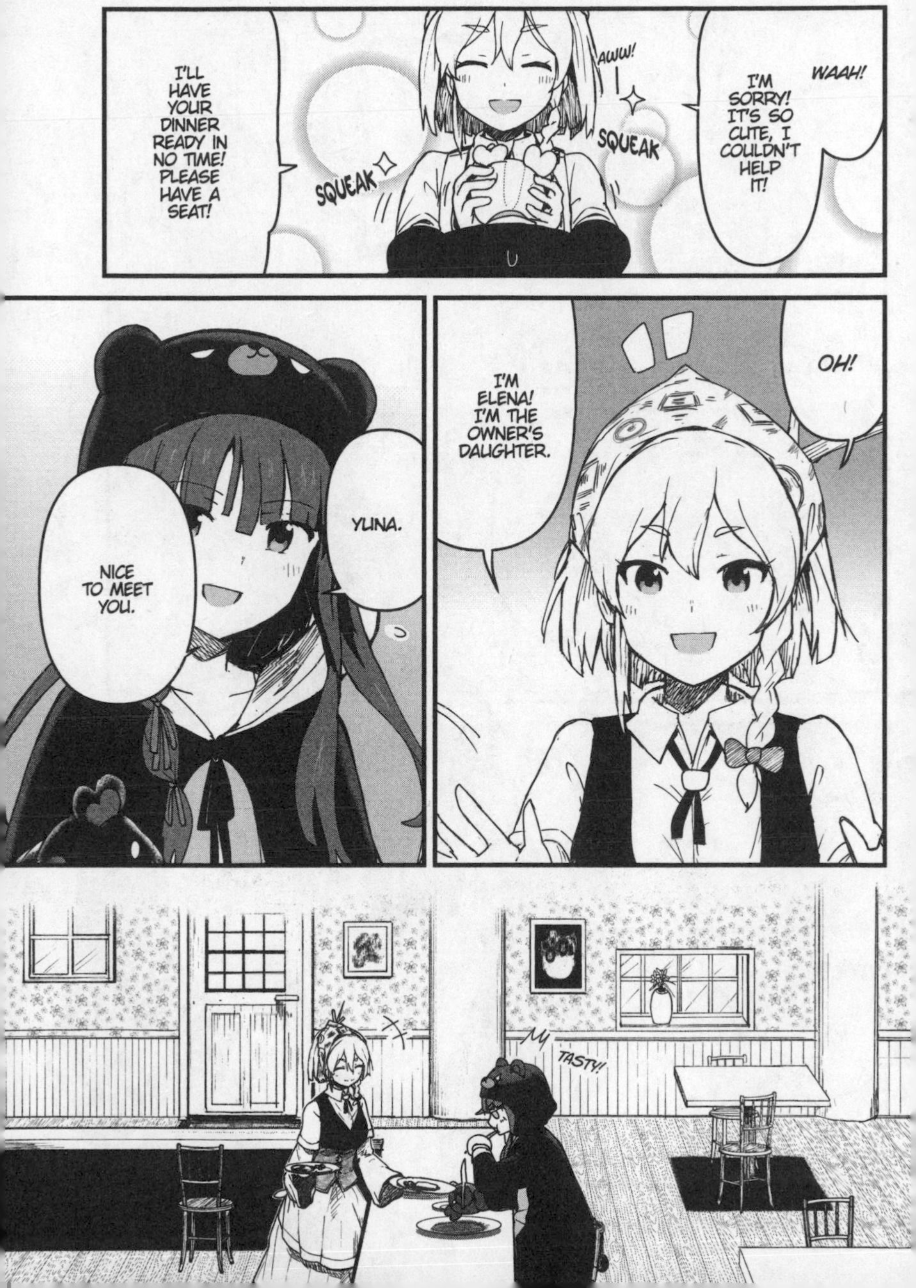
WAAH!
I'M SORRY! IT'S SO CUTE, I COULDN'T HELP IT!
AWW!
SQUEAK
SQUEAK
I'LL HAVE YOUR DINNER READY IN NO TIME! PLEASE HAVE A SEAT!
OH!
I'M ELENA! I'M THE OWNER'S DAUGHTER.
YUNA.
NICE TO MEET YOU.
TASTY!

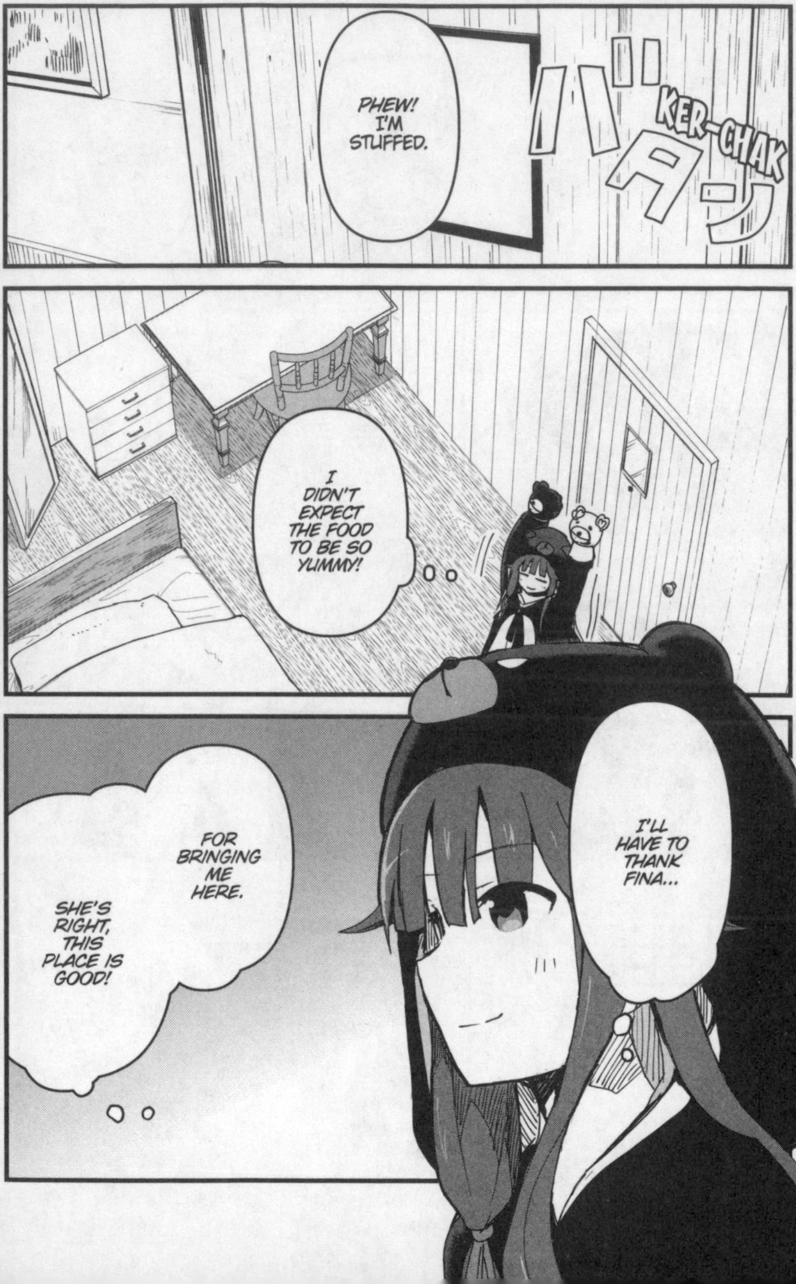
バターン
KER-CHAK
PHEW! I'M STUFFED.
I DIDN'T EXPECT THE FOOD TO BE SO YUMMY!
I'LL HAVE TO THANK FINA...
FOR BRINGING ME HERE.
SHE'S RIGHT, THIS PLACE IS GOOD!

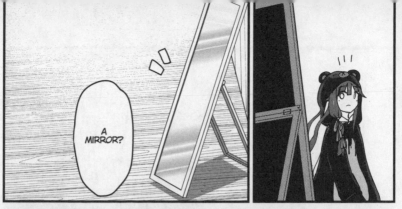

A MIRROR?

I NEVER DID SEE HOW I LOOK WEARING THIS.

I'D RATHER NOT, BUT MAYBE I SHOULD.

BUT I'M NERVOUS...

PEEK

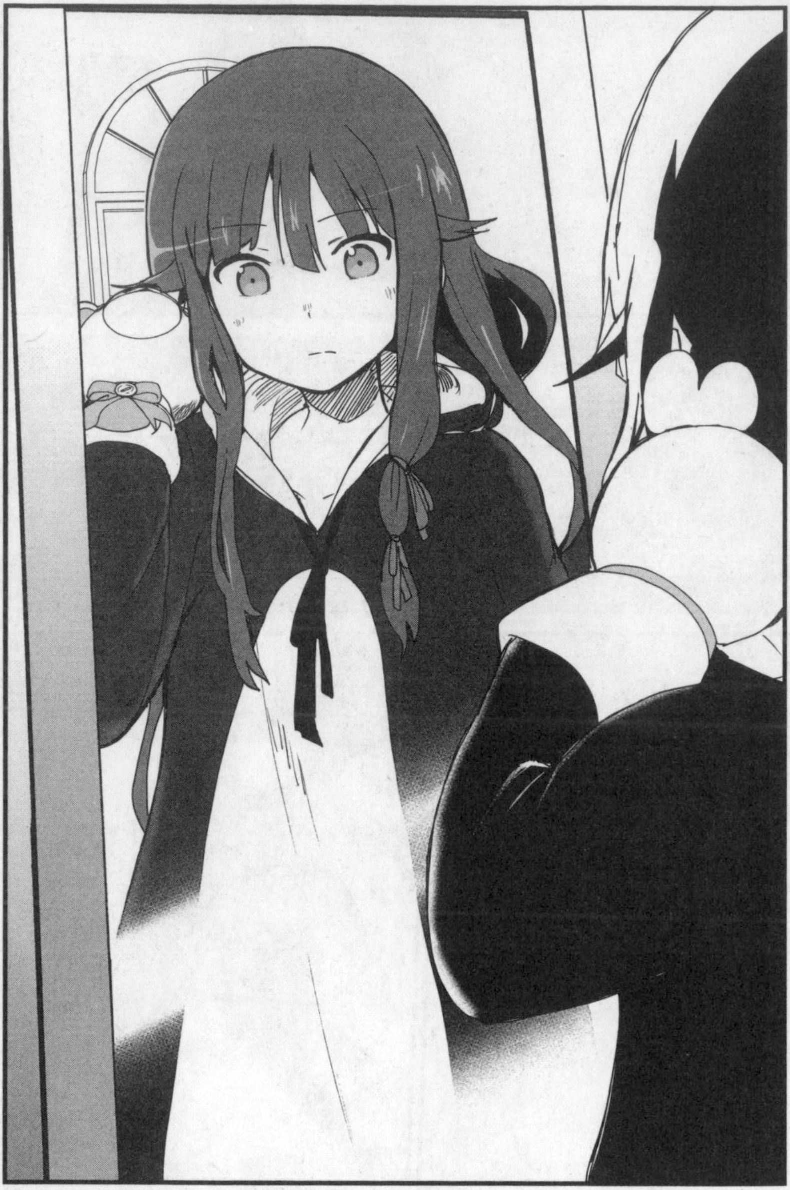

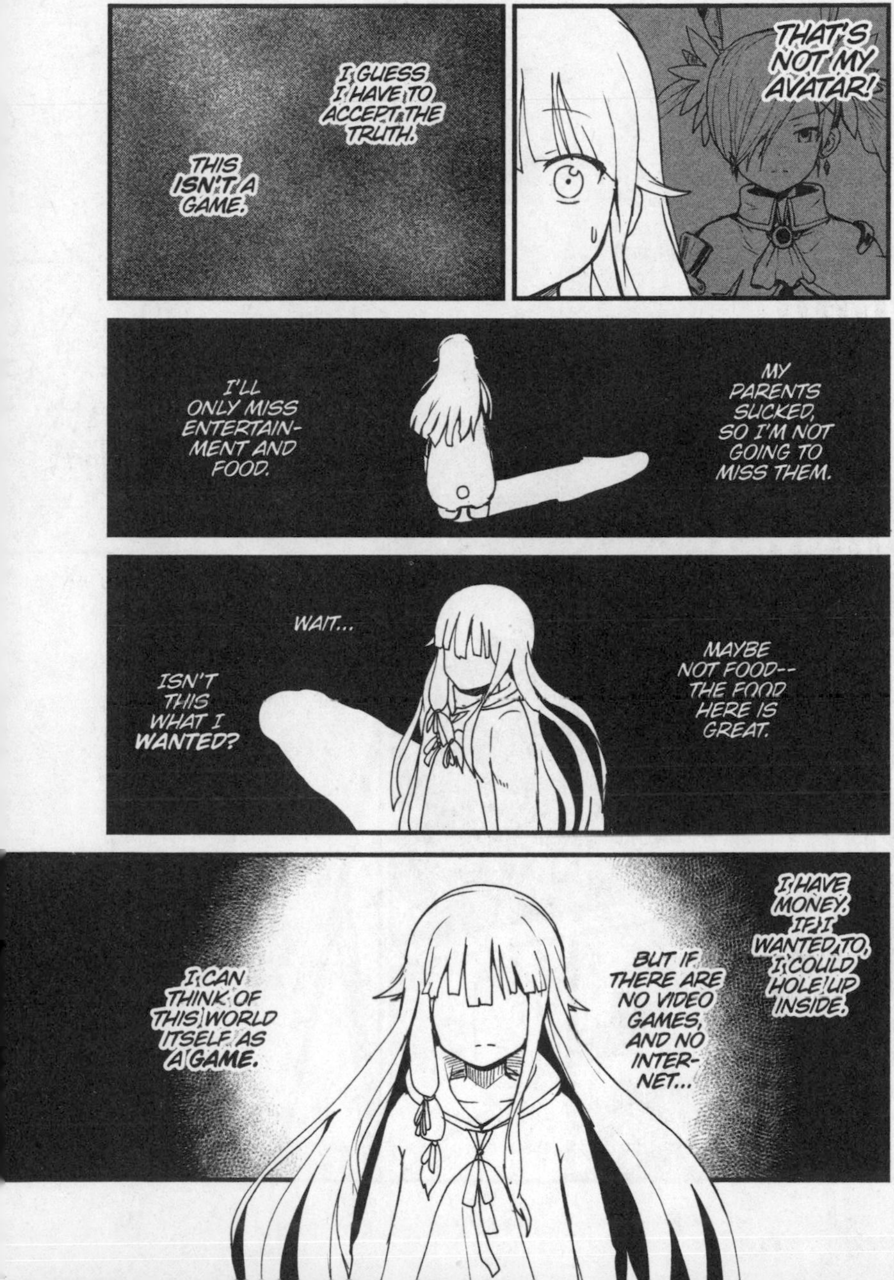
THAT'S NOT MY AVATAR!
I GUESS I HAVE TO ACCEPT THE TRUTH.
THIS ISN'T A GAME.
MY PARENTS SUCKED, SO I'M NOT GOING TO MISS THEM.
I'LL ONLY MISS ENTERTAIN-MENT AND FOOD.
MAYBE NOT FOOD-- THE FOOD HERE IS GREAT.
WAIT...
ISN'T THIS WHAT I WANTED?
I HAVE MONEY. IF I WANTED TO, I COULD HOLE UP INSIDE.
BUT IF THERE ARE NO VIDEO GAMES, AND NO INTER-NET...
I CAN THINK OF THIS WORLD ITSELF AS A GAME.

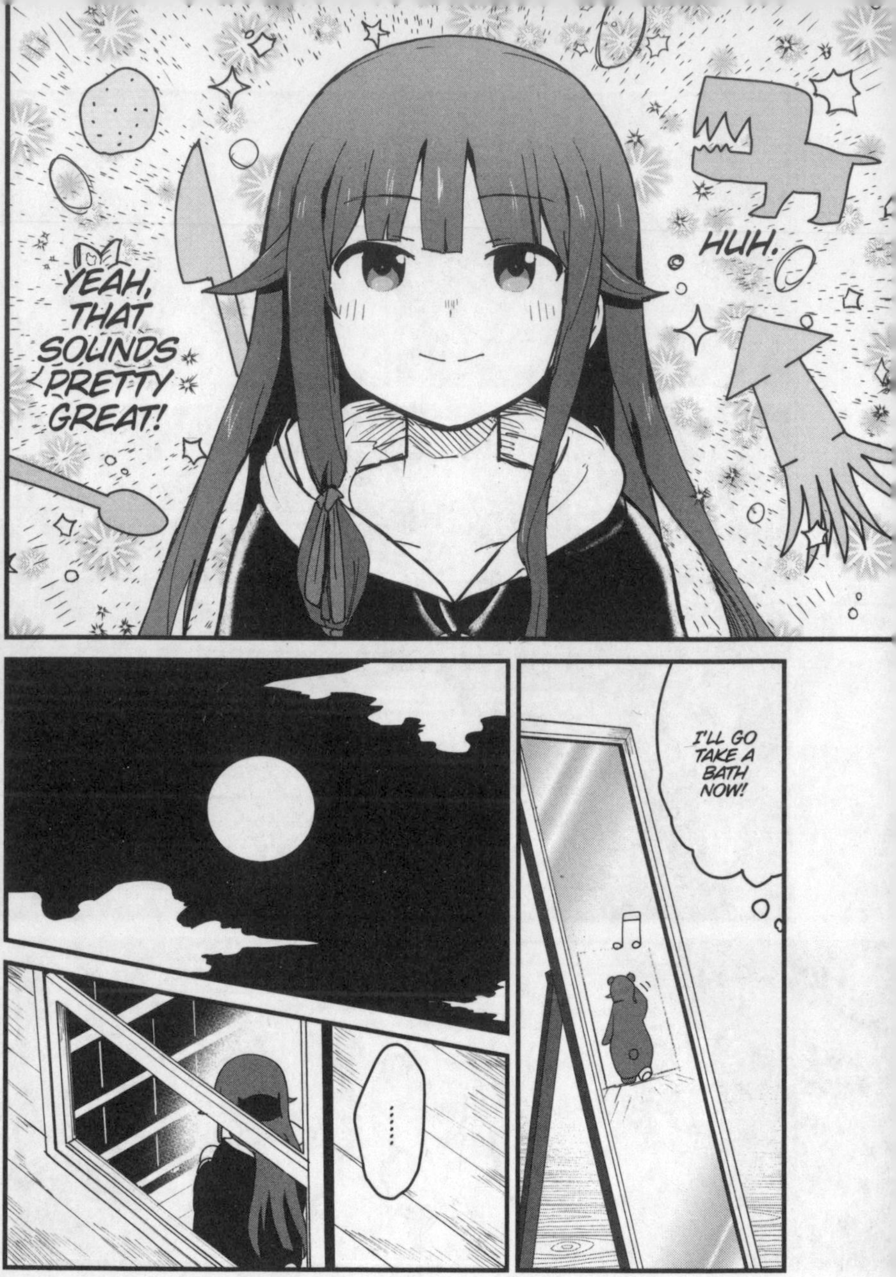
HUH.
YEAH, THAT SOUNDS PRETTY GREAT!
I'LL GO TAKE A BATH NOW!
......

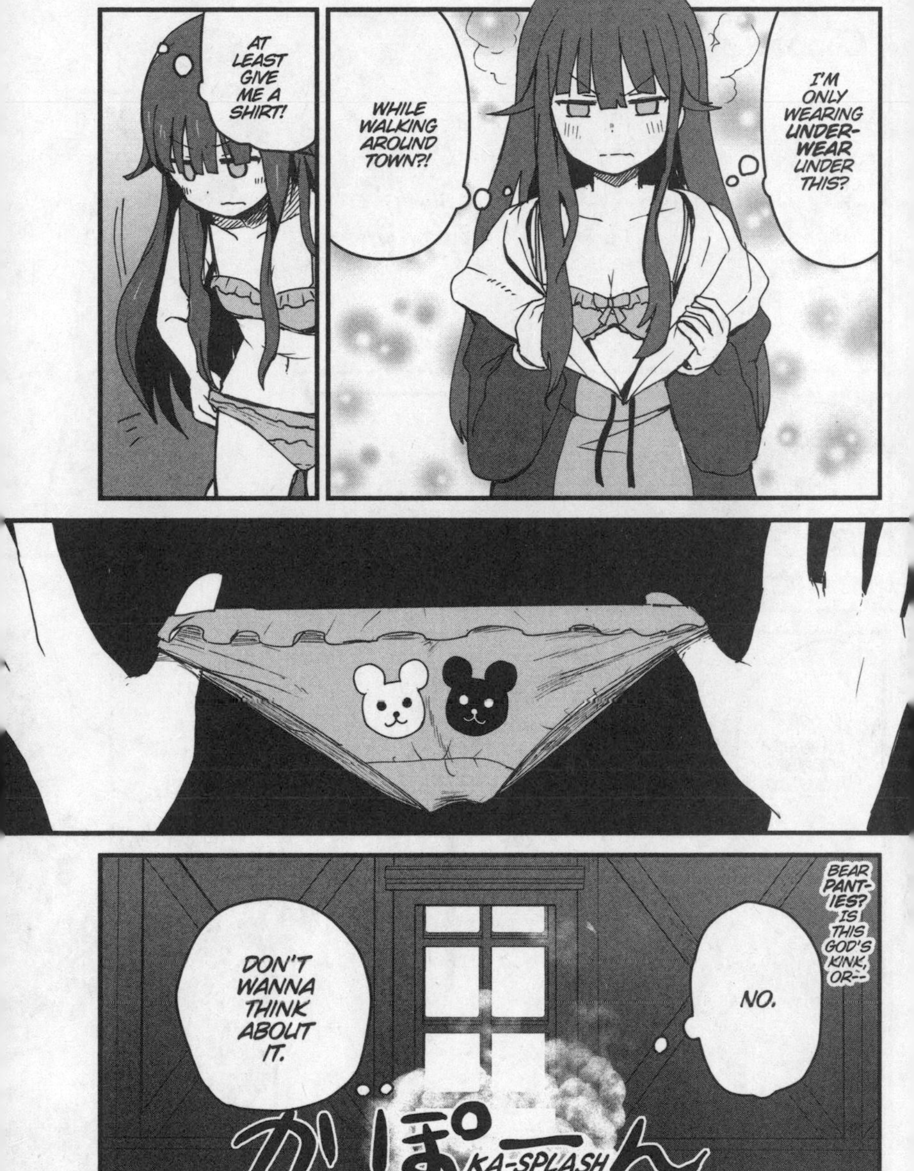
I'M ONLY WEARING UNDERWEAR UNDER THIS?
WHILE WALKING AROUND TOWN?!
AT LEAST GIVE ME A SHIRT!
BEAR PANTIES? IS THIS GOD'S KINK, OR--
NO.
DON'T WANNA THINK ABOUT IT.
かぽーん
KA-SPLASH

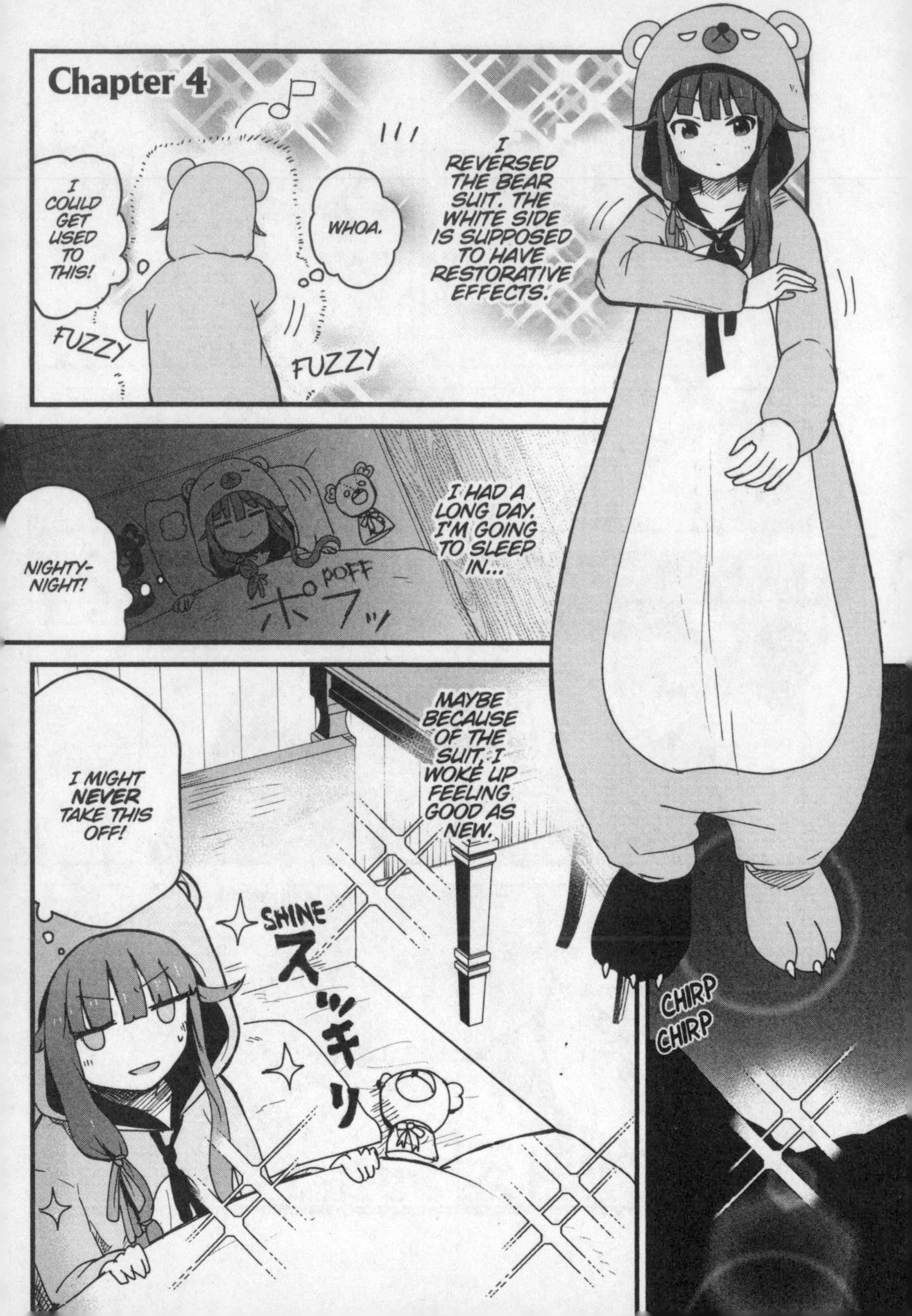
Chapter 4
I REVERSED THE BEAR SUIT. THE WHITE SIDE IS SUPPOSED TO HAVE RESTORATIVE EFFECTS.
WHOA.
I COULD GET USED TO THIS!
FUZZY
FUZZY
I HAD A LONG DAY. I'M GOING TO SLEEP IN...
POFF
ポフッ
NIGHTY-NIGHT!
MAYBE BECAUSE OF THE SUIT, I WOKE UP FEELING GOOD AS NEW.
CHIRP CHIRP
SHINE
スッキリ
I MIGHT NEVER TAKE THIS OFF!

YOU'RE A WHITE BEAR TODAY?
IT'S SO CUTE ON YOU!
UH, THANKS.
I FORGOT TO TURN IT BACK.
ALRIGHTY!
WHAT SHOULD I DO TODAY?
1. Buy clothes
2. Get an I.D.
3. Buy a weapon
4. Gather info
5. Test my strength
I THINK GETTING I.D. COMES FIRST.
ELENA-SAN, I CAN GET AN I.D. AT THE ADVENTURER'S GUILD, RIGHT?
YUP! THEY CAN MAKE THAT FOR YOU!
WHERE IS IT?

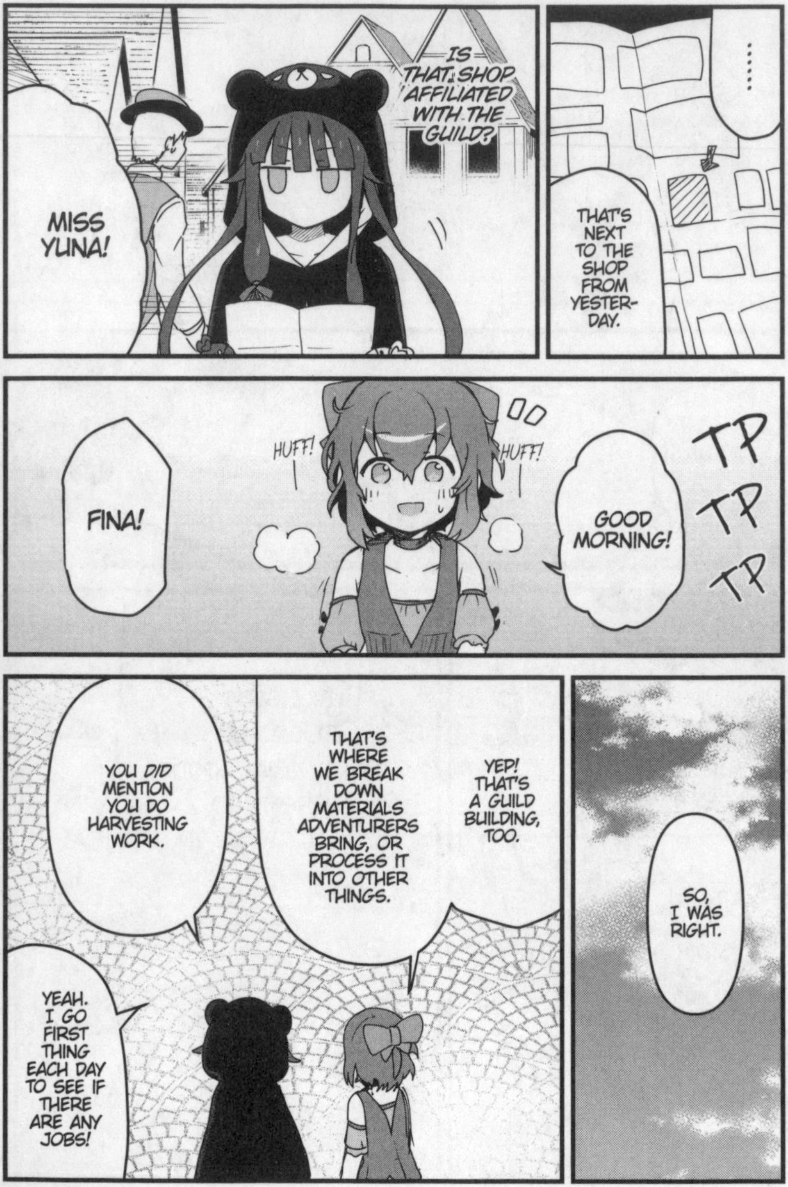
......
THAT'S NEXT TO THE SHOP FROM YESTER-DAY.
IS THAT SHOP AFFILIATED WITH THE GUILD?
MISS YUNA!
TP TP TP
GOOD MORNING!
HUFF! HUFF!
FINA!
SO, I WAS RIGHT.
YEP! THAT'S A GUILD BUILDING, TOO.
THAT'S WHERE WE BREAK DOWN MATERIALS ADVENTURERS BRING, OR PROCESS IT INTO OTHER THINGS.
YOU *DID* MENTION YOU DO HARVESTING WORK.
YEAH. I GO FIRST THING EACH DAY TO SEE IF THERE ARE ANY JOBS!

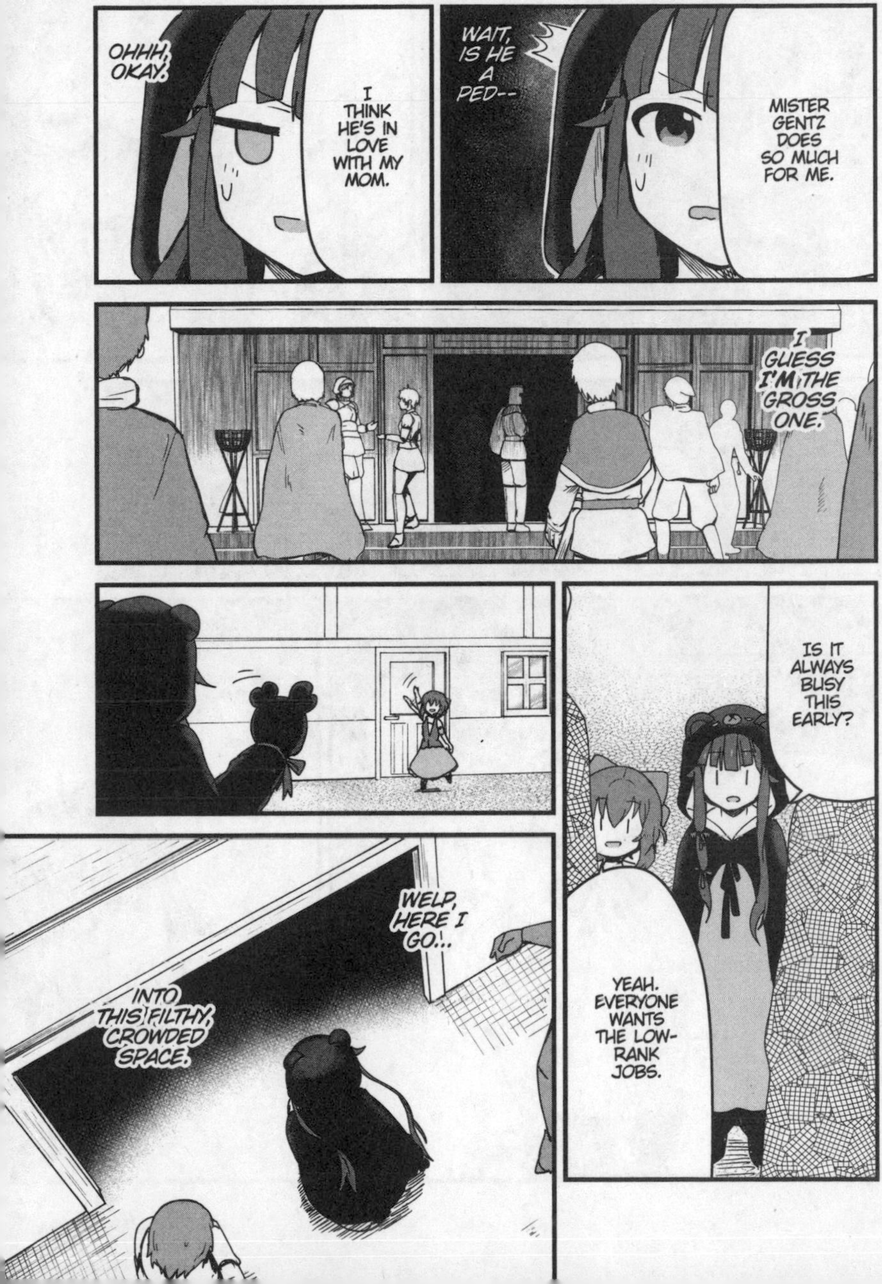
MISTER GENTZ DOES SO MUCH FOR ME.
WAIT, IS HE A PED--
I THINK HE'S IN LOVE WITH MY MOM.
OHHH, OKAY.
I GUESS I'M THE GROSS ONE.
IS IT ALWAYS BUSY THIS EARLY?
YEAH. EVERYONE WANTS THE LOW-RANK JOBS.
WELP, HERE I GO...
INTO THIS FILTHY, CROWDED SPACE.

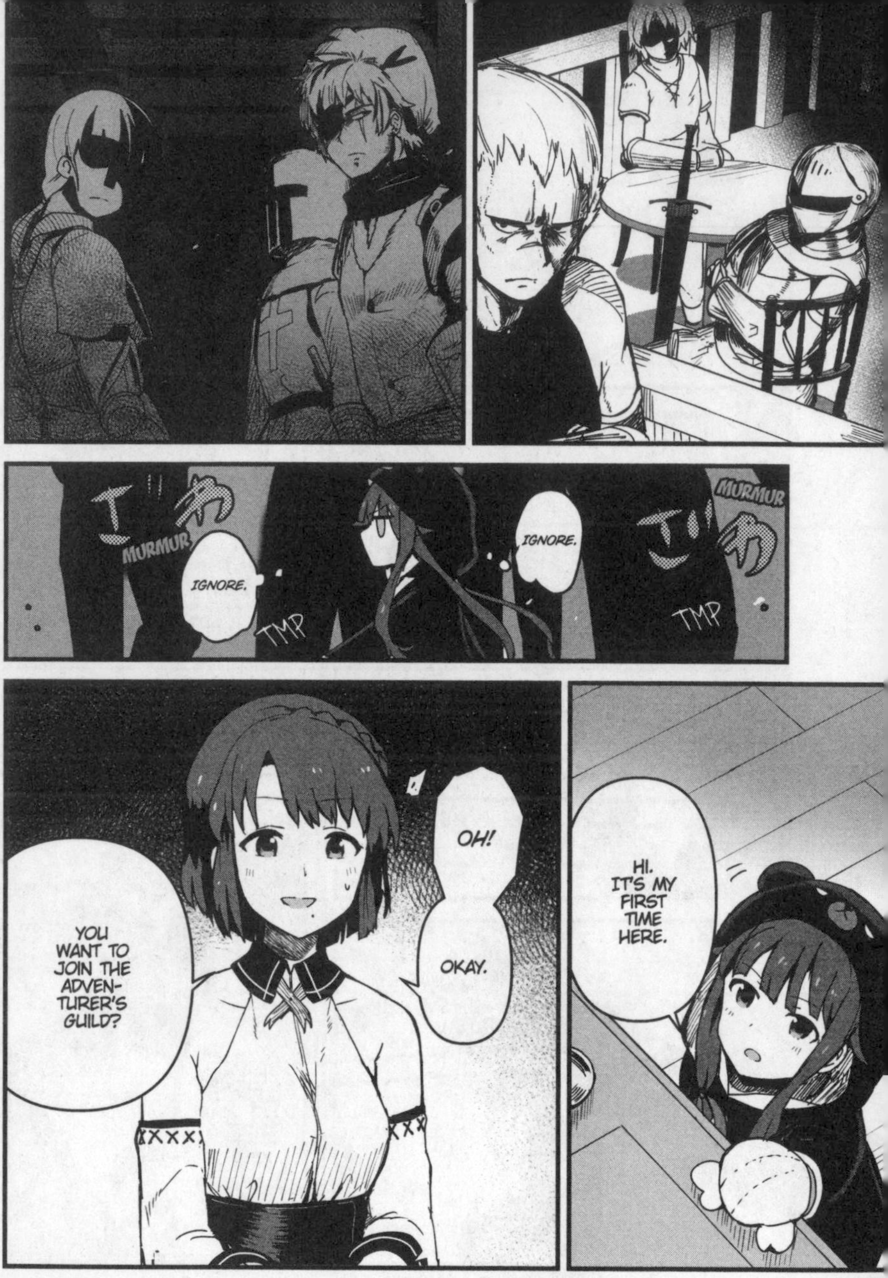
MURMUR
IGNORE.
TMP
IGNORE.
MURMUR
TMP
HI. IT'S MY FIRST TIME HERE.
OH!
OKAY.
YOU WANT TO JOIN THE ADVEN-TURER'S GUILD?

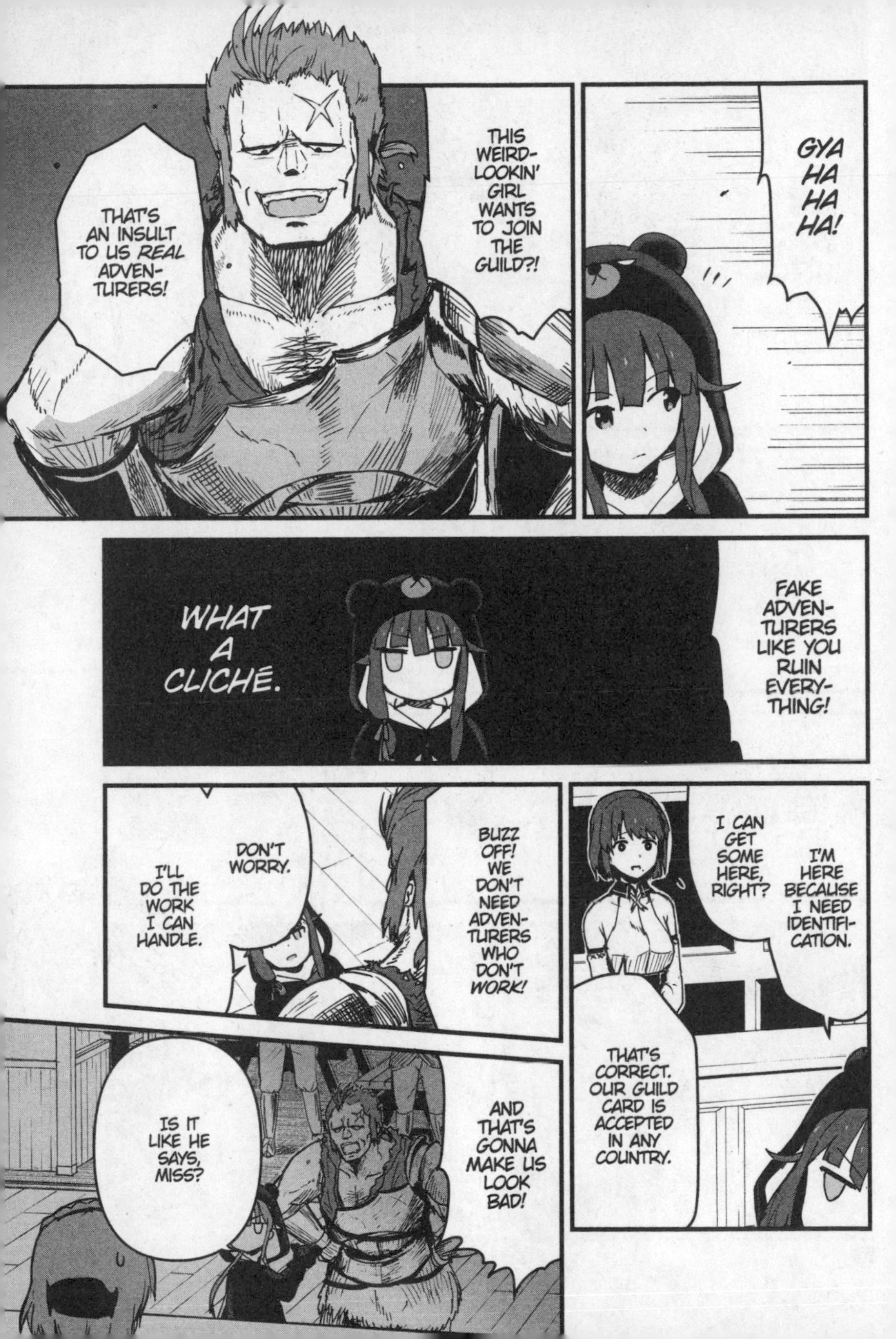

GYA HA HA HA!
THIS WEIRD-LOOKIN' GIRL WANTS TO JOIN THE GUILD?!
THAT'S AN INSULT TO US *REAL* ADVENTURERS!
FAKE ADVENTURERS LIKE YOU RUIN EVERYTHING!
WHAT A CLICHÉ.
I'M HERE BECAUSE I NEED IDENTIFICATION.
I CAN GET SOME HERE, RIGHT?
THAT'S CORRECT. OUR GUILD CARD IS ACCEPTED IN ANY COUNTRY.
BUZZ OFF! WE DON'T NEED ADVENTURERS WHO DON'T *WORK!*
DON'T WORRY.
I'LL DO THE WORK I CAN HANDLE.
AND THAT'S GONNA MAKE US LOOK BAD!
IS IT LIKE HE SAYS, MISS?

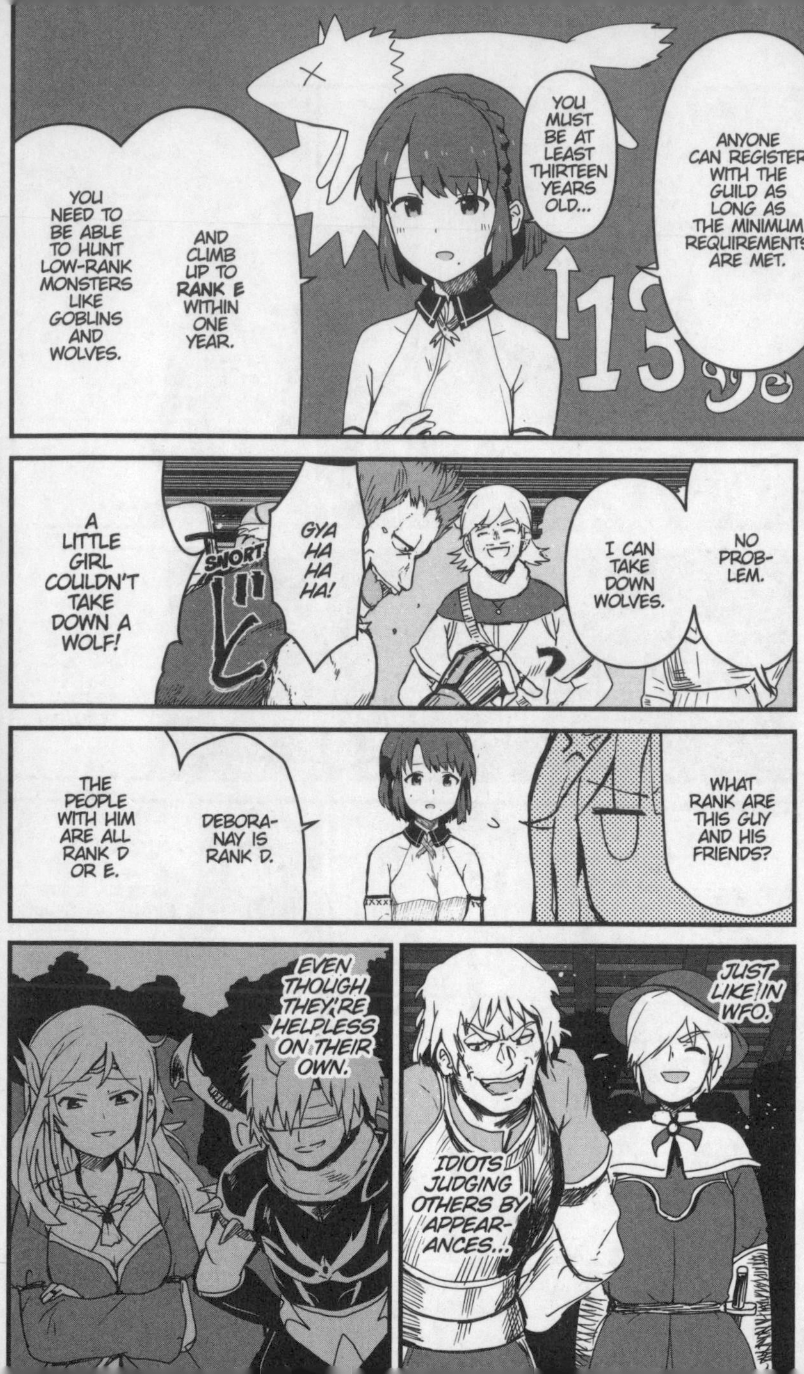
ANYONE CAN REGISTER WITH THE GUILD AS LONG AS THE MINIMUM REQUIREMENTS ARE MET.
YOU MUST BE AT LEAST THIRTEEN YEARS OLD...
13
YOU NEED TO BE ABLE TO HUNT LOW-RANK MONSTERS LIKE GOBLINS AND WOLVES.
AND CLIMB UP TO RANK E WITHIN ONE YEAR.
NO PROBLEM.
I CAN TAKE DOWN WOLVES.
GYA HA HA HA!
SNORT
A LITTLE GIRL COULDN'T TAKE DOWN A WOLF!
WHAT RANK ARE THIS GUY AND HIS FRIENDS?
DEBORANAY IS RANK D.
THE PEOPLE WITH HIM ARE ALL RANK D OR E.
JUST LIKE IN WFO.
IDIOTS JUDGING OTHERS BY APPEARANCES...
EVEN THOUGH THEY'RE HELPLESS ON THEIR OWN.

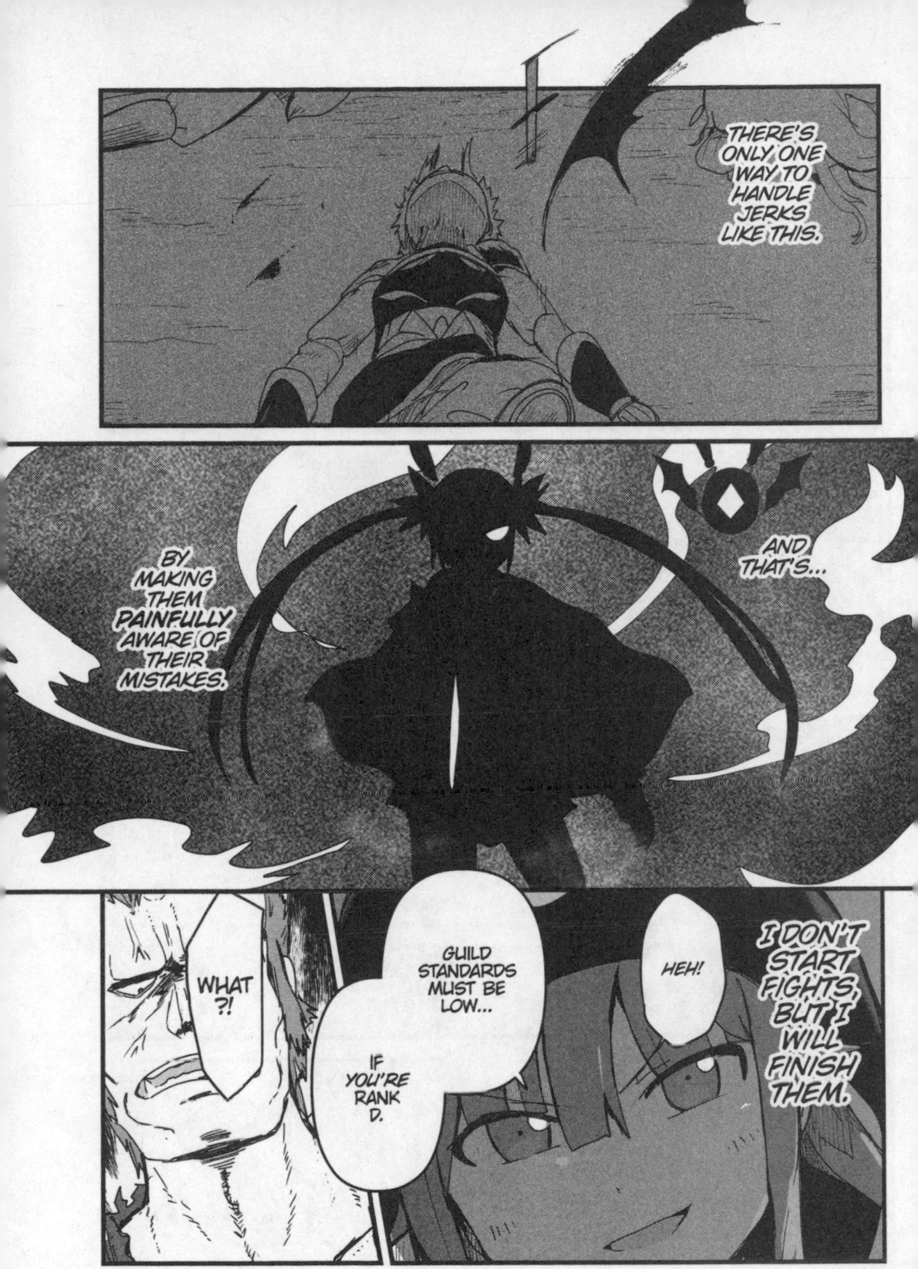
THERE'S ONLY ONE WAY TO HANDLE JERKS LIKE THIS.
AND THAT'S...
BY MAKING THEM PAINFULLY AWARE OF THEIR MISTAKES.
I DON'T START FIGHTS, BUT I WILL FINISH THEM.
HEH!
GUILD STANDARDS MUST BE LOW...
IF YOU'RE RANK D.
WHAT?!

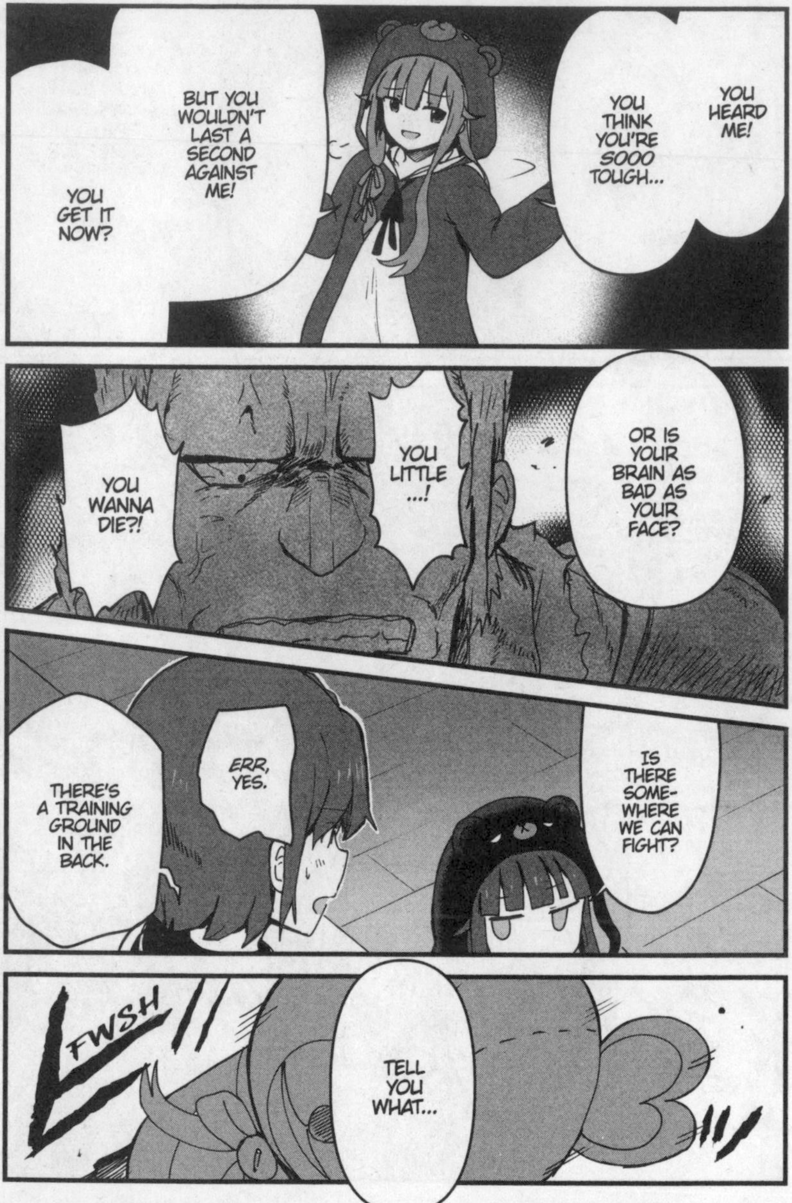
YOU HEARD ME!
YOU THINK YOU'RE SOOO TOUGH...
BUT YOU WOULDN'T LAST A SECOND AGAINST ME!
YOU GET IT NOW?
OR IS YOUR BRAIN AS BAD AS YOUR FACE?
YOU LITTLE ...!
YOU WANNA DIE?!
IS THERE SOME-WHERE WE CAN FIGHT?
ERR, YES.
THERE'S A TRAINING GROUND IN THE BACK.
TELL YOU WHAT...
FWSH

IF YOU CAN BEAT ME, I'LL GIVE UP ON BEING AN ADVENTURER!
IF *I* WIN, YOU *ALL* HAVE TO QUIT THE GUILD AND LEAVE!
PRETTY COCKY FOR A KID! ALL RIGHT.
IF YOU WIN, WE'LL QUIT!
AIN'T THAT RIGHT, FOLKS?!
YEAH!
HEH HEH!
YOU GOT ALL THAT, RIGHT?
YES, BUT YOU MIGHT WANT TO BACK DOWN.
THAT GUY'S A JERK, BUT HE'S STILL RANK D.

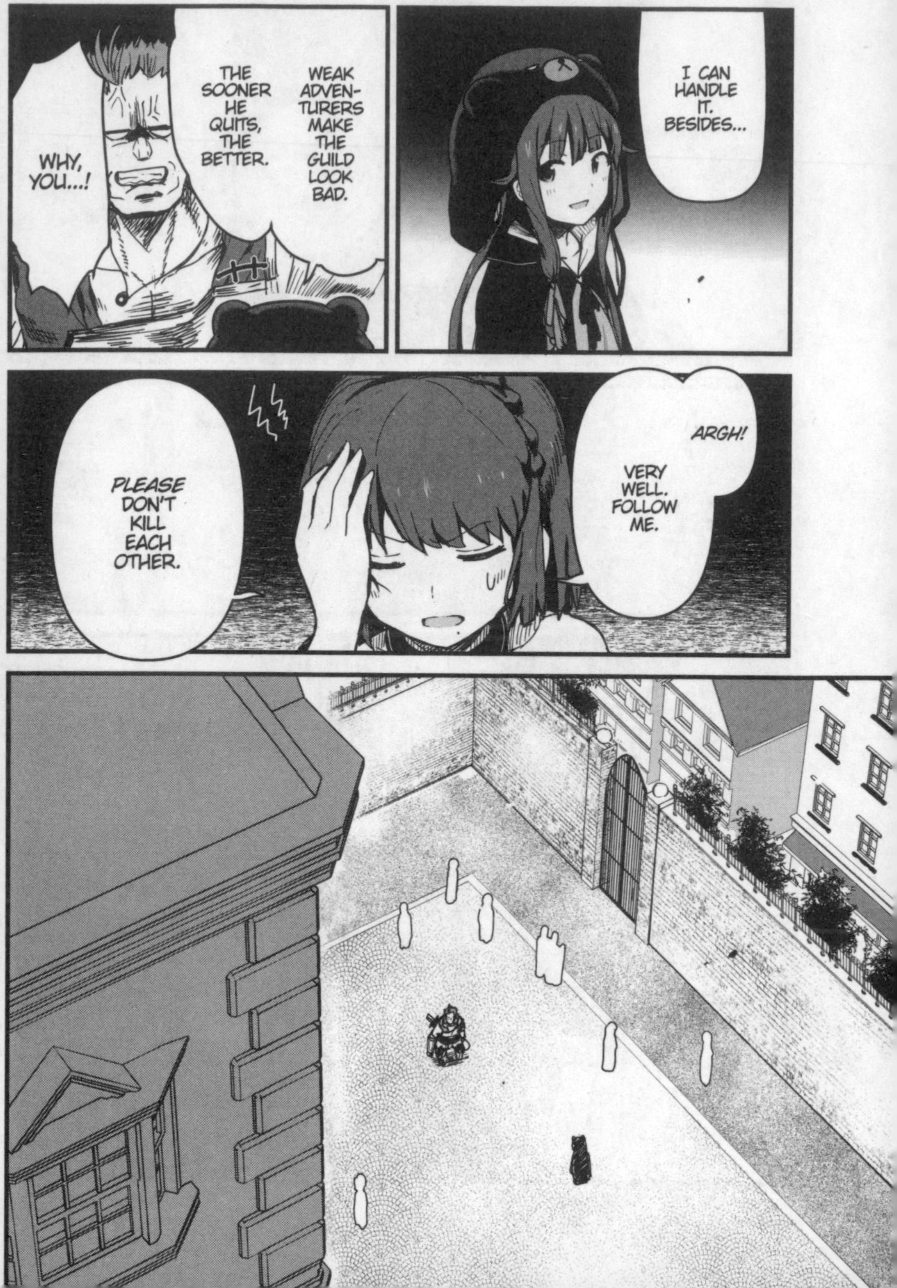
I CAN HANDLE IT. BESIDES...
WEAK ADVEN-TURERS MAKE THE GUILD LOOK BAD.
THE SOONER HE QUITS, THE BETTER.
WHY, YOU...!
ARGH!
VERY WELL. FOLLOW ME.
PLEASE DON'T KILL EACH OTHER.

WELL ?!

LET'S DO THIS!

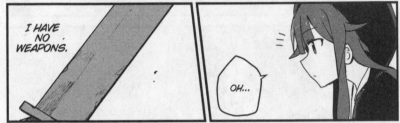

I HAVE NO WEAPONS.

OH...

MISS YUNA!

THAT STICK IS ALL I HAVE. I WONDER...

HMM.

COME AT ME! OR ARE YOU CHICKEN?!

SHUT UP. I'M THINKING.

HUH ?!

FINA!

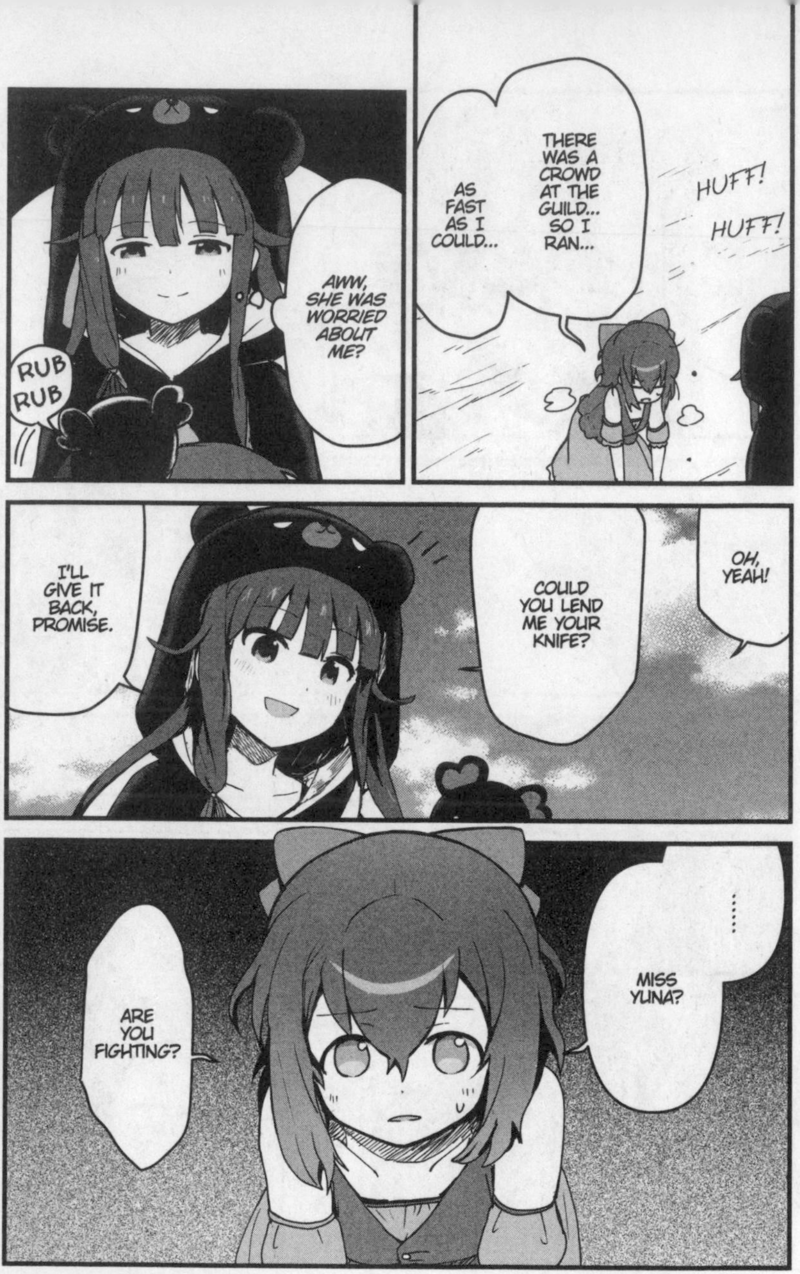
HUFF!
HUFF!
THERE WAS A CROWD AT THE GUILD... SO I RAN...
AS FAST AS I COULD...
AWW, SHE WAS WORRIED ABOUT ME?
RUB RUB
OH, YEAH!
COULD YOU LEND ME YOUR KNIFE?
I'LL GIVE IT BACK, PROMISE.
......
MISS YUNA?
ARE YOU FIGHTING?

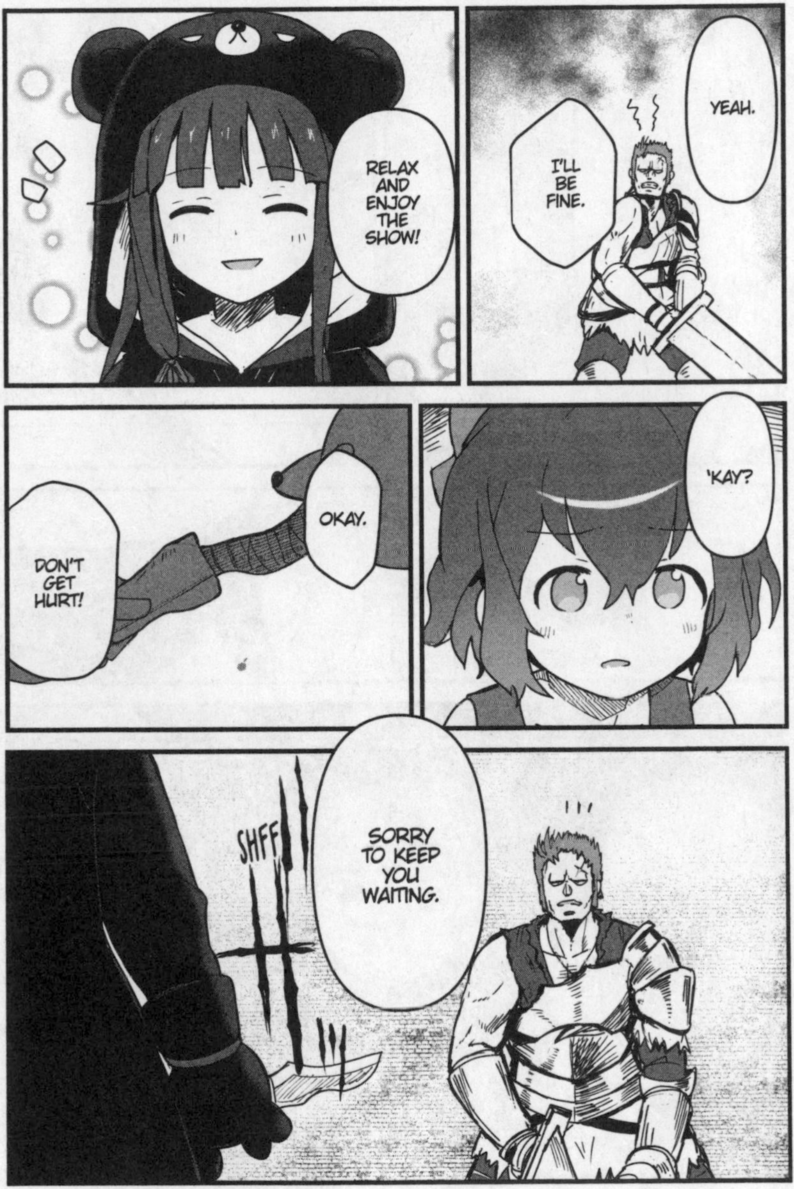
YEAH.
I'LL BE FINE.
RELAX AND ENJOY THE SHOW!
'KAY?
OKAY.
DON'T GET HURT!
SORRY TO KEEP YOU WAITING.
SHFF

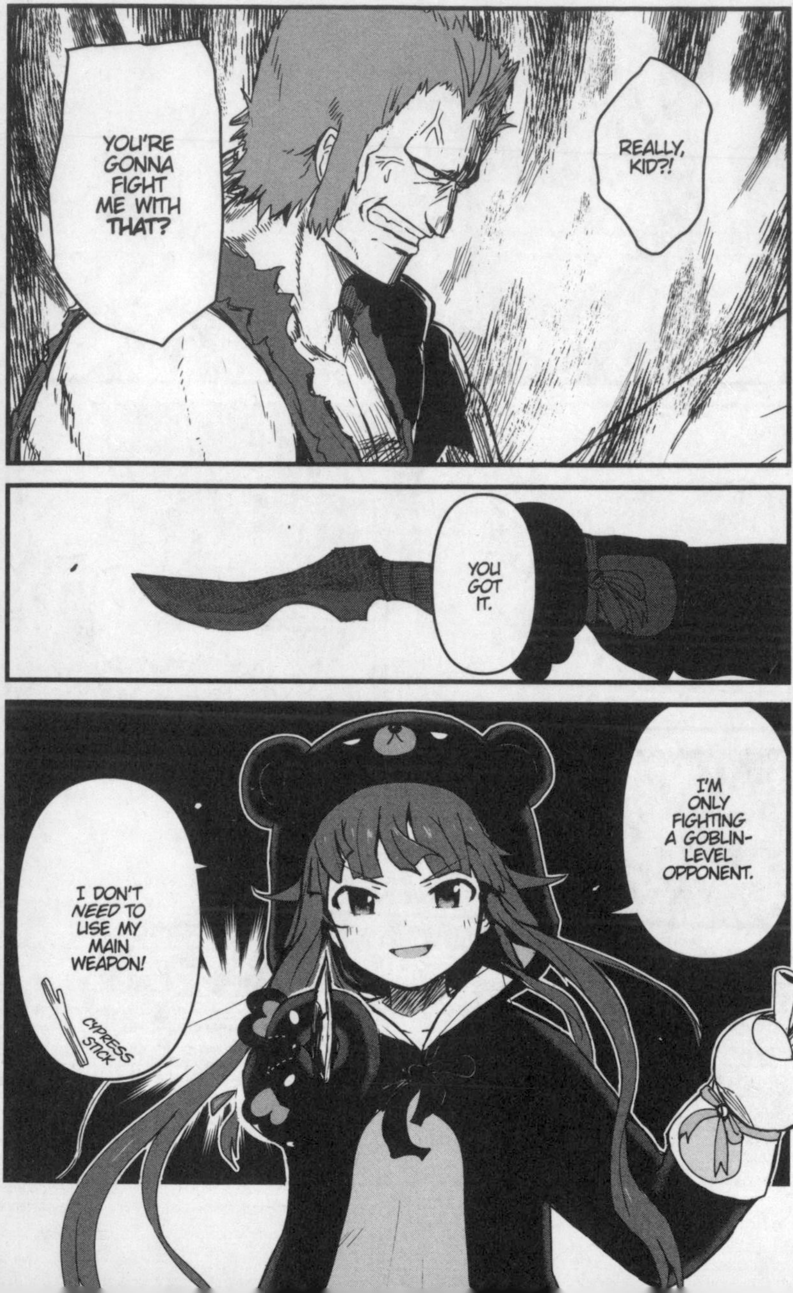
REALLY, KID?!
YOU'RE GONNA FIGHT ME WITH THAT?
YOU GOT IT.
I'M ONLY FIGHTING A GOBLIN-LEVEL OPPONENT.
I DON'T NEED TO USE MY MAIN WEAPON!
CYPRESS STICK

Chapter 5

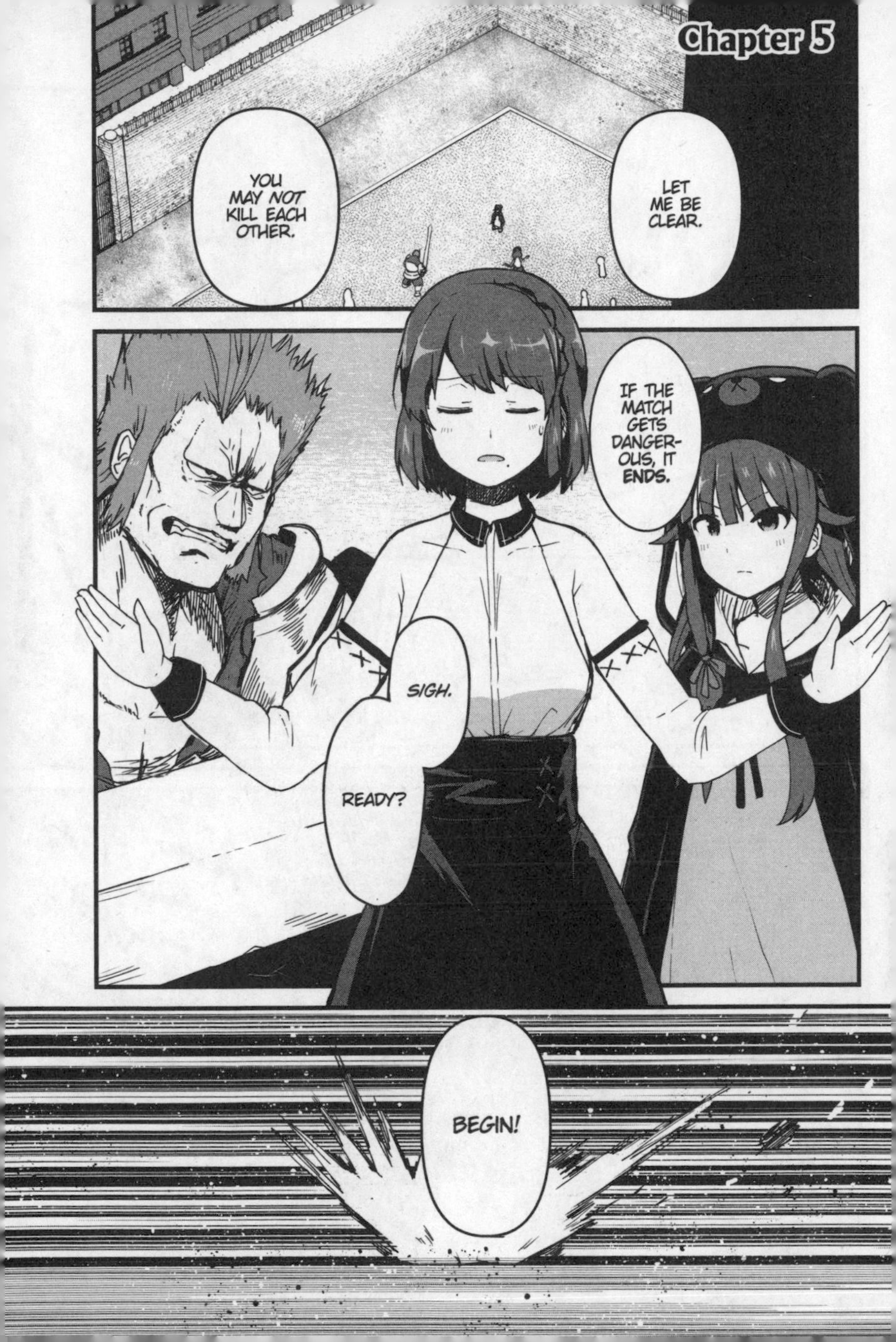
LET ME BE CLEAR.
YOU MAY NOT KILL EACH OTHER.
IF THE MATCH GETS DANGER-OUS, IT ENDS.
SIGH.
READY?
BEGIN!

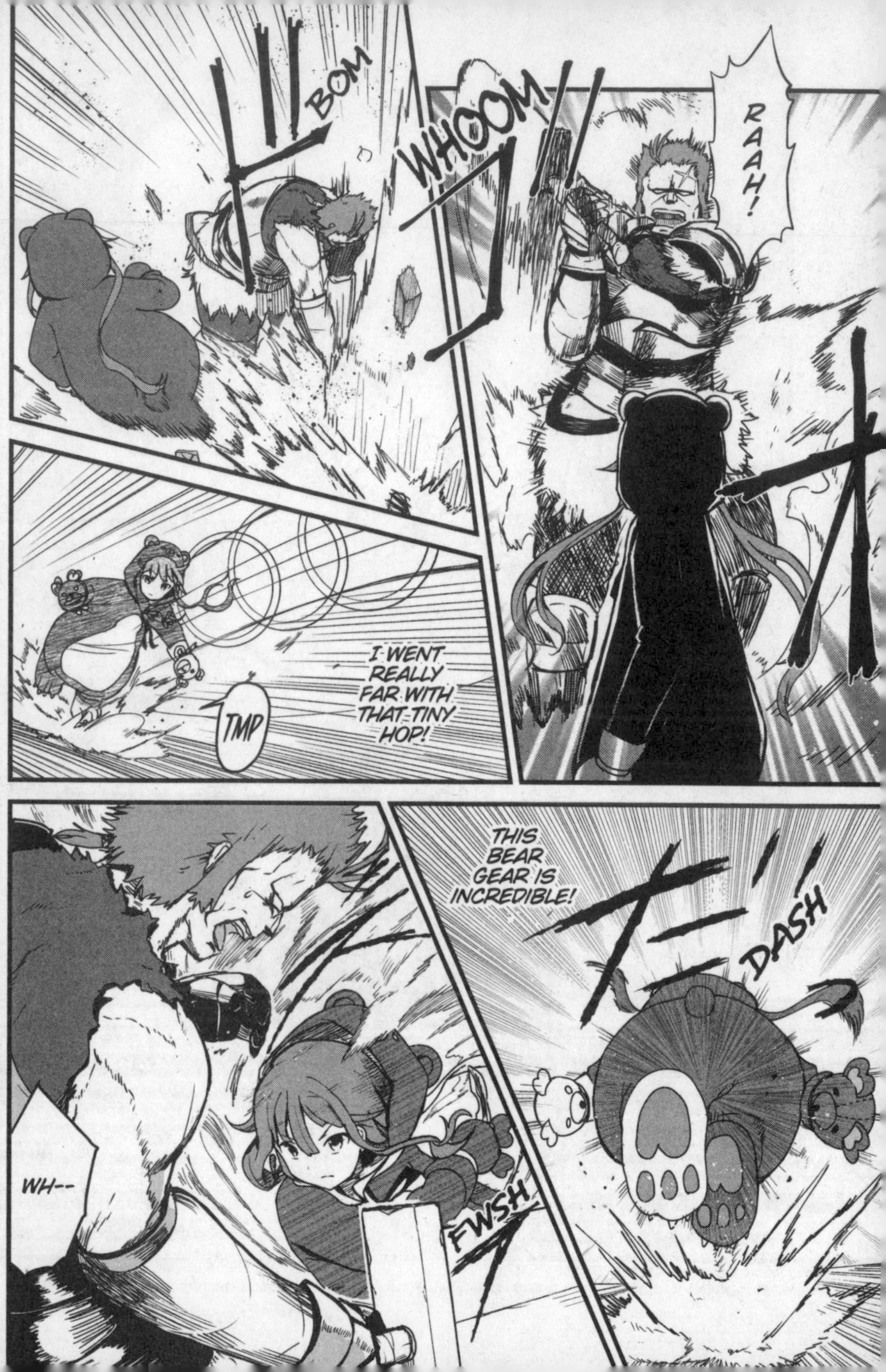
RAAAH!
WHOOM
BOM
I WENT REALLY FAR WITH THAT TINY HOP!
TMP
THIS BEAR GEAR IS INCREDIBLE!
DASH
FWSH
WH--

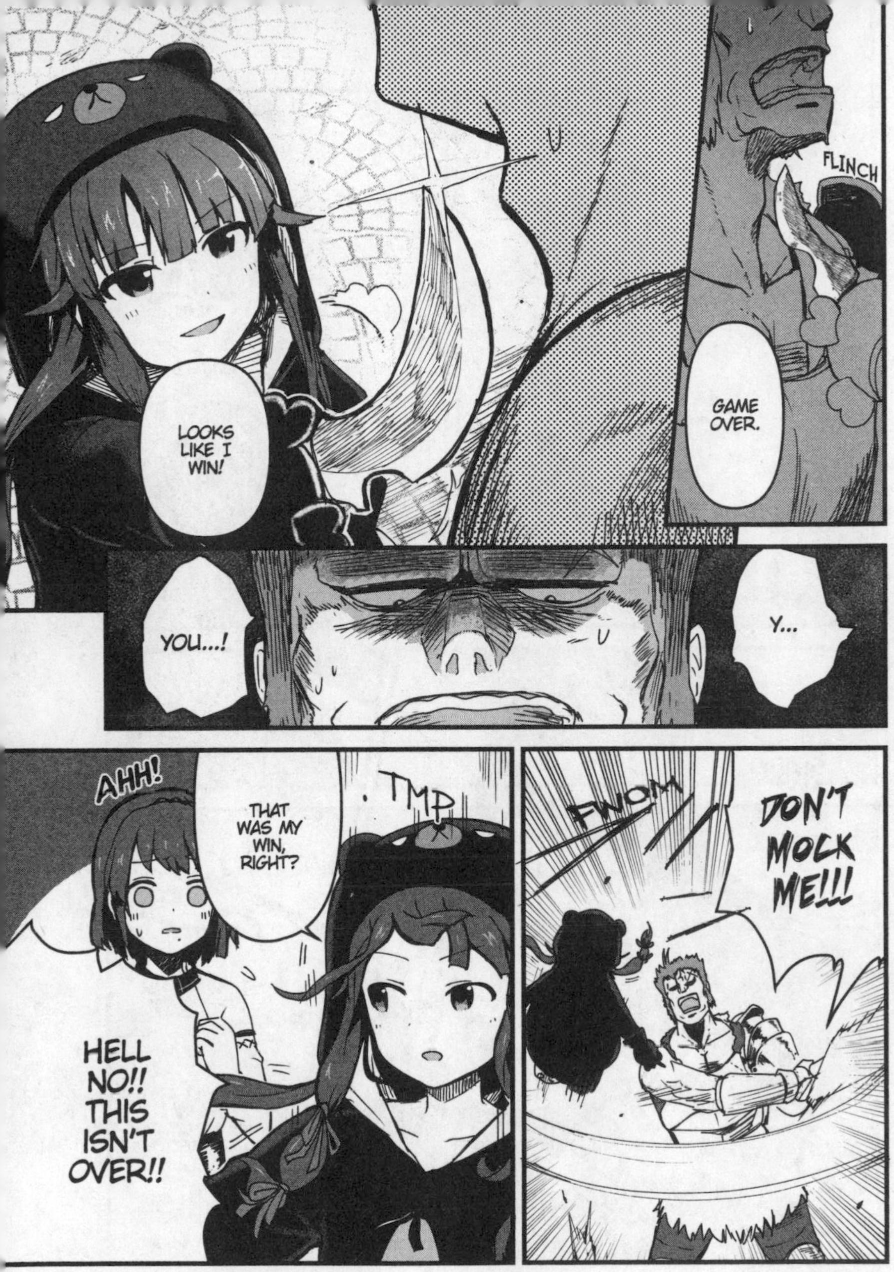
FLINCH
GAME OVER.
LOOKS LIKE I WIN!
Y...
YOU...!
FWOM
DON'T MOCK ME!!!
TMP
THAT WAS MY WIN, RIGHT?
AHH!
HELL NO!! THIS ISN'T OVER!!

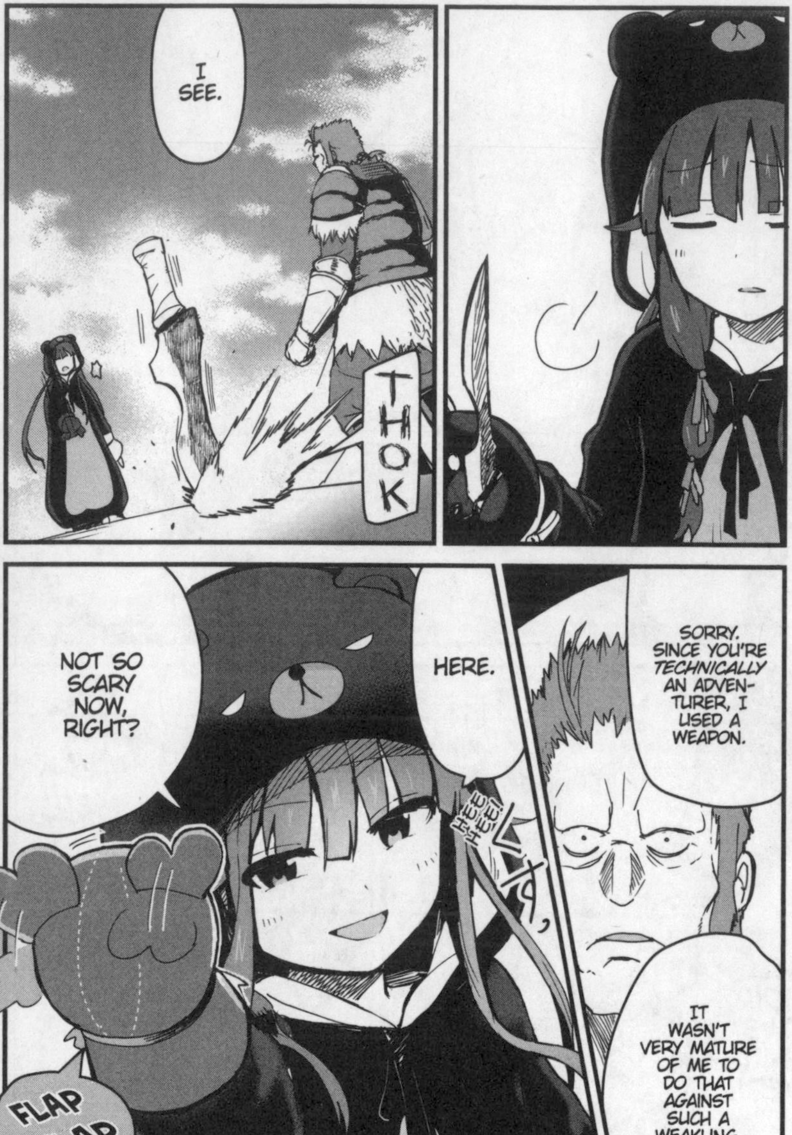
I SEE.
THOK
SORRY. SINCE YOU'RE *TECHNICALLY* AN ADVEN- TURER, I USED A WEAPON.
IT WASN'T VERY MATURE OF ME TO DO THAT AGAINST SUCH A WEAKLING.
HERE.
NOT SO SCARY NOW, RIGHT?
HEE HEE
FLAP FLAP

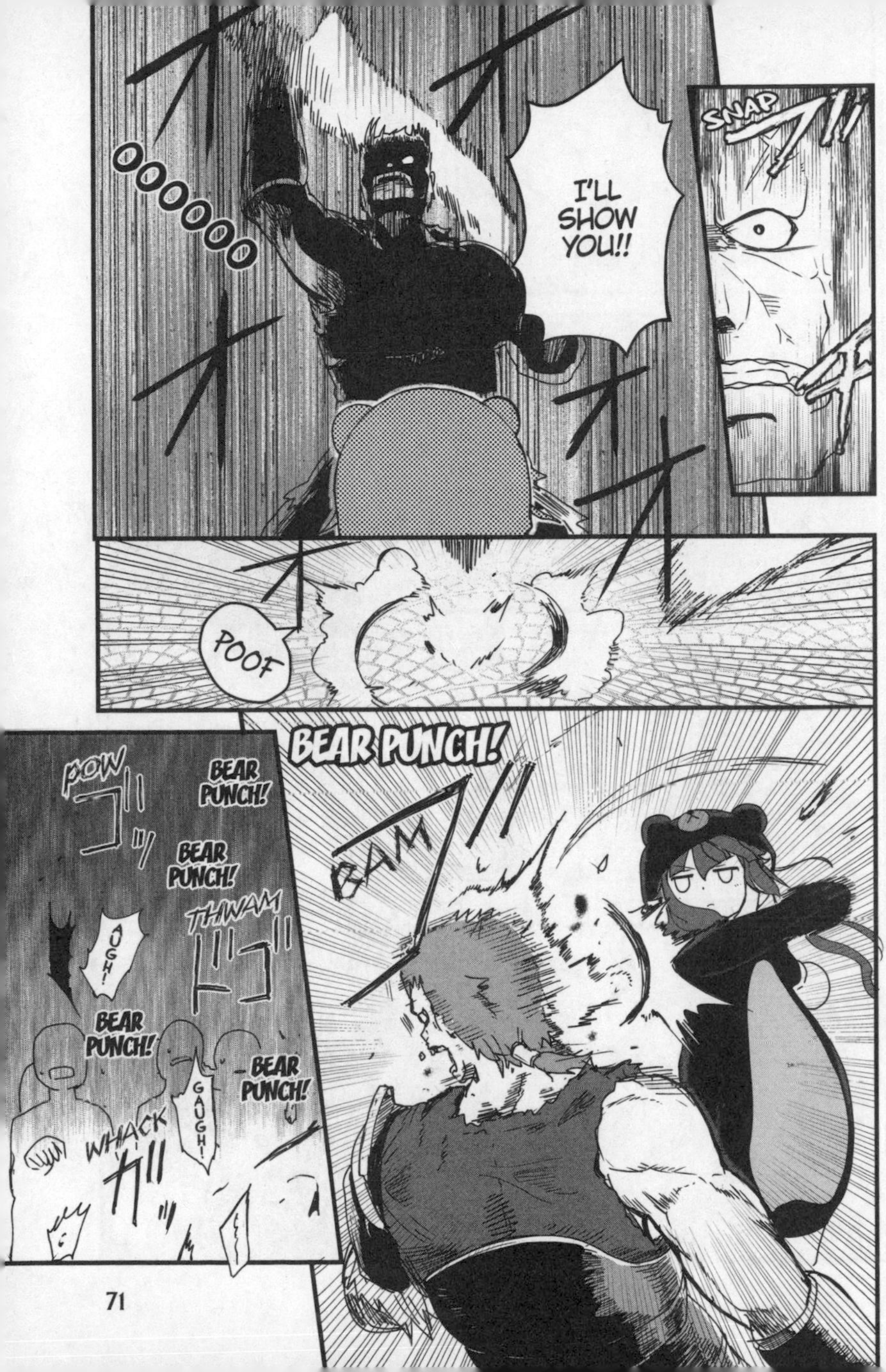
SNAP
OOOOOOO
I'LL SHOW YOU!!
POOF
BEAR PUNCH!
BAM
POW
BEAR PUNCH!
BEAR PUNCH!
THWAM
AUGH!
BEAR PUNCH!
BEAR PUNCH!
GAUGH!
WHACK

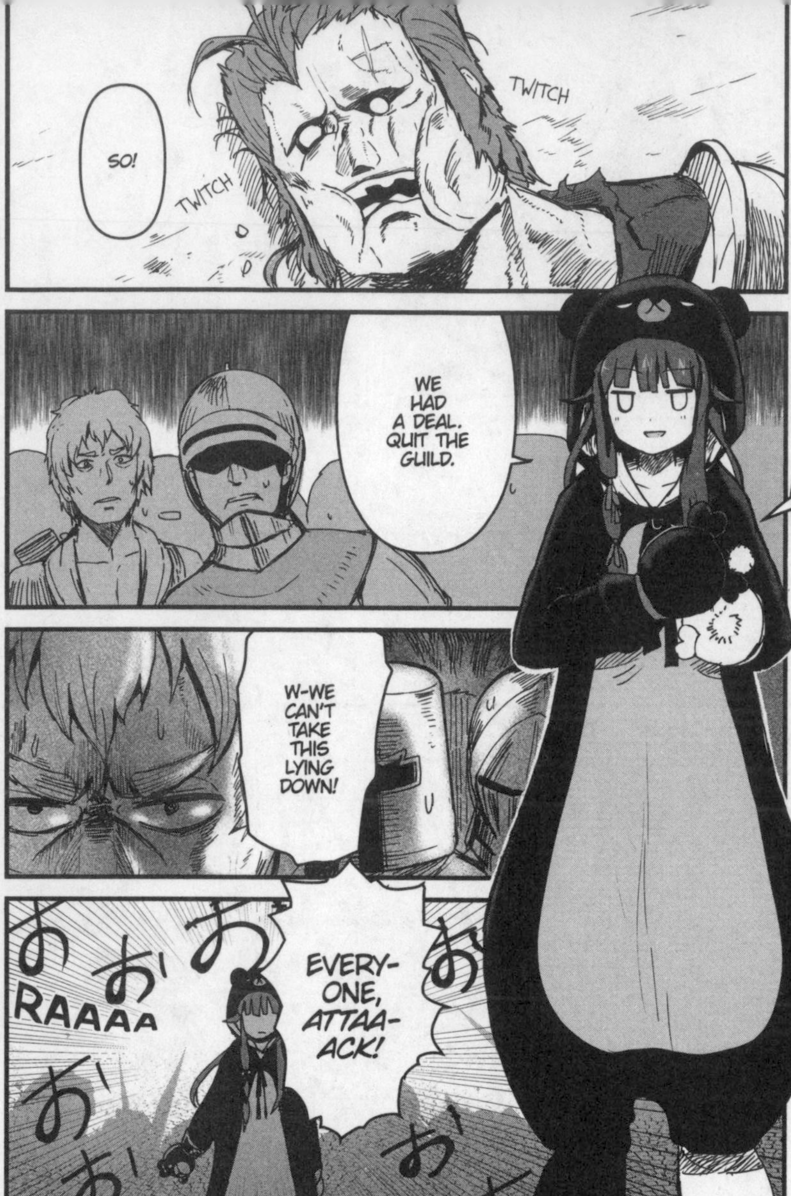
TWITCH
SO!
TWITCH
WE HAD A DEAL. QUIT THE GUILD.
PAFF
W-WE CAN'T TAKE THIS LYING DOWN!
EVERY-ONE, ATTAAA-ACK!
RAAAA
AAAHH!

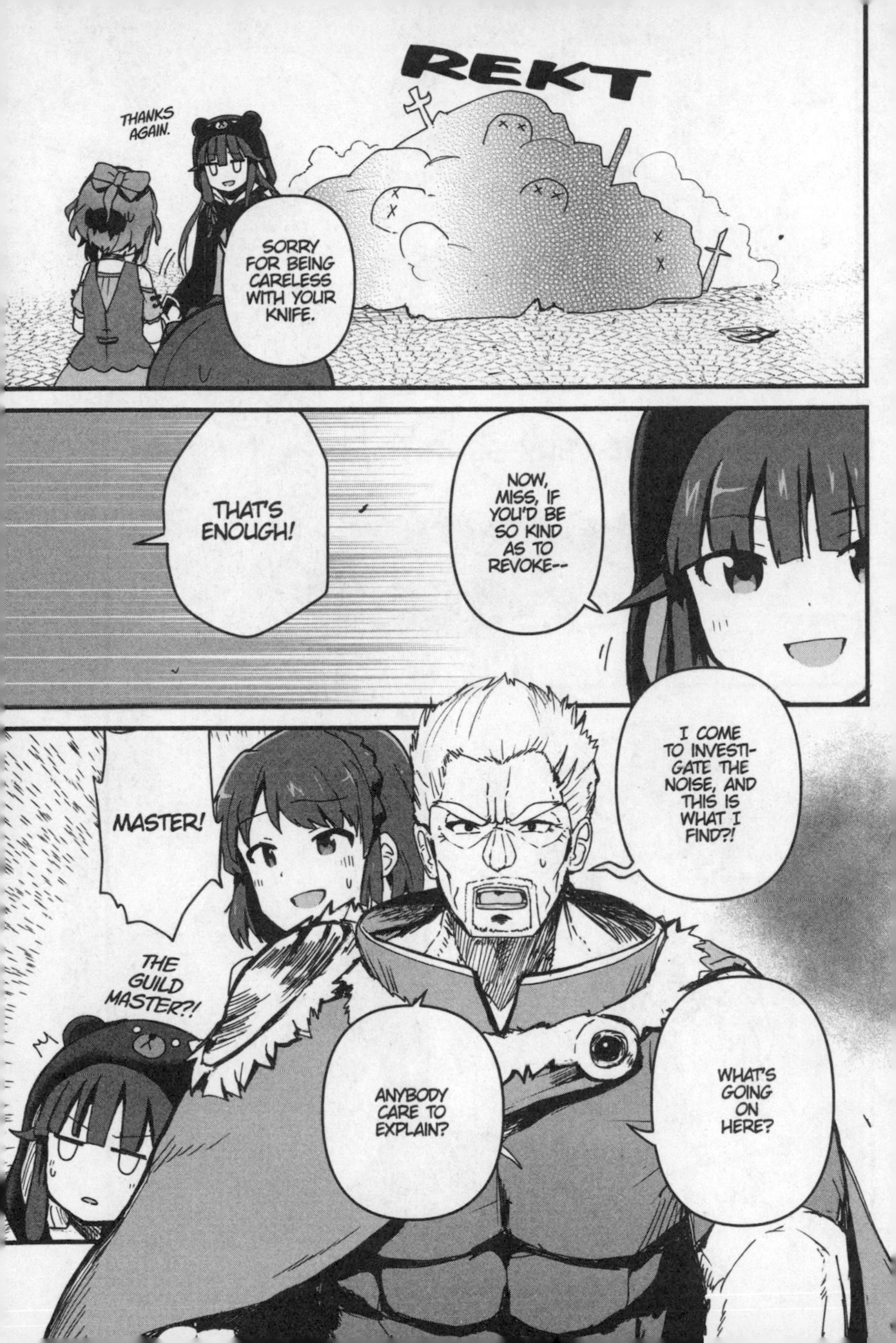
REKT
SORRY FOR BEING CARELESS WITH YOUR KNIFE.
THANKS AGAIN.
NOW, MISS, IF YOU'D BE SO KIND AS TO REVOKE--
THAT'S ENOUGH!
I COME TO INVESTI-GATE THE NOISE, AND THIS IS WHAT I FIND?!
WHAT'S GOING ON HERE?
ANYBODY CARE TO EXPLAIN?
MASTER!
THE GUILD MASTER?!

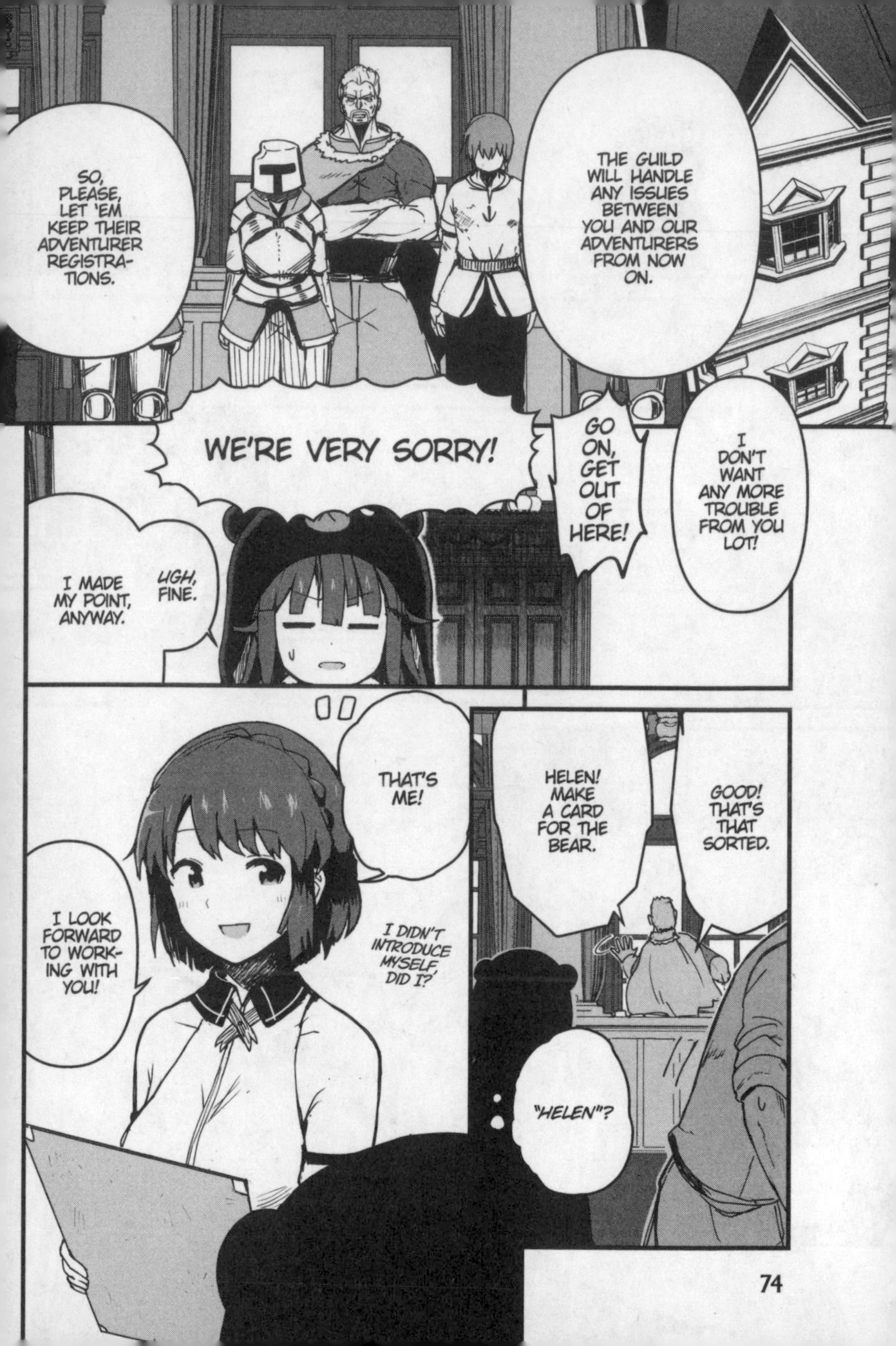
THE GUILD WILL HANDLE ANY ISSUES BETWEEN YOU AND OUR ADVENTURERS FROM NOW ON.
SO, PLEASE, LET 'EM KEEP THEIR ADVENTURER REGISTRA-TIONS.
WE'RE VERY SORRY!
I DON'T WANT ANY MORE TROUBLE FROM YOU LOT!
GO ON, GET OUT OF HERE!
UGH, FINE.
I MADE MY POINT, ANYWAY.
GOOD! THAT'S THAT SORTED.
HELEN! MAKE A CARD FOR THE BEAR.
"HELEN"?
THAT'S ME!
I DIDN'T INTRODUCE MYSELF, DID I?
I LOOK FORWARD TO WORK-ING WITH YOU!

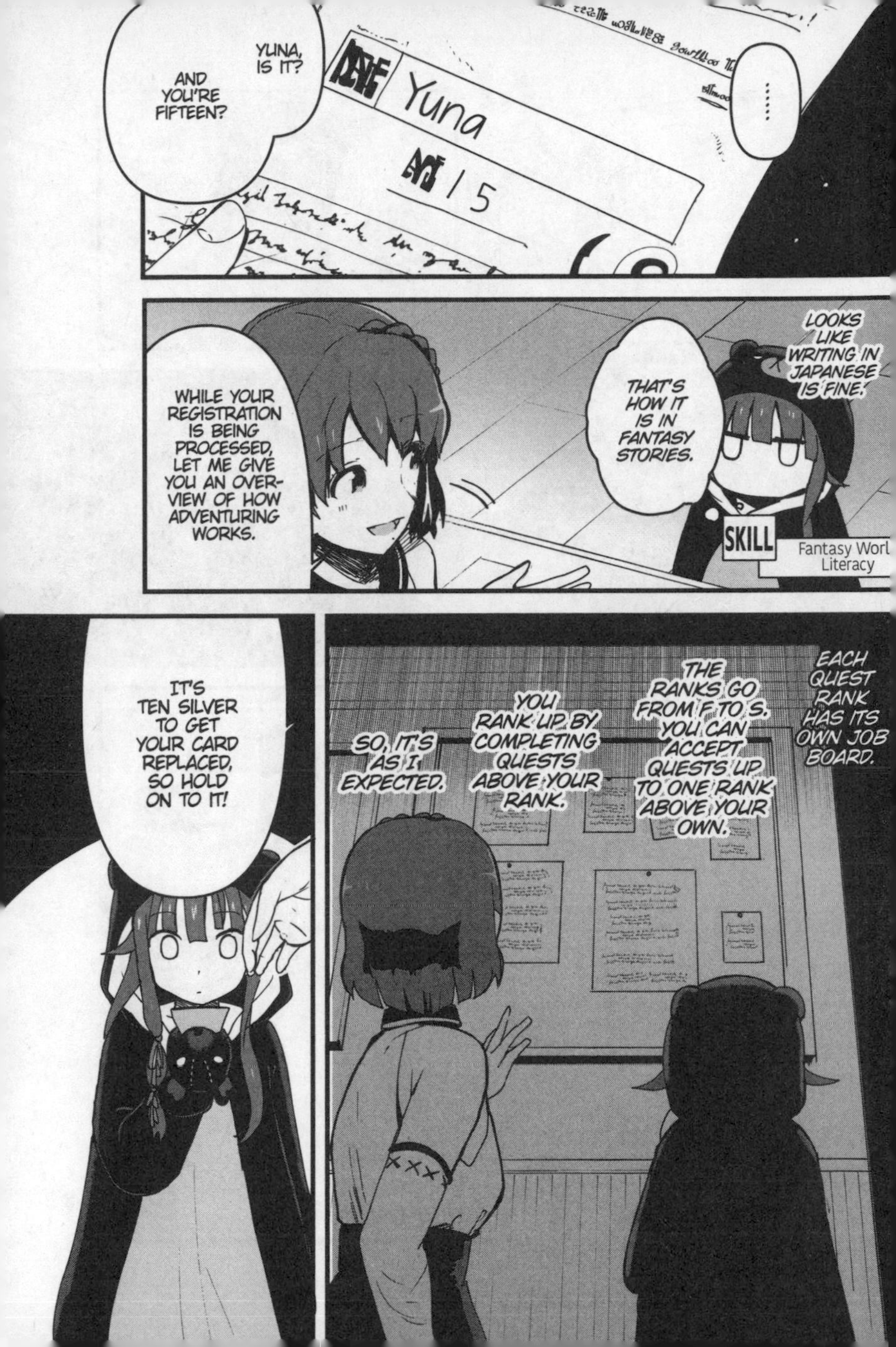
……
YUNA, IS IT?
AND YOU'RE FIFTEEN?
Yuna
/ 15
LOOKS LIKE WRITING IN JAPANESE IS FINE.
THAT'S HOW IT IS IN FANTASY STORIES.
SKILL
Fantasy Worl Literacy
WHILE YOUR REGISTRATION IS BEING PROCESSED, LET ME GIVE YOU AN OVER-VIEW OF HOW ADVENTURING WORKS.
EACH QUEST RANK HAS ITS OWN JOB BOARD.
THE RANKS GO FROM F TO S. YOU CAN ACCEPT QUESTS UP TO ONE RANK ABOVE YOUR OWN.
YOU RANK UP BY COMPLETING QUESTS ABOVE YOUR RANK.
SO, IT'S AS I EXPECTED.
IT'S TEN SILVER TO GET YOUR CARD REPLACED, SO HOLD ON TO IT!

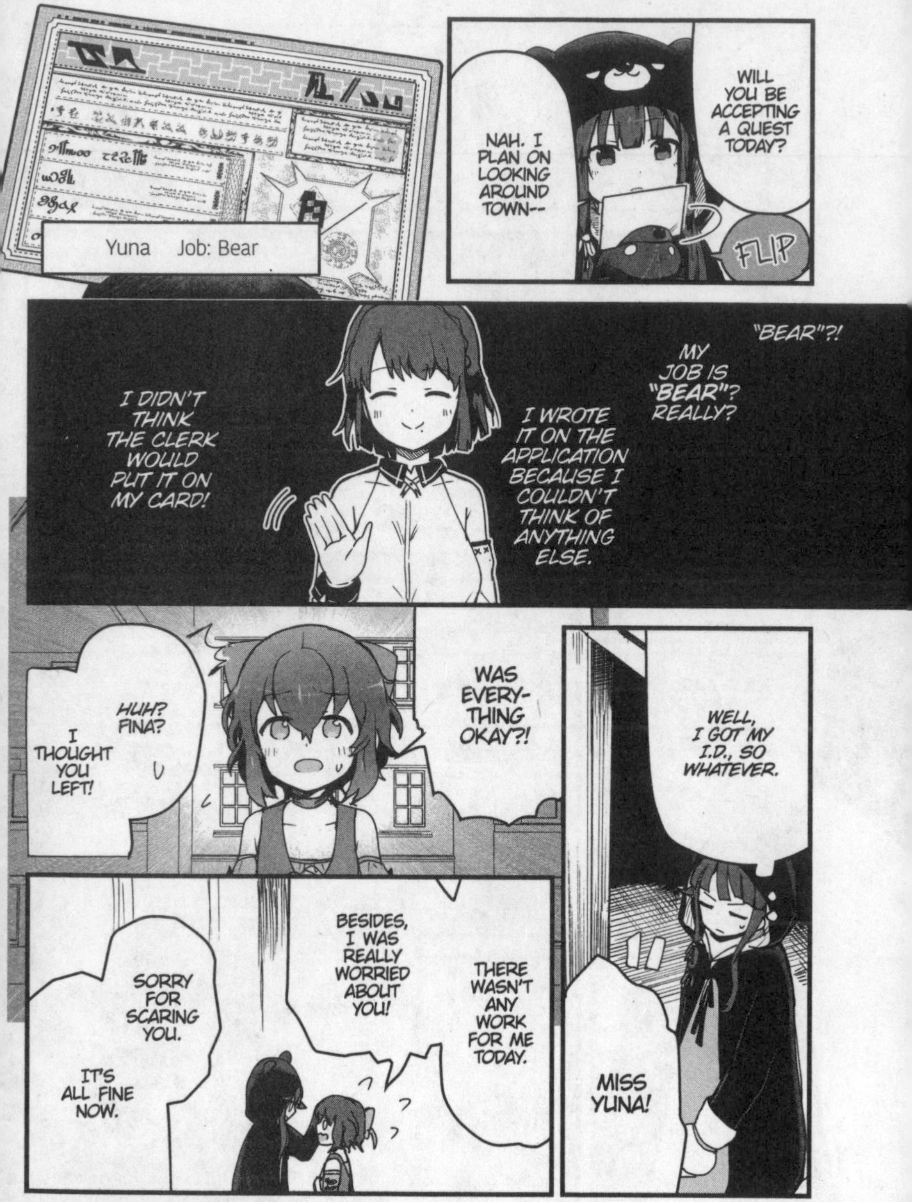
WILL YOU BE ACCEPTING A QUEST TODAY?
NAH. I PLAN ON LOOKING AROUND TOWN--
FLIP
Yuna Job: Bear
"BEAR"?!
MY JOB IS "BEAR"? REALLY?
I WROTE IT ON THE APPLICATION BECAUSE I COULDN'T THINK OF ANYTHING ELSE.
I DIDN'T THINK THE CLERK WOULD PUT IT ON MY CARD!
WELL, I GOT MY I.D., SO WHATEVER.
MISS YUNA!
WAS EVERY-THING OKAY?!
HUH? FINA? I THOUGHT YOU LEFT!
THERE WASN'T ANY WORK FOR ME TODAY.
BESIDES, I WAS REALLY WORRIED ABOUT YOU!
SORRY FOR SCARING YOU.
IT'S ALL FINE NOW.

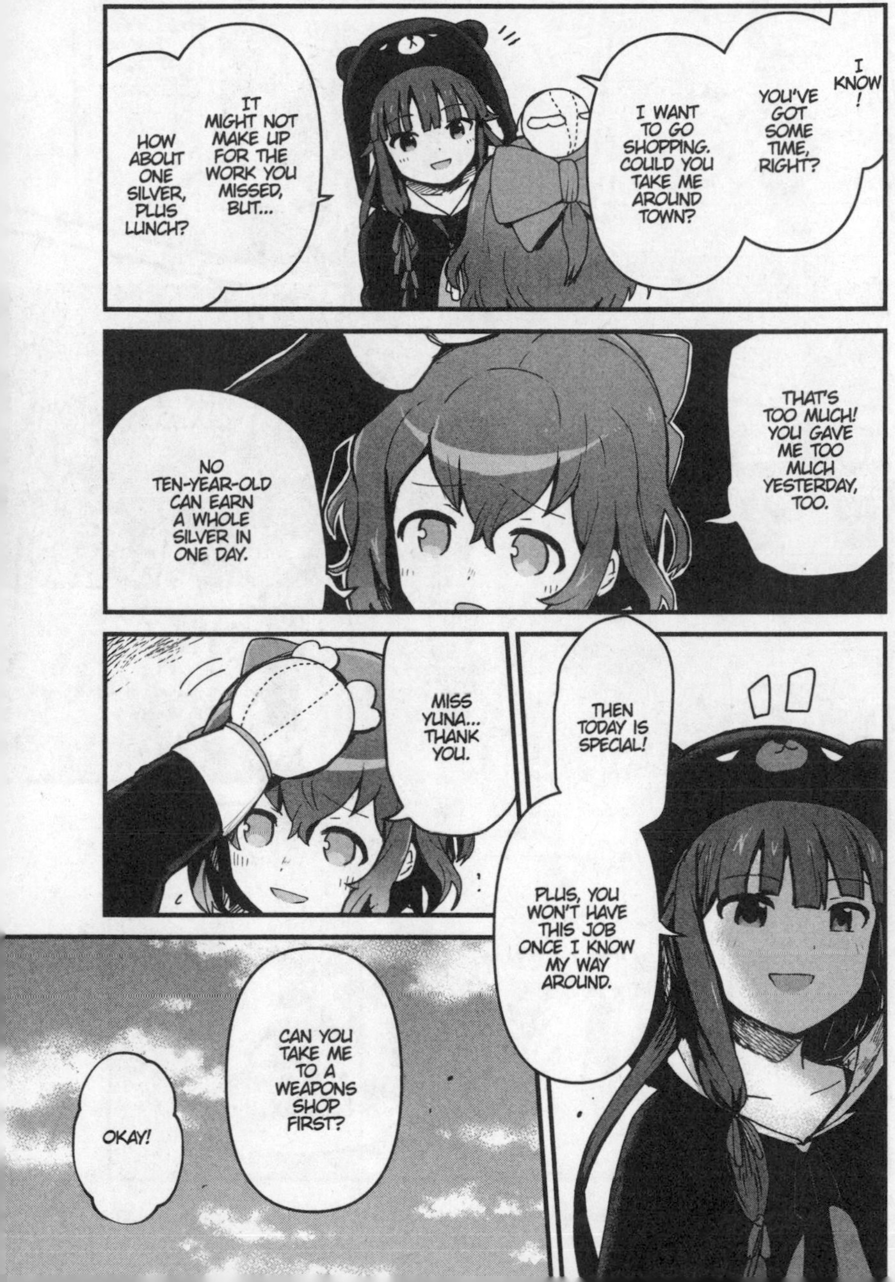
I KNOW!
YOU'VE GOT SOME TIME, RIGHT?
I WANT TO GO SHOPPING. COULD YOU TAKE ME AROUND TOWN?
IT MIGHT NOT MAKE UP FOR THE WORK YOU MISSED, BUT...
HOW ABOUT ONE SILVER, PLUS LUNCH?
THAT'S TOO MUCH! YOU GAVE ME TOO MUCH YESTERDAY, TOO.
NO TEN-YEAR-OLD CAN EARN A WHOLE SILVER IN ONE DAY.
THEN TODAY IS SPECIAL!
PLUS, YOU WON'T HAVE THIS JOB ONCE I KNOW MY WAY AROUND.
MISS YUNA... THANK YOU.
CAN YOU TAKE ME TO A WEAPONS SHOP FIRST?
OKAY!

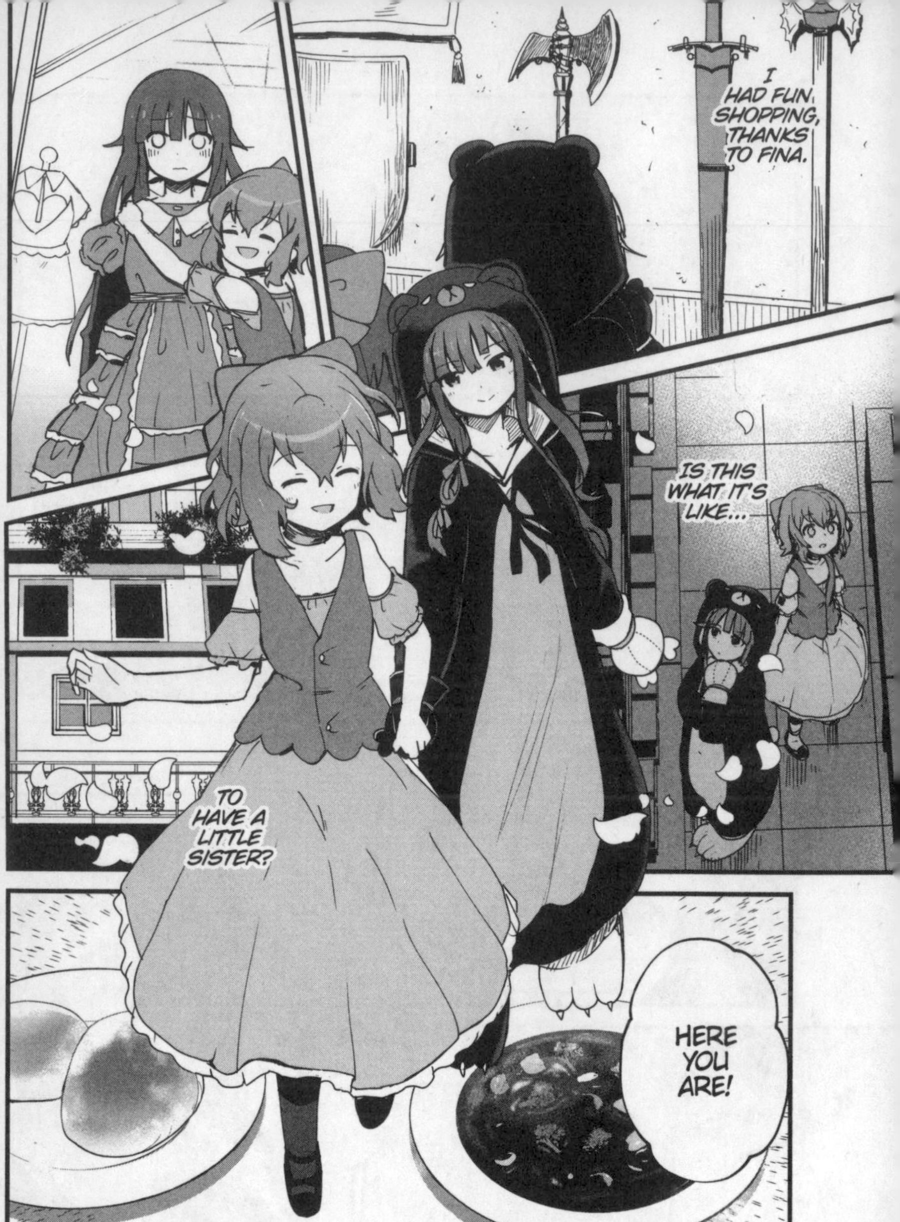
I HAD FUN SHOPPING, THANKS TO FINA.
IS THIS WHAT IT'S LIKE...
TO HAVE A LITTLE SISTER?
HERE YOU ARE!

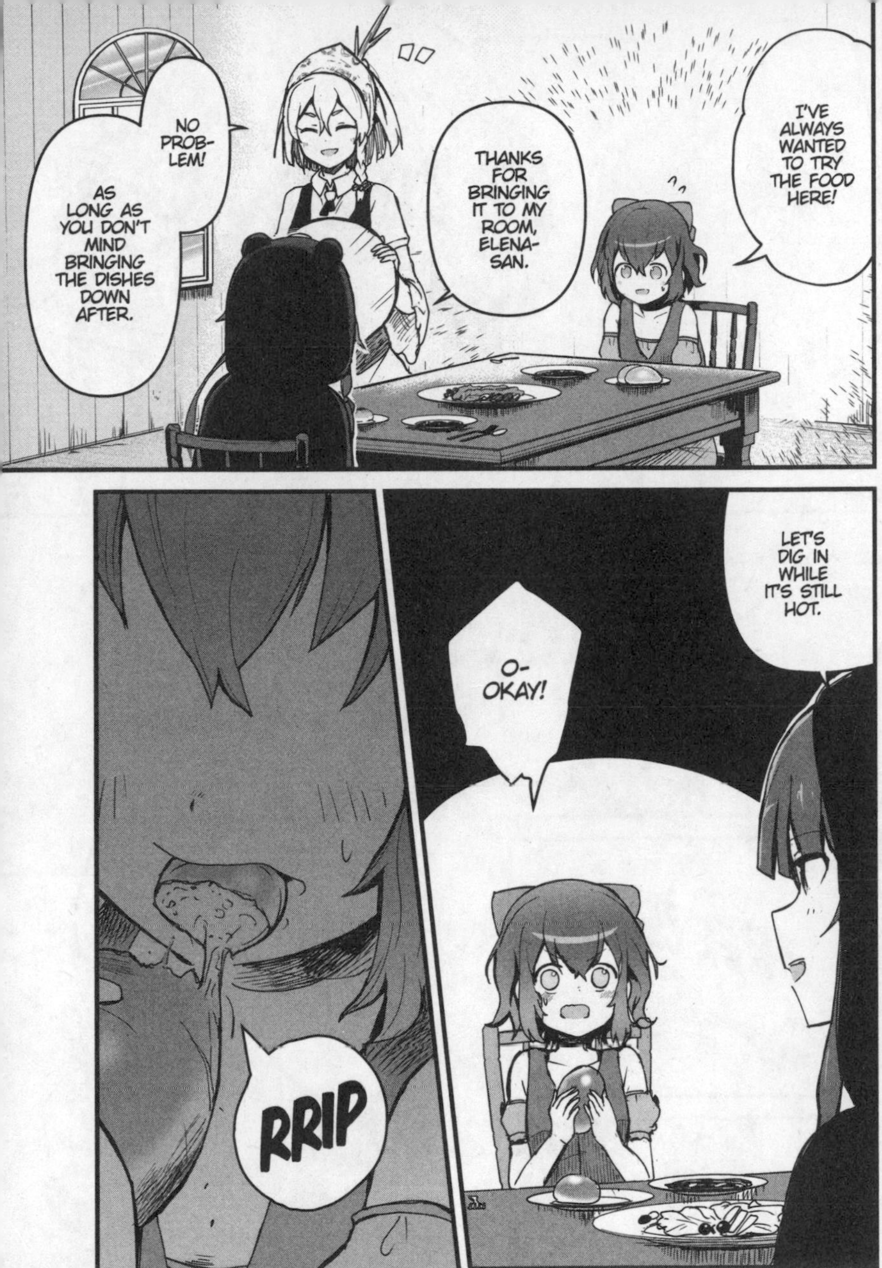
I'VE ALWAYS WANTED TO TRY THE FOOD HERE!
THANKS FOR BRINGING IT TO MY ROOM, ELENA-SAN.
NO PROB-LEM!
AS LONG AS YOU DON'T MIND BRINGING THE DISHES DOWN AFTER.
LET'S DIG IN WHILE IT'S STILL HOT.
O-OKAY!
RRIP

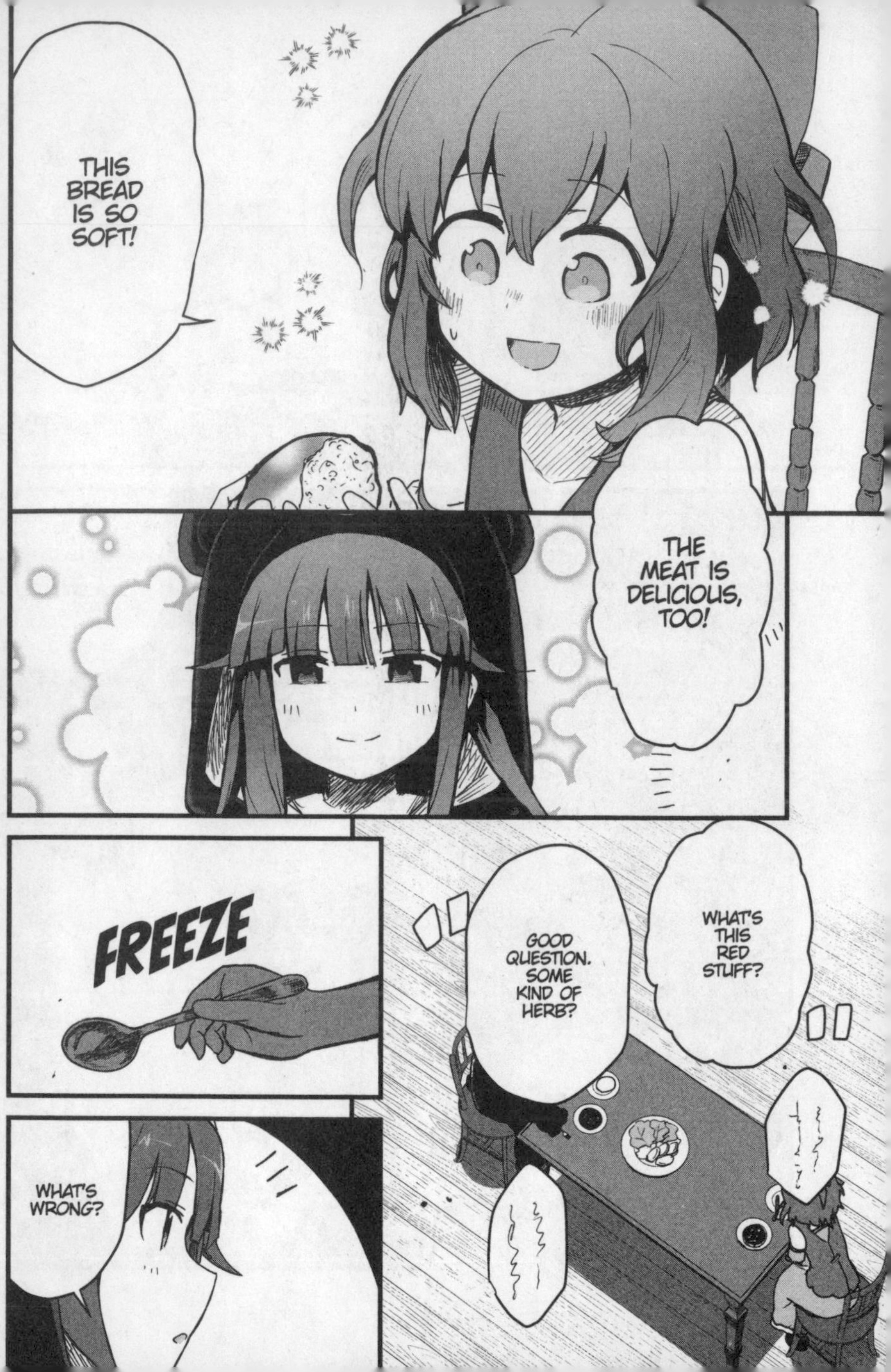
THIS BREAD IS SO SOFT!
THE MEAT IS DELICIOUS, TOO!
WHAT'S THIS RED STUFF?
GOOD QUESTION. SOME KIND OF HERB?
FREEZE
WHAT'S WRONG?

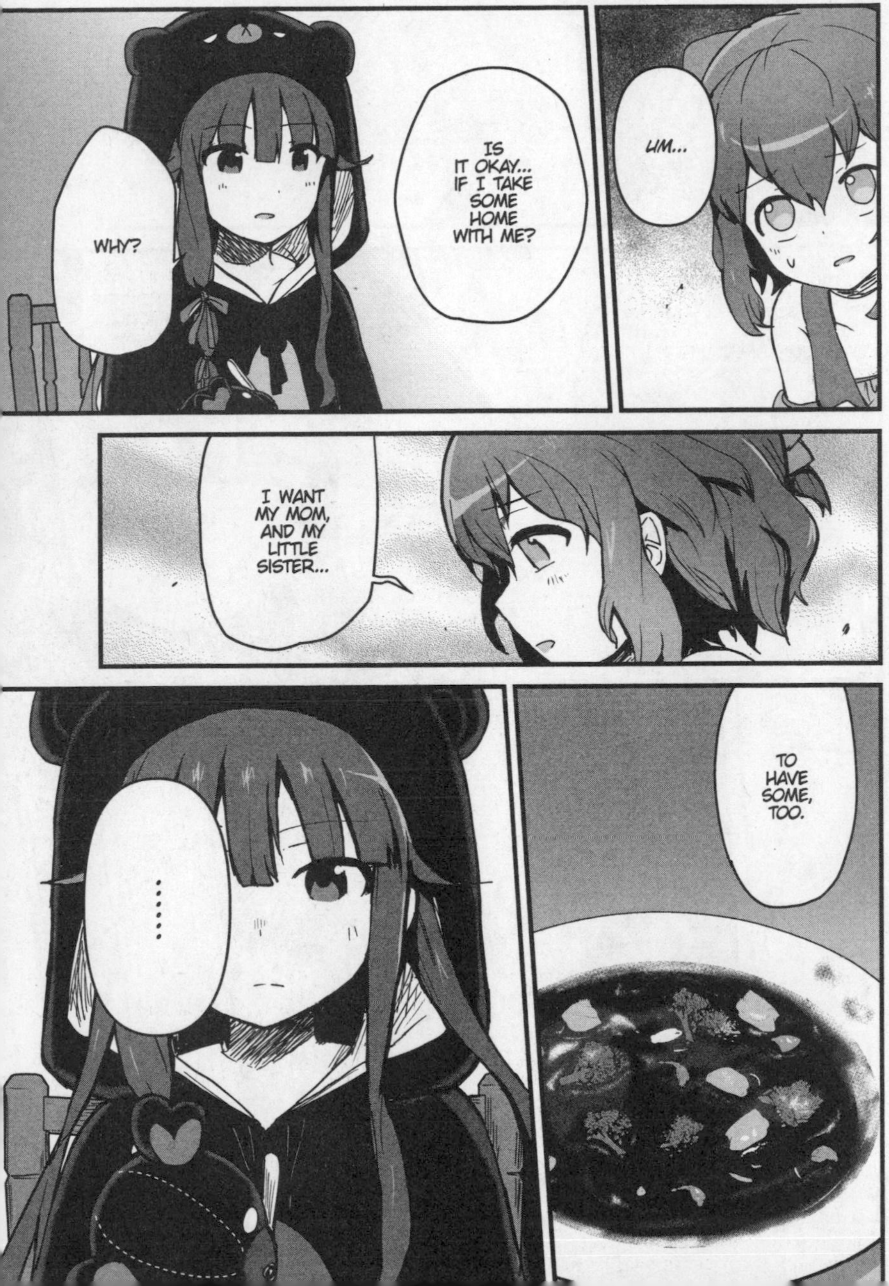
UM...
IS IT OKAY... IF I TAKE SOME HOME WITH ME?
WHY?
I WANT MY MOM, AND MY LITTLE SISTER...
TO HAVE SOME, TOO.
......

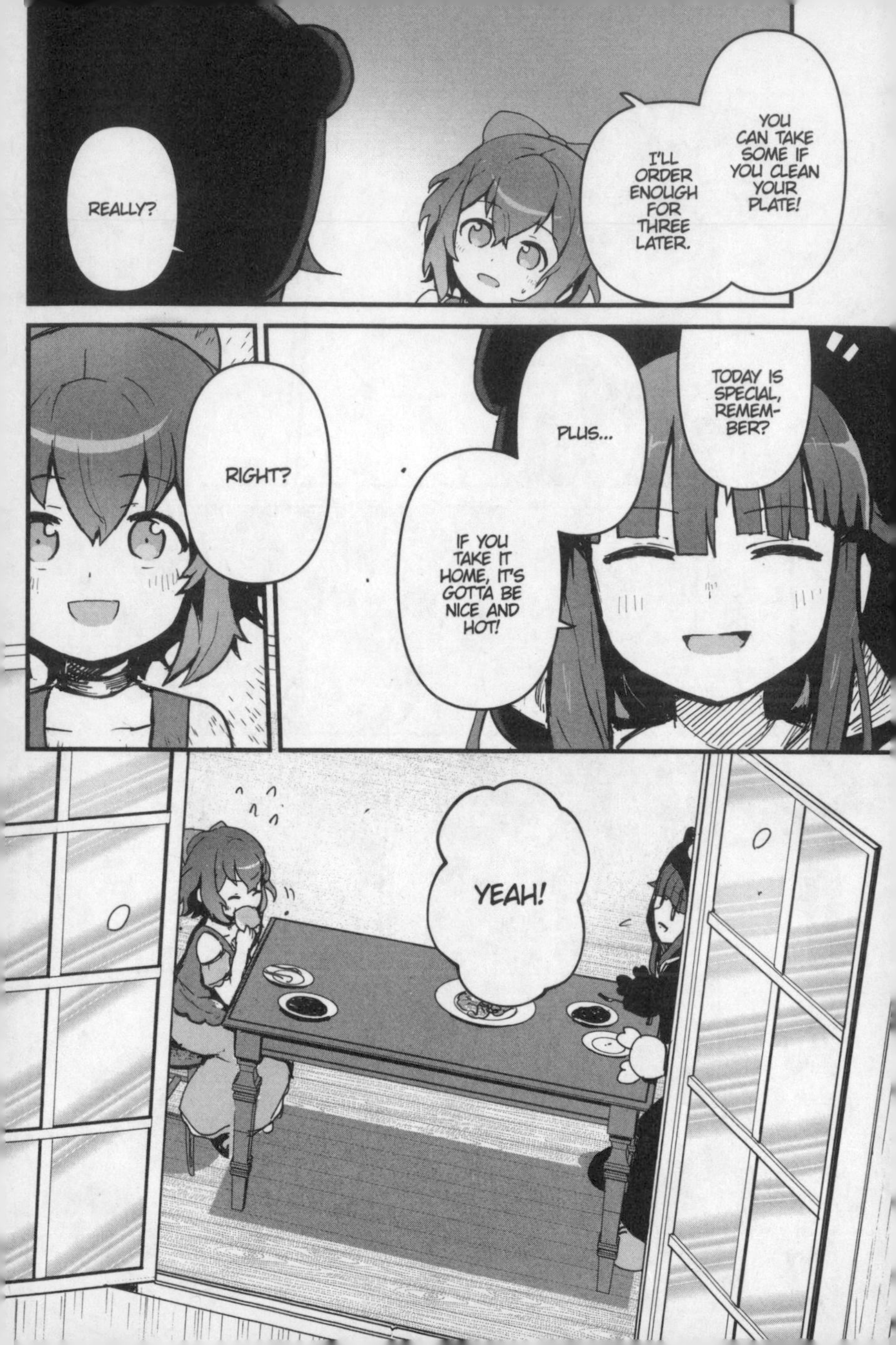
YOU CAN TAKE SOME IF YOU CLEAN YOUR PLATE!
I'LL ORDER ENOUGH FOR THREE LATER.
REALLY?
TODAY IS SPECIAL, REMEMBER?
PLUS...
IF YOU TAKE IT HOME, IT'S GOTTA BE NICE AND HOT!
RIGHT?
YEAH!

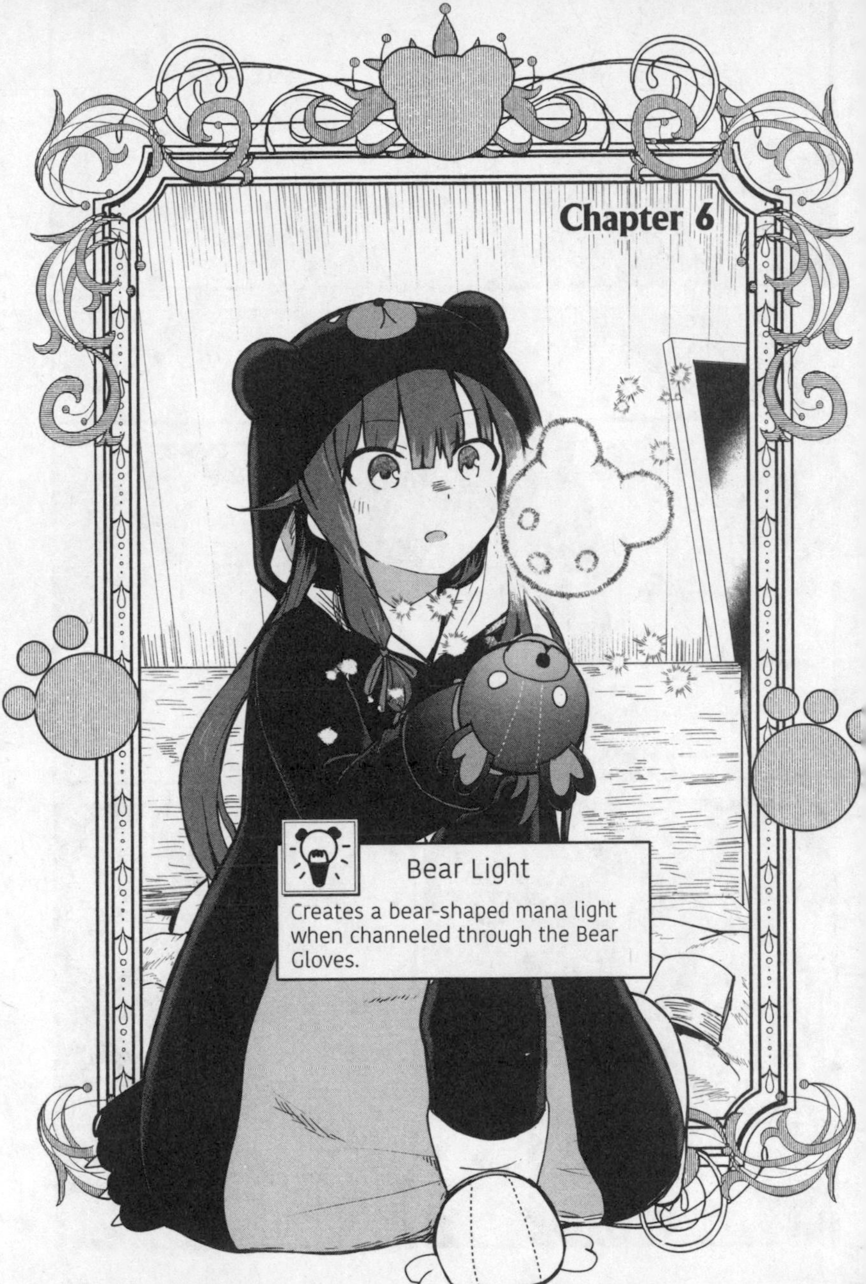
Chapter 6
Bear Light
Creates a bear-shaped mana light when channeled through the Bear Gloves.

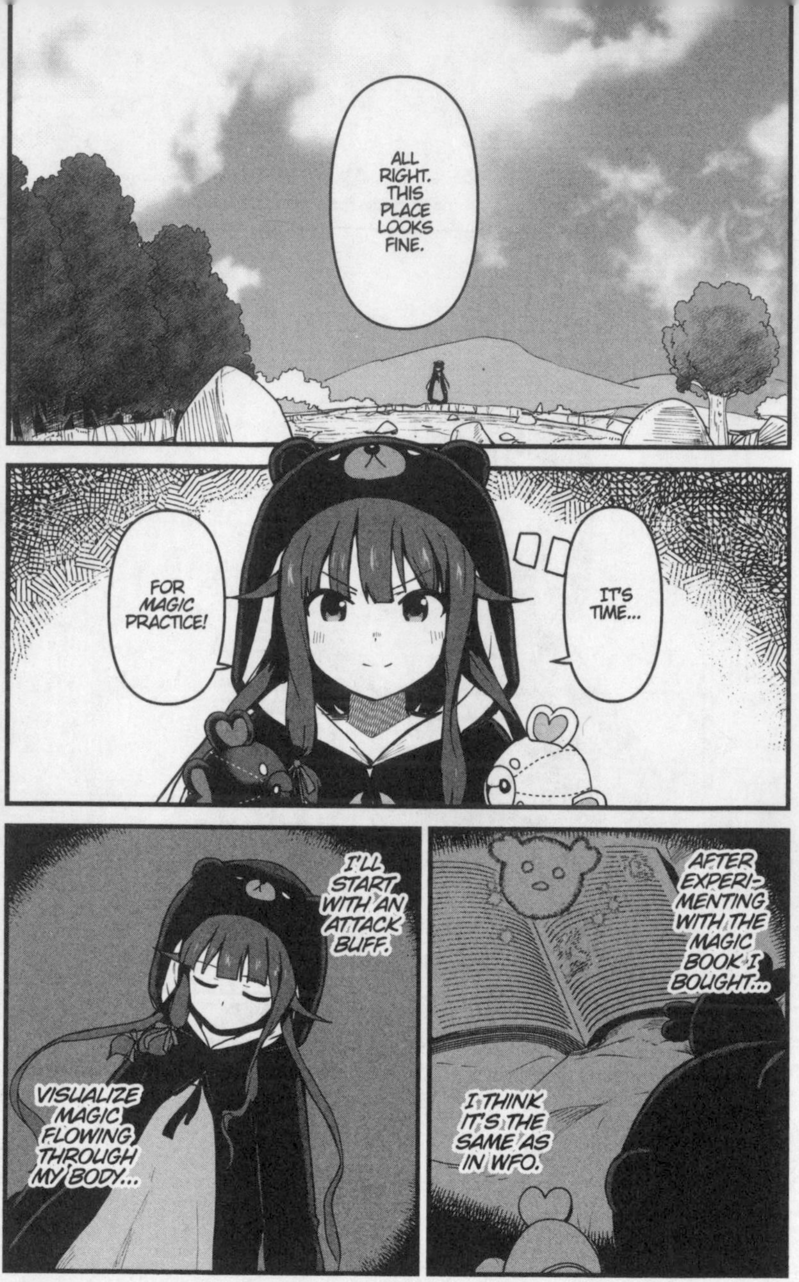
ALL RIGHT. THIS PLACE LOOKS FINE.
IT'S TIME...
FOR MAGIC PRACTICE!
AFTER EXPERI-MENTING WITH THE MAGIC BOOK I BOUGHT...
I THINK IT'S THE SAME AS IN WFO.
I'LL START WITH AN ATTACK BUFF.
VISUALIZE MAGIC FLOWING THROUGH MY BODY...

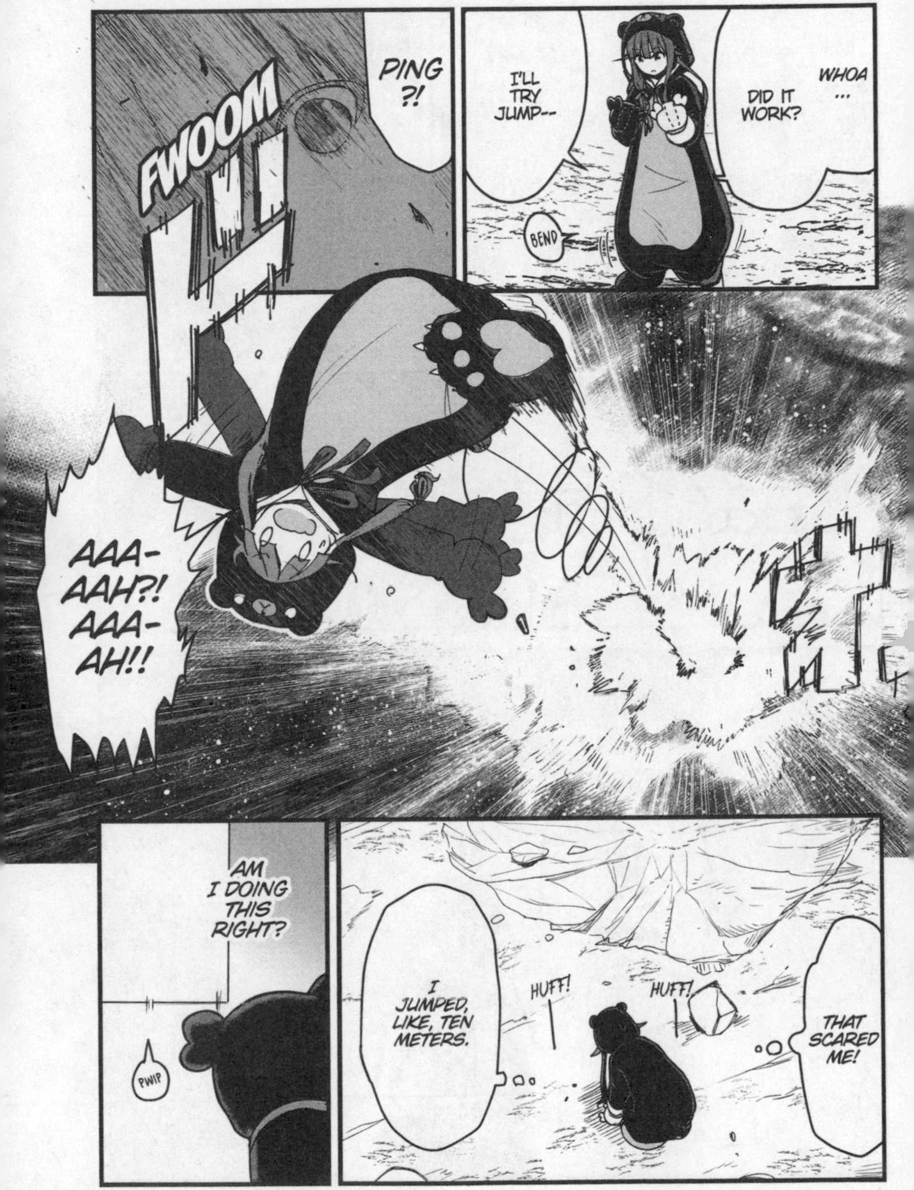
WHOA ...
DID IT WORK?
I'LL TRY JUMP--
BEND
PING ?!
FWOOM
AAA-AAH?! AAA-AH!!
THAT SCARED ME!
HUFF!
HUFF!
I JUMPED, LIKE, TEN METERS.
AM I DOING THIS RIGHT?
PWIP

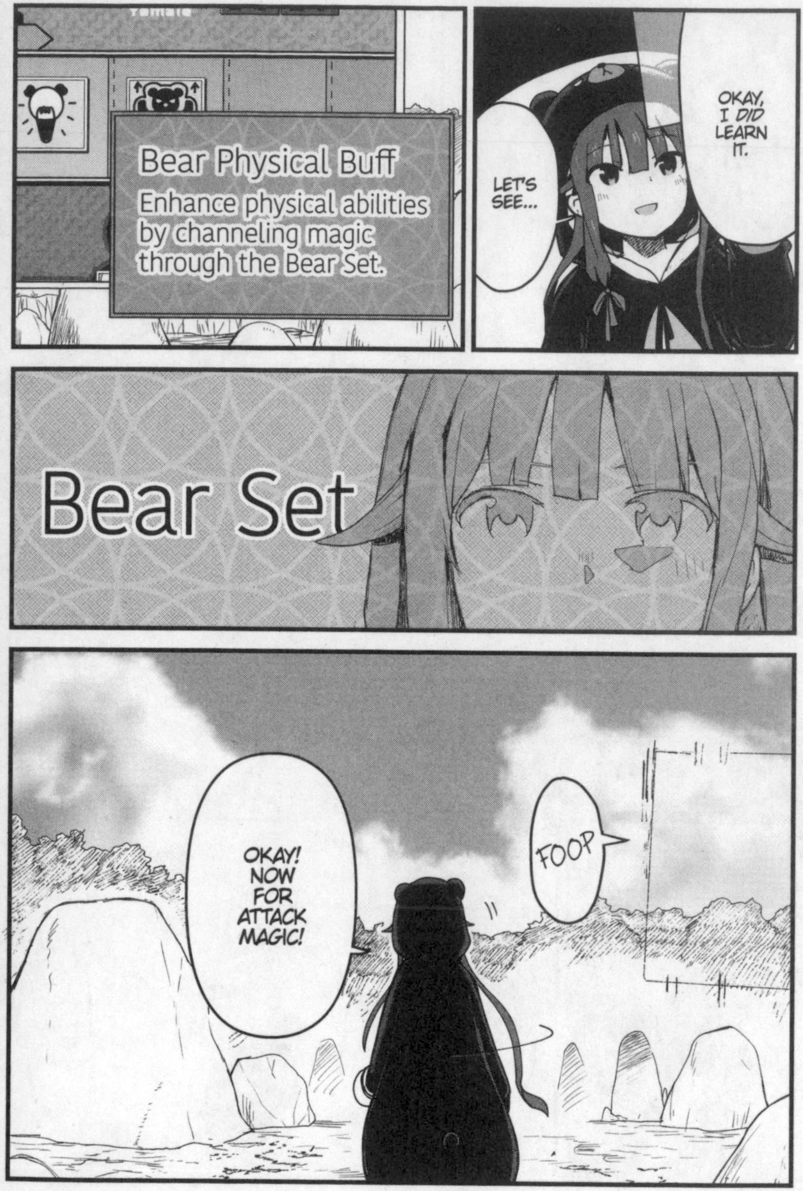

OKAY, I *DID* LEARN IT.
LET'S SEE...
Bear Physical Buff
Enhance physical abilities by channeling magic through the Bear Set.
Bear Set
FOOP
OKAY! NOW FOR ATTACK MAGIC!

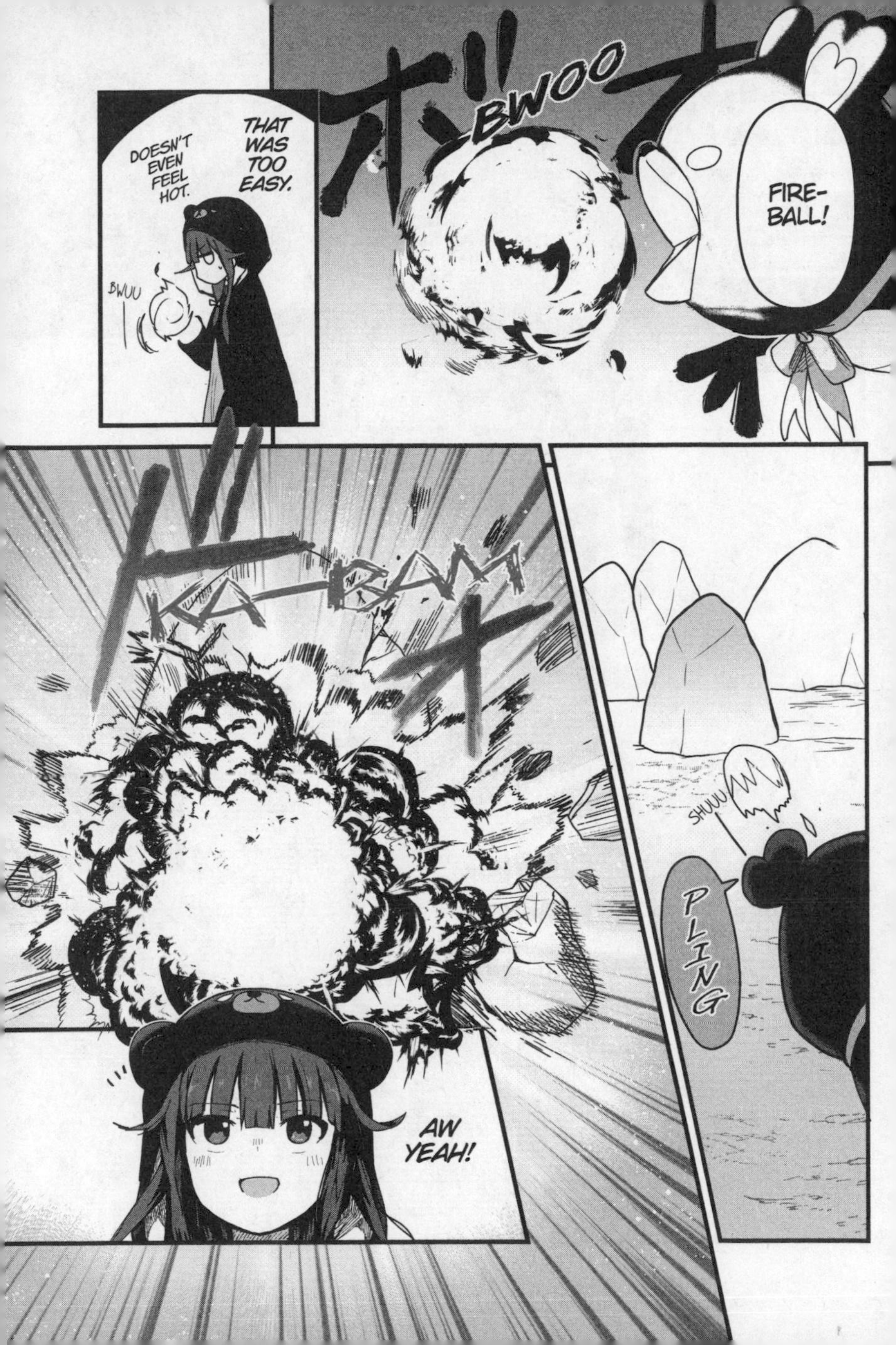
FIRE-BALL!
BWOO
THAT WAS TOO EASY.
DOESN'T EVEN FEEL HOT.
BWUU
SHUUU
PLING
KA-BAM
AW YEAH!

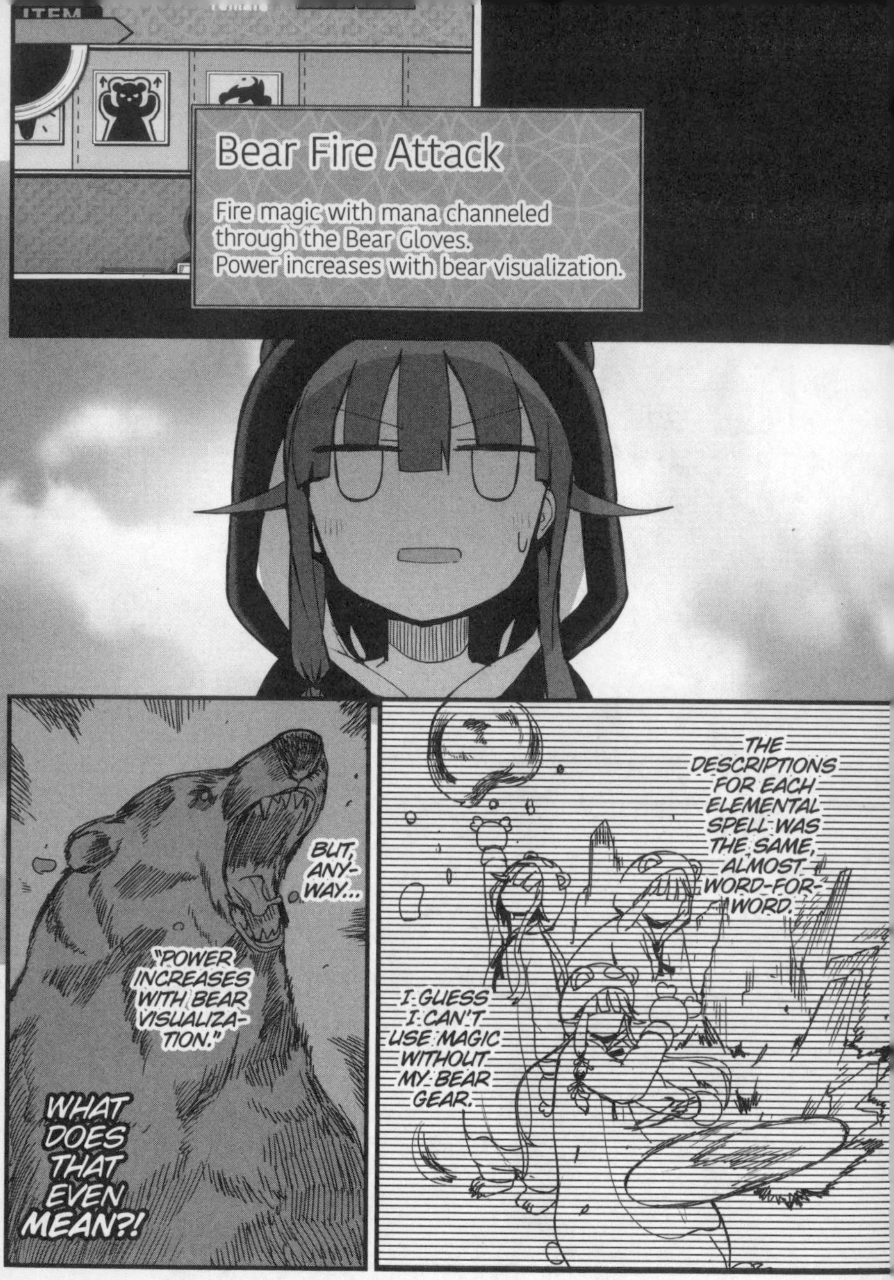
Bear Fire Attack
Fire magic with mana channeled through the Bear Gloves. Power increases with bear visualization.
THE DESCRIPTIONS FOR EACH ELEMENTAL SPELL WAS THE SAME, ALMOST WORD-FOR-WORD.
I GUESS I CAN'T USE MAGIC WITHOUT MY BEAR GEAR.
BUT, ANYWAY...
"POWER INCREASES WITH BEAR VISUALIZATION."
WHAT DOES THAT EVEN MEAN?!

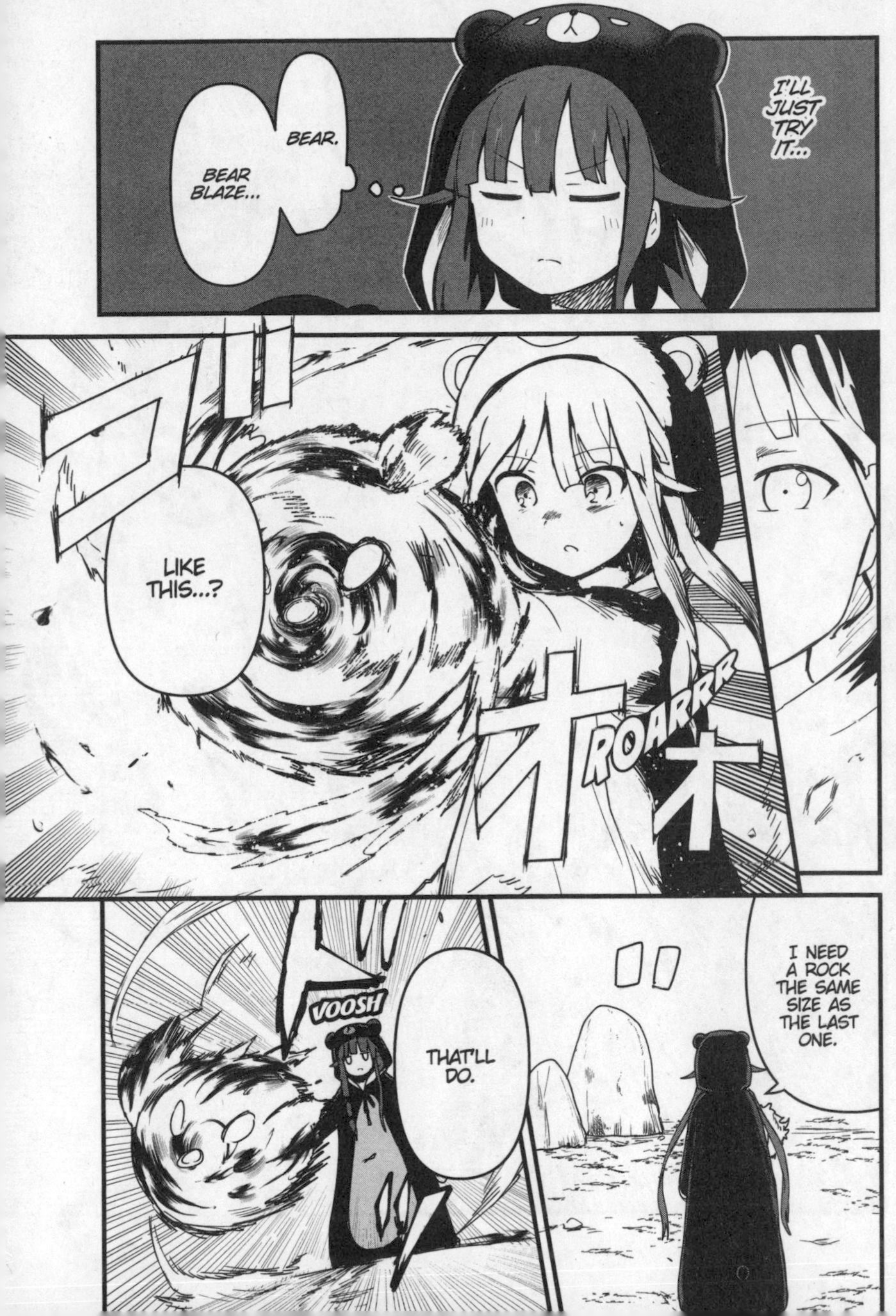

I'LL JUST TRY IT...
BEAR.
BEAR BLAZE...
LIKE THIS...?
ROARRR
I NEED A ROCK THE SAME SIZE AS THE LAST ONE.
THAT'LL DO.
VOOSH

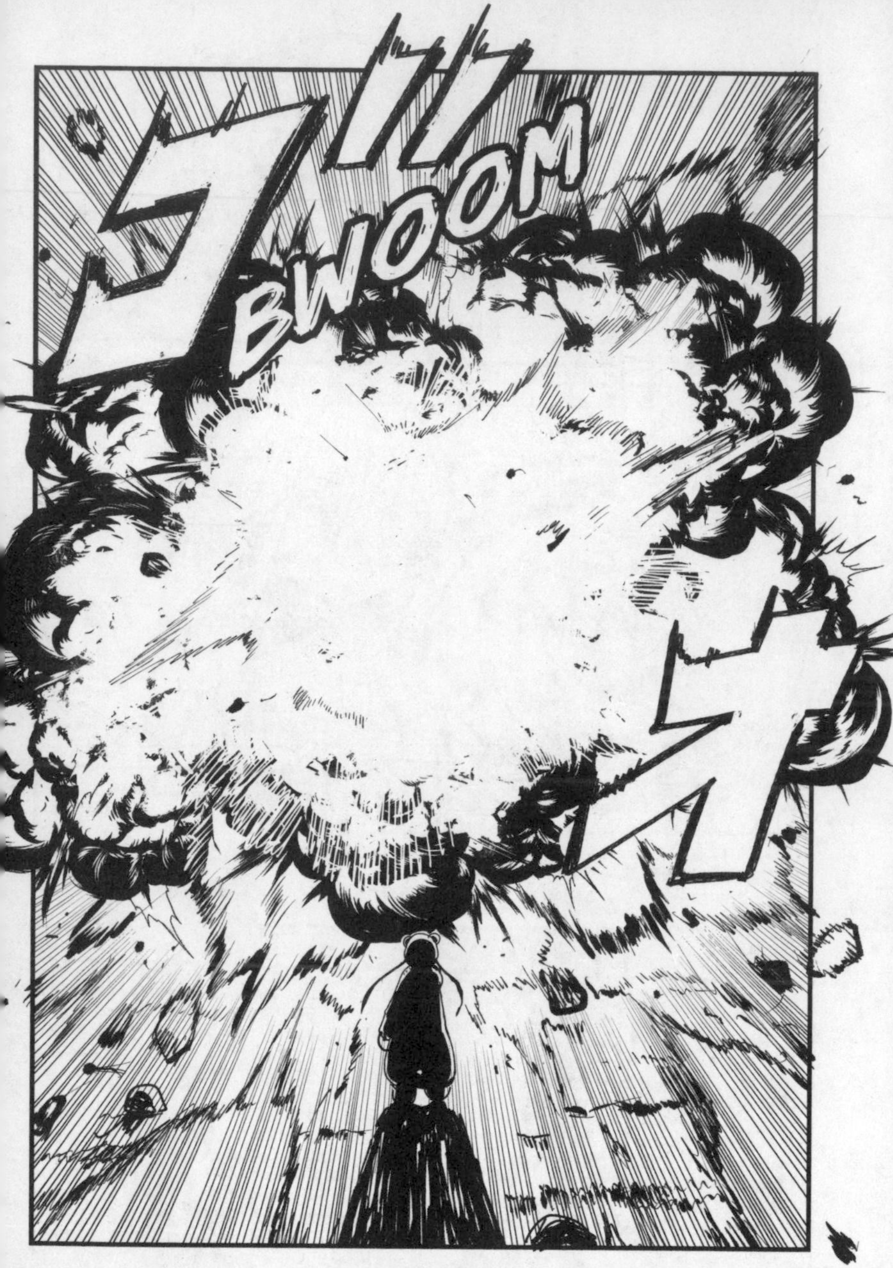
BWOOM

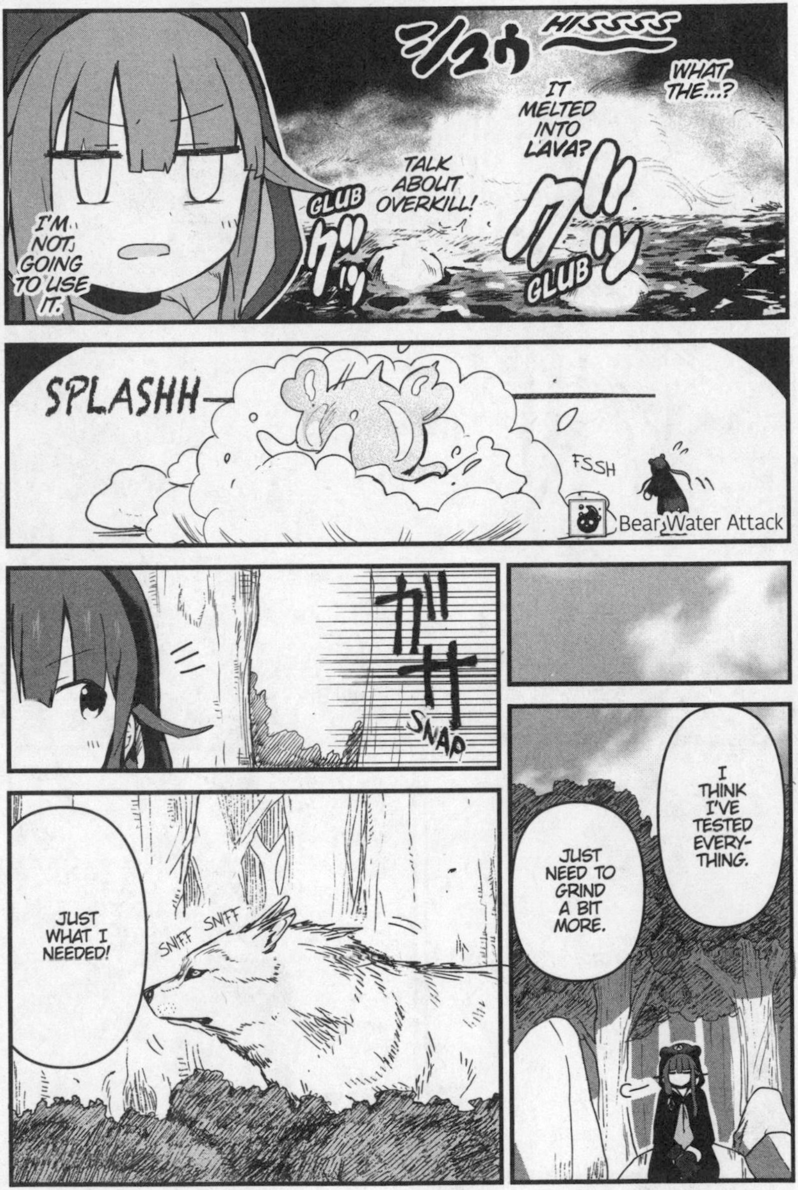
HISSSS
WHAT THE...?
IT MELTED INTO LAVA?
GLUB
TALK ABOUT OVERKILL!
GLUB
I'M NOT GOING TO USE IT.
SPLASHH
FSSH
Bear Water Attack
I THINK I'VE TESTED EVERY-THING.
JUST NEED TO GRIND A BIT MORE.
SNAP
SNIFF SNIFF
JUST WHAT I NEEDED!

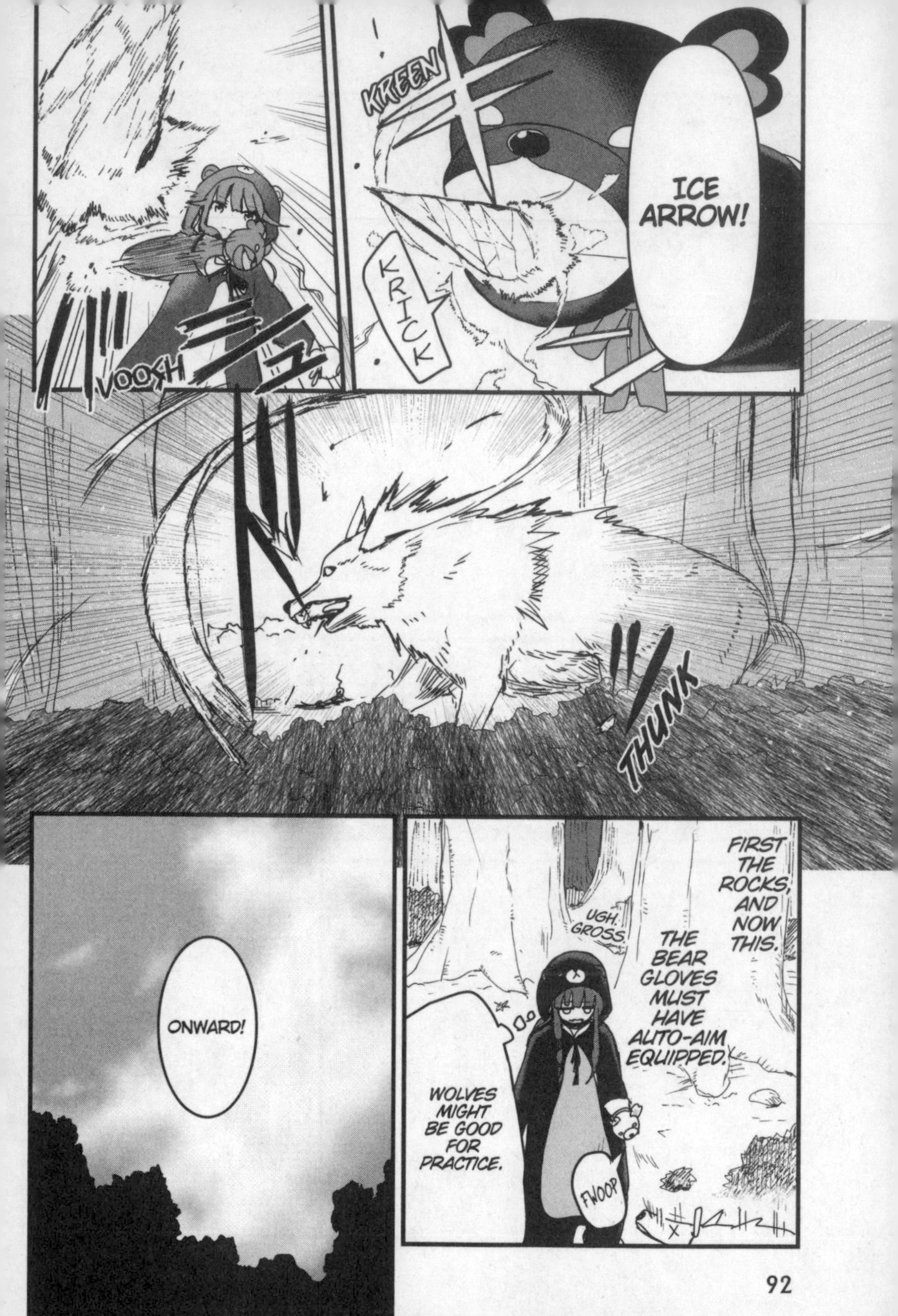
ICE ARROW!
KREEN
KRICK
VOOSH
THUNK
FIRST THE ROCKS, AND NOW THIS.
UGH. GROSS.
THE BEAR GLOVES MUST HAVE AUTO-AIM EQUIPPED.
WOLVES MIGHT BE GOOD FOR PRACTICE.
FWOOP
ONWARD!

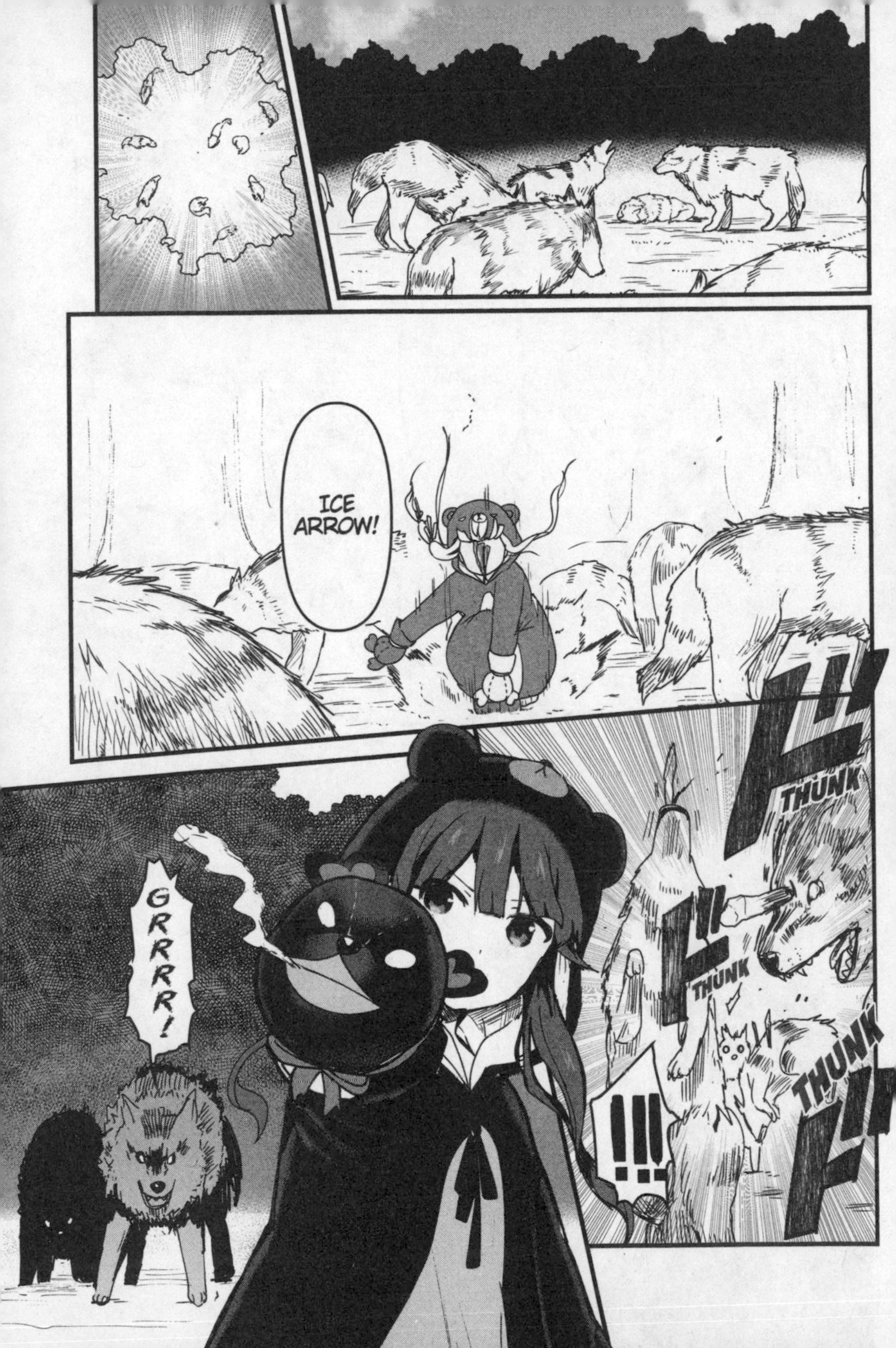
ICE ARROW!
THUNK
THUNK
THUNK
!!!
GRRRR!

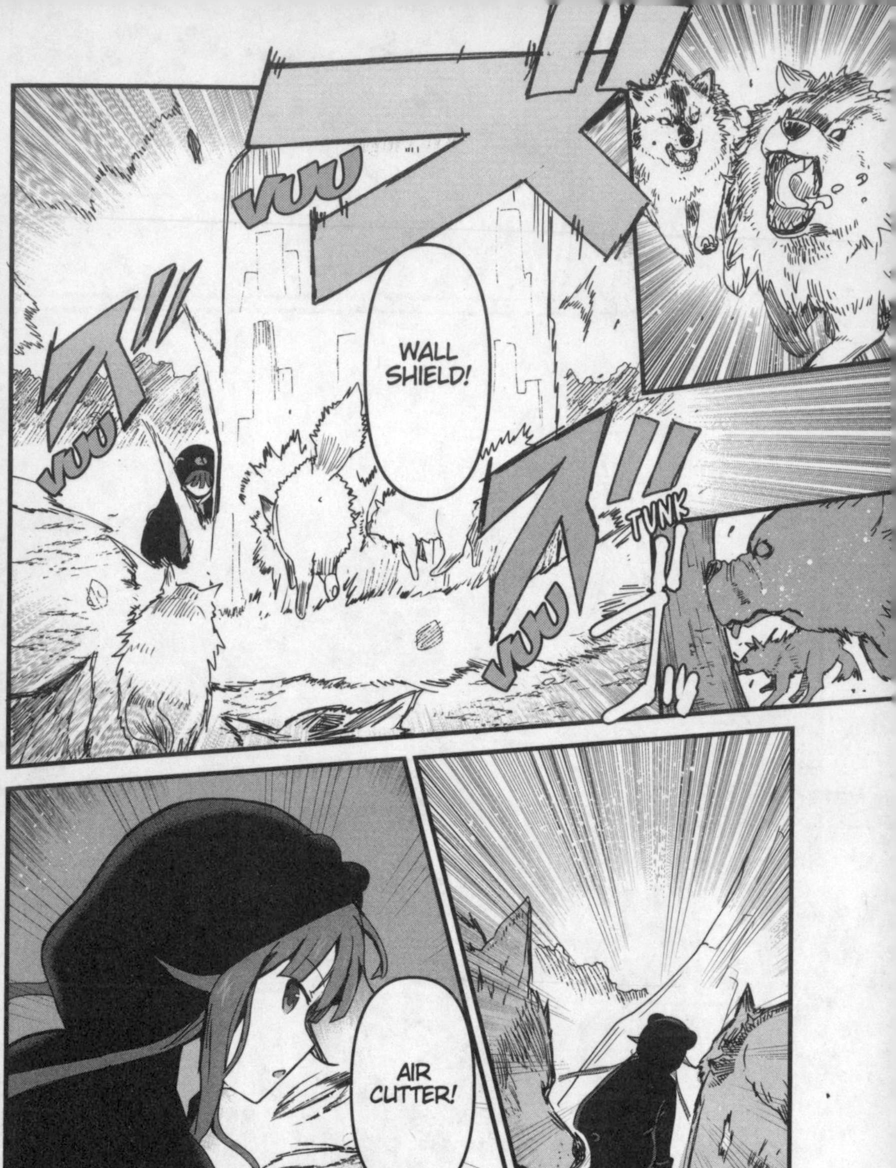
VUU
WALL SHIELD!
TUNK
VUU
VUU
AIR CUTTER!

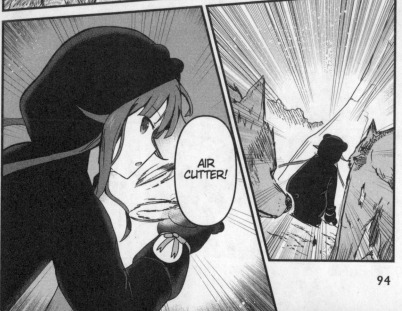

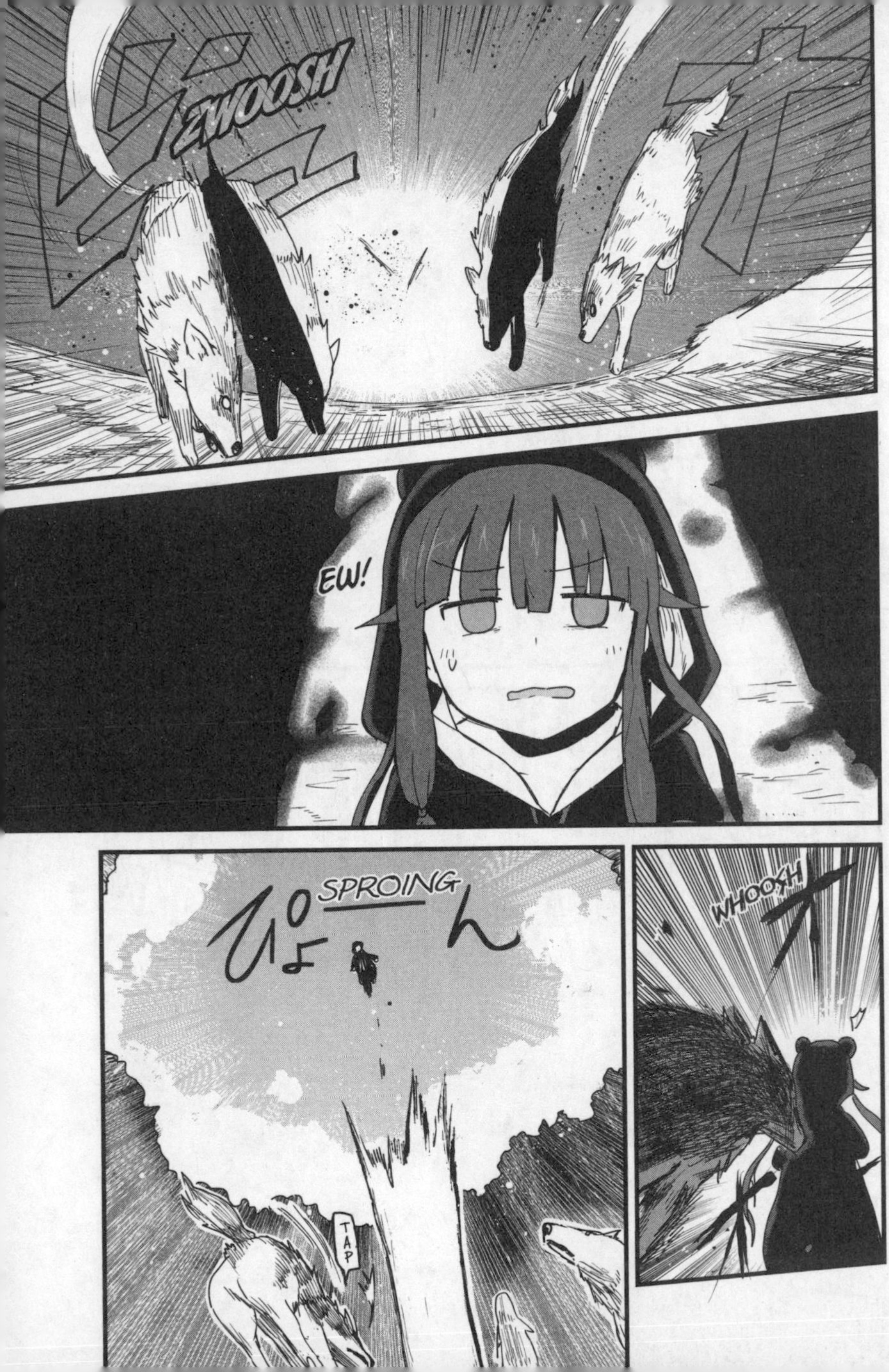
SWOOSH
EW!
WHOOSH
SPROING
ぴょん
TAP

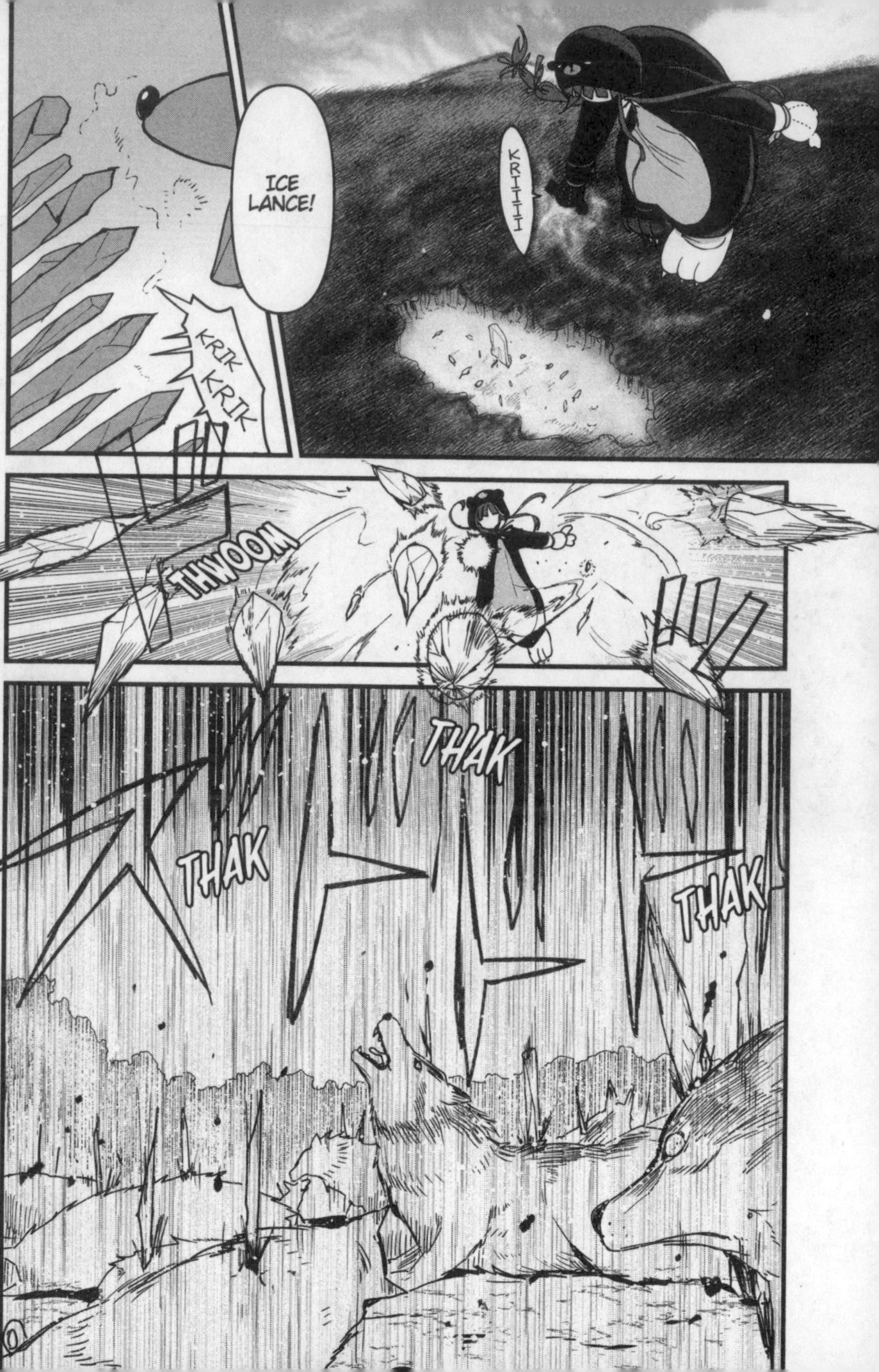
KRIIIII
ICE LANCE!
KRIK KRIK
THWOOM
THAK
THAK
THAK

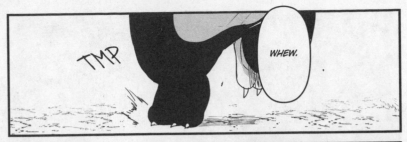

WHEW.

TMP

THAT WAS... ABOUT FORTY WOLVES?

DECENT GRIND SESH, I'D SAY.

ANY-HOO...

THAT LEAVES...

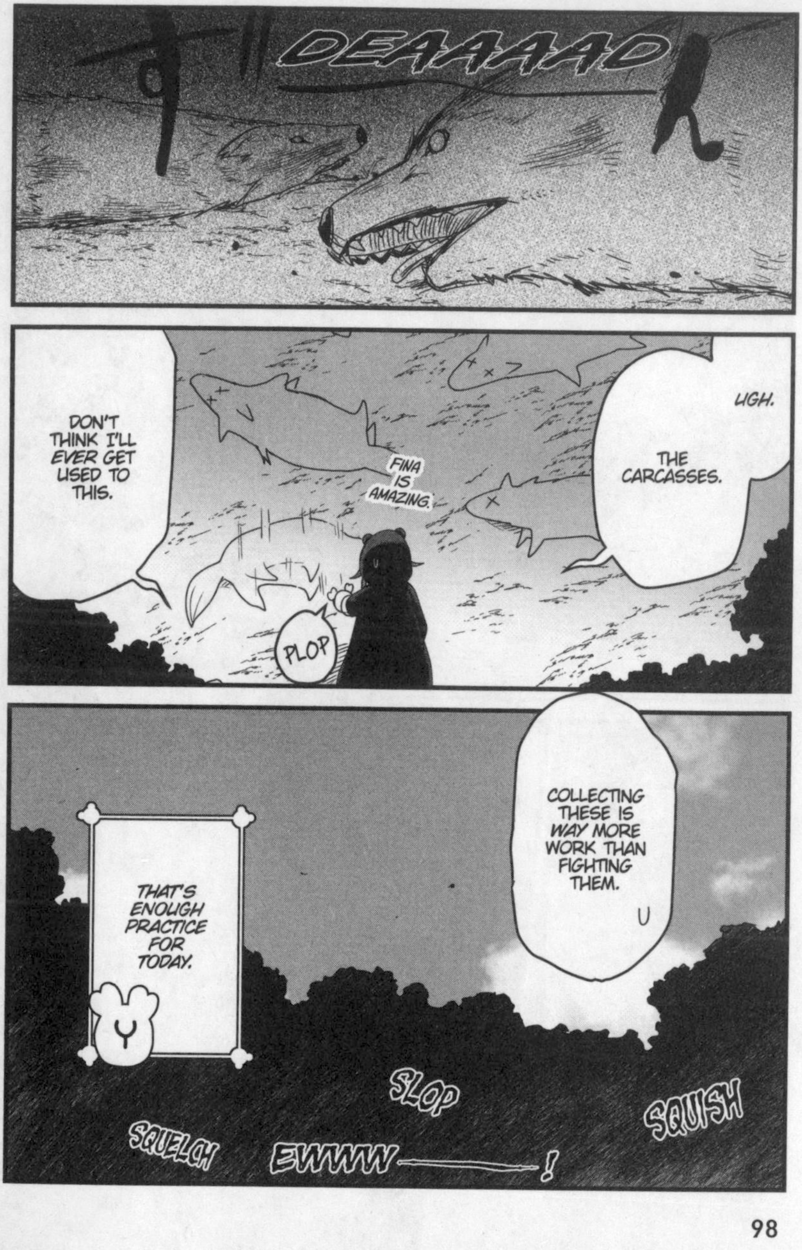
DEAAAAD
UGH.
THE CARCASSES.
FINA IS AMAZING.
DON'T THINK I'LL EVER GET USED TO THIS.
PLOP
COLLECTING THESE IS WAY MORE WORK THAN FIGHTING THEM.
THAT'S ENOUGH PRACTICE FOR TODAY.
SQUISH
SLOP
EWWWW—!
SQUELCH

Chapter 7

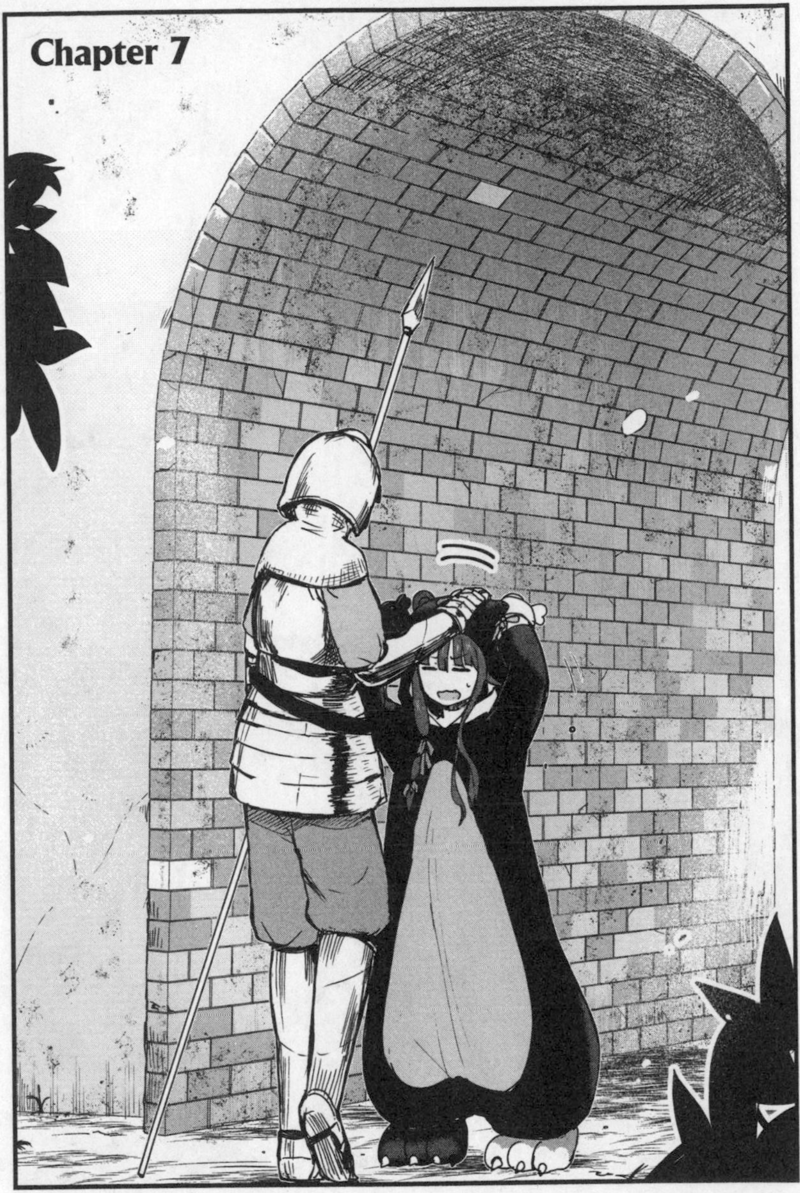

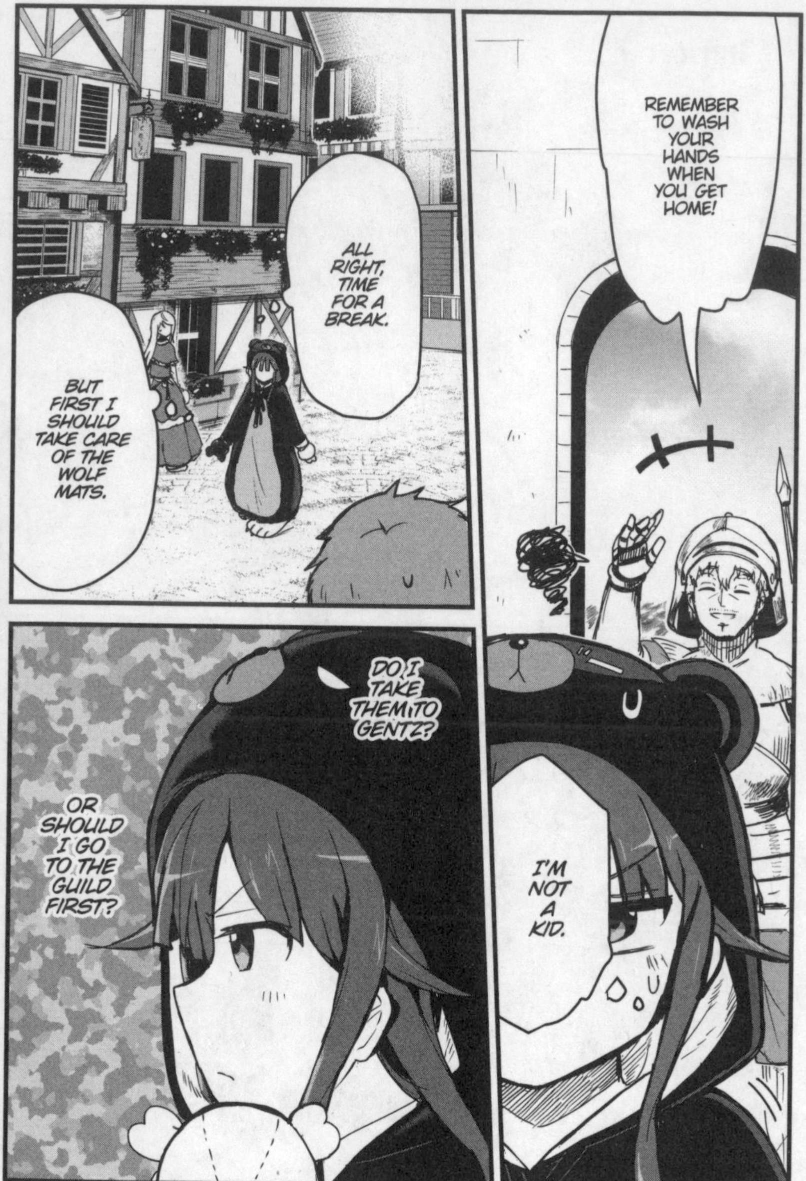
REMEMBER TO WASH YOUR HANDS WHEN YOU GET HOME!
ALL RIGHT, TIME FOR A BREAK.
BUT FIRST I SHOULD TAKE CARE OF THE WOLF MATS.
I'M NOT A KID.
DO I TAKE THEM TO GENTZ?
OR SHOULD I GO TO THE GUILD FIRST?

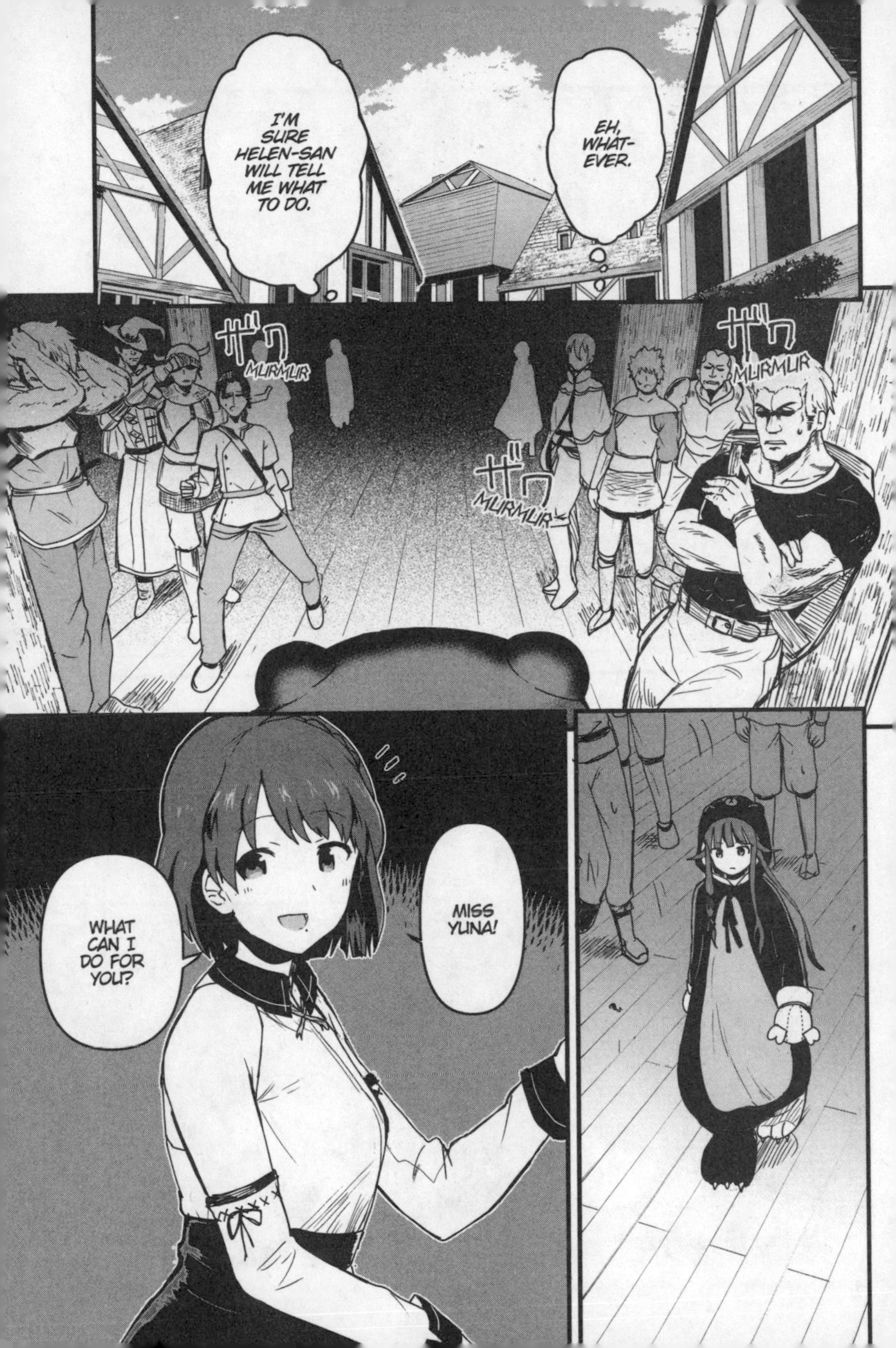
EH, WHATEVER.
I'M SURE HELEN-SAN WILL TELL ME WHAT TO DO.
ザワ
MURMUR
ザワ
MURMUR
ザワ
MURMUR
MISS YUNA!
WHAT CAN I DO FOR YOU?

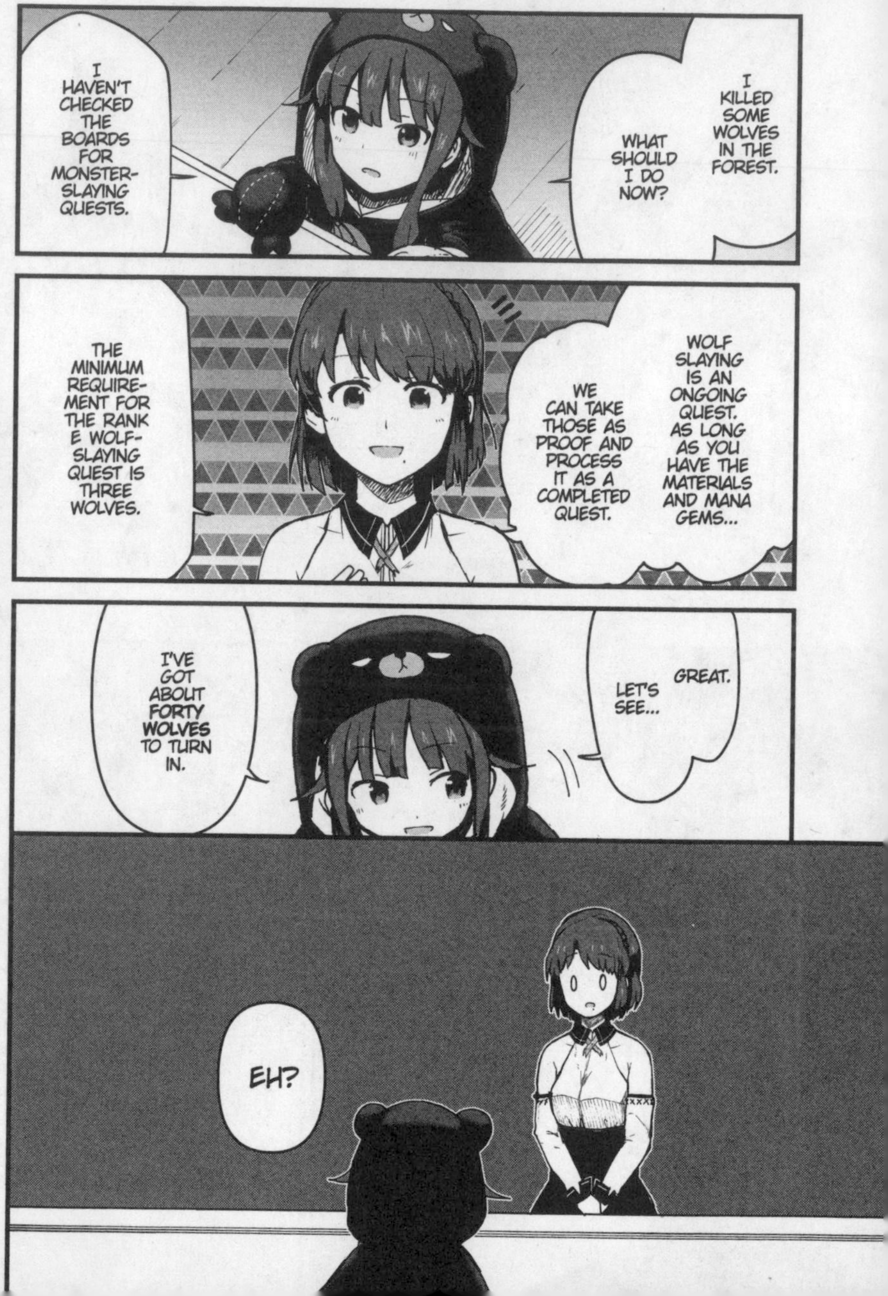
I KILLED SOME WOLVES IN THE FOREST.
WHAT SHOULD I DO NOW?
I HAVEN'T CHECKED THE BOARDS FOR MONSTER-SLAYING QUESTS.
WOLF SLAYING IS AN ONGOING QUEST. AS LONG AS YOU HAVE THE MATERIALS AND MANA GEMS...
WE CAN TAKE THOSE AS PROOF AND PROCESS IT AS A COMPLETED QUEST.
THE MINIMUM REQUIREMENT FOR THE RANK E WOLF-SLAYING QUEST IS THREE WOLVES.
GREAT.
LET'S SEE...
I'VE GOT ABOUT FORTY WOLVES TO TURN IN.
EH?

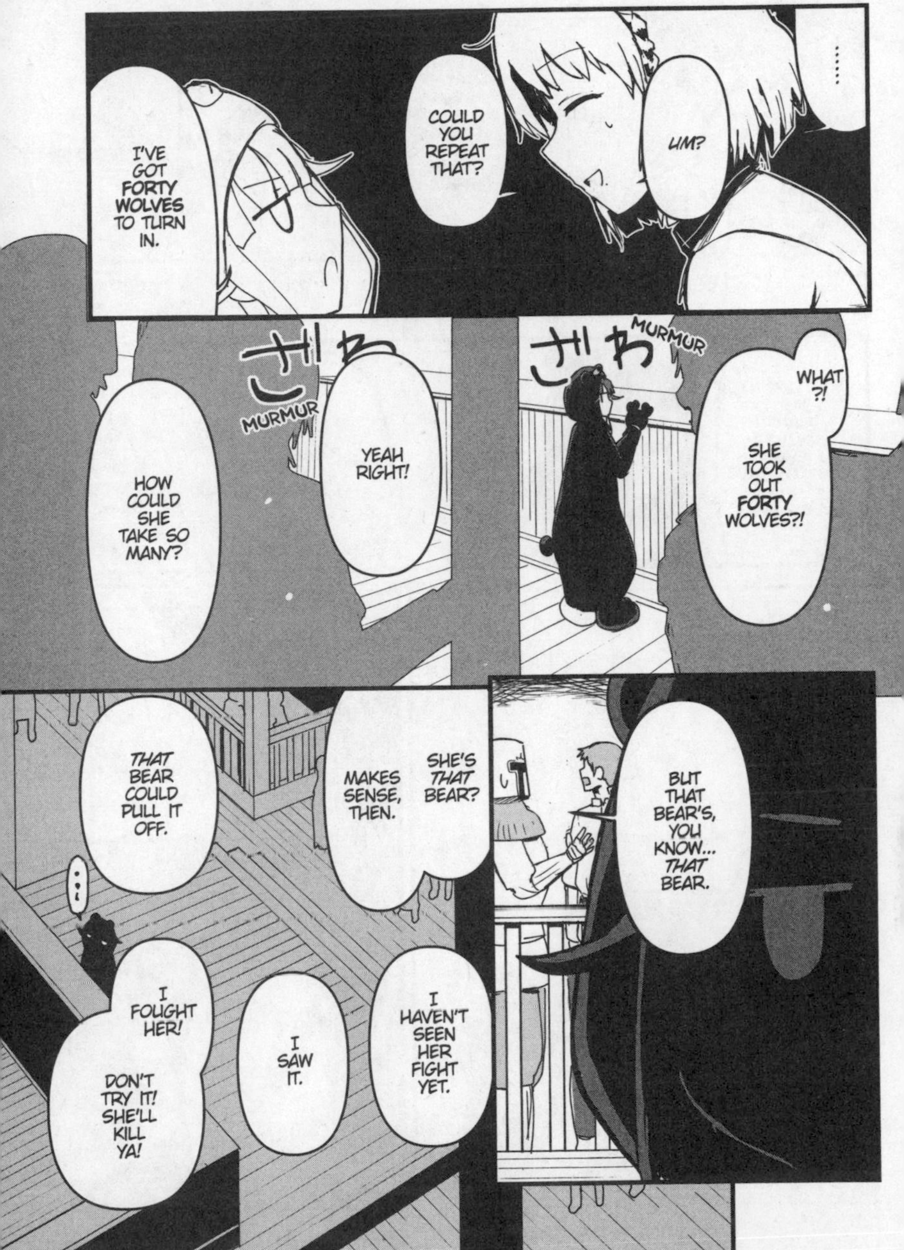
......
UM?
COULD YOU REPEAT THAT?
I'VE GOT FORTY WOLVES TO TURN IN.
ざわ
MURMUR
WHAT?! SHE TOOK OUT FORTY WOLVES?!
ざわ
MURMUR
YEAH RIGHT!
HOW COULD SHE TAKE SO MANY?
BUT THAT BEAR'S, YOU KNOW... *THAT* BEAR.
SHE'S *THAT* BEAR?
MAKES SENSE, THEN.
THAT BEAR COULD PULL IT OFF.
I HAVEN'T SEEN HER FIGHT YET.
I SAW IT.
I FOUGHT HER! DON'T TRY IT! SHE'LL KILL YA!
...?

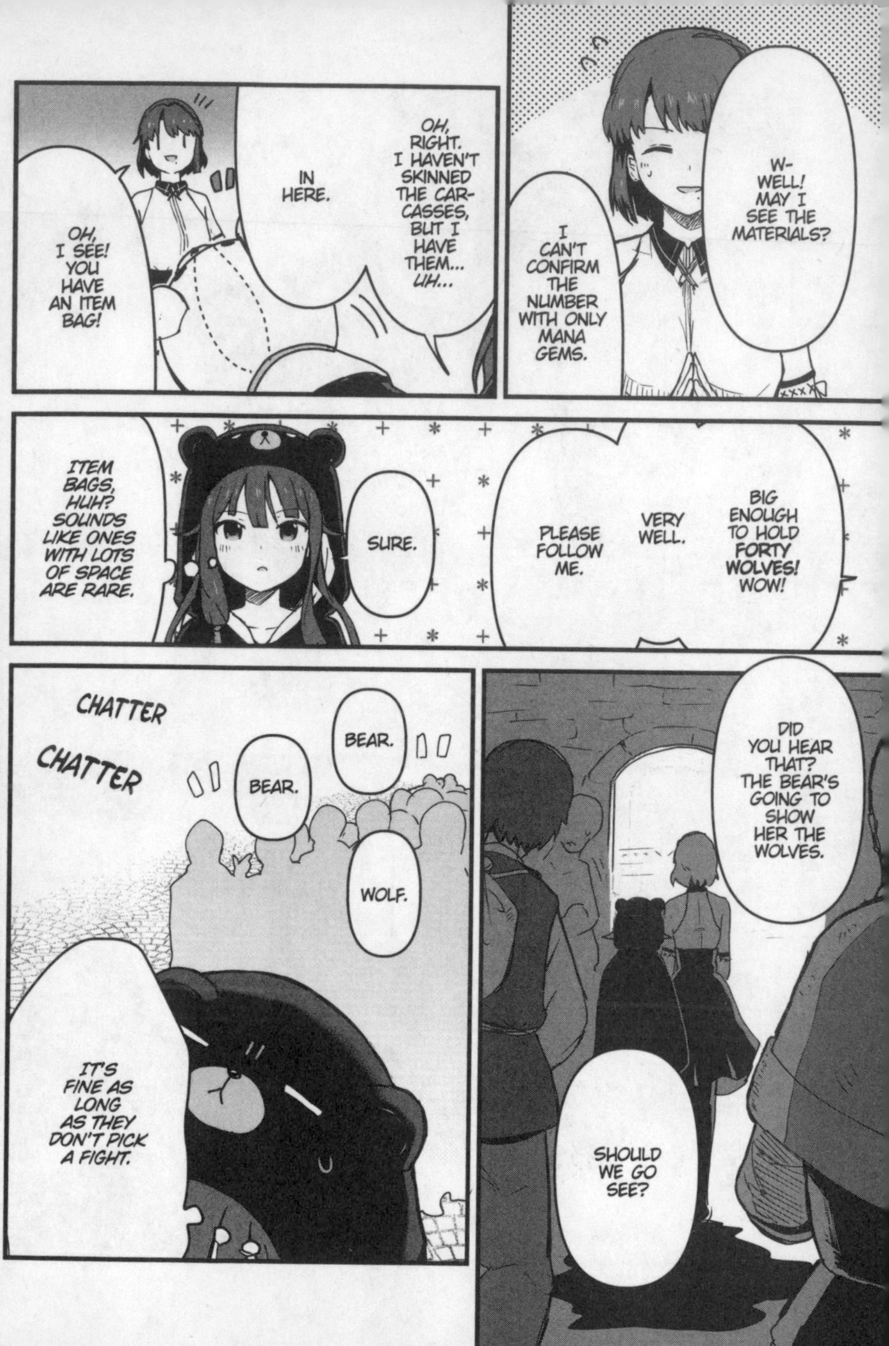
W-WELL! MAY I SEE THE MATERIALS?
I CAN'T CONFIRM THE NUMBER WITH ONLY MANA GEMS.
OH, RIGHT. I HAVEN'T SKINNED THE CAR-CASSES, BUT I HAVE THEM... UH...
IN HERE.
OH, I SEE! YOU HAVE AN ITEM BAG!
BIG ENOUGH TO HOLD FORTY WOLVES! WOW!
VERY WELL.
PLEASE FOLLOW ME.
SURE.
ITEM BAGS, HUH? SOUNDS LIKE ONES WITH LOTS OF SPACE ARE RARE.
DID YOU HEAR THAT? THE BEAR'S GOING TO SHOW HER THE WOLVES.
SHOULD WE GO SEE?
CHATTER
CHATTER
BEAR.
BEAR.
WOLF.
IT'S FINE AS LONG AS THEY DON'T PICK A FIGHT.

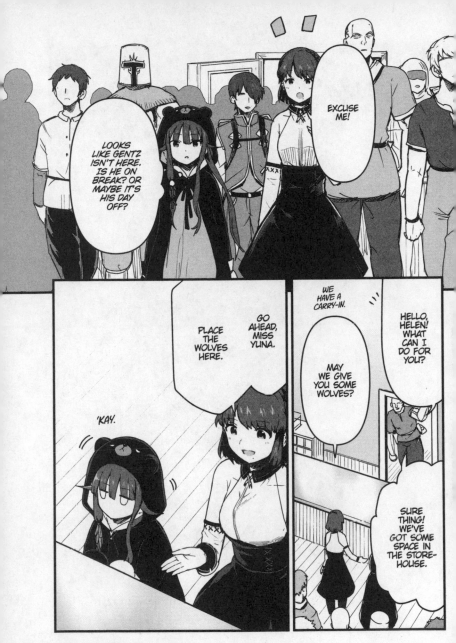

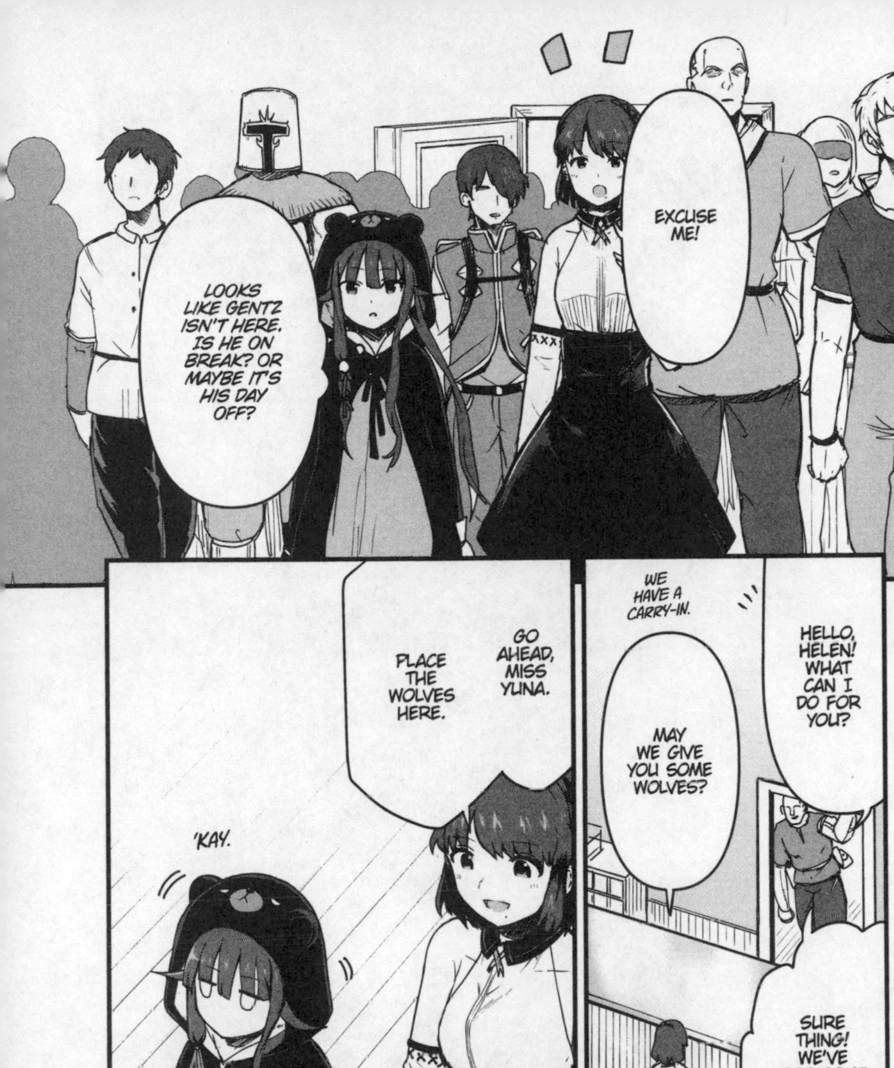
EXCUSE ME!
LOOKS LIKE GENTZ ISN'T HERE. IS HE ON BREAK? OR MAYBE IT'S HIS DAY OFF?
HELLO, HELEN! WHAT CAN I DO FOR YOU?
WE HAVE A CARRY-IN.
MAY WE GIVE YOU SOME WOLVES?
SURE THING! WE'VE GOT SOME SPACE IN THE STORE-HOUSE.
GO AHEAD, MISS YUNA.
PLACE THE WOLVES HERE.
'KAY.

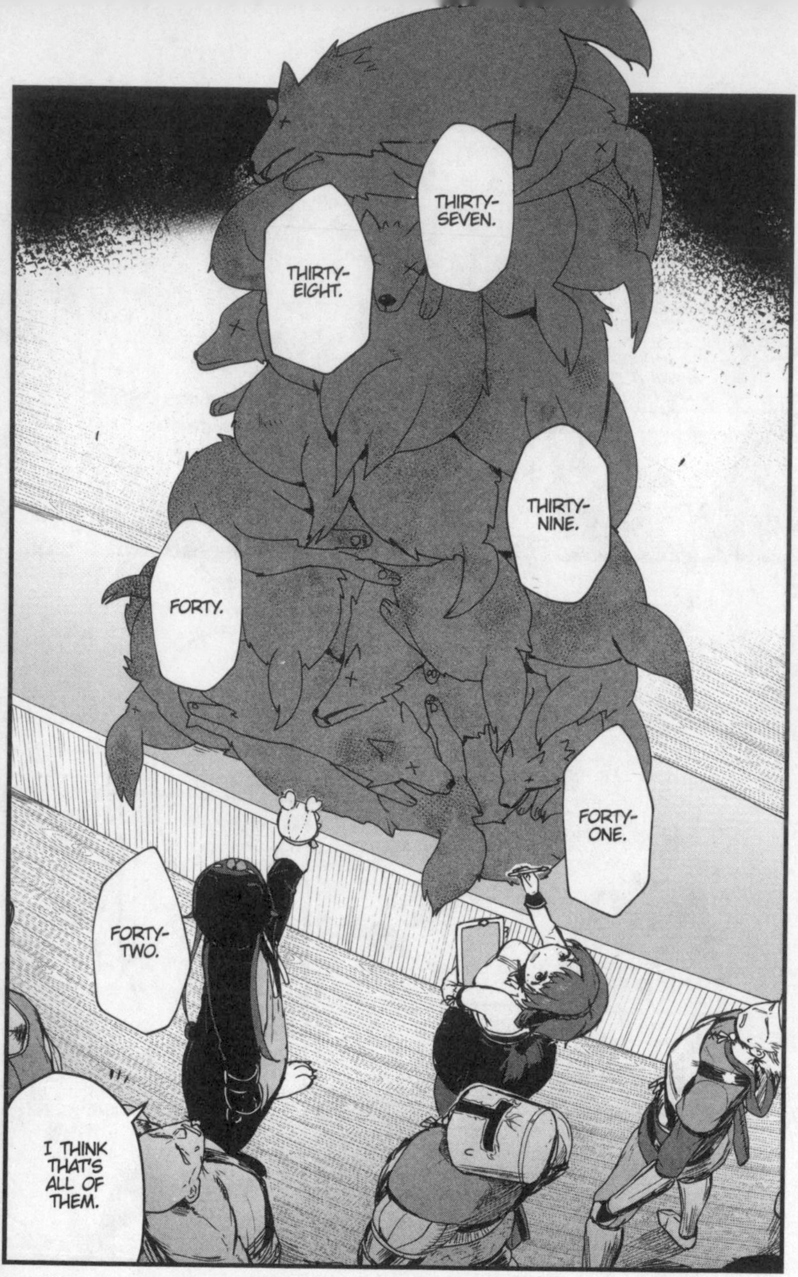
THIRTY-SEVEN.
THIRTY-EIGHT.
THIRTY-NINE.
FORTY.
FORTY-ONE.
FORTY-TWO.
I THINK THAT'S ALL OF THEM.

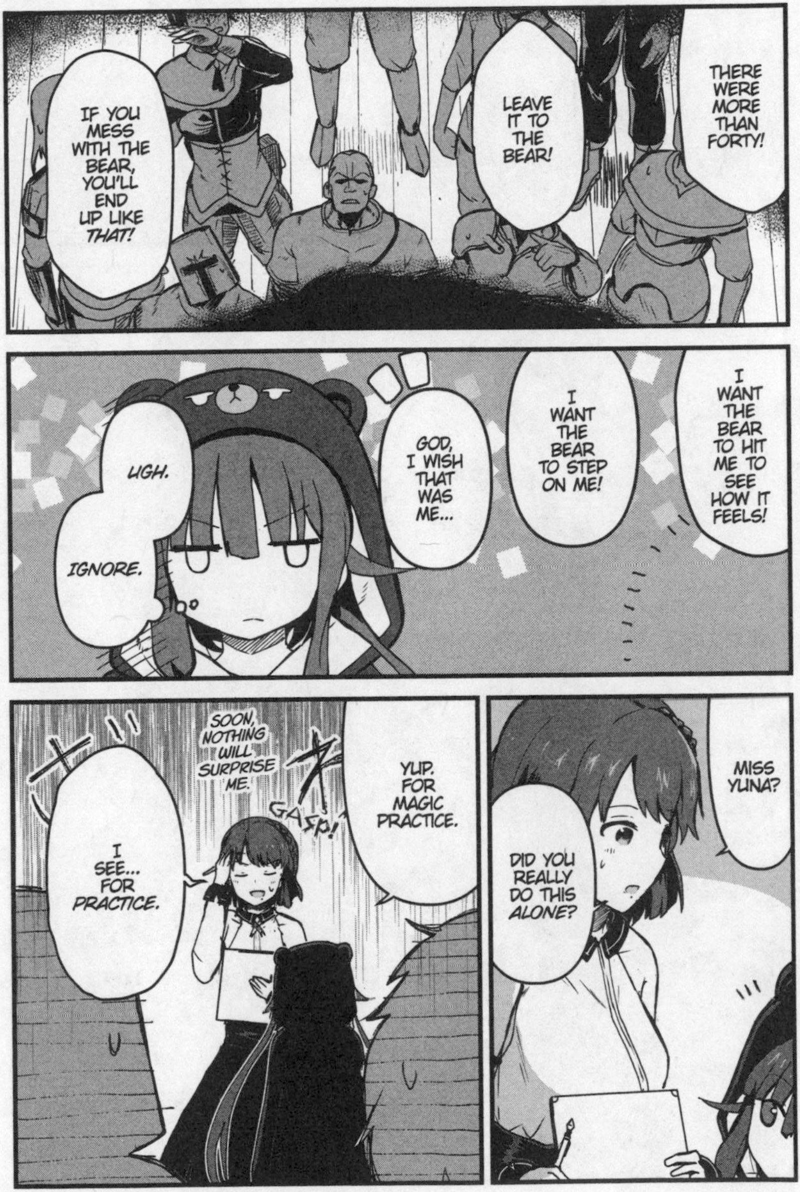
THERE WERE MORE THAN FORTY!
LEAVE IT TO THE BEAR!
IF YOU MESS WITH THE BEAR, YOU'LL END UP LIKE *THAT!*
I WANT THE BEAR TO HIT ME TO SEE HOW IT FEELS!
I WANT THE BEAR TO STEP ON ME!
GOD, I WISH THAT WAS ME...
UGH.
IGNORE.
MISS YUNA?
DID YOU REALLY DO THIS *ALONE?*
YUP. FOR MAGIC PRACTICE.
SOON, NOTHING WILL SURPRISE ME.
GASP!
I SEE... FOR *PRACTICE.*

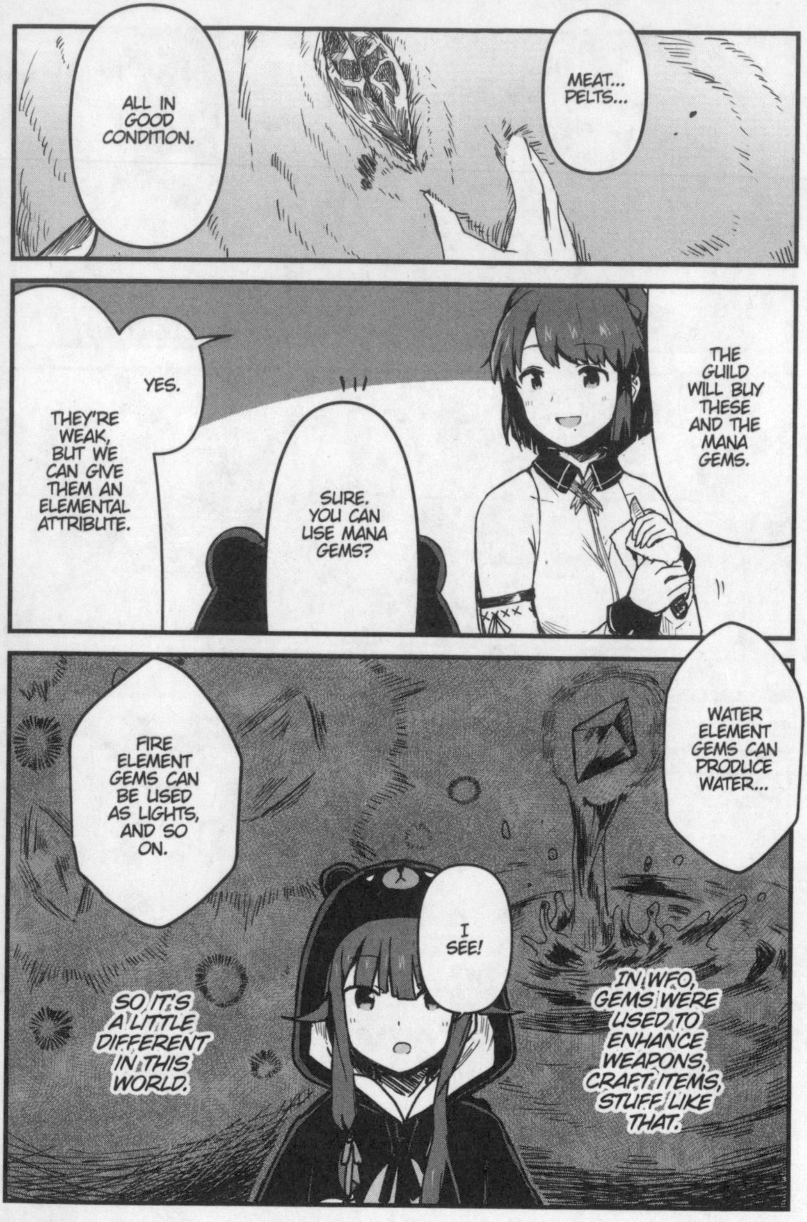
MEAT... PELTS...
ALL IN GOOD CONDITION.
THE GUILD WILL BUY THESE AND THE MANA GEMS.
SURE. YOU CAN USE MANA GEMS?
YES.
THEY'RE WEAK, BUT WE CAN GIVE THEM AN ELEMENTAL ATTRIBUTE.
WATER ELEMENT GEMS CAN PRODUCE WATER...
FIRE ELEMENT GEMS CAN BE USED AS LIGHTS, AND SO ON.
I SEE!
IN WFO, GEMS WERE USED TO ENHANCE WEAPONS, CRAFT ITEMS, STUFF LIKE THAT.
SO IT'S A LITTLE DIFFERENT IN THIS WORLD.

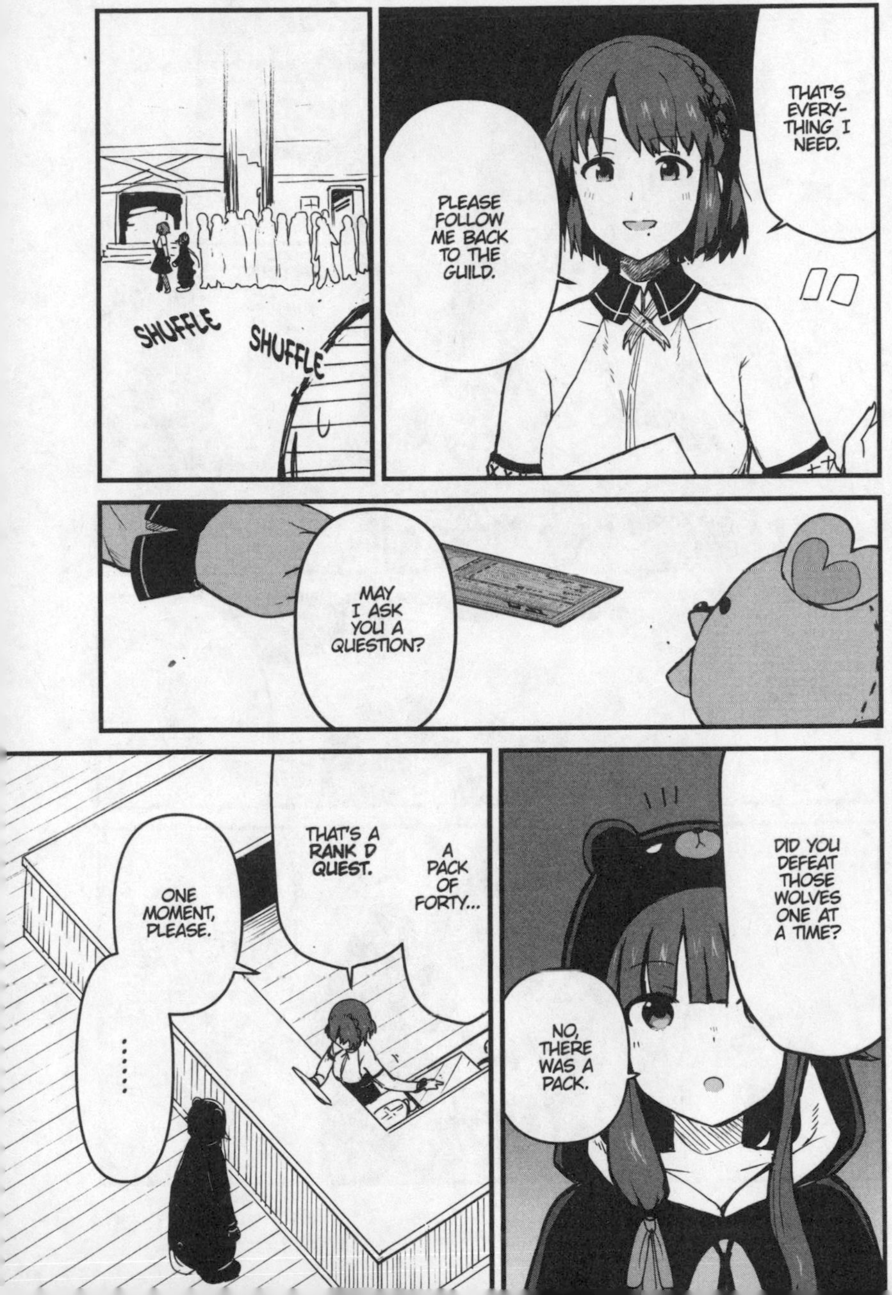
THAT'S EVERY-THING I NEED.
PLEASE FOLLOW ME BACK TO THE GUILD.
SHUFFLE
SHUFFLE
MAY I ASK YOU A QUESTION?
DID YOU DEFEAT THOSE WOLVES ONE AT A TIME?
NO, THERE WAS A PACK.
A PACK OF FORTY...
THAT'S A RANK D QUEST.
ONE MOMENT, PLEASE.
......

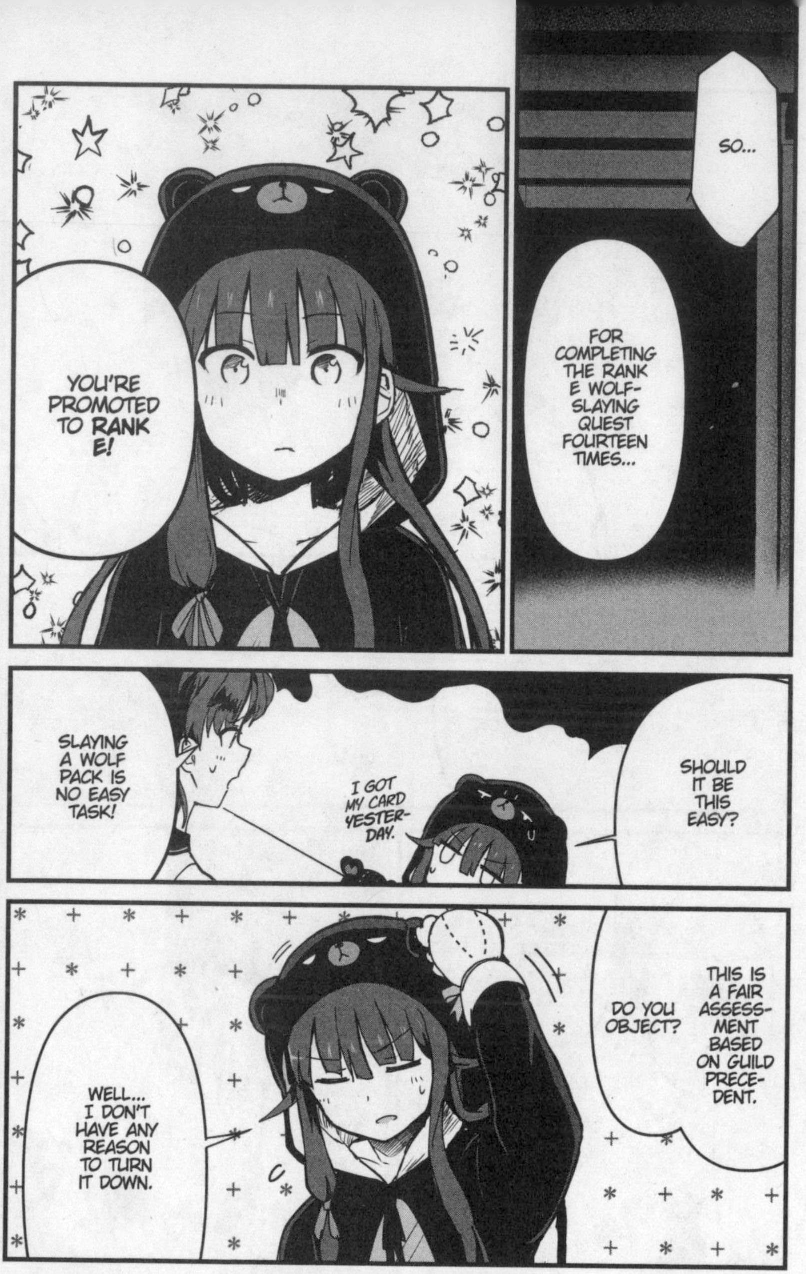
SO...
FOR COMPLETING THE RANK E WOLF-SLAYING QUEST FOURTEEN TIMES...
YOU'RE PROMOTED TO RANK E!
SHOULD IT BE THIS EASY?
I GOT MY CARD YESTER-DAY.
SLAYING A WOLF PACK IS NO EASY TASK!
THIS IS A FAIR ASSESS-MENT BASED ON GUILD PRECE-DENT.
DO YOU OBJECT?
WELL... I DON'T HAVE ANY REASON TO TURN IT DOWN.

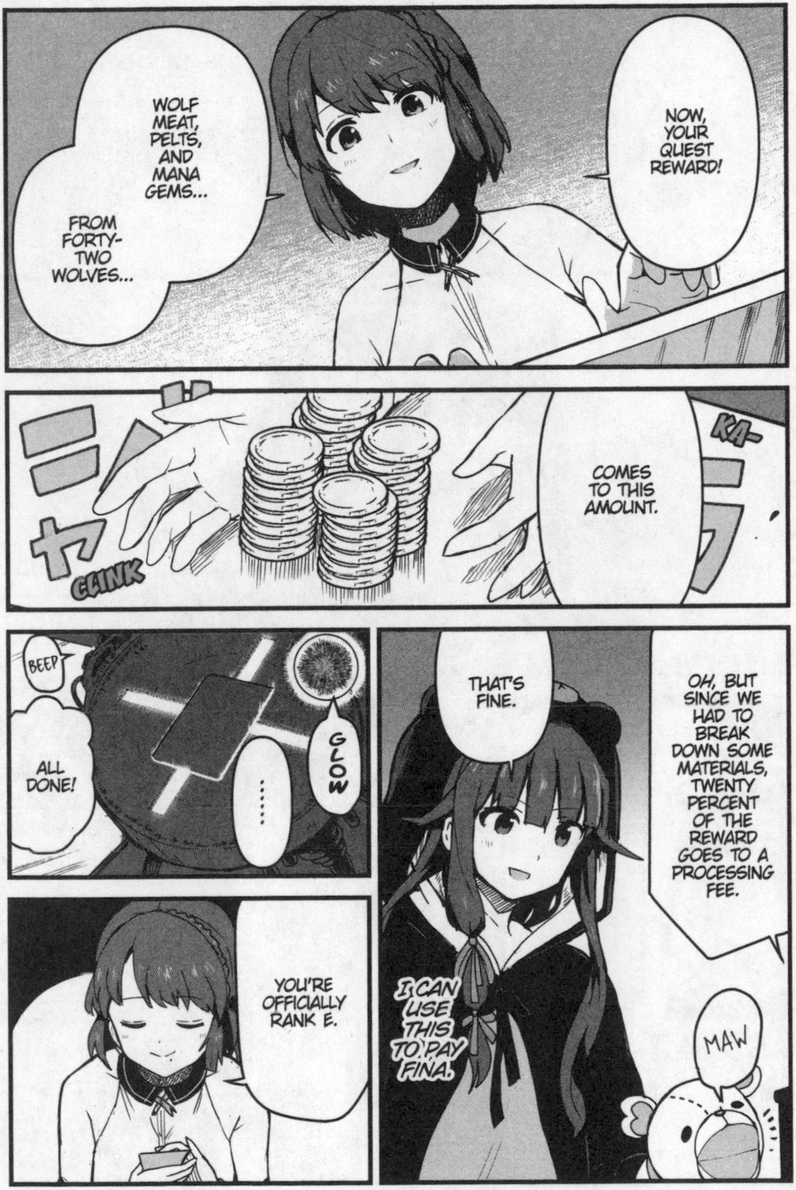
NOW, YOUR QUEST REWARD!
WOLF MEAT, PELTS, AND MANA GEMS...
FROM FORTY-TWO WOLVES...
KA-
COMES TO THIS AMOUNT.
CLINK
OH, BUT SINCE WE HAD TO BREAK DOWN SOME MATERIALS, TWENTY PERCENT OF THE REWARD GOES TO A PROCESSING FEE.
THAT'S FINE.
I CAN USE THIS TO PAY FINA.
MAW
GLOW
......
BEEP
ALL DONE!
YOU'RE OFFICIALLY RANK E.

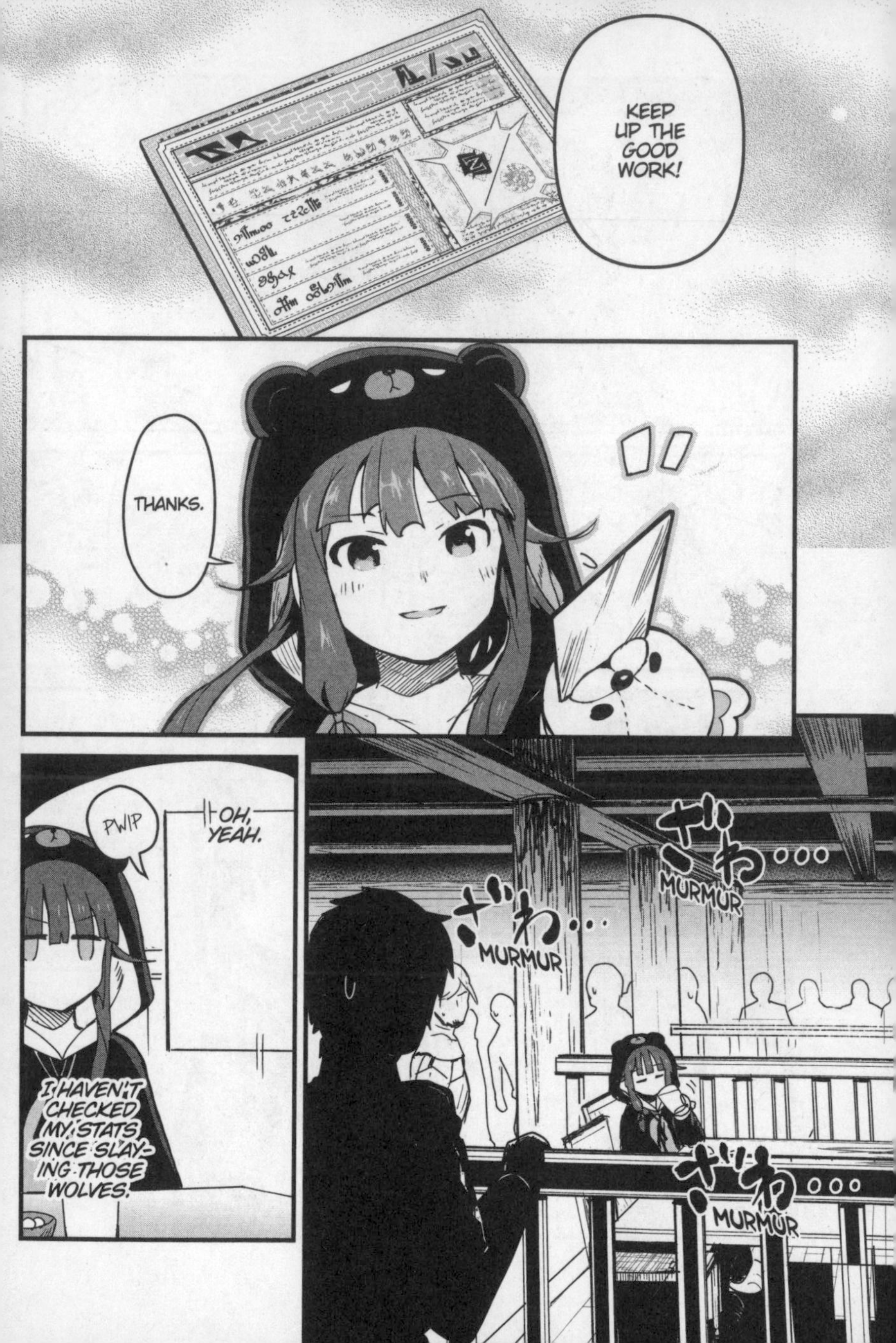

KEEP UP THE GOOD WORK!
THANKS.
ざわ…
MURMUR
ざわ…
MURMUR
ざわ…
MURMUR
PWIP
OH, YEAH.
I HAVEN'T CHECKED MY STATS SINCE SLAYING THOSE WOLVES.

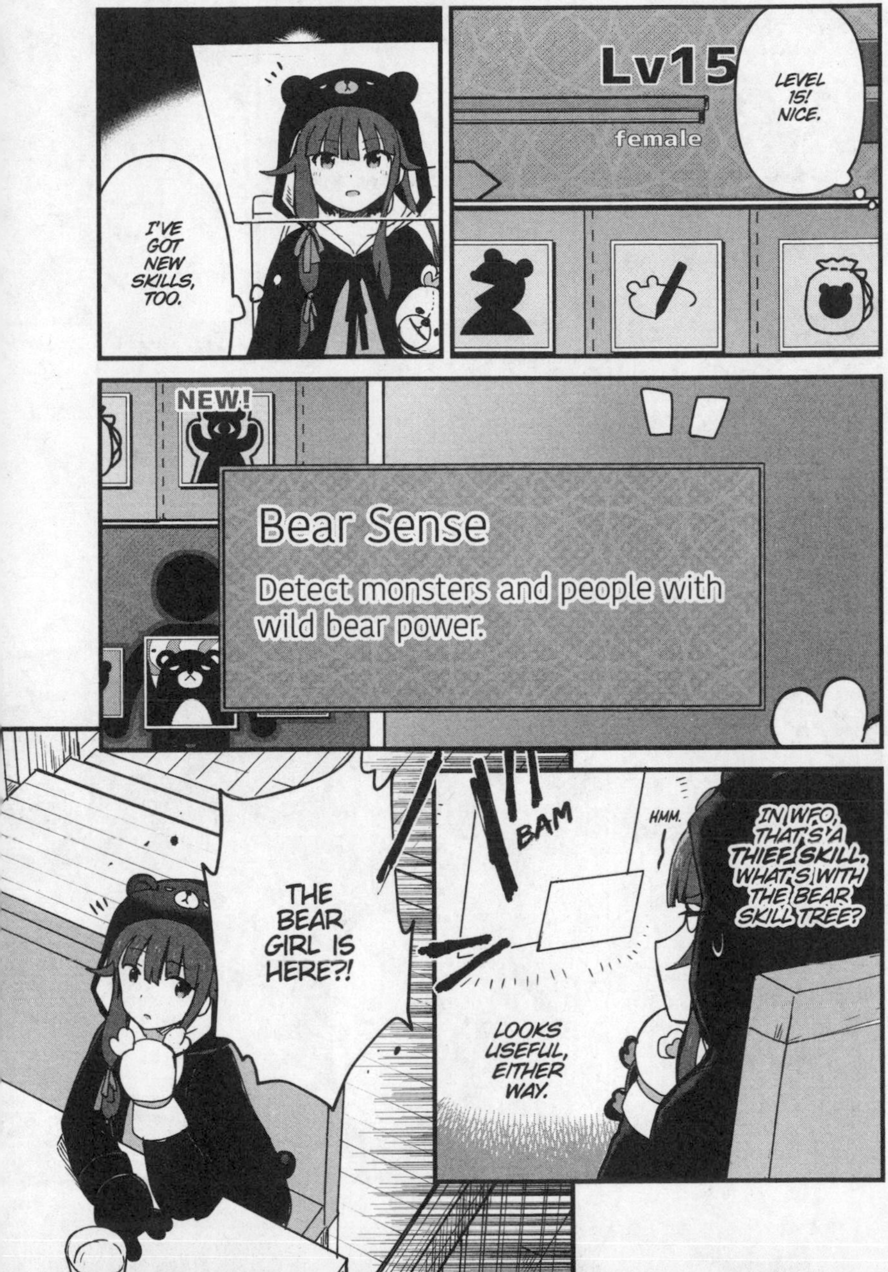
Lv15
female
LEVEL 15! NICE.
I'VE GOT NEW SKILLS, TOO.
NEW!
Bear Sense
Detect monsters and people with wild bear power.
BAM
HMM.
IN WFO, THAT'S A THIEF SKILL. WHAT'S WITH THE BEAR SKILL TREE?
LOOKS USEFUL, EITHER WAY.
THE BEAR GIRL IS HERE?!

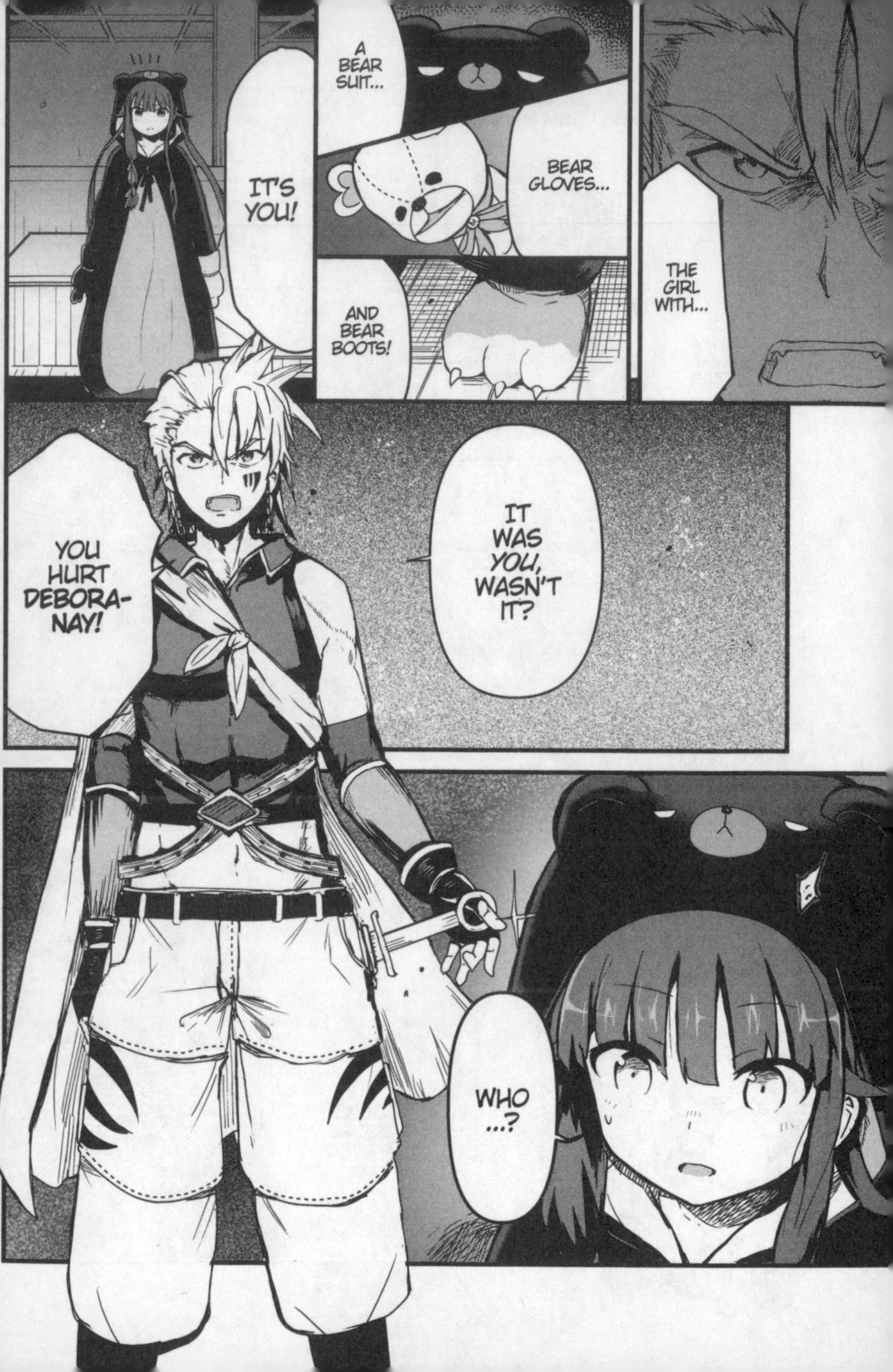
THE GIRL WITH...
A BEAR SUIT...
BEAR GLOVES...
AND BEAR BOOTS!
IT'S YOU!
IT WAS YOU, WASN'T IT?
YOU HURT DEBORA-NAY!
WHO ...?

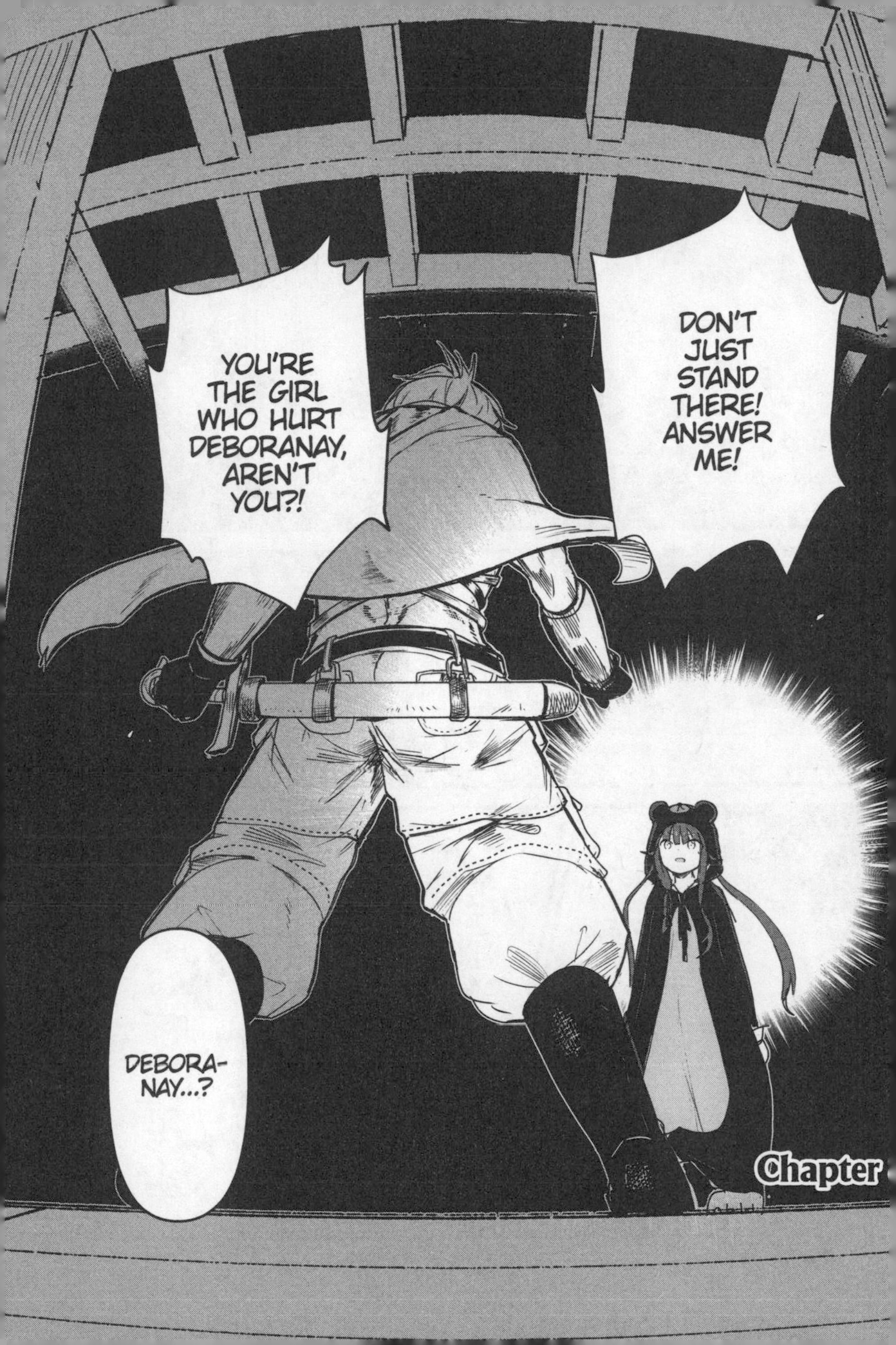
DON'T JUST STAND THERE! ANSWER ME!
YOU'RE THE GIRL WHO HURT DEBORANAY, AREN'T YOU?!
DEBORA-NAY...?
Chapter

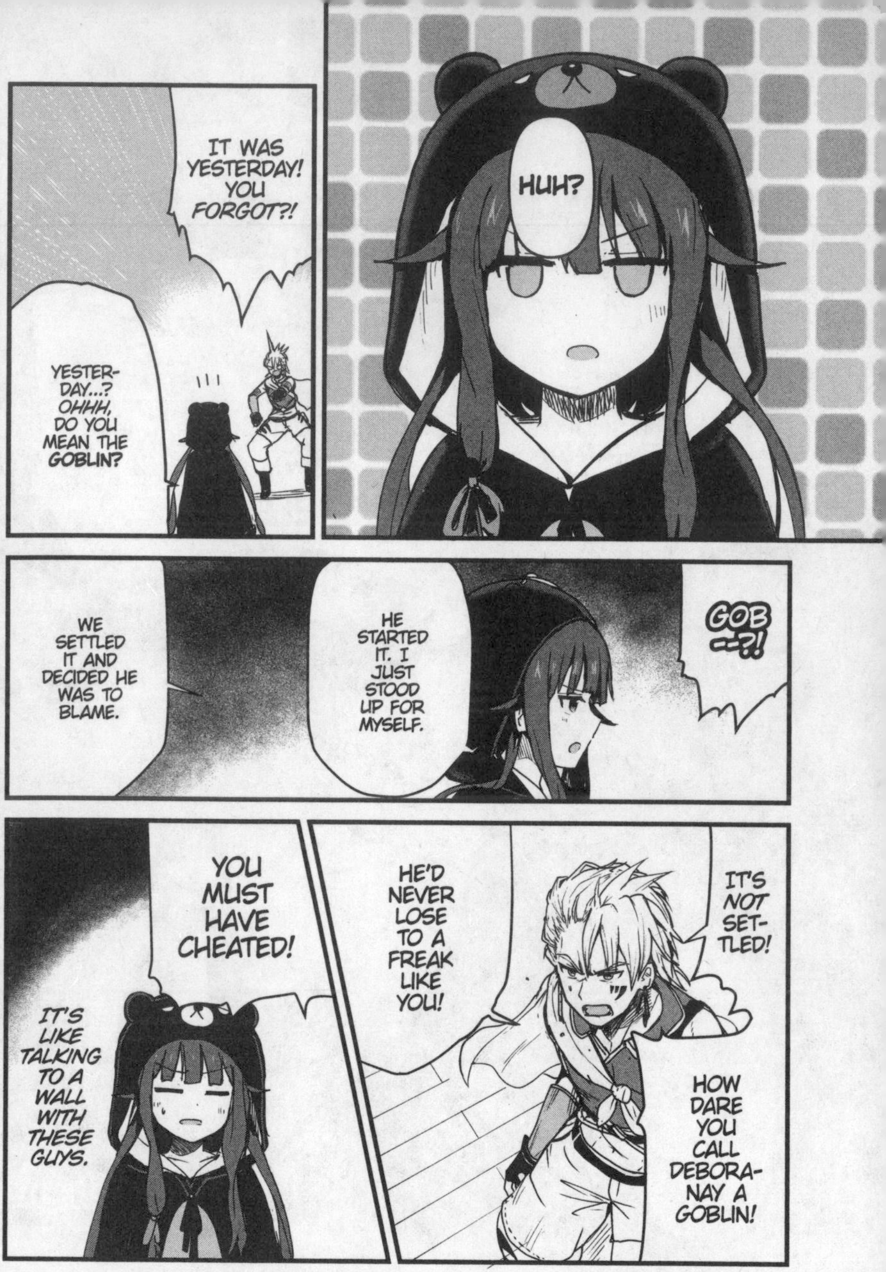
HUH?
IT WAS YESTERDAY! YOU FORGOT?!
YESTERDAY...? OHHH, DO YOU MEAN THE GOBLIN?
GOB--?!
HE STARTED IT. I JUST STOOD UP FOR MYSELF.
WE SETTLED IT AND DECIDED HE WAS TO BLAME.
IT'S NOT SETTLED!
HE'D NEVER LOSE TO A FREAK LIKE YOU!
HOW DARE YOU CALL DEBORANAY A GOBLIN!
YOU MUST HAVE CHEATED!
IT'S LIKE TALKING TO A WALL WITH THESE GUYS.

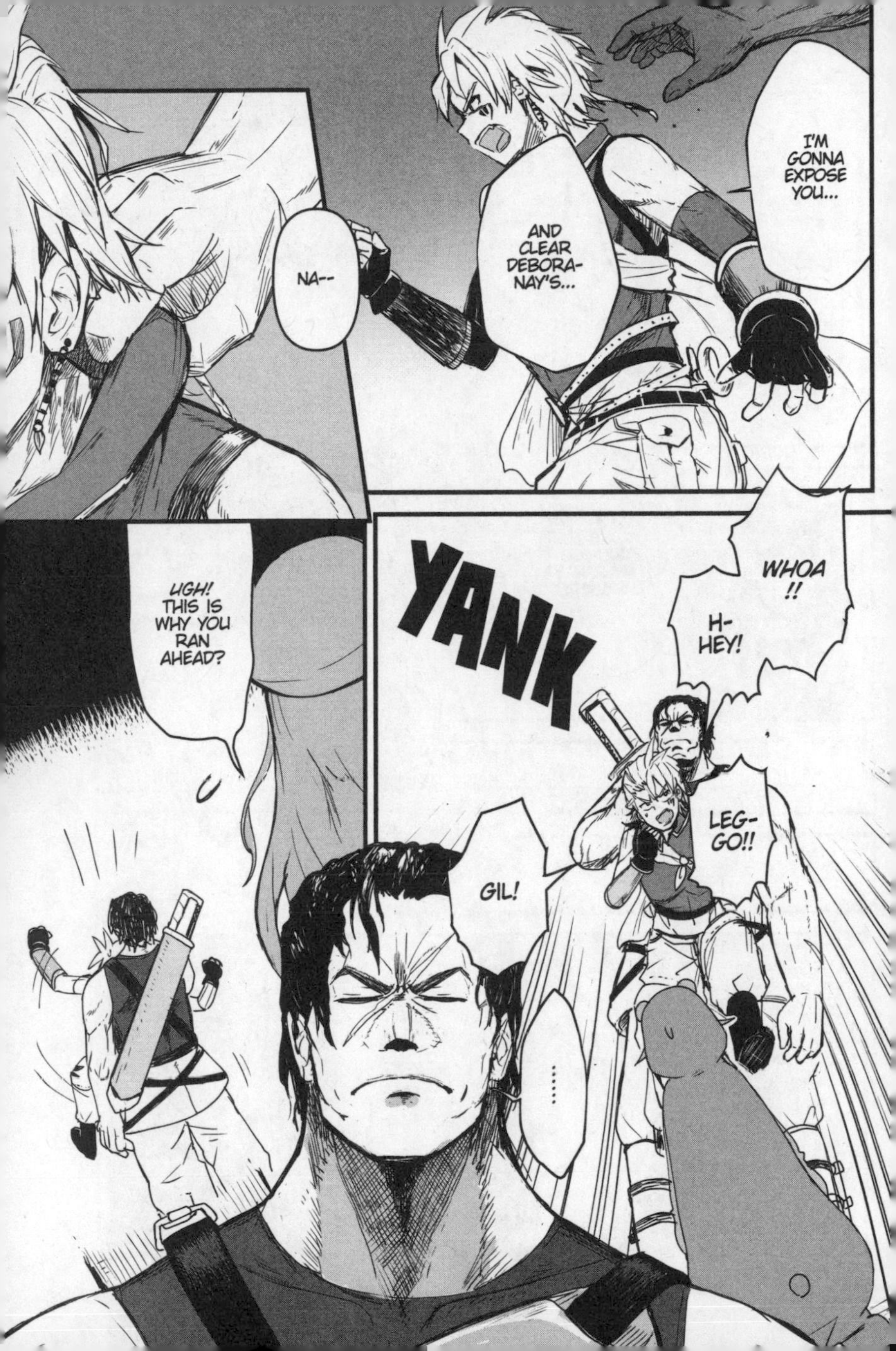
I'M GONNA EXPOSE YOU...
AND CLEAR DEBORA-NAY'S...
NA--
YANK
WHOA!!
H-HEY!
LEG-GO!!
UGH! THIS IS WHY YOU RAN AHEAD?
GIL!
......

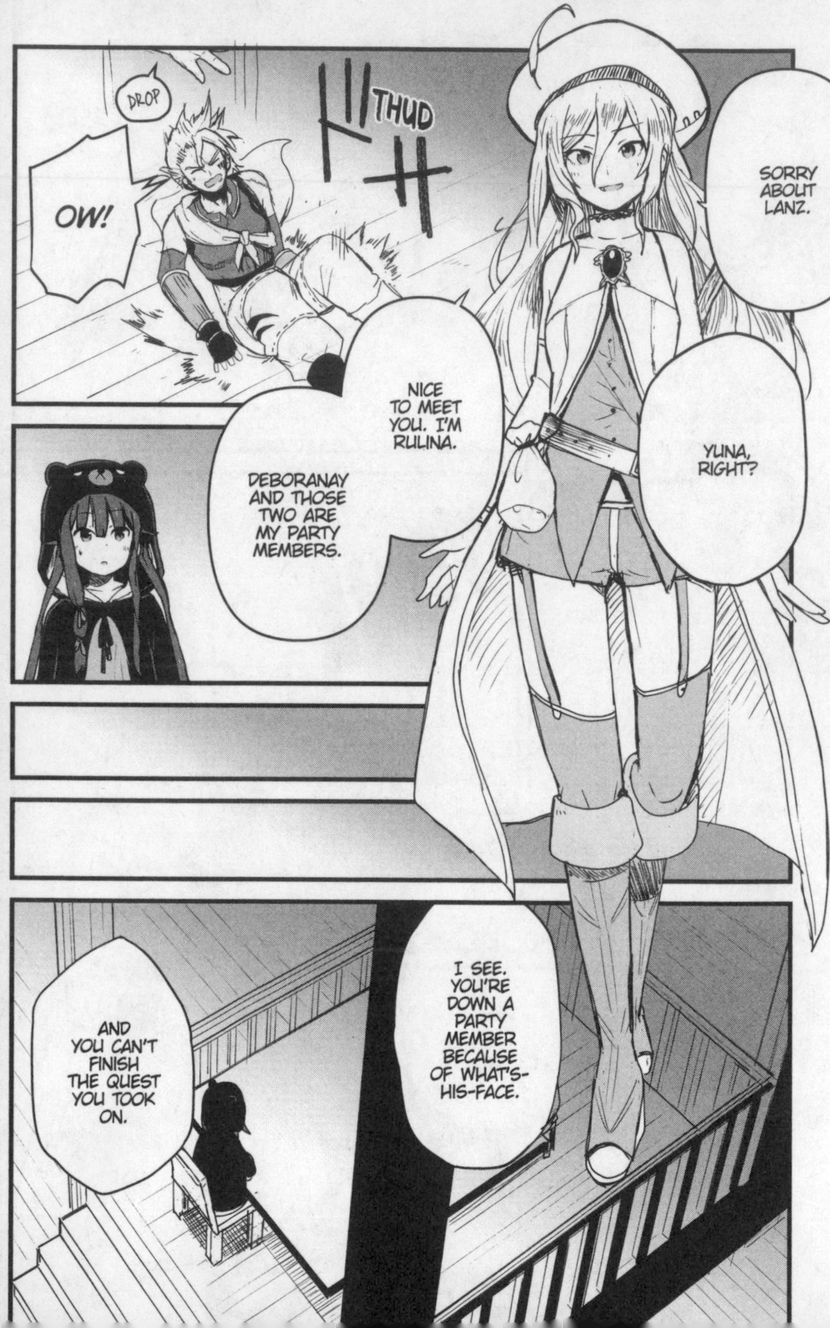
THUD
DROP
OW!
SORRY ABOUT LANZ.
YUNA, RIGHT?
NICE TO MEET YOU. I'M RULINA.
DEBORANAY AND THOSE TWO ARE MY PARTY MEMBERS.
I SEE. YOU'RE DOWN A PARTY MEMBER BECAUSE OF WHAT'S-HIS-FACE.
AND YOU CAN'T FINISH THE QUEST YOU TOOK ON.

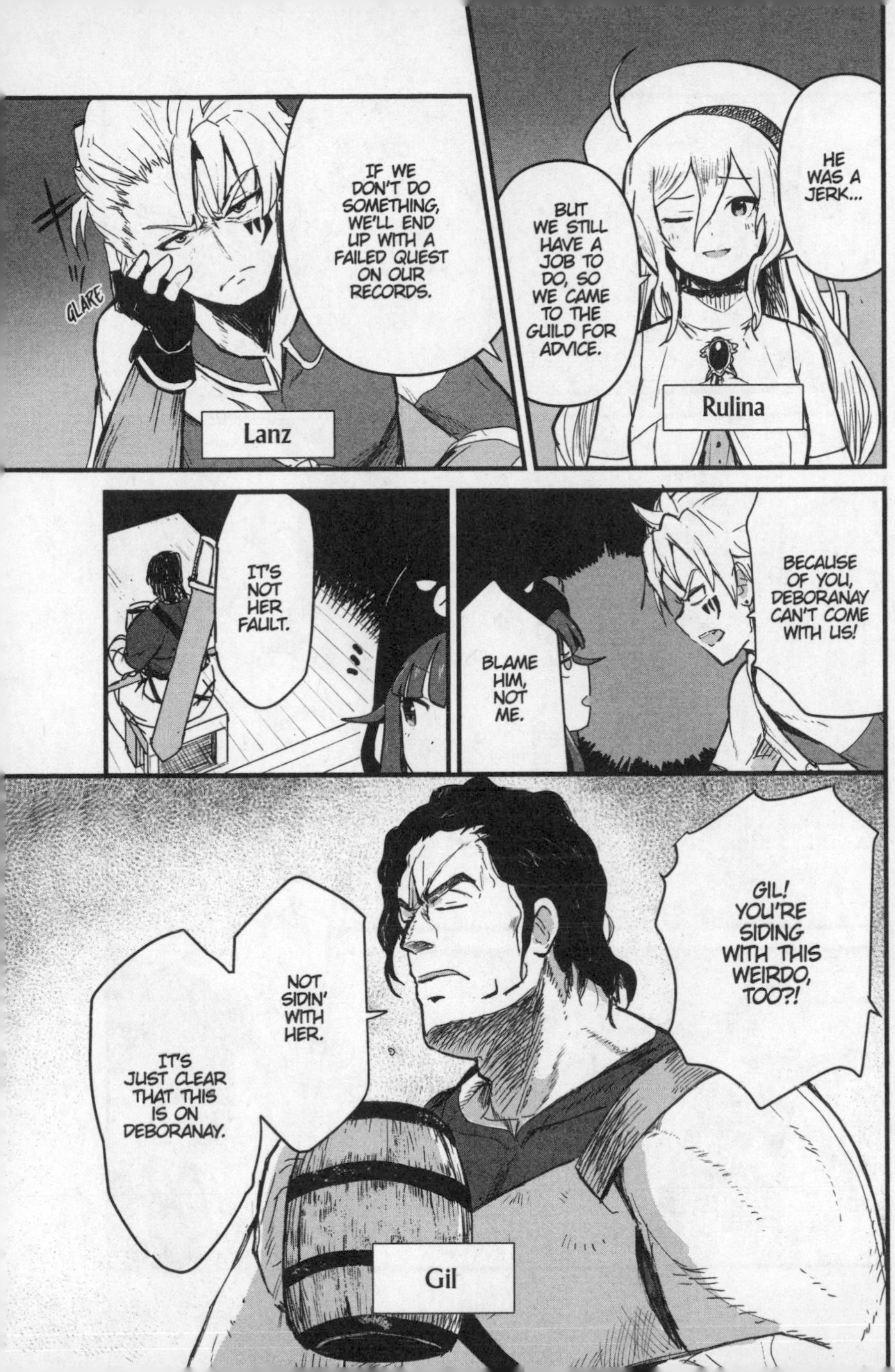
HE WAS A JERK...
BUT WE STILL HAVE A JOB TO DO, SO WE CAME TO THE GUILD FOR ADVICE.
Rulina
IF WE DON'T DO SOMETHING, WE'LL END UP WITH A FAILED QUEST ON OUR RECORDS.
GLARE
Lanz
BECAUSE OF YOU, DEBORANAY CAN'T COME WITH US!
BLAME HIM, NOT ME.
IT'S NOT HER FAULT.
GIL! YOU'RE SIDING WITH THIS WEIRDO, TOO?!
NOT SIDIN' WITH HER.
IT'S JUST CLEAR THAT THIS IS ON DEBORANAY.
Gil

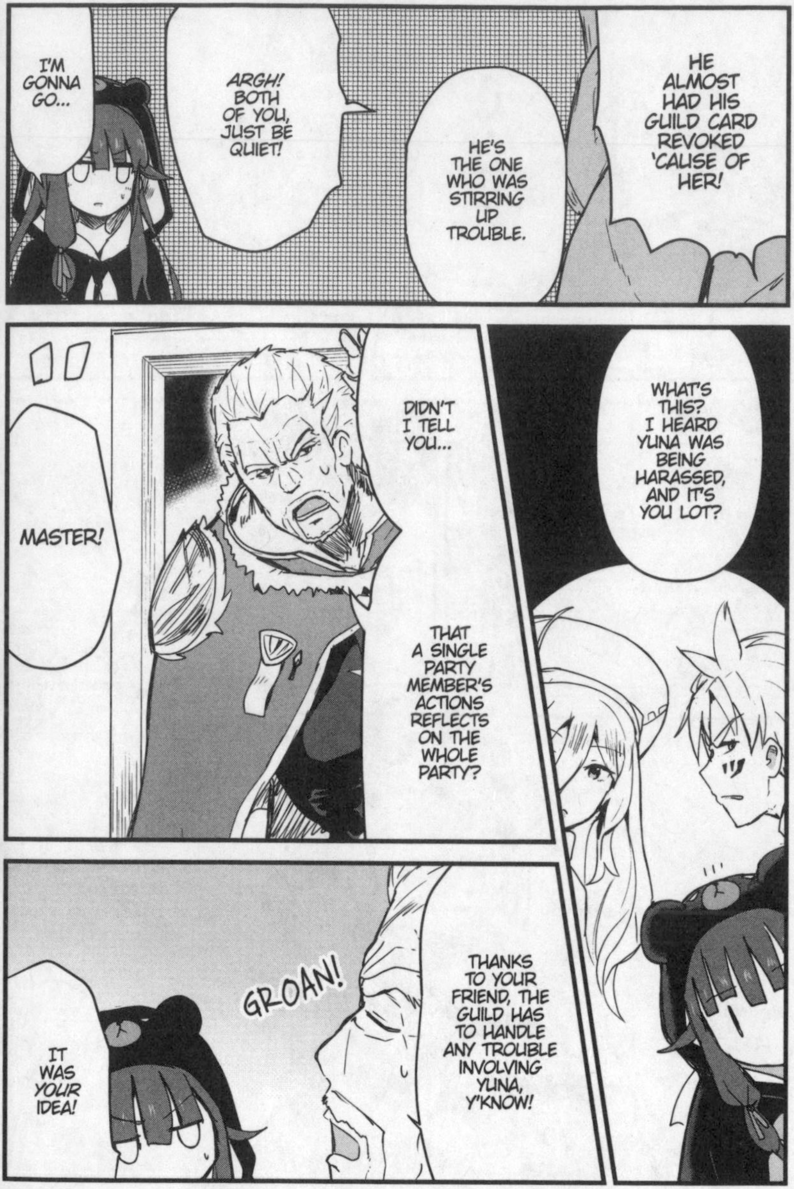
HE ALMOST HAD HIS GUILD CARD REVOKED 'CAUSE OF HER!
HE'S THE ONE WHO WAS STIRRING UP TROUBLE.
ARGH! BOTH OF YOU, JUST BE QUIET!
I'M GONNA GO...
WHAT'S THIS? I HEARD YUNA WAS BEING HARASSED, AND IT'S YOU LOT?
DIDN'T I TELL YOU...
THAT A SINGLE PARTY MEMBER'S ACTIONS REFLECTS ON THE WHOLE PARTY?
MASTER!
THANKS TO YOUR FRIEND, THE GUILD HAS TO HANDLE ANY TROUBLE INVOLVING YUNA, Y'KNOW!
GROAN!
IT WAS YOUR IDEA!

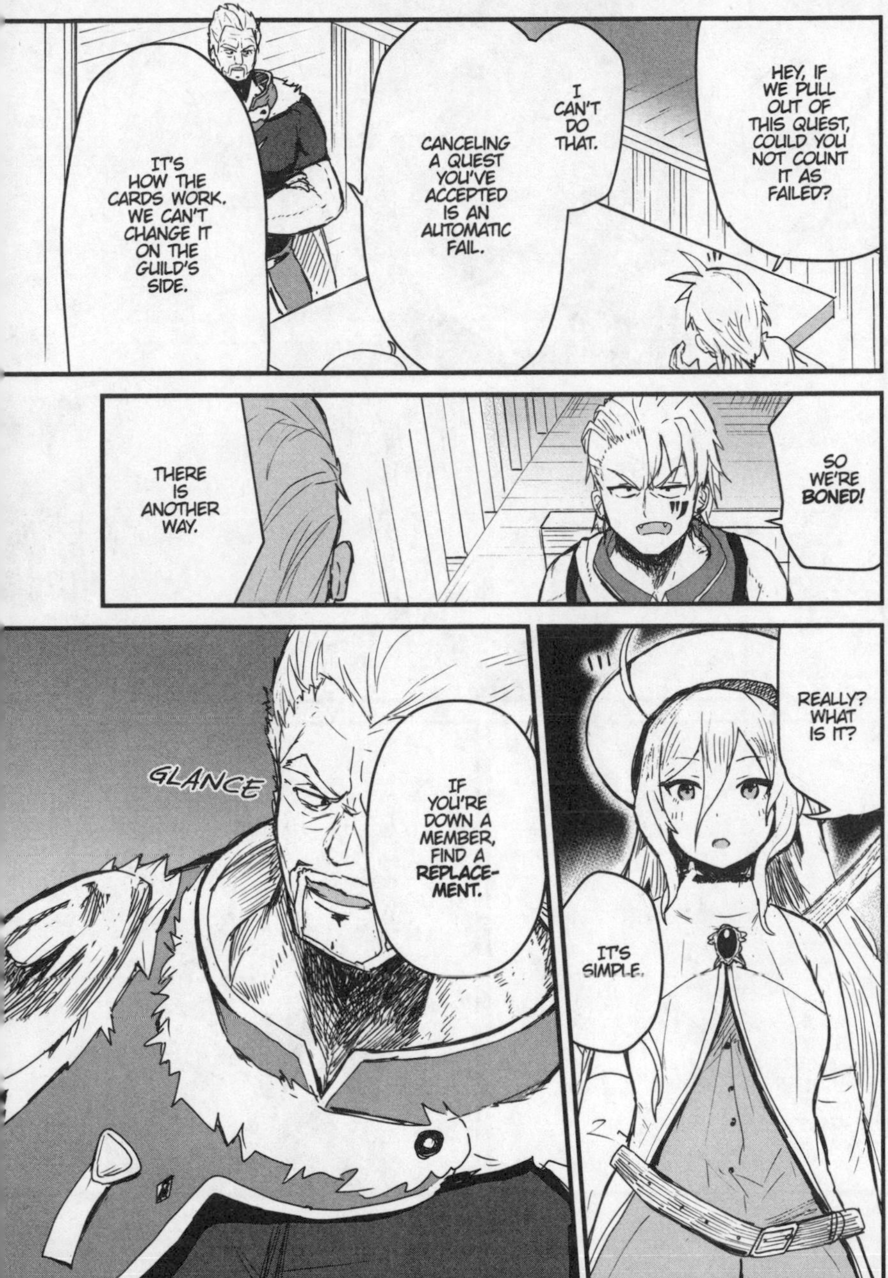
HEY, IF WE PULL OUT OF THIS QUEST, COULD YOU NOT COUNT IT AS FAILED?
I CAN'T DO THAT.
CANCELING A QUEST YOU'VE ACCEPTED IS AN AUTOMATIC FAIL.
IT'S HOW THE CARDS WORK. WE CAN'T CHANGE IT ON THE GUILD'S SIDE.
SO WE'RE BONED!
THERE IS ANOTHER WAY.
REALLY? WHAT IS IT?
IT'S SIMPLE.
GLANCE
IF YOU'RE DOWN A MEMBER, FIND A REPLACEMENT.

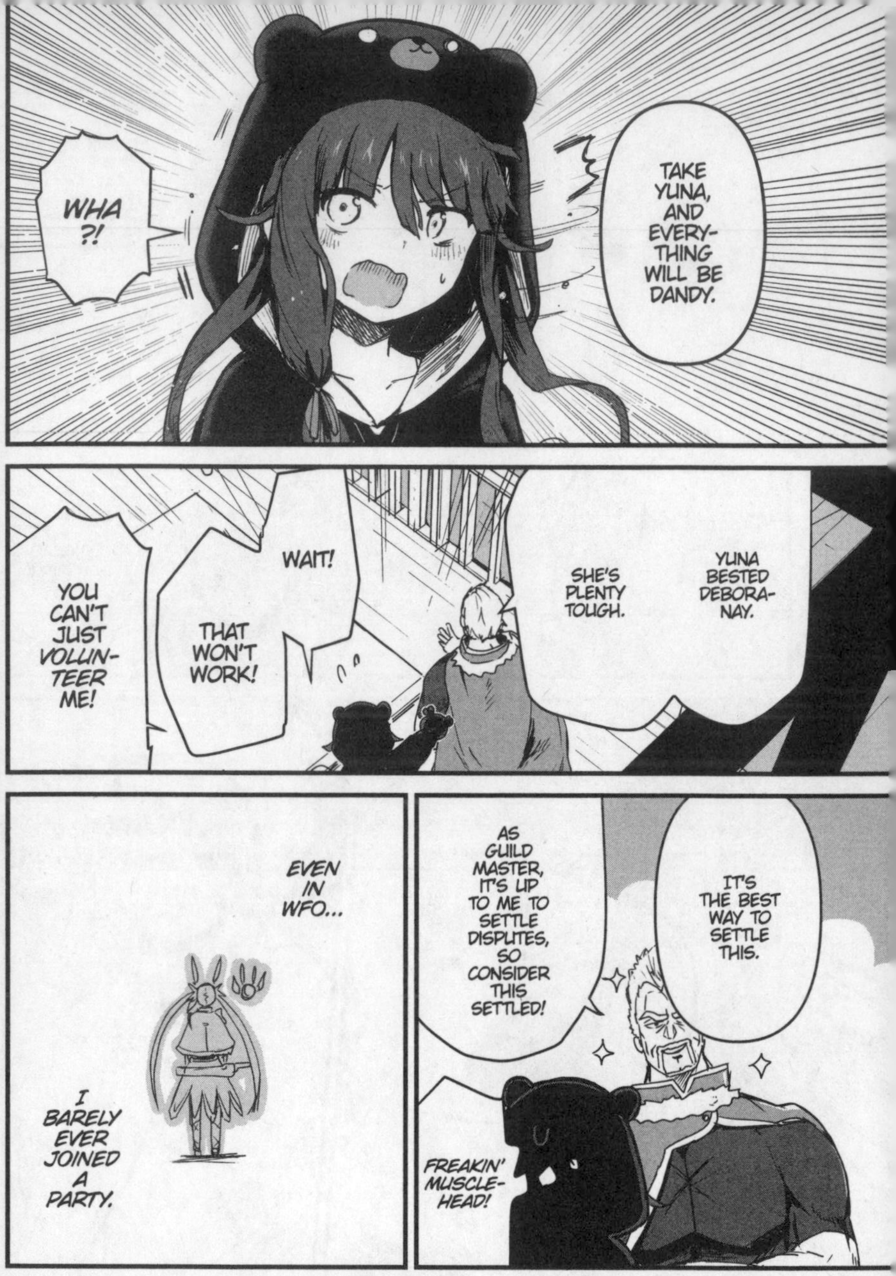
TAKE YUNA, AND EVERYTHING WILL BE DANDY.
WHA?!
YUNA BESTED DEBORANAY.
SHE'S PLENTY TOUGH.
WAIT!
THAT WON'T WORK!
YOU CAN'T JUST VOLUNTEER ME!
IT'S THE BEST WAY TO SETTLE THIS.
AS GUILD MASTER, IT'S UP TO ME TO SETTLE DISPUTES, SO CONSIDER THIS SETTLED!
FREAKIN' MUSCLE-HEAD!
EVEN IN WFO...
I BARELY EVER JOINED A PARTY.

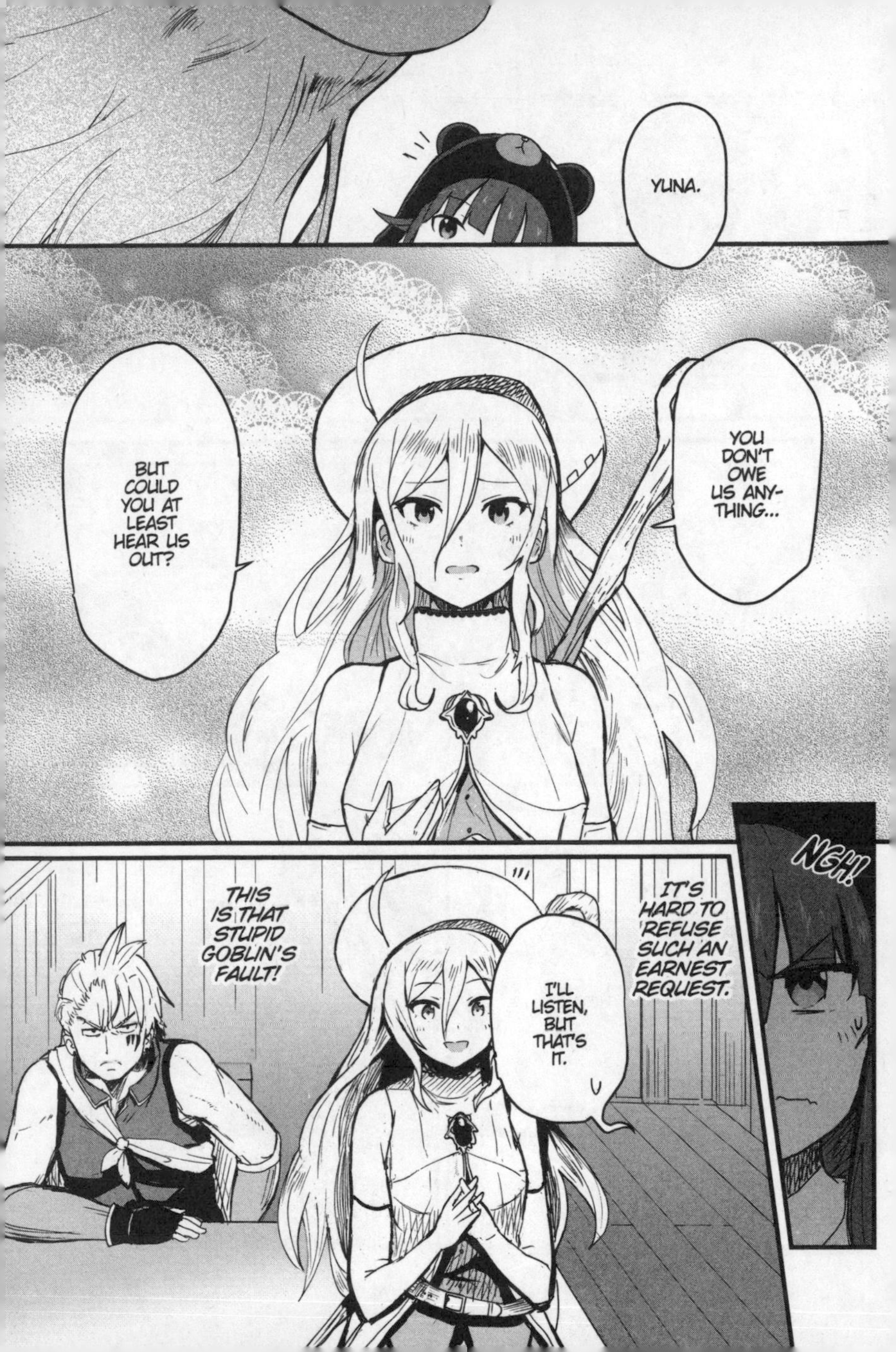
YUNA.
YOU DON'T OWE US ANY-THING...
BUT COULD YOU AT LEAST HEAR US OUT?
NGH!
IT'S HARD TO REFUSE SUCH AN EARNEST REQUEST.
I'LL LISTEN, BUT THAT'S IT.
THIS IS THAT STUPID GOBLIN'S FAULT!

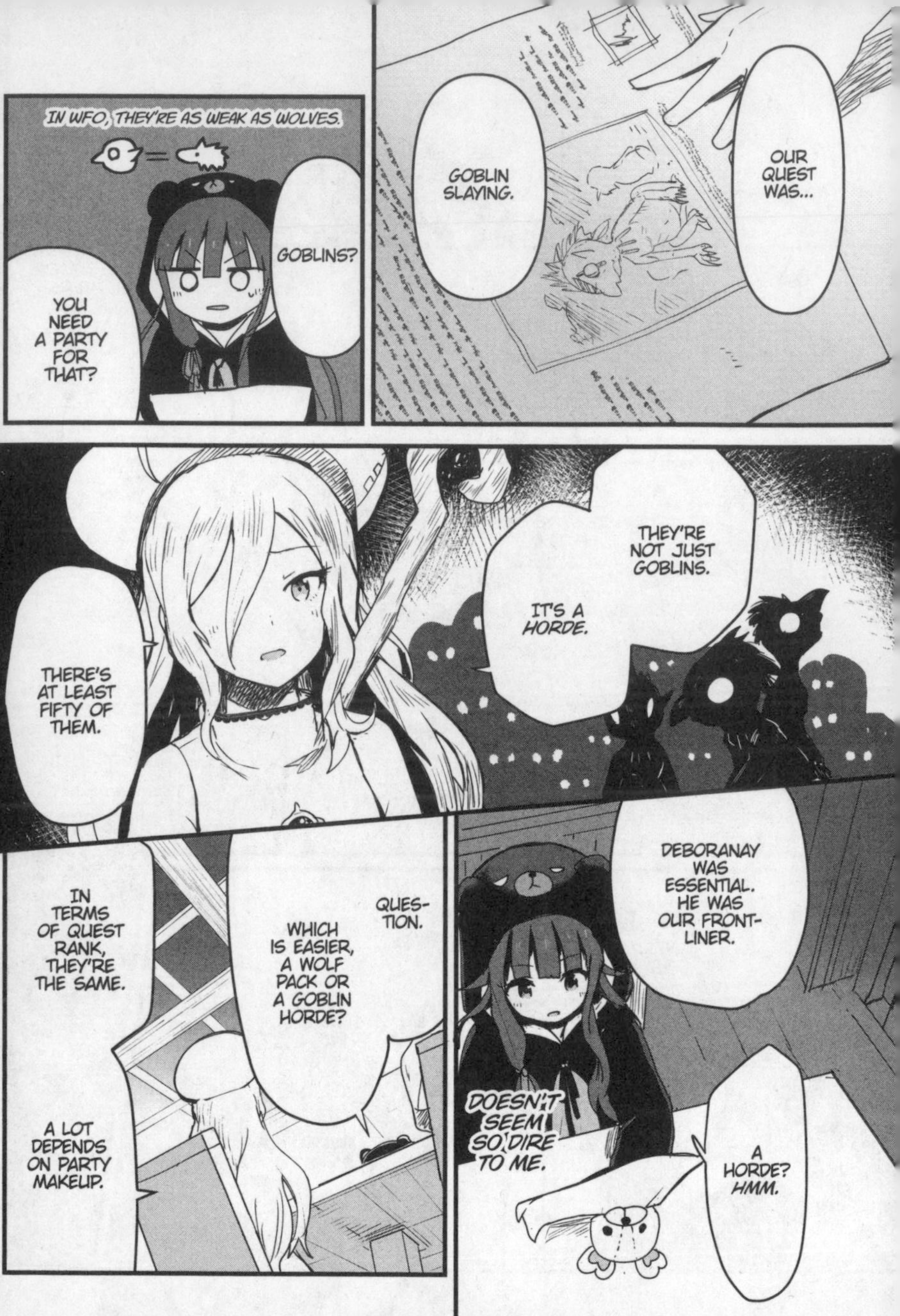
OUR QUEST WAS...
GOBLIN SLAYING.
IN WFO, THEY'RE AS WEAK AS WOLVES.
GOBLINS?
YOU NEED A PARTY FOR THAT?
THEY'RE NOT JUST GOBLINS.
IT'S A HORDE.
THERE'S AT LEAST FIFTY OF THEM.
DEBORANAY WAS ESSENTIAL. HE WAS OUR FRONT-LINER.
A HORDE? HMM.
DOESN'T SEEM SO DIRE TO ME.
QUES-TION.
WHICH IS EASIER, A WOLF PACK OR A GOBLIN HORDE?
IN TERMS OF QUEST RANK, THEY'RE THE SAME.
A LOT DEPENDS ON PARTY MAKEUP.

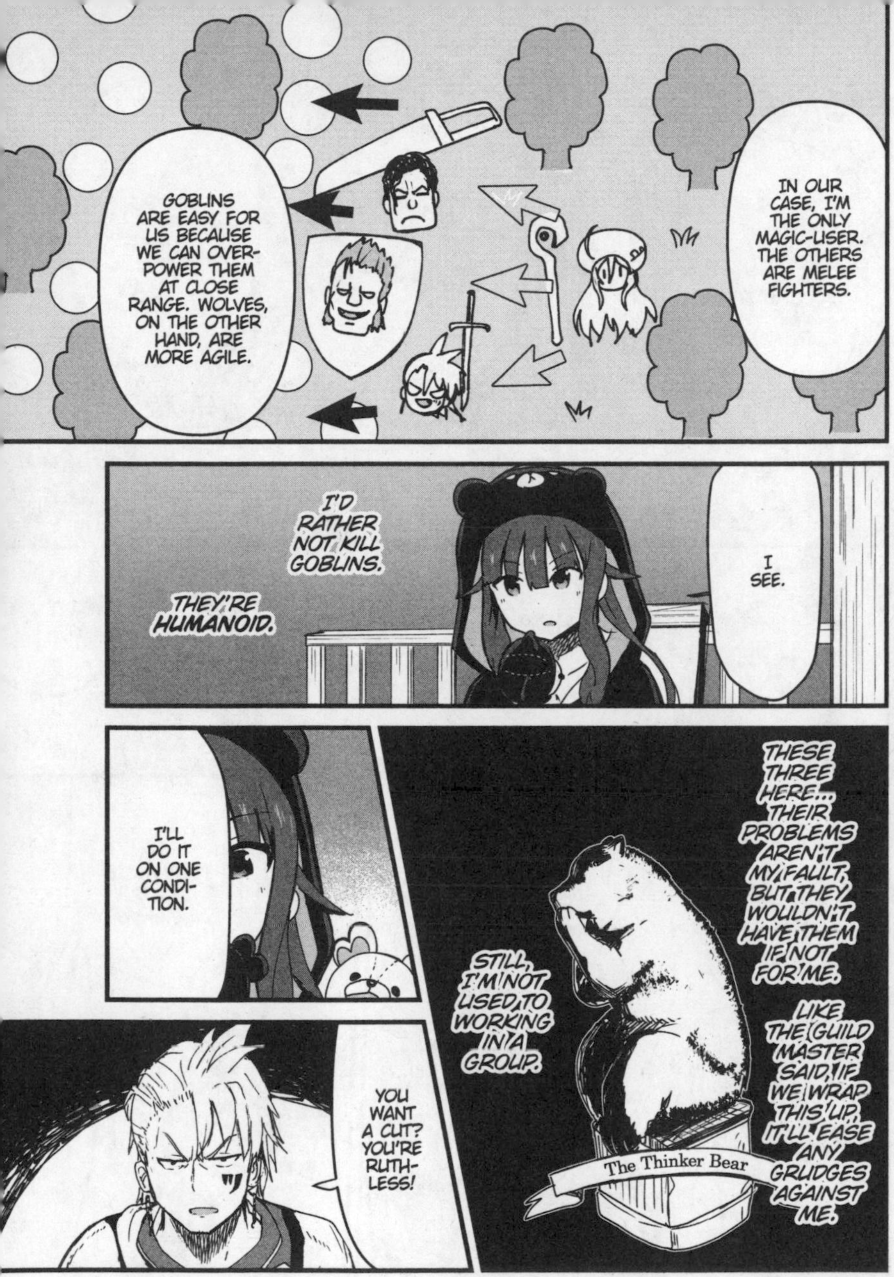
IN OUR CASE, I'M THE ONLY MAGIC-USER. THE OTHERS ARE MELEE FIGHTERS.
GOBLINS ARE EASY FOR US BECAUSE WE CAN OVER-POWER THEM AT CLOSE RANGE. WOLVES, ON THE OTHER HAND, ARE MORE AGILE.
I SEE.
I'D RATHER NOT KILL GOBLINS.
THEY'RE HUMANOID.
THESE THREE HERE... THEIR PROBLEMS AREN'T MY FAULT, BUT THEY WOULDN'T HAVE THEM IF NOT FOR ME.
LIKE THE GUILD MASTER SAID, IF WE WRAP THIS UP, IT'LL EASE ANY GRUDGES AGAINST ME.
STILL, I'M NOT USED TO WORKING IN A GROUP.
The Thinker Bear
I'LL DO IT ON ONE CONDITION.
YOU WANT A CUT? YOU'RE RUTHLESS!

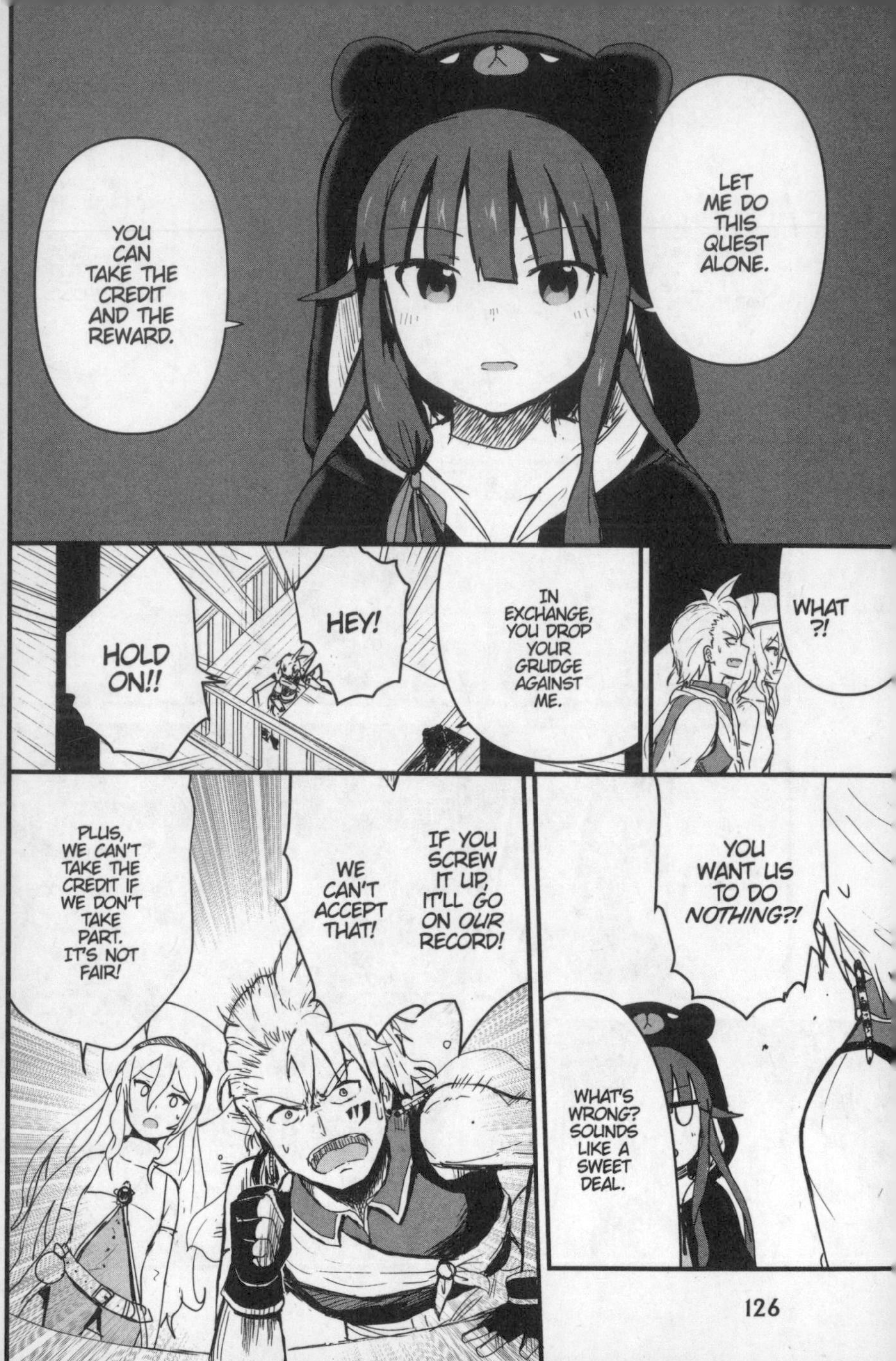

LET ME DO THIS QUEST ALONE.
YOU CAN TAKE THE CREDIT AND THE REWARD.
WHAT?!
IN EXCHANGE, YOU DROP YOUR GRUDGE AGAINST ME.
HEY!
HOLD ON!!
YOU WANT US TO DO *NOTHING?!*
WHAT'S WRONG? SOUNDS LIKE A SWEET DEAL.
IF YOU SCREW IT UP, IT'LL GO ON *OUR* RECORD!
WE CAN'T ACCEPT THAT!
PLUS, WE CAN'T TAKE THE CREDIT IF WE DON'T TAKE PART. IT'S NOT FAIR!

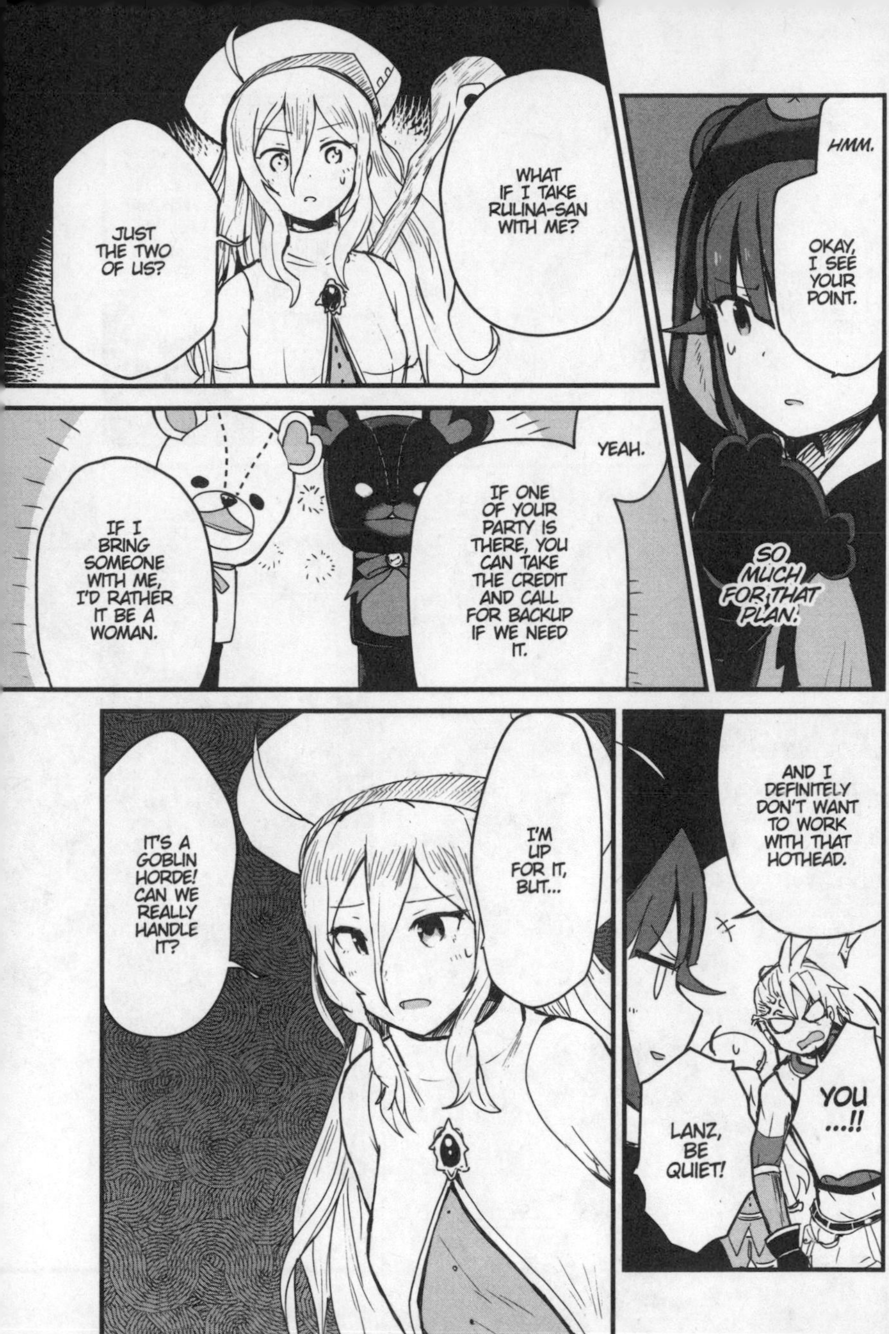
WHAT IF I TAKE RULINA-SAN WITH ME?
JUST THE TWO OF US?
YEAH.
IF ONE OF YOUR PARTY IS THERE, YOU CAN TAKE THE CREDIT AND CALL FOR BACKUP IF WE NEED IT.
IF I BRING SOMEONE WITH ME, I'D RATHER IT BE A WOMAN.
HMM.
OKAY, I SEE YOUR POINT.
SO MUCH FOR THAT PLAN.
AND I DEFINITELY DON'T WANT TO WORK WITH THAT HOTHEAD.
YOU ...!!
LANZ, BE QUIET!
I'M UP FOR IT, BUT...
IT'S A GOBLIN HORDE! CAN WE REALLY HANDLE IT?

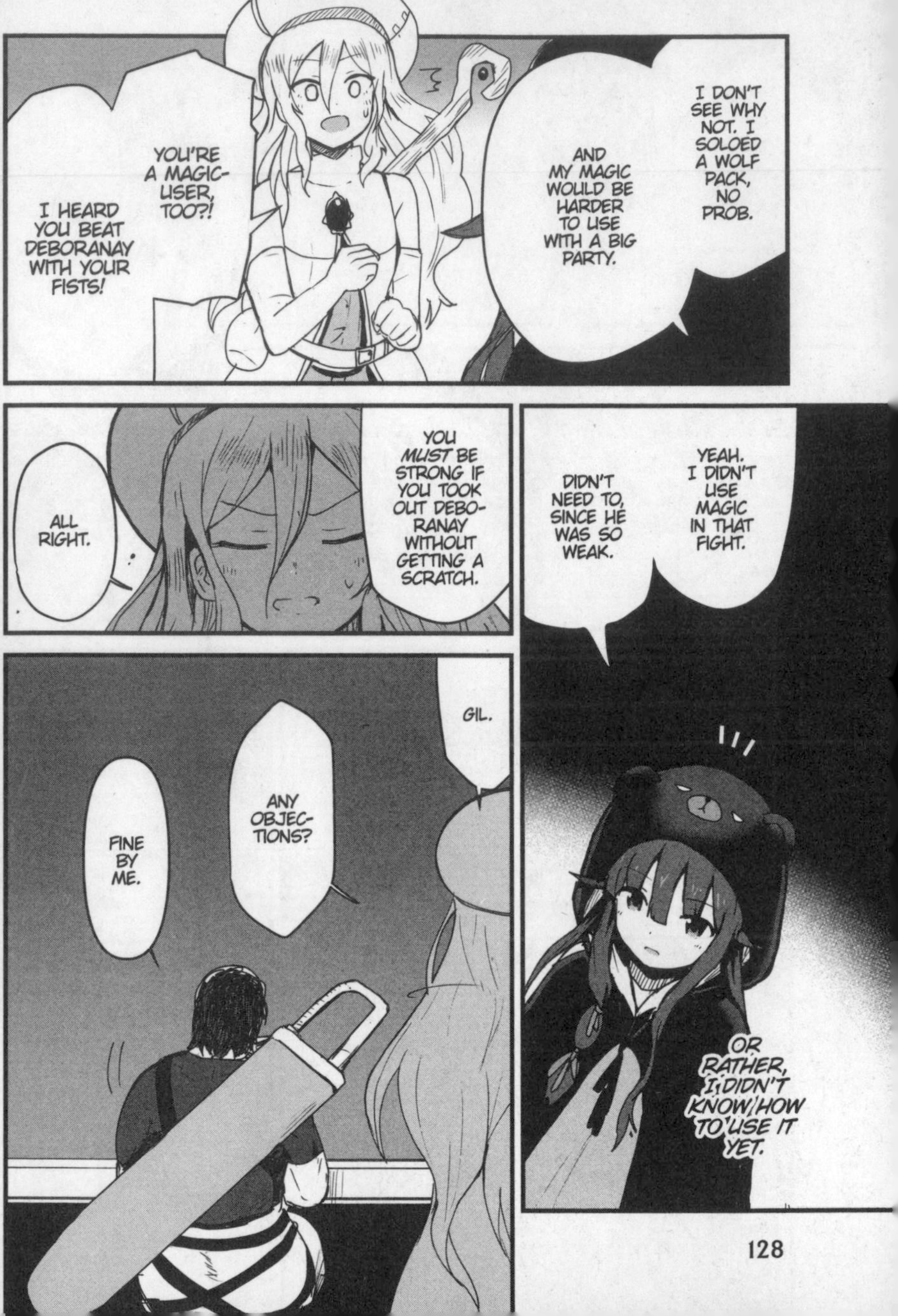
I DON'T SEE WHY NOT. I SOLOED A WOLF PACK, NO PROB.
AND MY MAGIC WOULD BE HARDER TO USE WITH A BIG PARTY.
YOU'RE A MAGIC-USER, TOO?!
I HEARD YOU BEAT DEBORANAY WITH YOUR FISTS!
YEAH. I DIDN'T USE MAGIC IN THAT FIGHT.
DIDN'T NEED TO, SINCE HE WAS SO WEAK.
OR RATHER, I DIDN'T KNOW HOW TO USE IT YET.
YOU *MUST* BE STRONG IF YOU TOOK OUT DEBORANAY WITHOUT GETTING A SCRATCH.
ALL RIGHT.
GIL.
ANY OBJECTIONS?
FINE BY ME.

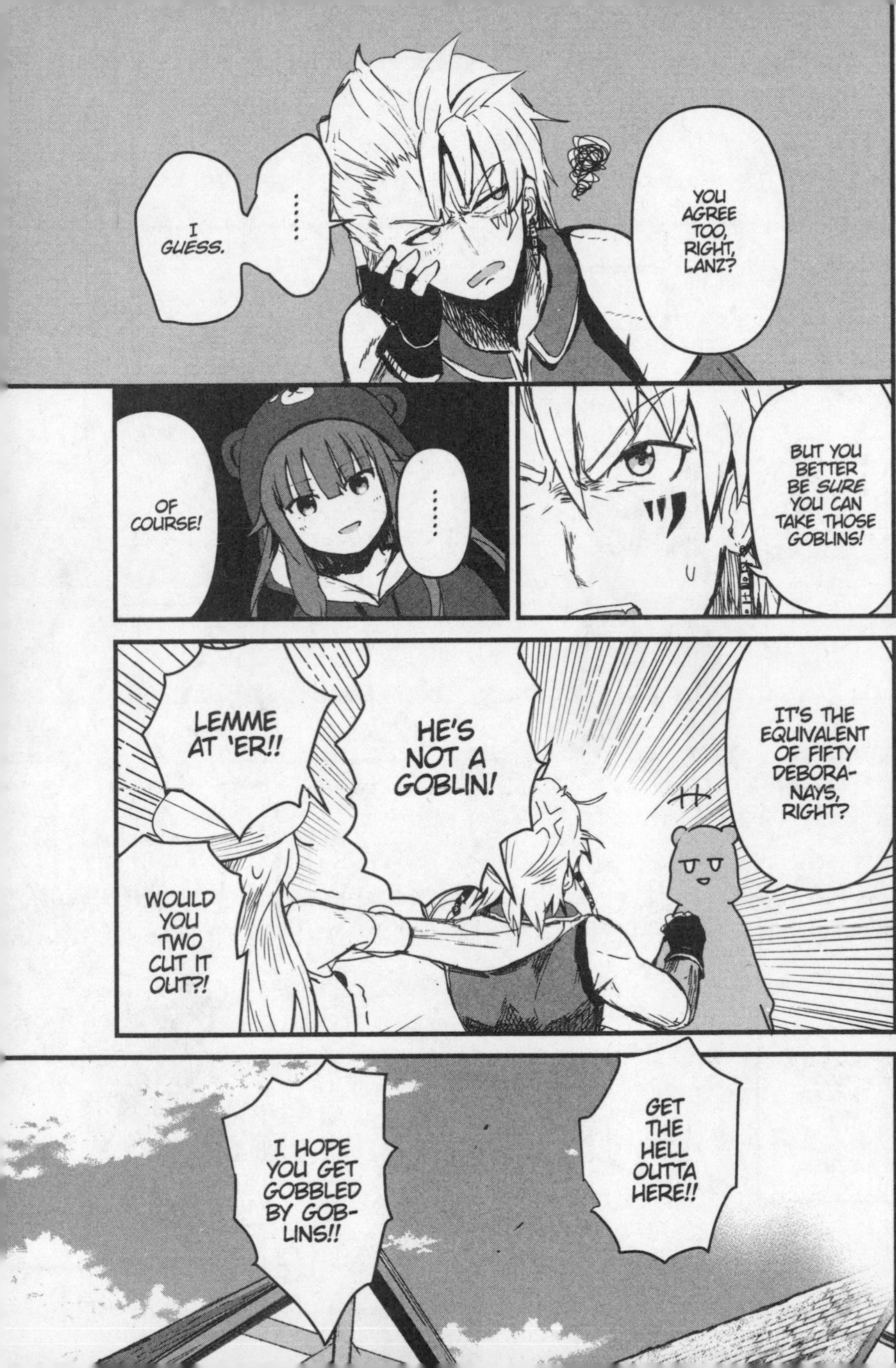
YOU AGREE TOO, RIGHT, LANZ?
......
I GUESS.
BUT YOU BETTER BE *SURE* YOU CAN TAKE THOSE GOBLINS!
......
OF COURSE!
IT'S THE EQUIVALENT OF FIFTY DEBORA-NAYS, RIGHT?
HE'S NOT A GOBLIN!
LEMME AT 'ER!!
WOULD YOU TWO CUT IT OUT?!
GET THE HELL OUTTA HERE!!
I HOPE YOU GET GOBBLED BY GOB-LINS!!

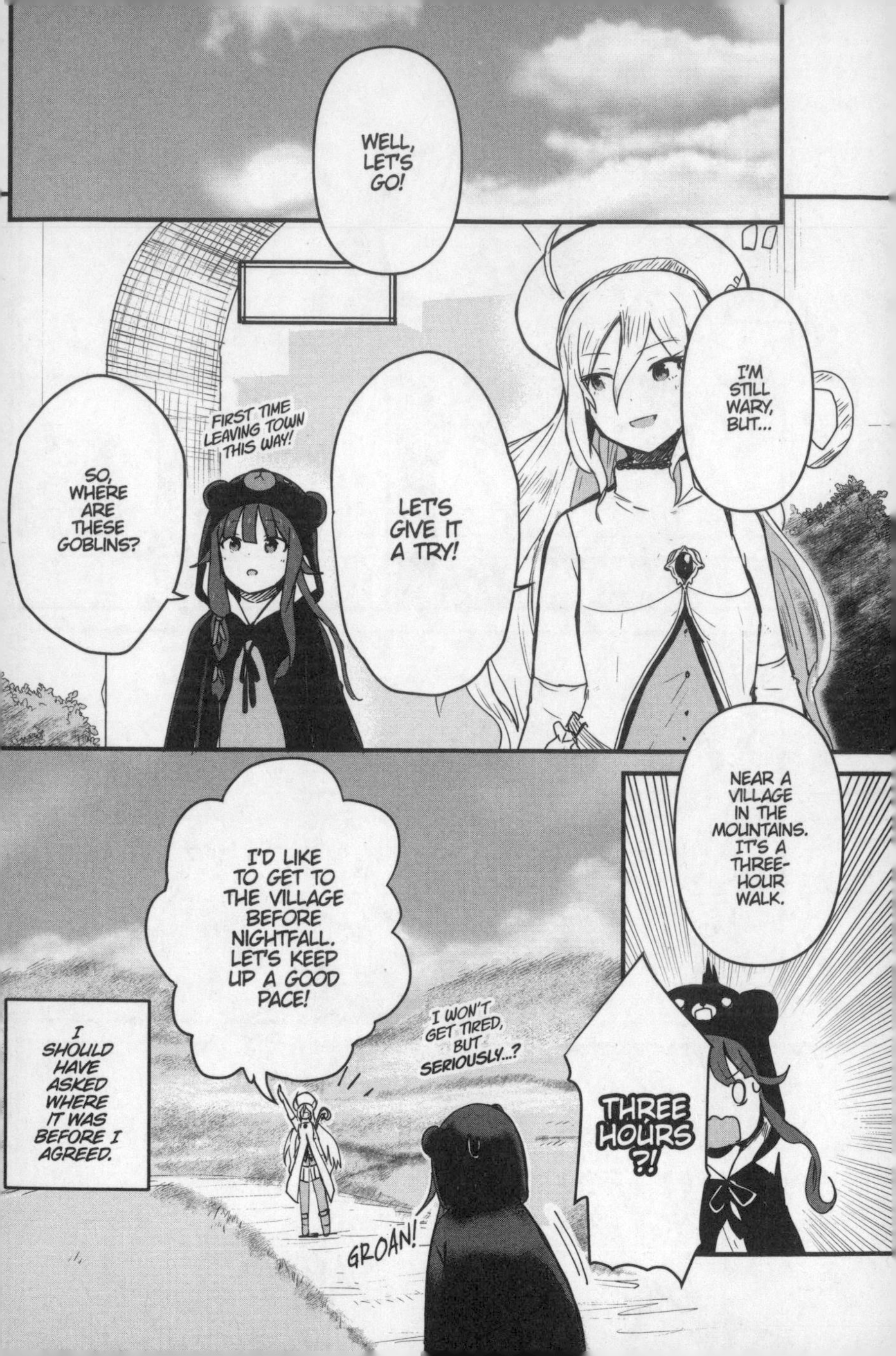
WELL, LET'S GO!
I'M STILL WARY, BUT...
LET'S GIVE IT A TRY!
FIRST TIME LEAVING TOWN THIS WAY!
SO, WHERE ARE THESE GOBLINS?
NEAR A VILLAGE IN THE MOUNTAINS. IT'S A THREE-HOUR WALK.
THREE HOURS?!
I'D LIKE TO GET TO THE VILLAGE BEFORE NIGHTFALL. LET'S KEEP UP A GOOD PACE!
I WON'T GET TIRED, BUT SERIOUSLY...?
GROAN!
I SHOULD HAVE ASKED WHERE IT WAS BEFORE I AGREED.

Chapter 9

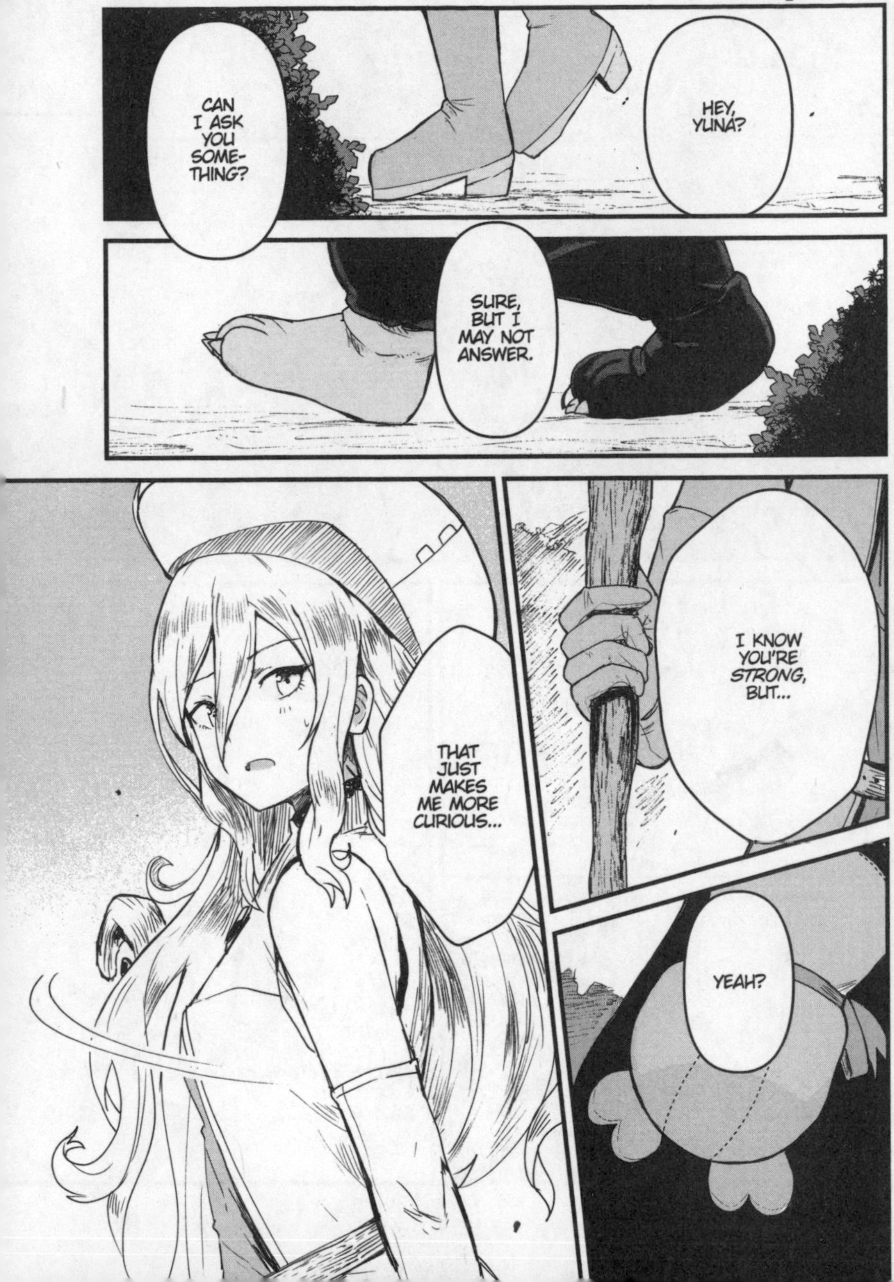
HEY, YUNA?
CAN I ASK YOU SOMETHING?
SURE, BUT I MAY NOT ANSWER.
I KNOW YOU'RE STRONG, BUT...
YEAH?
THAT JUST MAKES ME MORE CURIOUS...

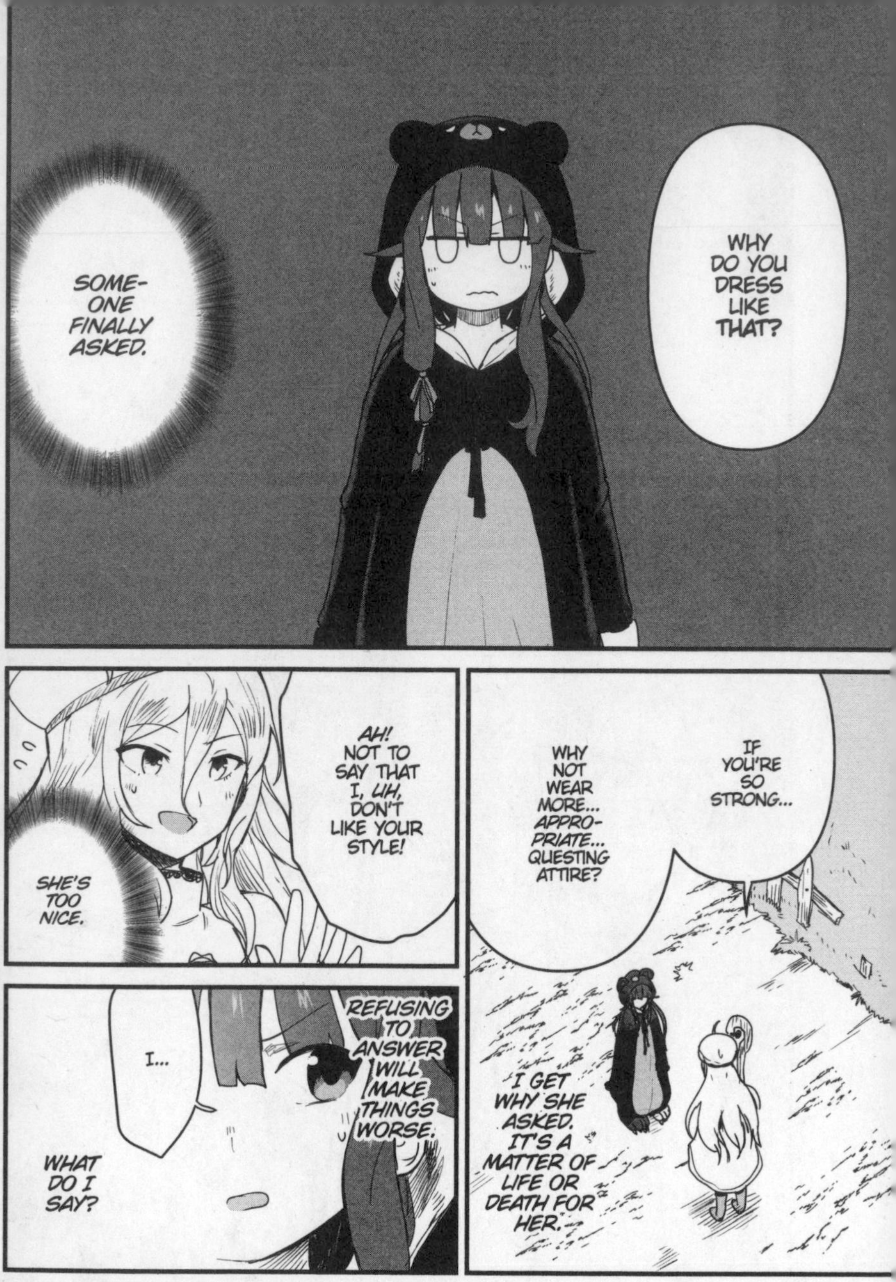
WHY DO YOU DRESS LIKE THAT?
SOME-ONE FINALLY ASKED.
IF YOU'RE SO STRONG...
WHY NOT WEAR MORE... APPROPRIATE... QUESTING ATTIRE?
I GET WHY SHE ASKED. IT'S A MATTER OF LIFE OR DEATH FOR HER.
AH! NOT TO SAY THAT I, UH, DON'T LIKE YOUR STYLE!
SHE'S TOO NICE.
REFUSING TO ANSWER WILL MAKE THINGS WORSE.
I...
WHAT DO I SAY?

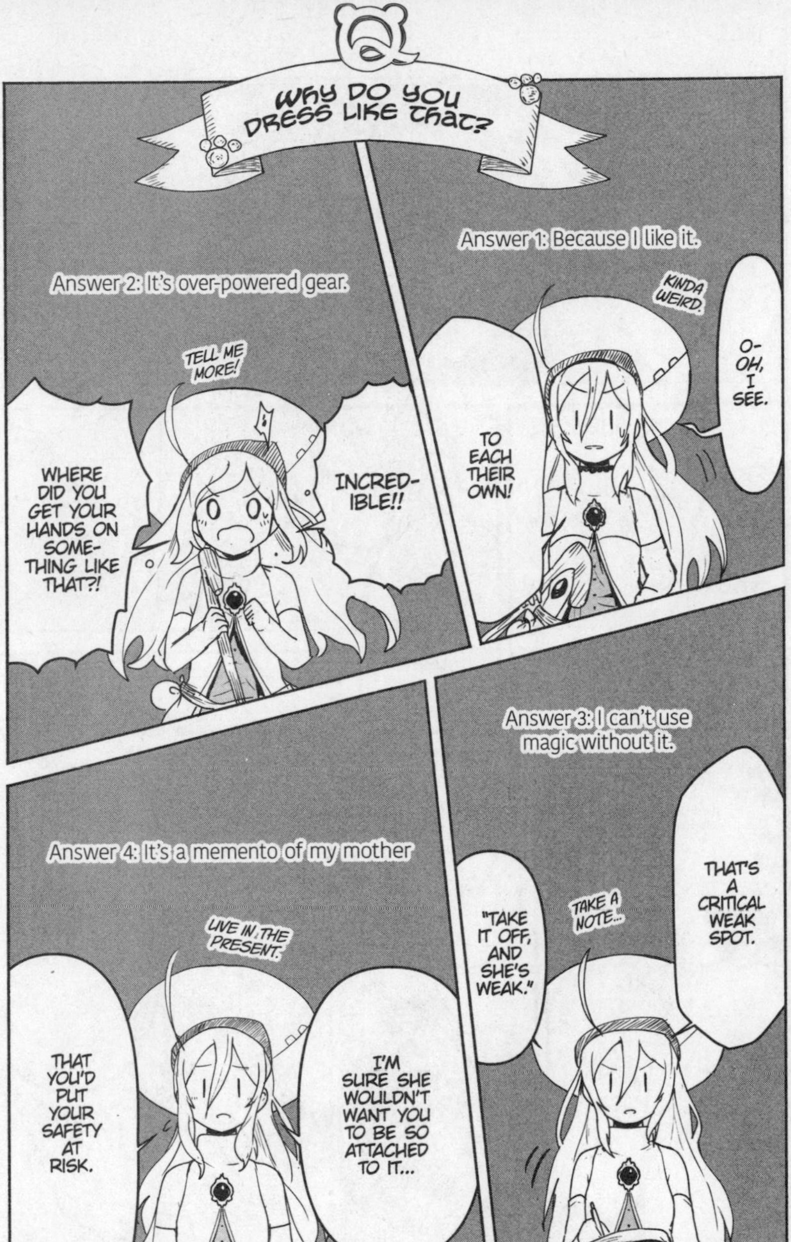
WHY DO YOU DRESS LIKE THAT?
Answer 1: Because I like it.
O-OH, I SEE.
KINDA WEIRD.
TO EACH THEIR OWN!
Answer 2: It's over-powered gear.
INCREDIBLE!!
TELL ME MORE!
WHERE DID YOU GET YOUR HANDS ON SOMETHING LIKE THAT?!
Answer 3: I can't use magic without it.
THAT'S A CRITICAL WEAK SPOT.
TAKE A NOTE...
"TAKE IT OFF, AND SHE'S WEAK."
Answer 4: It's a memento of my mother
I'M SURE SHE WOULDN'T WANT YOU TO BE SO ATTACHED TO IT...
LIVE IN THE PRESENT.
THAT YOU'D PUT YOUR SAFETY AT RISK.

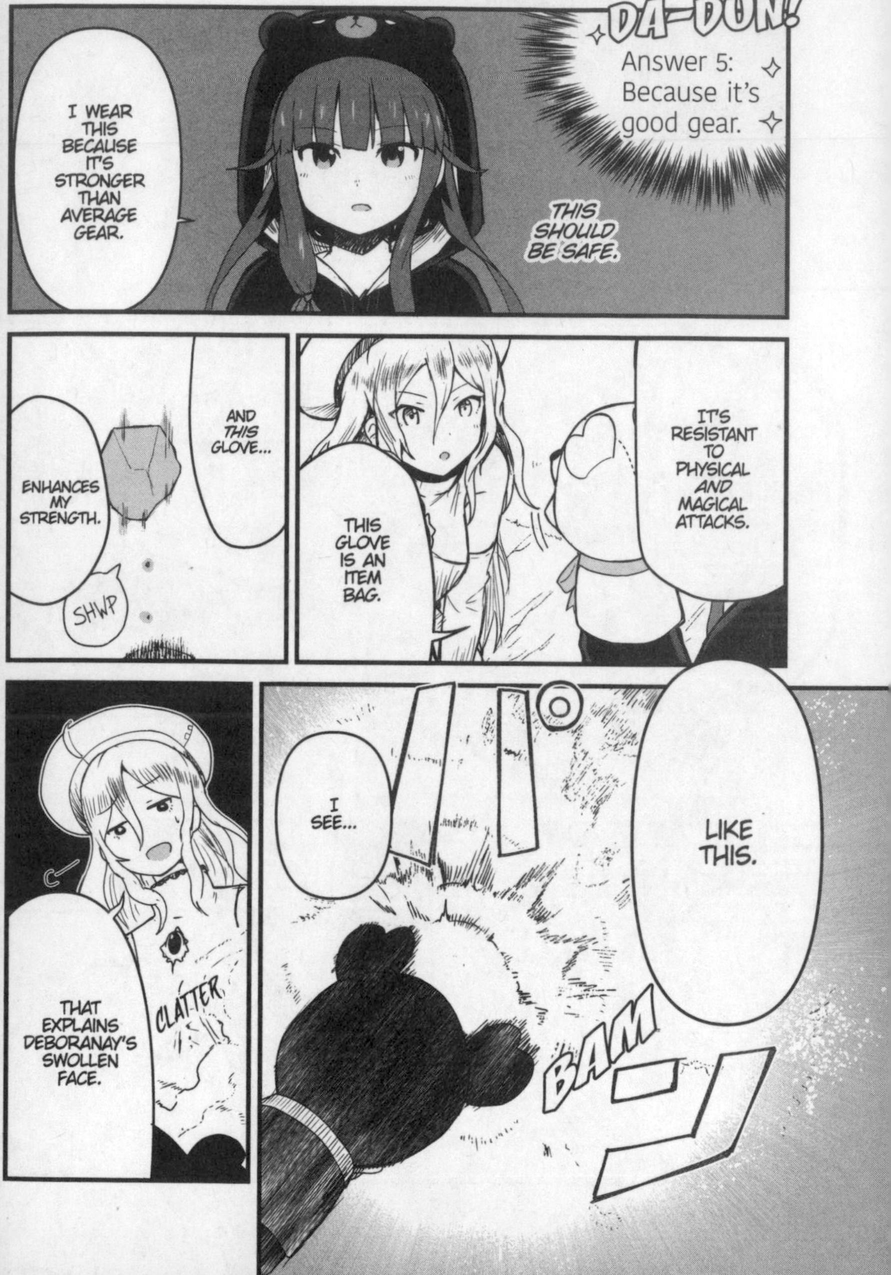
DA-DUN!
Answer 5: Because it's good gear.
THIS SHOULD BE SAFE.
I WEAR THIS BECAUSE IT'S STRONGER THAN AVERAGE GEAR.
IT'S RESISTANT TO PHYSICAL AND MAGICAL ATTACKS.
THIS GLOVE IS AN ITEM BAG.
AND THIS GLOVE...
ENHANCES MY STRENGTH.
SHWP
LIKE THIS.
I SEE...
BAM
CLATTER
THAT EXPLAINS DEBORANAY'S SWOLLEN FACE.

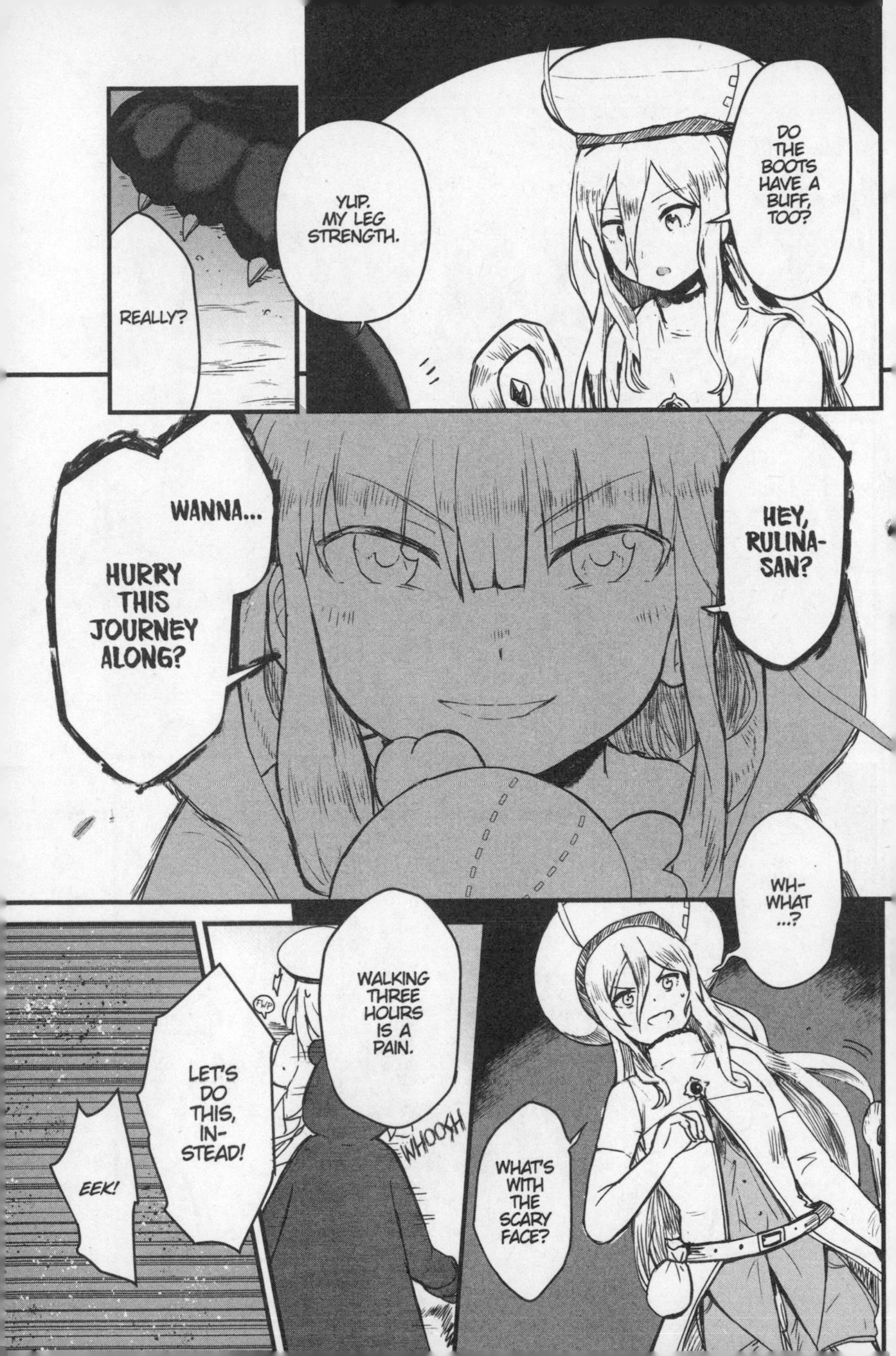
DO THE BOOTS HAVE A BUFF, TOO?
YUP. MY LEG STRENGTH.
REALLY?
HEY, RULINA-SAN?
WANNA...
HURRY THIS JOURNEY ALONG?
WH-WHAT ...?
WHAT'S WITH THE SCARY FACE?
WALKING THREE HOURS IS A PAIN.
FWP
LET'S DO THIS, IN-STEAD!
WHOOSH
EEK!

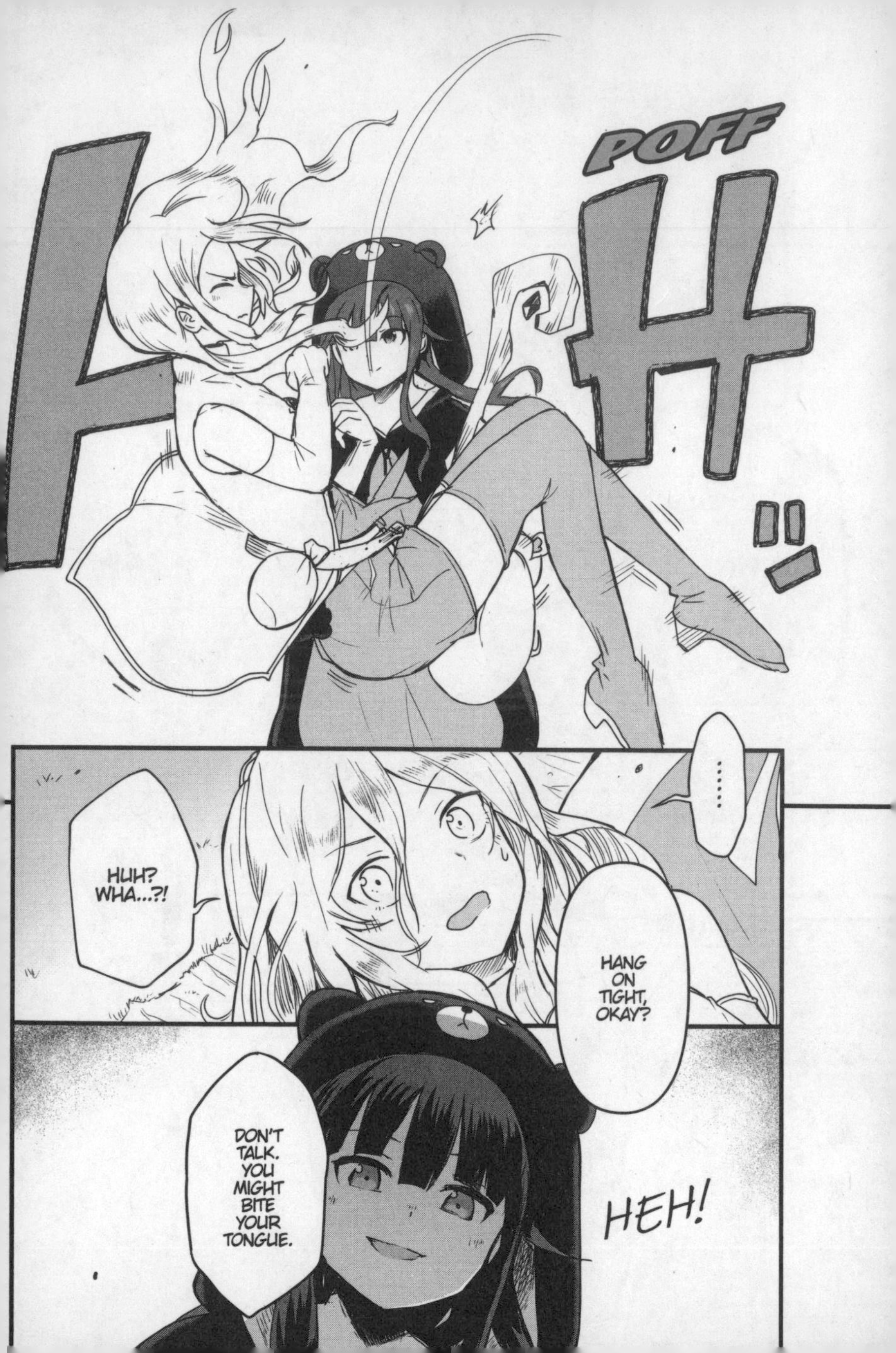
POFF
......
HUH? WHA...?!
HANG ON TIGHT, OKAY?
DON'T TALK. YOU MIGHT BITE YOUR TONGUE.
HEH!

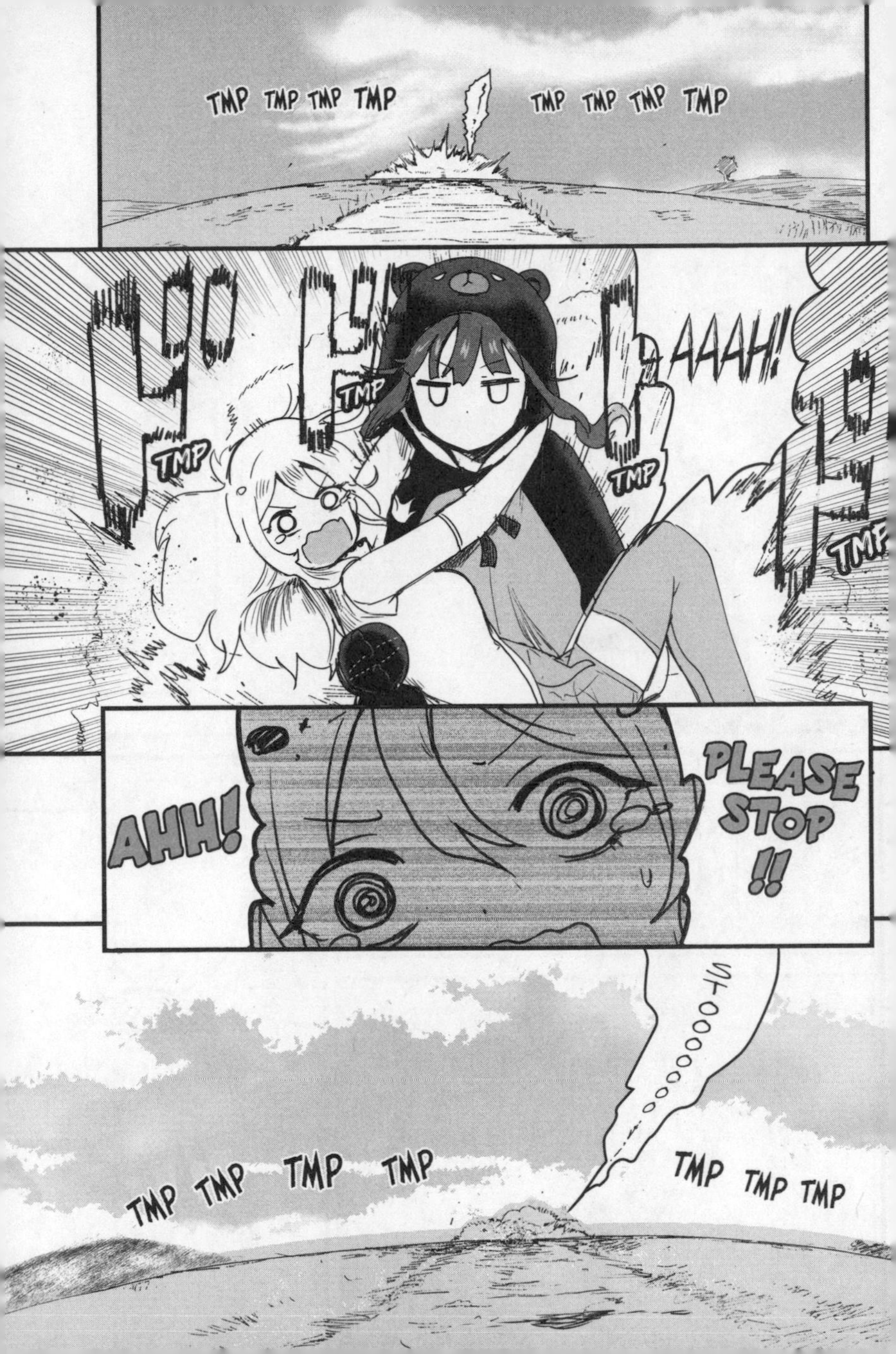
TMP TMP TMP TMP
TMP TMP TMP TMP
AAAH!
TMP
TMP
TMP
TMP
PLEASE STOP !!
AHH!
STOOOOOOO
TMP TMP TMP
TMP TMP TMP TMP

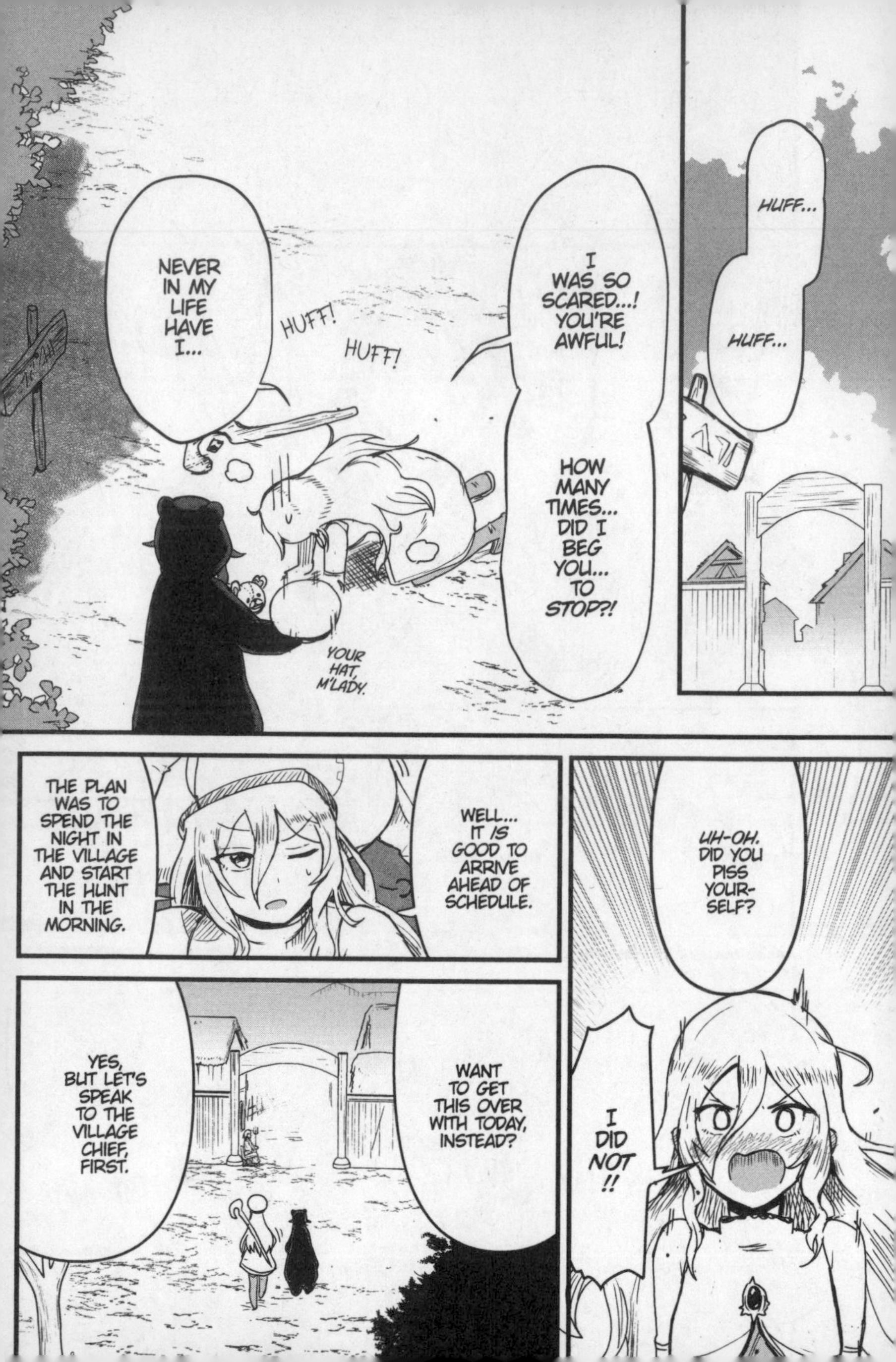
HUFF...
HUFF...
I WAS SO SCARED...! YOU'RE AWFUL!
HOW MANY TIMES... DID I BEG YOU... TO STOP?!
NEVER IN MY LIFE HAVE I...
HUFF!
HUFF!
YOUR HAT, M'LADY.
UH-OH. DID YOU PISS YOURSELF?
I DID *NOT*!!
WELL... IT *IS* GOOD TO ARRIVE AHEAD OF SCHEDULE.
THE PLAN WAS TO SPEND THE NIGHT IN THE VILLAGE AND START THE HUNT IN THE MORNING.
WANT TO GET THIS OVER WITH TODAY, INSTEAD?
YES, BUT LET'S SPEAK TO THE VILLAGE CHIEF, FIRST.

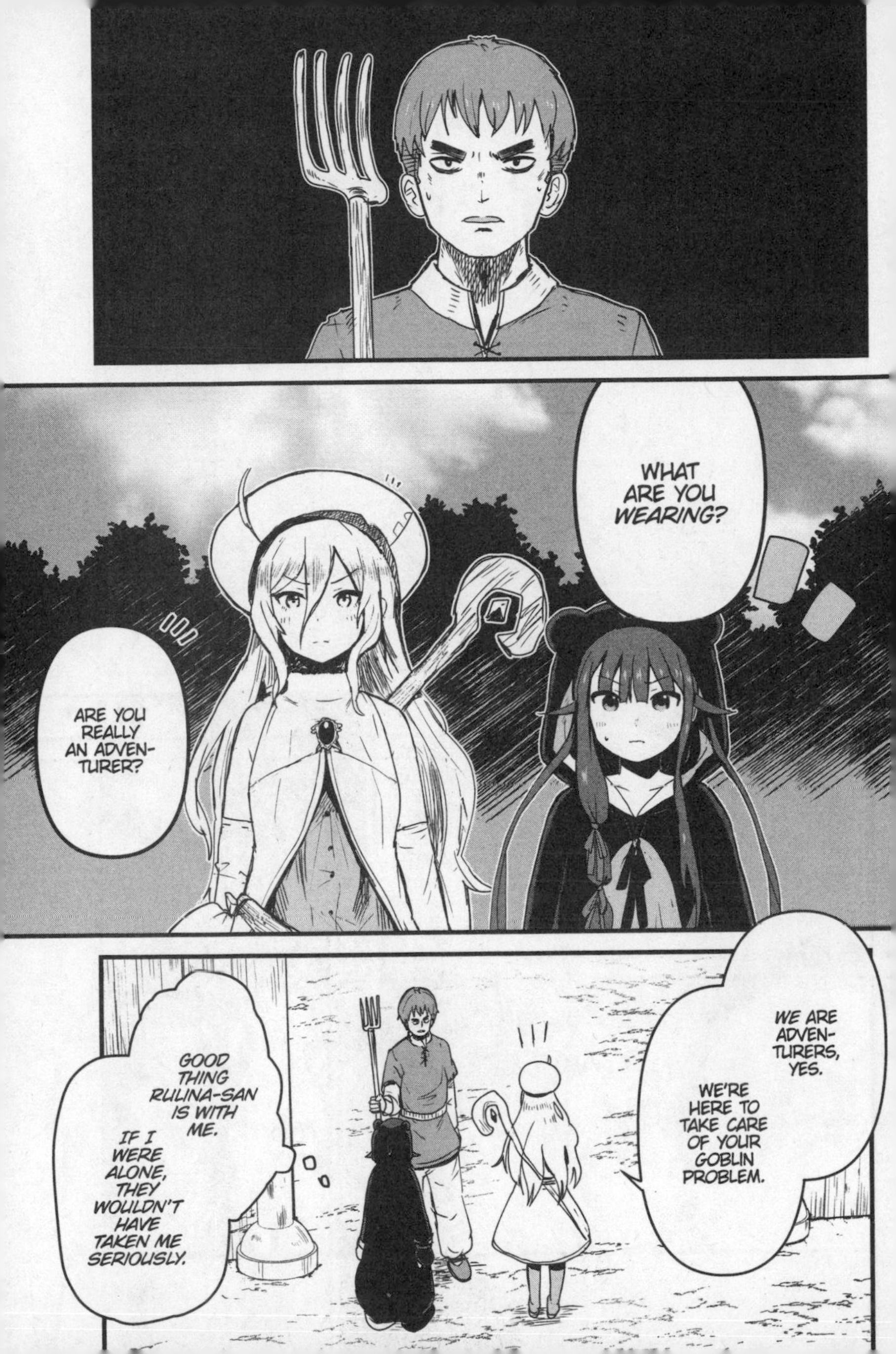
WHAT ARE YOU WEARING?
ARE YOU REALLY AN ADVEN-TURER?
WE ARE ADVEN-TURERS, YES.
WE'RE HERE TO TAKE CARE OF YOUR GOBLIN PROBLEM.
GOOD THING RULINA-SAN IS WITH ME.
IF I WERE ALONE, THEY WOULDN'T HAVE TAKEN ME SERIOUSLY.

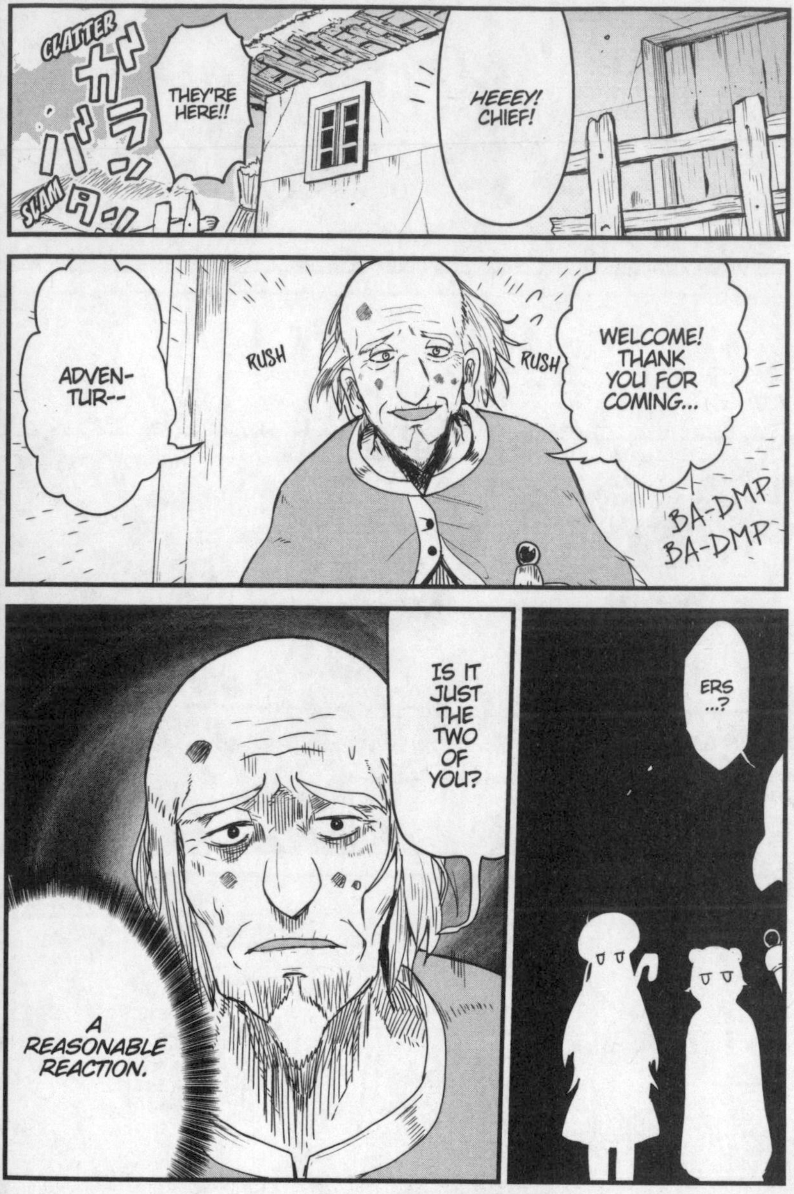
HEEEY! CHIEF!
THEY'RE HERE!!
CLATTER
SLAM
WELCOME! THANK YOU FOR COMING...
RUSH
RUSH
BA-DMP BA-DMP
ADVEN-TUR--
ERS ...?
IS IT JUST THE TWO OF YOU?
A REASONABLE REACTION.

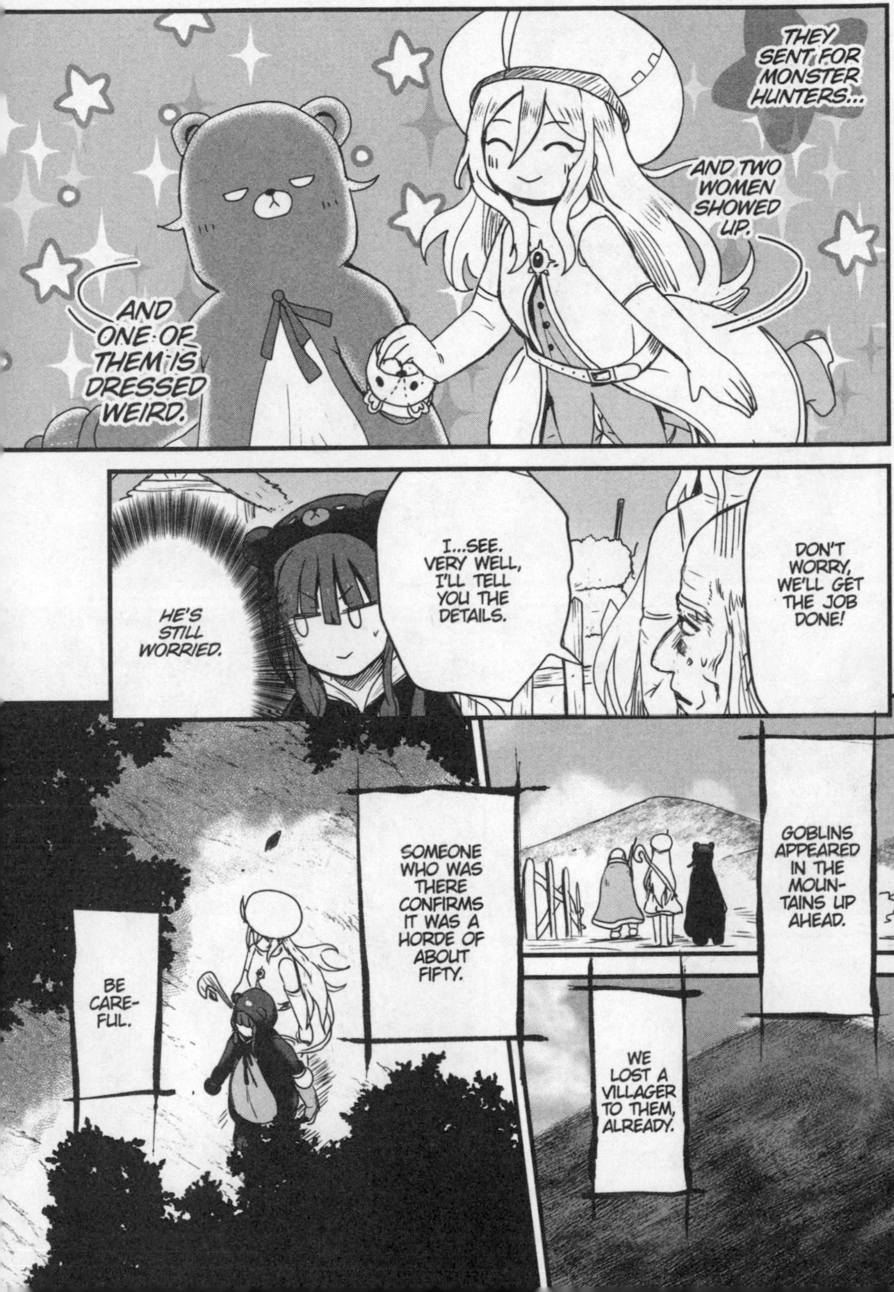
THEY SENT FOR MONSTER HUNTERS...
AND TWO WOMEN SHOWED UP.
AND ONE OF THEM IS DRESSED WEIRD.
DON'T WORRY, WE'LL GET THE JOB DONE!
I...SEE. VERY WELL, I'LL TELL YOU THE DETAILS.
HE'S STILL WORRIED.
GOBLINS APPEARED IN THE MOUN-TAINS UP AHEAD.
WE LOST A VILLAGER TO THEM, ALREADY.
SOMEONE WHO WAS THERE CONFIRMS IT WAS A HORDE OF ABOUT FIFTY.
BE CARE-FUL.

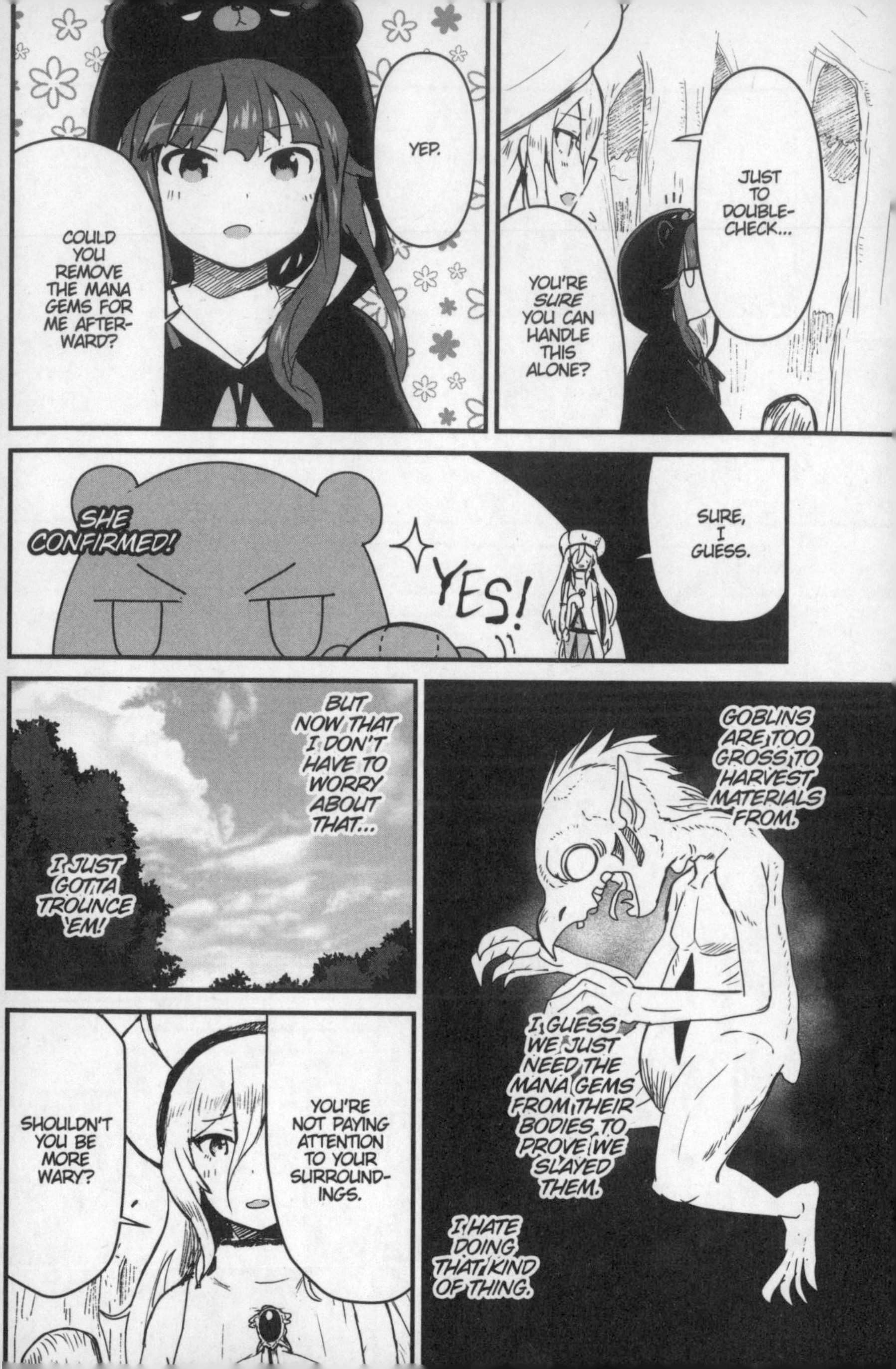
JUST TO DOUBLE-CHECK...
YOU'RE SURE YOU CAN HANDLE THIS ALONE?
YEP.
COULD YOU REMOVE THE MANA GEMS FOR ME AFTERWARD?
SURE, I GUESS.
YES!
SHE CONFIRMED!
GOBLINS ARE TOO GROSS TO HARVEST MATERIALS FROM.
I GUESS WE JUST NEED THE MANA GEMS FROM THEIR BODIES TO PROVE WE SLAYED THEM.
I HATE DOING THAT KIND OF THING.
BUT NOW THAT I DON'T HAVE TO WORRY ABOUT THAT...
I JUST GOTTA TROUNCE EM!
YOU'RE NOT PAYING ATTENTION TO YOUR SURROUNDINGS.
SHOULDN'T YOU BE MORE WARY?

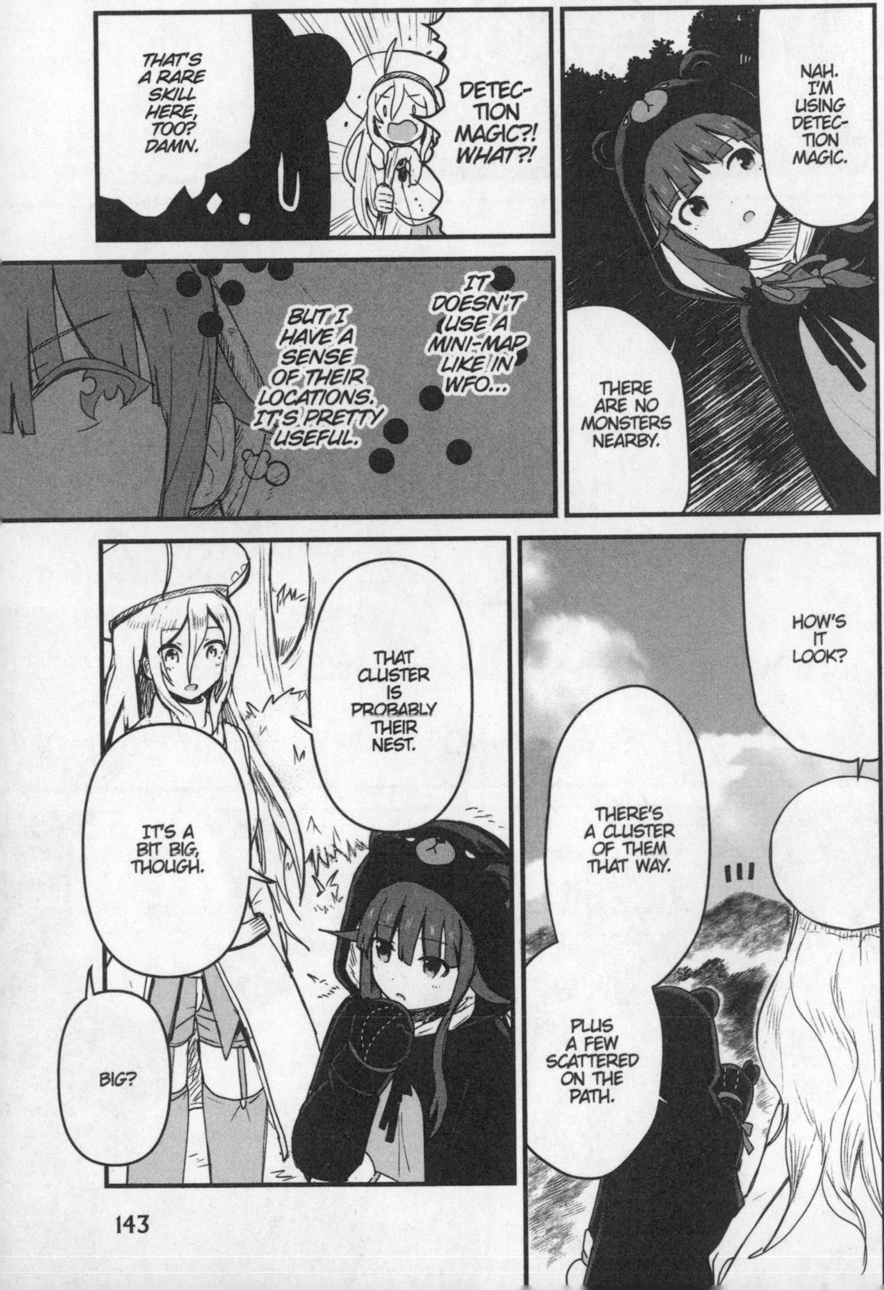
NAH. I'M USING DETECTION MAGIC.
THERE ARE NO MONSTERS NEARBY.
DETECTION MAGIC?! WHAT?!
THAT'S A RARE SKILL HERE, TOO? DAMN.
IT DOESN'T USE A MINI-MAP LIKE IN WFO...
BUT I HAVE A SENSE OF THEIR LOCATIONS. IT'S PRETTY USEFUL.
HOW'S IT LOOK?
THERE'S A CLUSTER OF THEM THAT WAY.
PLUS A FEW SCATTERED ON THE PATH.
THAT CLUSTER IS PROBABLY THEIR NEST.
IT'S A BIT BIG, THOUGH.
BIG?

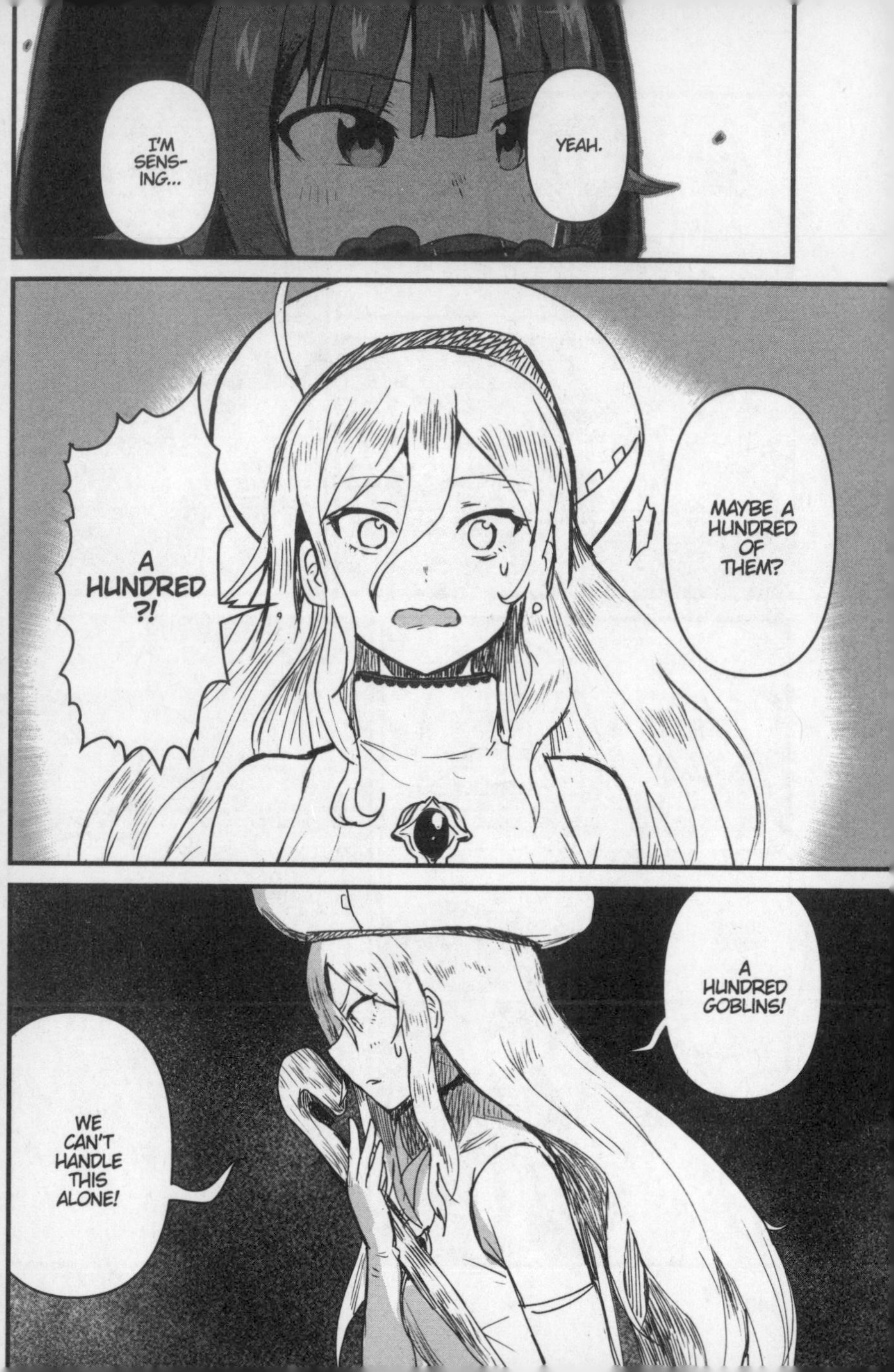
YEAH.
I'M SENSING...
MAYBE A HUNDRED OF THEM?
A HUNDRED?!
A HUNDRED GOBLINS!
WE CAN'T HANDLE THIS ALONE!

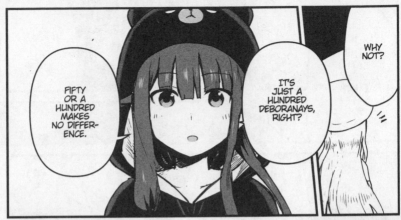

WHY NOT?
IT'S JUST A HUNDRED DEBORANAYS, RIGHT?
FIFTY OR A HUNDRED MAKES NO DIFFER-ENCE.
......
ARE YOU SERIOUS?
I'M SERIOUS.
UGH...

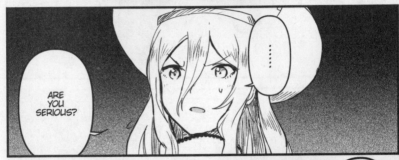

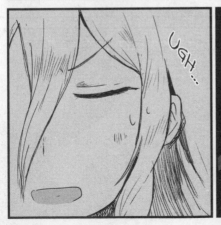

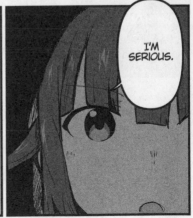

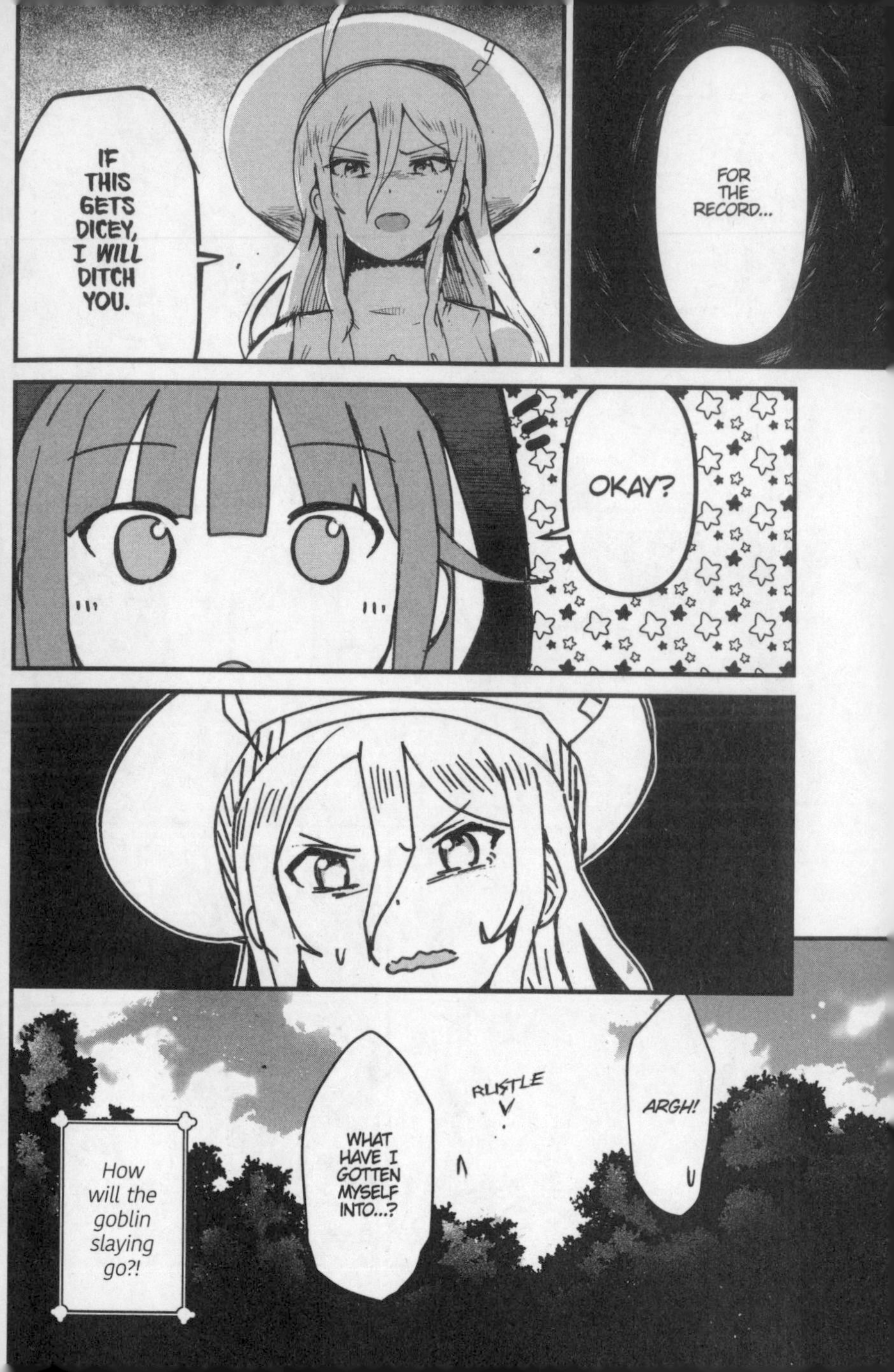
FOR THE RECORD...
IF THIS GETS DICEY, I WILL DITCH YOU.
OKAY?
ARGH!
RUSTLE
WHAT HAVE I GOTTEN MYSELF INTO...?
How will the goblin slaying go?!

Chapter 10

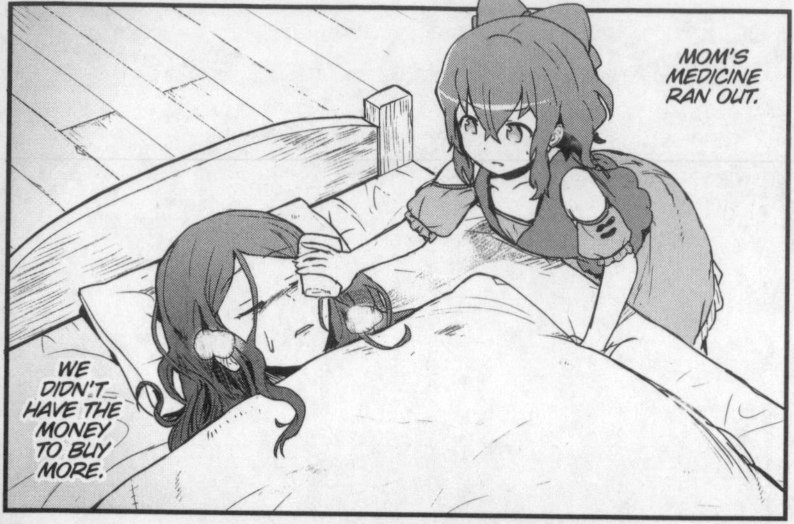
MOM'S MEDICINE RAN OUT.
WE DIDN'T HAVE THE MONEY TO BUY MORE.

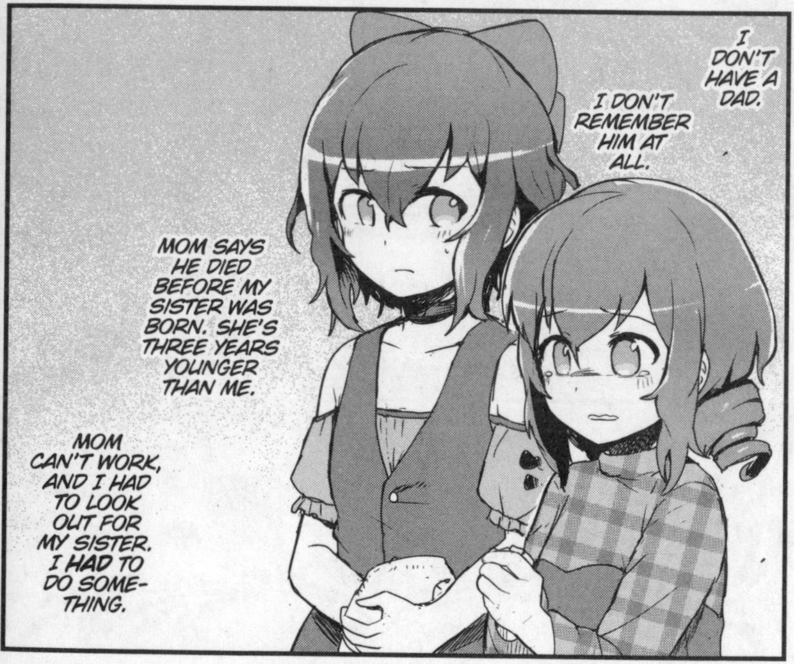
I DON'T HAVE A DAD.
I DON'T REMEMBER HIM AT ALL.
MOM SAYS HE DIED BEFORE MY SISTER WAS BORN. SHE'S THREE YEARS YOUNGER THAN ME.
MOM CAN'T WORK, AND I HAD TO LOOK OUT FOR MY SISTER. I HAD TO DO SOME-THING.

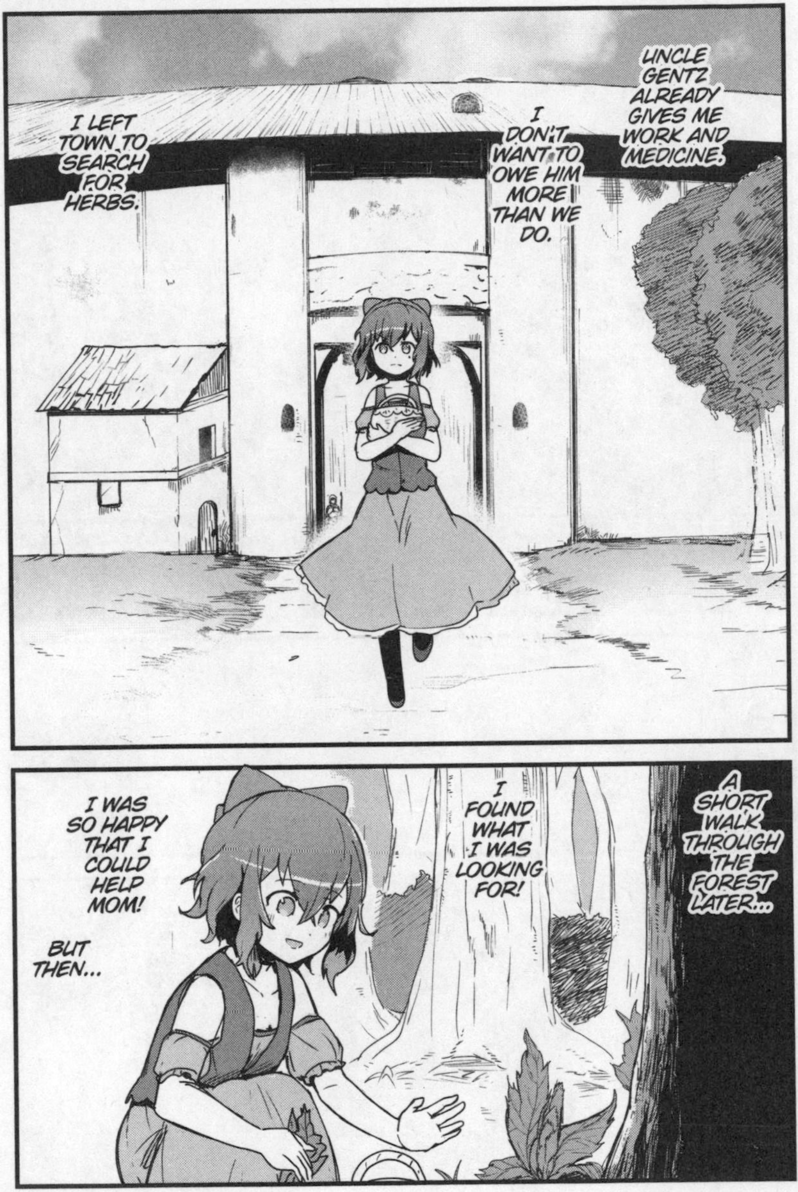
UNCLE GENTZ ALREADY GIVES ME WORK AND MEDICINE.
I DON'T WANT TO OWE HIM MORE THAN WE DO.
I LEFT TOWN TO SEARCH FOR HERBS.
A SHORT WALK THROUGH THE FOREST LATER...
I FOUND WHAT I WAS LOOKING FOR!
I WAS SO HAPPY THAT I COULD HELP MOM!
BUT THEN...

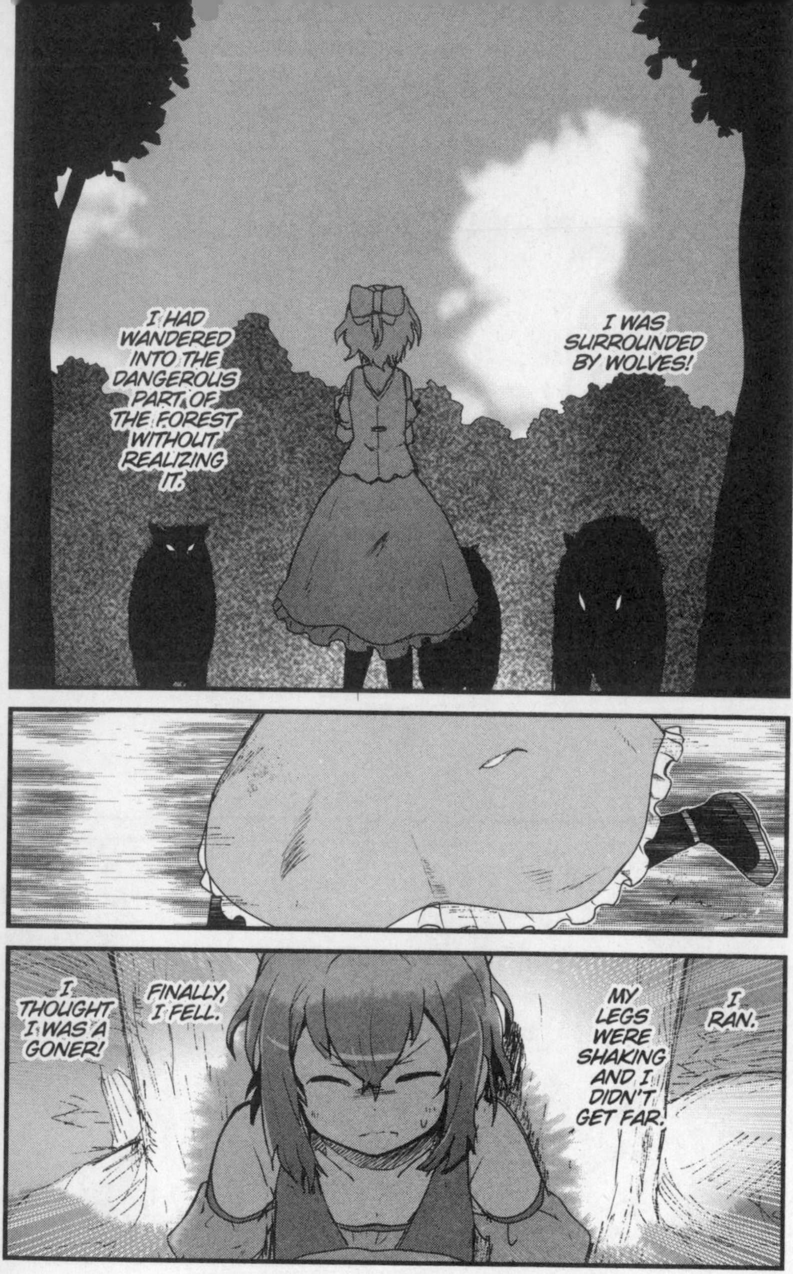
I WAS SURROUNDED BY WOLVES!
I HAD WANDERED INTO THE DANGEROUS PART OF THE FOREST WITHOUT REALIZING IT.
I RAN.
MY LEGS WERE SHAKING AND I DIDN'T GET FAR.
FINALLY, I FELL.
I THOUGHT I WAS A GONER!

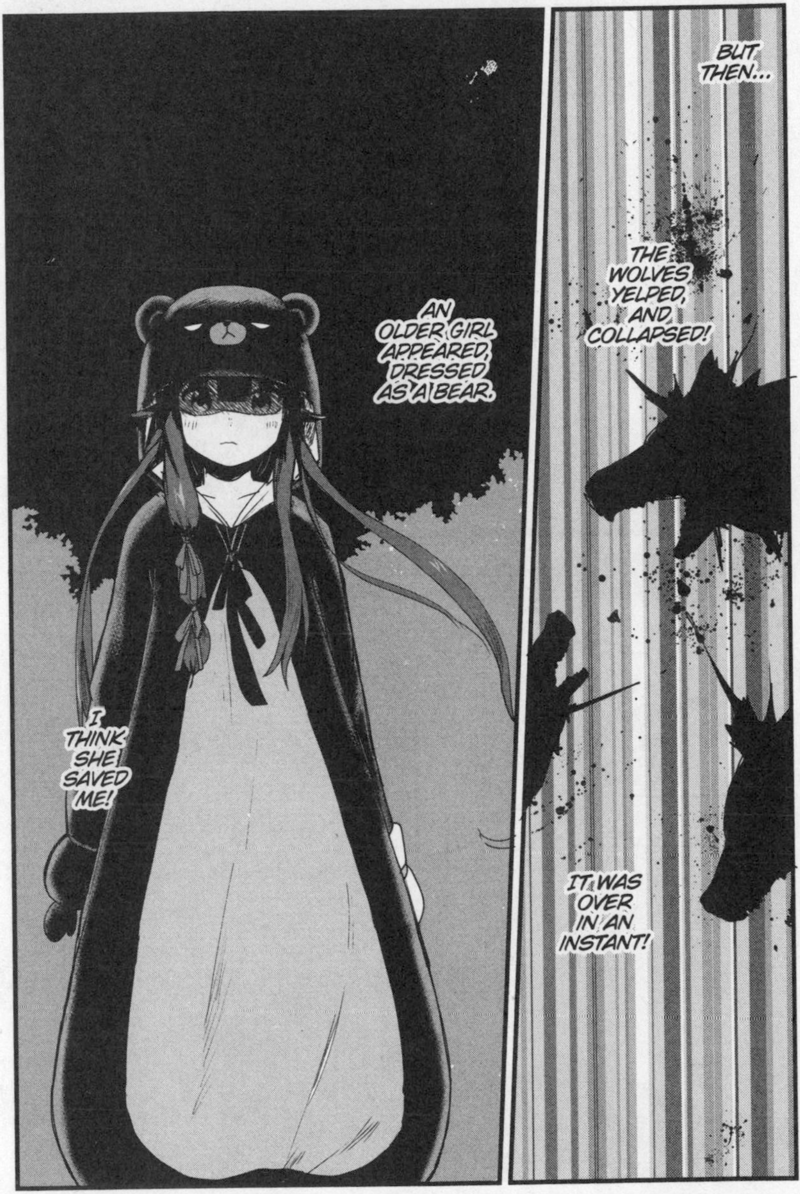
BUT THEN...
THE WOLVES YELPED, AND COLLAPSED!
IT WAS OVER IN AN INSTANT!
AN OLDER GIRL APPEARED, DRESSED AS A BEAR.
I THINK SHE SAVED ME!

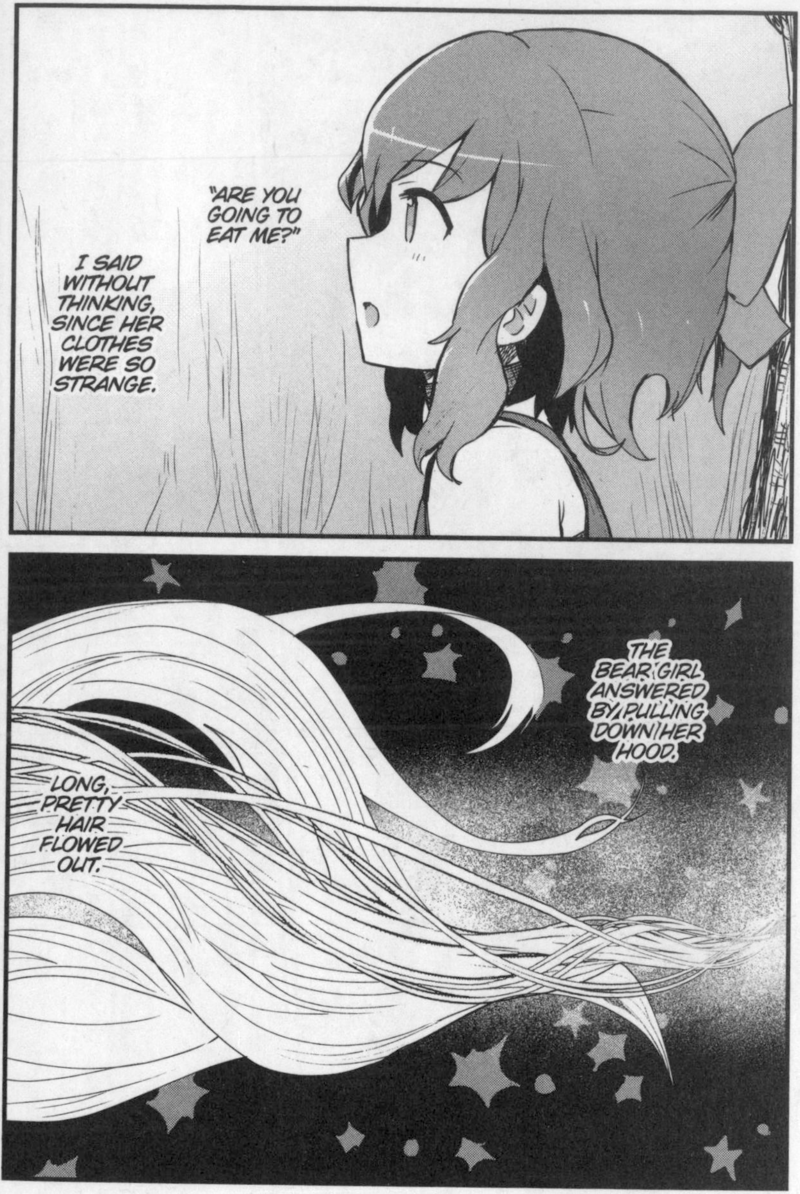
"ARE YOU GOING TO EAT ME?"
I SAID WITHOUT THINKING, SINCE HER CLOTHES WERE SO STRANGE.
THE BEAR GIRL ANSWERED BY PULLING DOWN HER HOOD.
LONG, PRETTY HAIR FLOWED OUT.

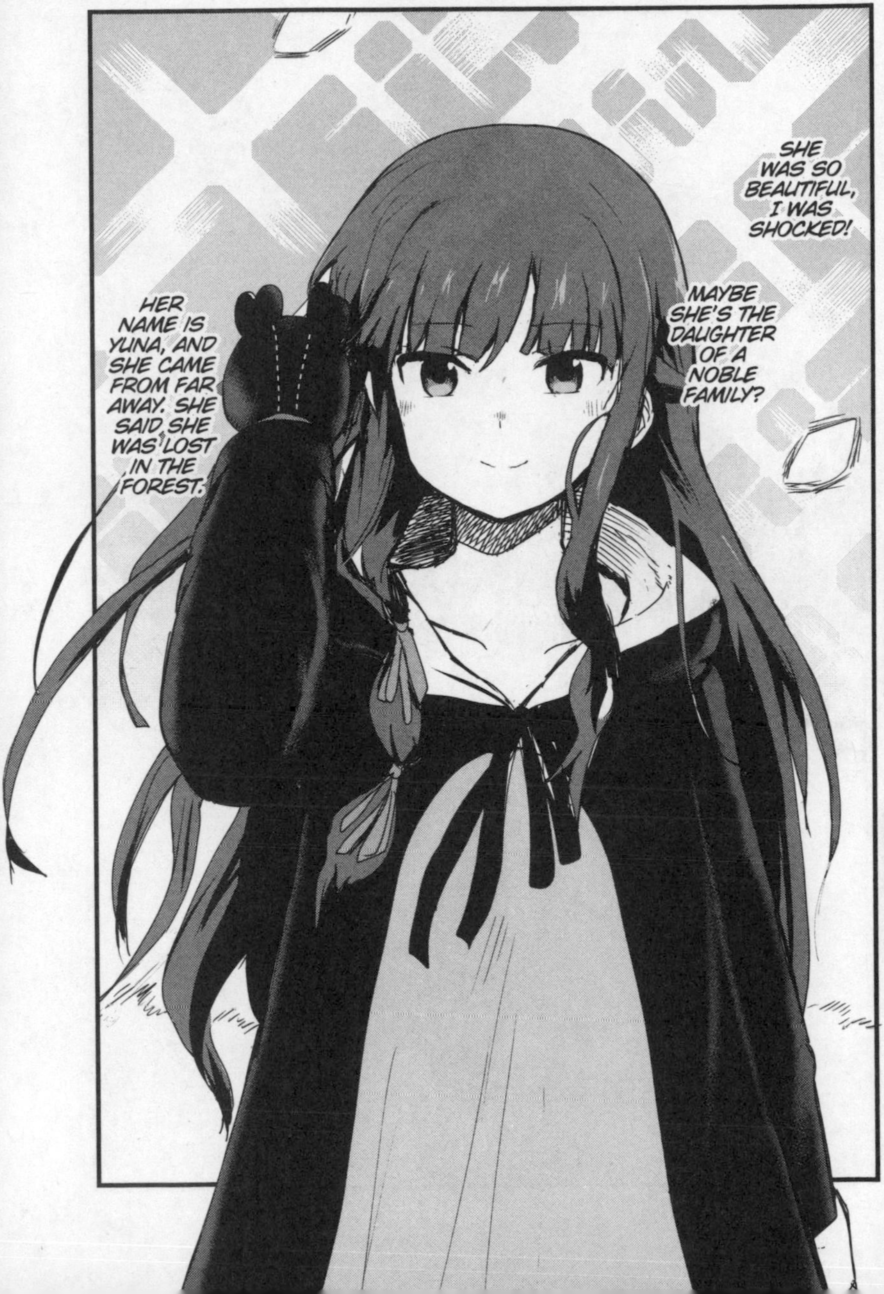
SHE WAS SO BEAUTIFUL, I WAS SHOCKED!
MAYBE SHE'S THE DAUGHTER OF A NOBLE FAMILY?
HER NAME IS YUNA, AND SHE CAME FROM FAR AWAY. SHE SAID SHE WAS LOST IN THE FOREST.

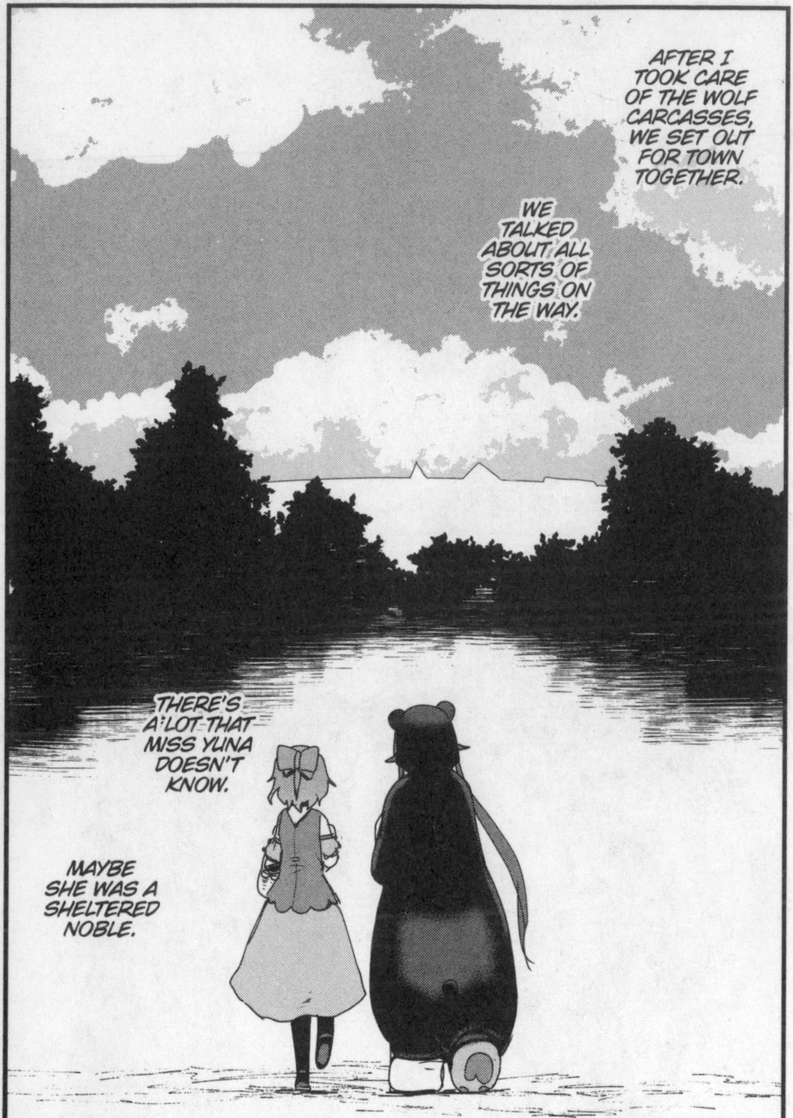
AFTER I TOOK CARE OF THE WOLF CARCASSES, WE SET OUT FOR TOWN TOGETHER.
WE TALKED ABOUT ALL SORTS OF THINGS ON THE WAY.
THERE'S A LOT THAT MISS YUNA DOESN'T KNOW.
MAYBE SHE WAS A SHELTERED NOBLE.

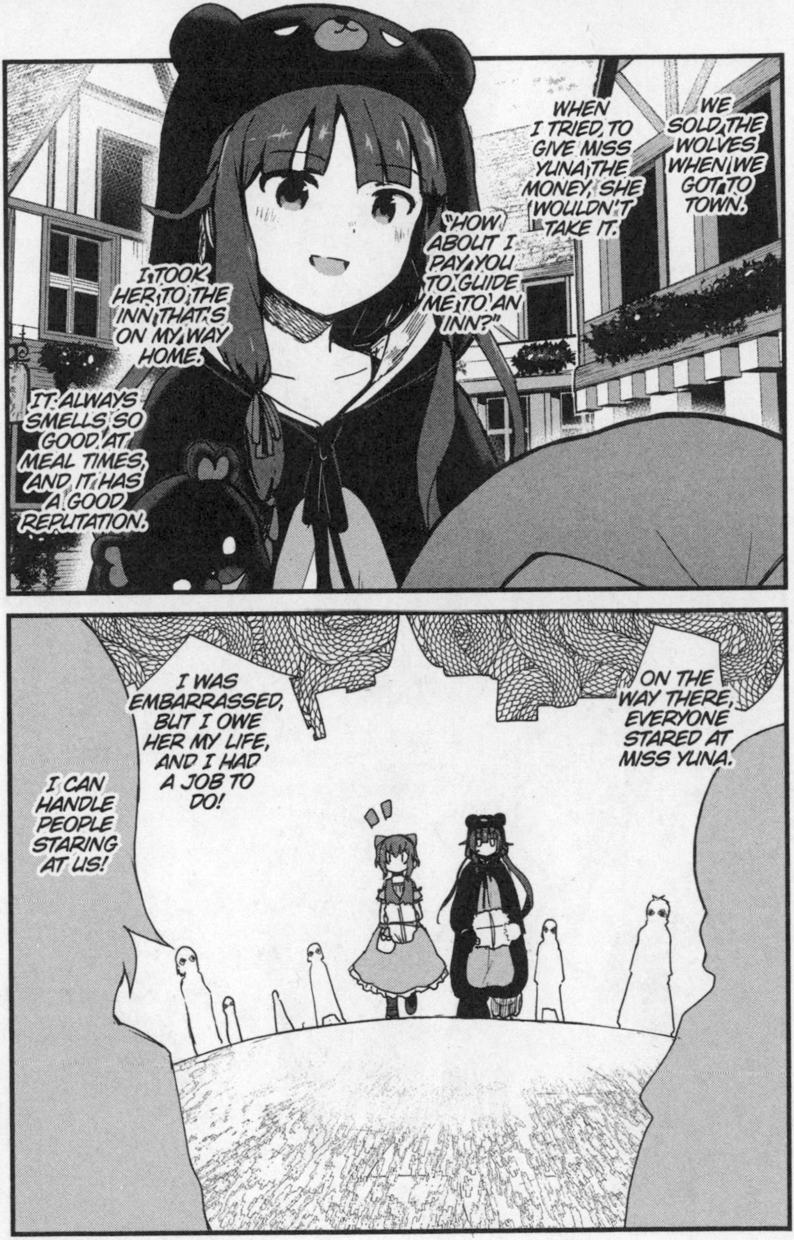
WE SOLD THE WOLVES WHEN WE GOT TO TOWN.
WHEN I TRIED TO GIVE MISS YUNA THE MONEY, SHE WOULDN'T TAKE IT.
"HOW ABOUT I PAY YOU TO GUIDE ME TO AN INN?"
I TOOK HER TO THE INN THAT'S ON MY WAY HOME.
IT ALWAYS SMELLS SO GOOD AT MEAL TIMES, AND IT HAS A GOOD REPUTATION.
ON THE WAY THERE, EVERYONE STARED AT MISS YUNA.
I WAS EMBARRASSED, BUT I OWE HER MY LIFE, AND I HAD A JOB TO DO!
I CAN HANDLE PEOPLE STARING AT US!

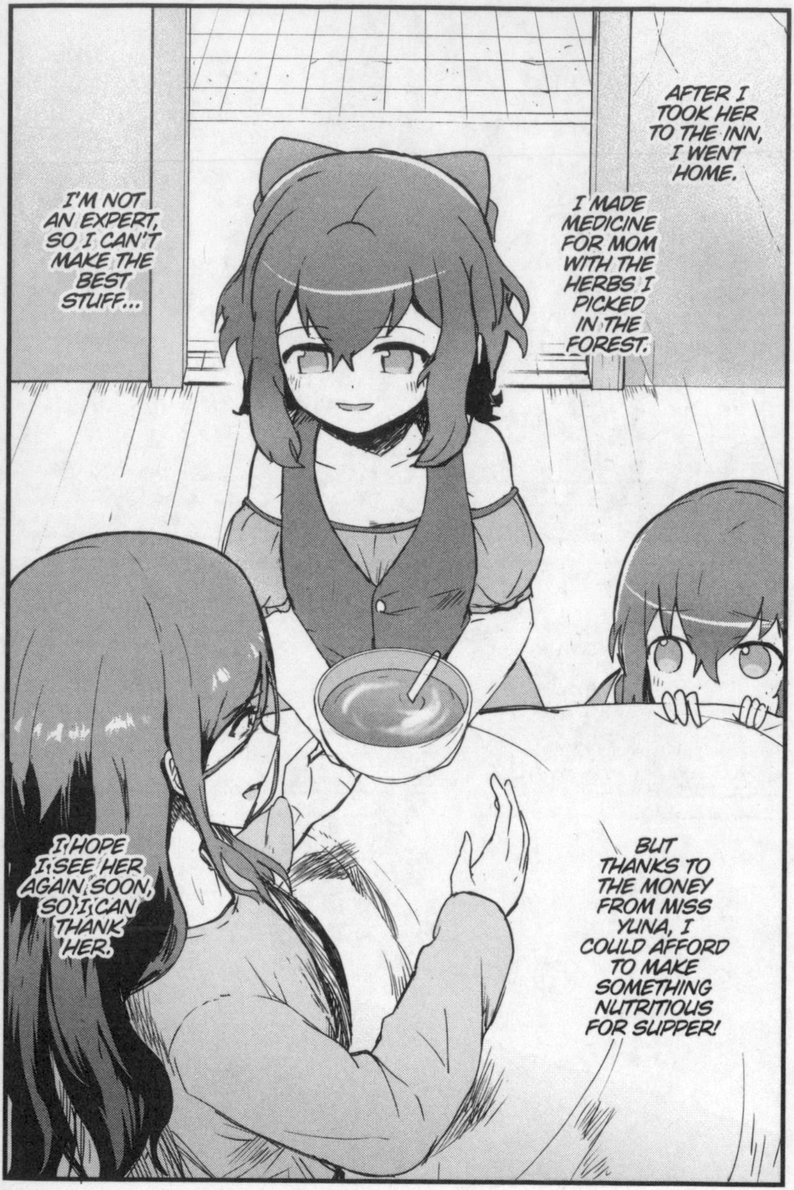
AFTER I TOOK HER TO THE INN, I WENT HOME.
I MADE MEDICINE FOR MOM WITH THE HERBS I PICKED IN THE FOREST.
I'M NOT AN EXPERT, SO I CAN'T MAKE THE BEST STUFF...
BUT THANKS TO THE MONEY FROM MISS YUNA, I COULD AFFORD TO MAKE SOMETHING NUTRITIOUS FOR SUPPER!
I HOPE I SEE HER AGAIN SOON, SO I CAN THANK HER.

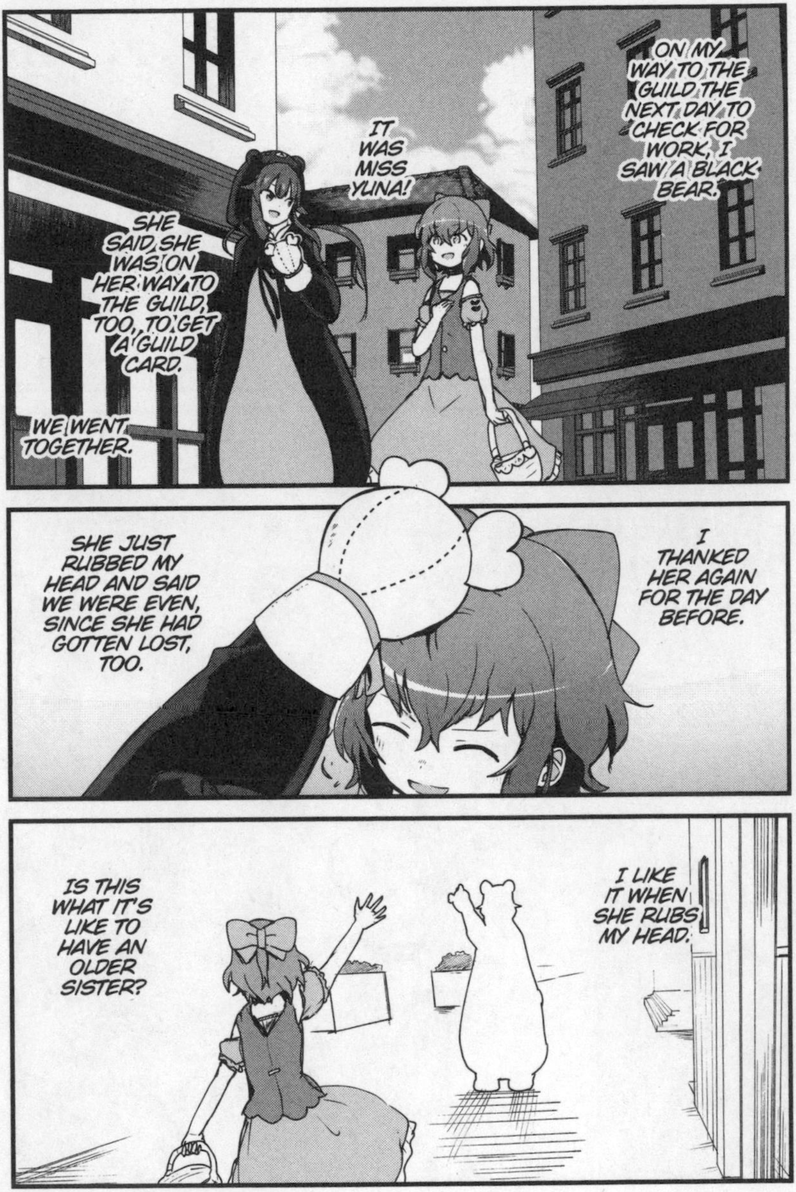
ON MY WAY TO THE GUILD THE NEXT DAY TO CHECK FOR WORK, I SAW A BLACK BEAR.
IT WAS MISS YUNA!
SHE SAID SHE WAS ON HER WAY TO THE GUILD, TOO, TO GET A GUILD CARD.
WE WENT TOGETHER.
I THANKED HER AGAIN FOR THE DAY BEFORE.
SHE JUST RUBBED MY HEAD AND SAID WE WERE EVEN, SINCE SHE HAD GOTTEN LOST, TOO.
I LIKE IT WHEN SHE RUBS MY HEAD.
IS THIS WHAT IT'S LIKE TO HAVE AN OLDER SISTER?

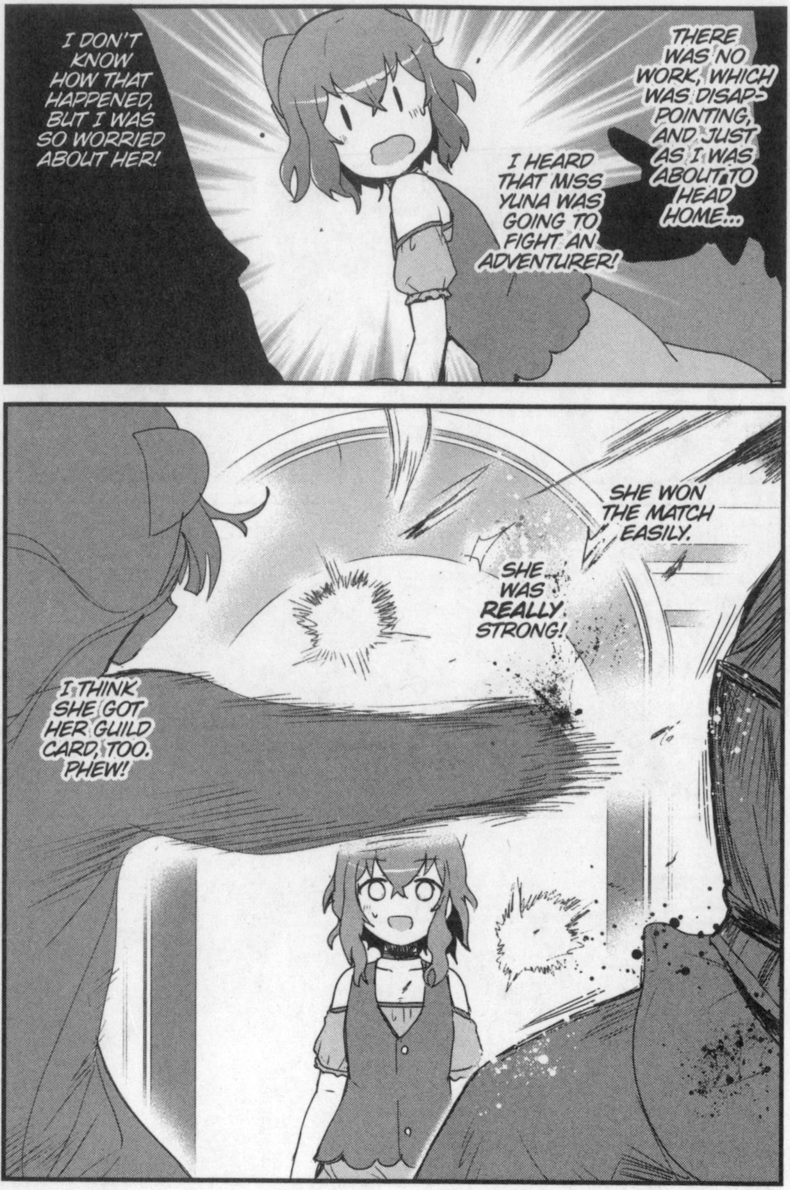
THERE WAS NO WORK, WHICH WAS DISAPPOINTING, AND JUST AS I WAS ABOUT TO HEAD HOME...
I HEARD THAT MISS YUNA WAS GOING TO FIGHT AN ADVENTURER!
I DON'T KNOW HOW THAT HAPPENED, BUT I WAS SO WORRIED ABOUT HER!
SHE WON THE MATCH EASILY.
SHE WAS REALLY STRONG!
I THINK SHE GOT HER GUILD CARD, TOO. PHEW!

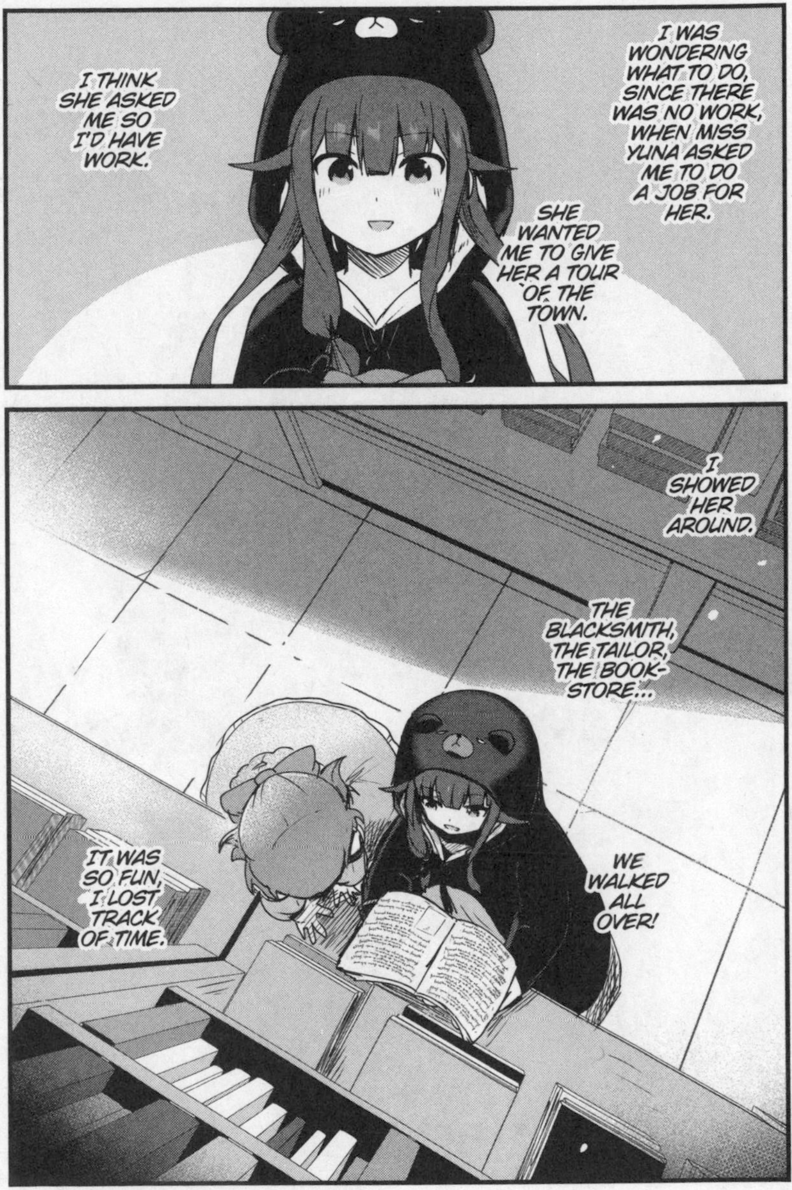
I WAS WONDERING WHAT TO DO, SINCE THERE WAS NO WORK, WHEN MISS YUNA ASKED ME TO DO A JOB FOR HER.
SHE WANTED ME TO GIVE HER A TOUR OF THE TOWN.
I THINK SHE ASKED ME SO I'D HAVE WORK.
I SHOWED HER AROUND.
THE BLACKSMITH, THE TAILOR, THE BOOK-STORE...
WE WALKED ALL OVER!
IT WAS SO FUN, I LOST TRACK OF TIME.

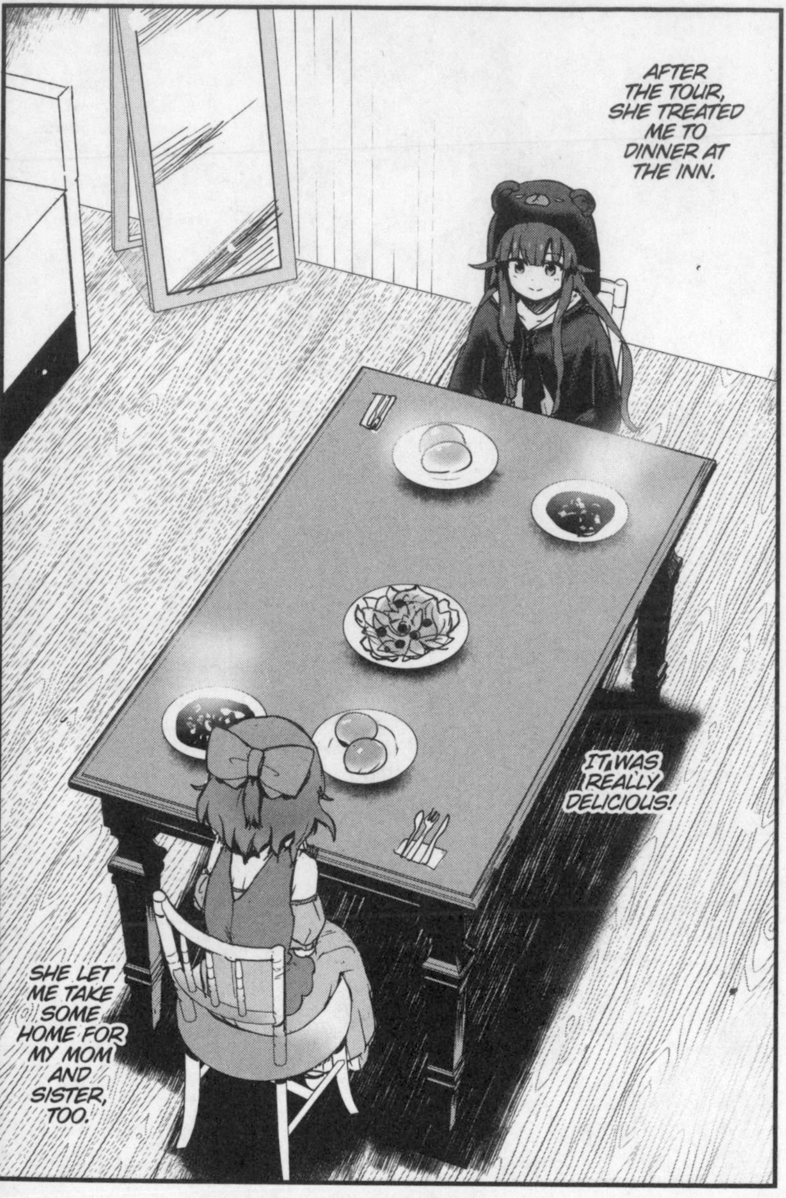
AFTER THE TOUR, SHE TREATED ME TO DINNER AT THE INN.
IT WAS REALLY DELICIOUS!
SHE LET ME TAKE SOME HOME FOR MY MOM AND SISTER, TOO.

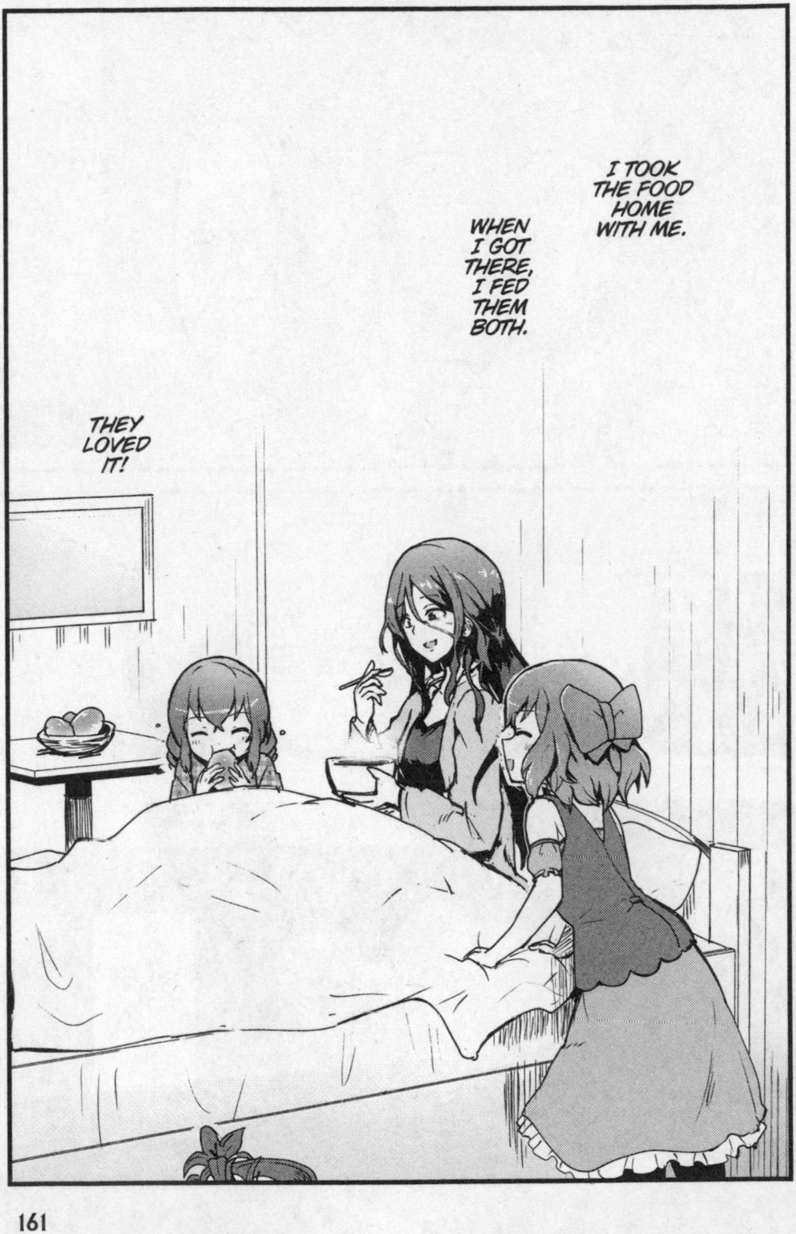
I TOOK THE FOOD HOME WITH ME.
WHEN I GOT THERE, I FED THEM BOTH.
THEY LOVED IT!

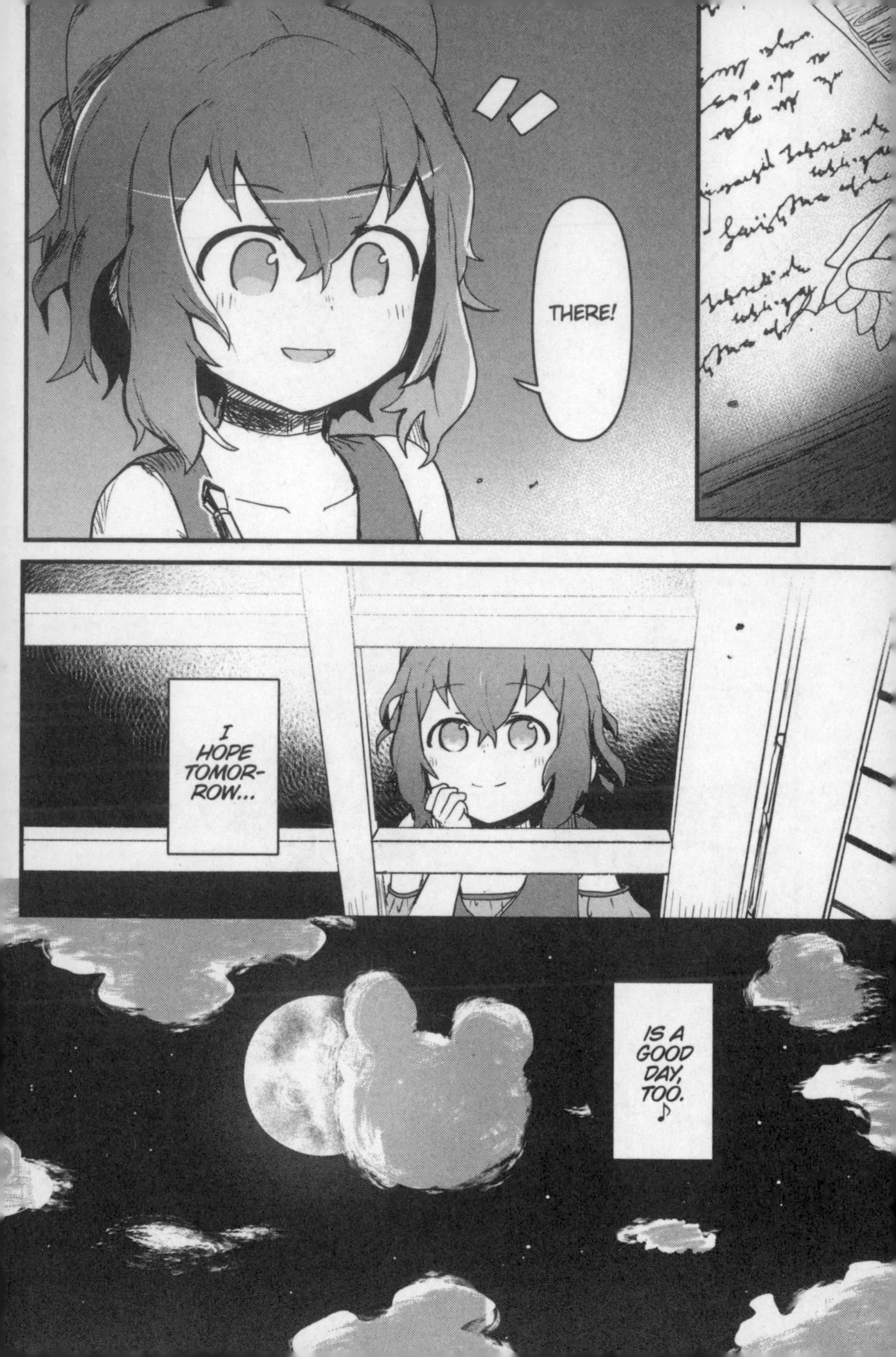
THERE!
I HOPE TOMORROW...
IS A GOOD DAY, TOO. ♪

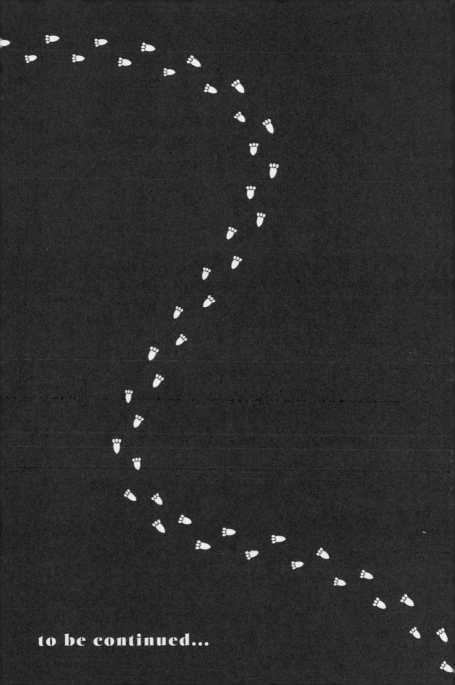

to be continued...

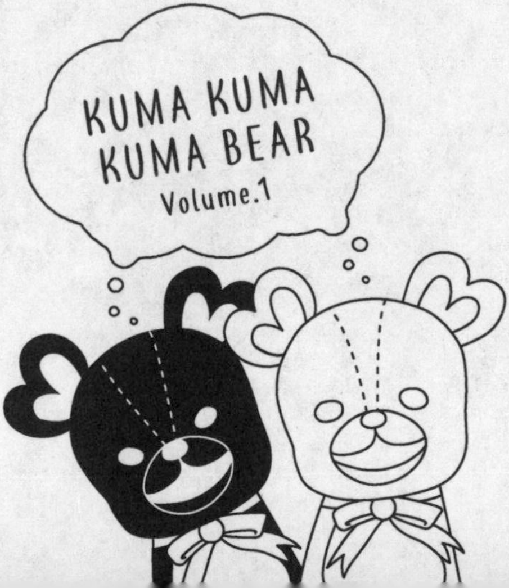
KUMA KUMA
KUMA BEAR
Volume.1

Yuna's Story

Written by Kumanano

I play games all day long. I don't even go to school.

School is a boring waste of time. I have more fun playing games or reading manga and novels. Studying? I can do that at home. Money? I already earn enough to support myself. Thinking that way, it felt pointless to go to school. Once I started middle school, I stopped going at all.

My parents got on my case for it, at first. They said it made them look bad. Then I gave them money, so they shut up. Now, they're traveling overseas on my dime.

For the first time in a while, I'm going to visit my Grandpa. He has a big house with a huge garden in the Tokyo Metropolitan area.

"I heard you're not going to school, Yuna," Grandpa nags as soon as he sees me.

Did my parents tell him? No...they wouldn't bother. He must have looked into it himself.

"It's a pain."

"A pain?"

"Yep."

Grandpa sighs.

We've had this conversation countless times. I guess he still hasn't given up, even after my parents did. Sometimes you gotta know when to quit.

"You have to go to school, even if it's a pain."

"I can study at home." I like to think I'm smart for my age.

"School isn't just for studying. It's for making friends, too."

"Don't need 'em."

"Building friendships is important!"

"Don't need 'em."

"When you're an adult, the friends you've had in your youth become priceless assets."

"Don't need 'em."

He sighs again.

I don't hate my Grandpa, but he always lectures me. I'd rather not visit him if I can help it, but I have a favor to ask him this time.

"What brings you out here today, out of the blue?"

"Grandpa, I want to move out."

"You want to live with me?"

I shake my head. "I can live on my own."

"Yuna, you're still a child."

"Grandpa, I'm fifteen. Maybe I'm not an adult yet, but I'm not a little kid. I make my own money, and take care of myself." I'm more independent than my parents. I've been cooking, doing laundry, and taking care of myself ever since I was small. "I can pay my own rent, but I need an adult to co-sign."

I don't want to live with my parents anymore. Grandpa's place would be better, but he nags so much I don't want to live with him.

"I'm not worried about the rent. I know that you make a living. I can't say that I like it, though."

"Stocks are a real job." Lots of people make a living as day traders. I'm one of them. I've already made billions of yen, enough to live well for the rest of my life. But if I keep living with my parents, they'll take my money down the drain with them. There's nothing to gain by living with those people. "Grandpa, *please*," I beg, making puppy-dog eyes. His weakness.

Grandpa hesitates, but gives in. "All right, fine. Do you know where you want to live?"

"I want an apartment building with tight security." Insurance, in case my parents find me. "Other than that, I'm happy as long as I have a bedroom, a library, and a gaming room."

"You really love your books and games."

"Books let me escape reality, and in games, you can get stronger with a little effort. Give it time, and you can stand up for yourself when people mess with you." I make sure that anyone who picks a fight wishes they'd never crossed me.

If you game all day long, some people will mock you for it. They call you a NEET, or a waste of space. I've been accused of wasting my parents' money, even though I pay for everything in-game with money I earned myself. I think they're jealous of how I have money *and* freedom. With time and some financial investment, my character got stronger. Some might say I'm one of the top players. I did it all with time and my money I earned for myself.

Grandpa is stunned by my answer.

"I'd like to keep my address a secret from Mom and Dad."

"You're leaving without saying anything to them?"

"Talking to them would defeat the point. They're adults. They shouldn't need to rely on their kid, right?"

"Where *are* your parents, anyway?"

"Overseas. I gave them money to take a trip."

Grandpa sighs yet again.

I sent them off with a hundred million yen, which I think is fair compensation. I'd like to move out while they're gone.

"How did those two fools have a child as clever as you?" Grandpa places a hand on my head.

Grandpa is the president of a big company. His third son is my father, the disappointment. My mother is a gold digger who married him for money.

I'm nothing like my parents.

"I got it from you, Grandpa."

There's a pleased look on Grandpa's face. I'm not buttering him up—I really do think I take after him the most. In his lifetime, he turned his company into one of the best in the field. I respect him, which is why I can turn to him for things like this.

"Why don't you come work for me, Yuna?"

"Nah. Too much trouble."

"If only you hadn't gotten *that* trait from your parents..."

My talent with the stock market, among other things, comes from my Grandpa, but I think I got my laziness and penchant for self-indulgence from my parents. I have no desire to change that about myself. Maybe it's genetic? If so, maybe I do take after my parents, after all.

"I think that I could leave my business to you, one day."

"Sounds like a lot of work. Plus, wouldn't my uncles be mad at you for that? I don't want it enough to fight them for it."

Grandpa's eldest son, my uncle, is supposed to carry on the business. He wants his own son to take after him, too. I can already see the chaos that would ensue if I made a play for it. I don't want to deal with that crap. Most of all, managing a business would be a lot of work. Playing games is more fun.

"Would you take on a supporting role for your uncles?"

"They'd never listen to *me*...but I could run a video game department! I'd get them to make games I want to play."

"Video games, huh? You really do love those."

"They help me forget the unfortunate things about reality."

"You should make some connections, Yuna."

"I know. I could probably get along with people who aren't interested in my power or money. If I find someone like that, I'll talk to them." People flock to places with money and power like moths to flame.

"It's too bad you weren't born to my eldest son, Yuna."

"If you say that, I'll start feeling bad for my cousin. Besides, he's more social than me. Much better for running a business."

Grandpa doesn't say anything to that.

My cousin has been working hard to live up to my uncle. He doesn't need me getting in the way of it. I've never been to any of the company parties, and I never wanted to, either. Even before that, no one wanted the daughter of those deadbeat parents working at Grandpa's company.

My relatives hate my parents because they're money-grubbers. They hate me, too, because I'm related to them. They think the apple doesn't fall far from the tree. If they knew I came to Grandpa today, they'd think it was to ask for money. I'm antisocial by nature, so I've never given them a reason to believe otherwise. I have no relationship with my other relatives, and only a few people know about what I've made on the stock market.

"All right. I'll talk to some realtors. You can pick out whichever property you like."

"Thanks, Grandpa."

Grandpa brought me a list of apartments the next day.

"These are all close to your place," I pointed out. All of the buildings were in the same neighborhood as Grandpa.

"I won't tell your parents as long as you stay where I can keep an eye on you. That's my only condition."

If I stay home all the time, odds are I won't run into anyone. I accept Grandpa's condition and pick a building with tight security. It's big for just one person, but it'll do.

Grandpa takes care of the lease paperwork for me, and I finish moving before my parents return from their travels.

"All right! Time for games."

I turn my computer on.

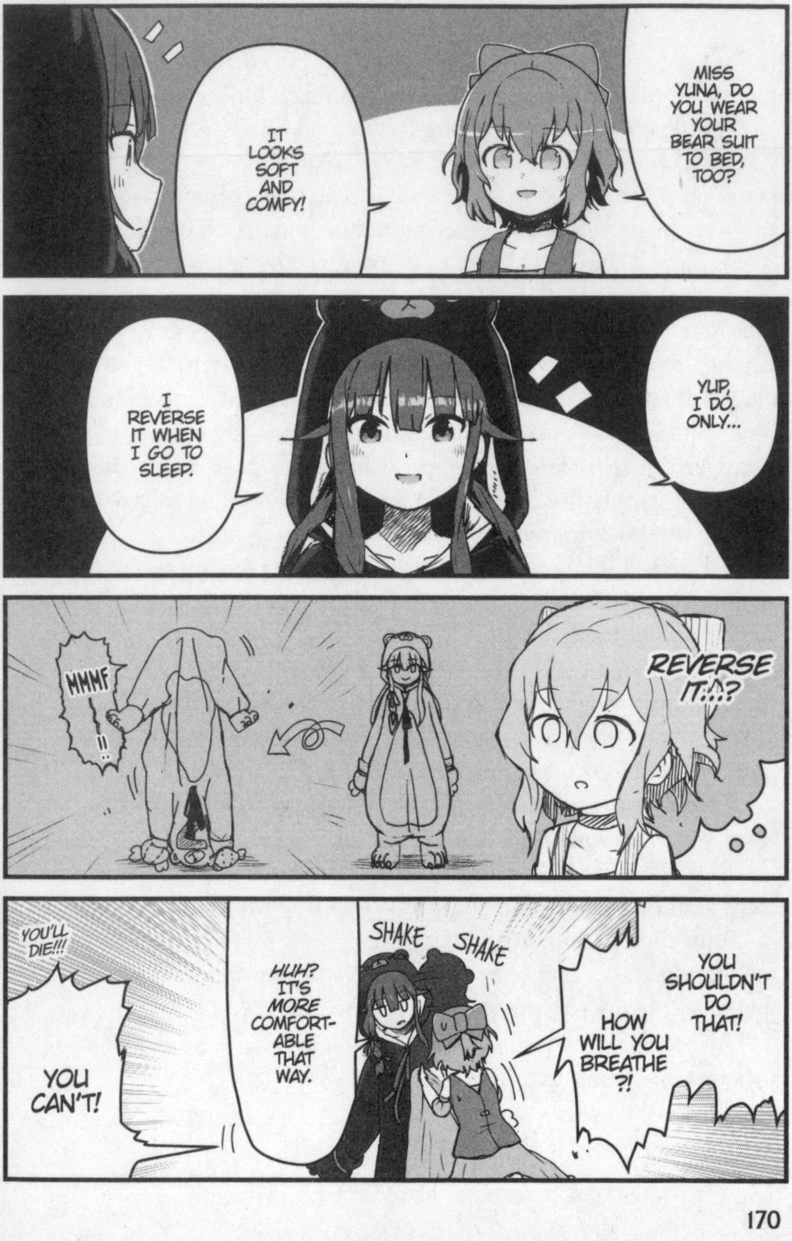
MISS YUNA, DO YOU WEAR YOUR BEAR SUIT TO BED, TOO?
IT LOOKS SOFT AND COMFY!
YUP, I DO. ONLY...
I REVERSE IT WHEN I GO TO SLEEP.
REVERSE IT...?
MMMF !!
YOU SHOULDN'T DO THAT!
HOW WILL YOU BREATHE?!
SHAKE
SHAKE
HUH? IT'S MORE COMFORT-ABLE THAT WAY.
YOU'LL DIE!!!
YOU CAN'T!

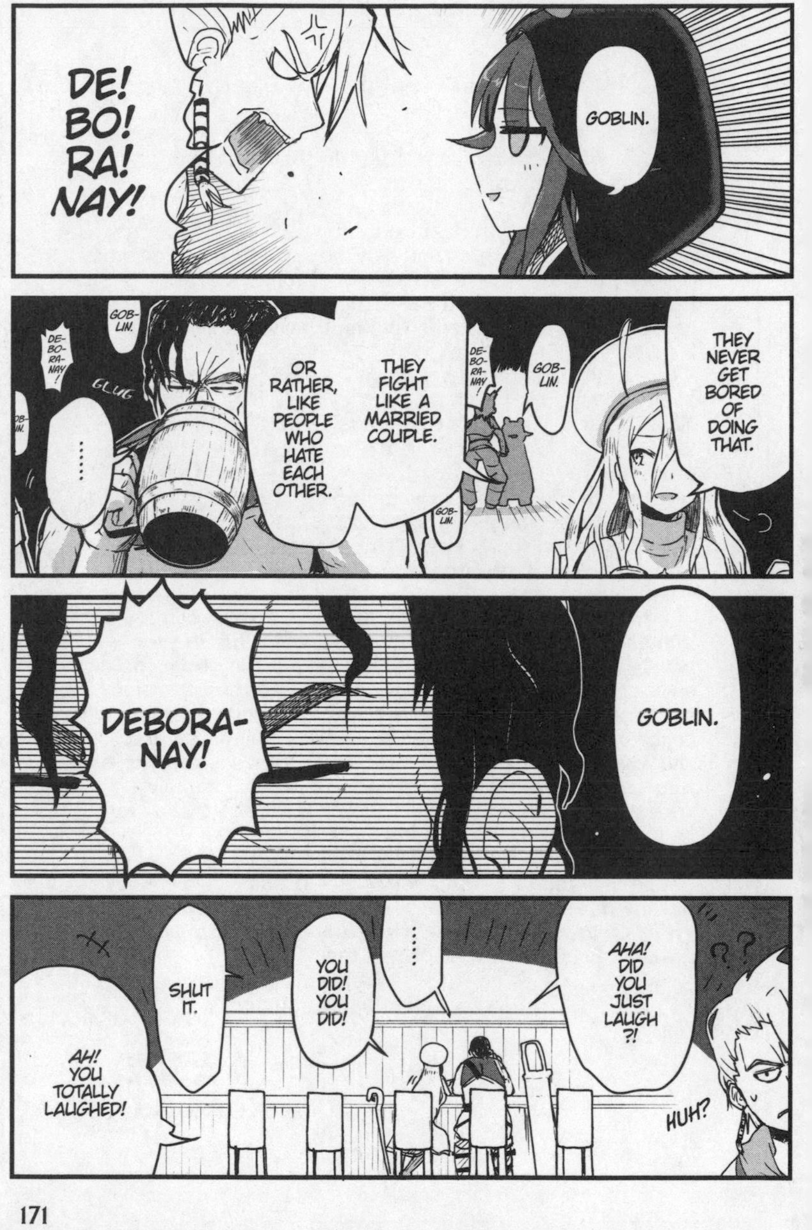
GOBLIN.
DE! BO! RA! NAY!
THEY NEVER GET BORED OF DOING THAT.
GOB-LIN.
DE-BO-RA-NAY!
GOB-LIN.
THEY FIGHT LIKE A MARRIED COUPLE.
OR RATHER, LIKE PEOPLE WHO HATE EACH OTHER.
......
GOB-LIN.
DE-BO-RA-NAY!
GLUG
GOBLIN.
DEBORA-NAY!
HUH?
AHA! DID YOU JUST LAUGH?!
......
YOU DID! YOU DID!
SHUT IT.
AH! YOU TOTALLY LAUGHED!

Nice to meet you! I'm Kumanano!

Thank you so much for picking up the *Kuma Kuma Kuma Bear* manga.

I heard about the manga adaptation when I visited my publisher to autograph copies of the seventh novel. It had come up before that the series would make a great manga, but it seemed like a difficult project, so nothing came of it. So I was thrilled when I heard the news!

Adapting the story to a manga, though, is a lot of work! I have to account for characters' clothing, facial expressions, body types, the fantasy world's architecture, and knickknacks. Everything that's accounted for vaguely in prose has to be defined by the art. Every time I see the results, I'm touched by how incredible it is! I love seeing Yuna and her friends' expressions. Thank you very much to Sergei-sensei for drawing this manga! Please keep taking good care of Yuna and the others.

I wrote about Yuna's past for the first time in this manga. We barely touch on her real-world life in the novels. All we know is that she makes money from the stock market, and her parents are terrible people. As a matter of fact, I hadn't put much thought into Yuna's backstory when I started writing. All I knew was that she was going to another world, so I didn't want her to be someone who would want to go back. What I came up with was a talented recluse. She's a strong girl who can be independent and look after herself.

Yuna is going to make a lot of new friends as she enjoys her life in another world. Please follow her adventures! We're up to ten volumes of the *Kuma Kuma Kuma Bear* novels--I hope you'll read those, too!

Thanks for your ongoing support!

くまなの
Kumanano

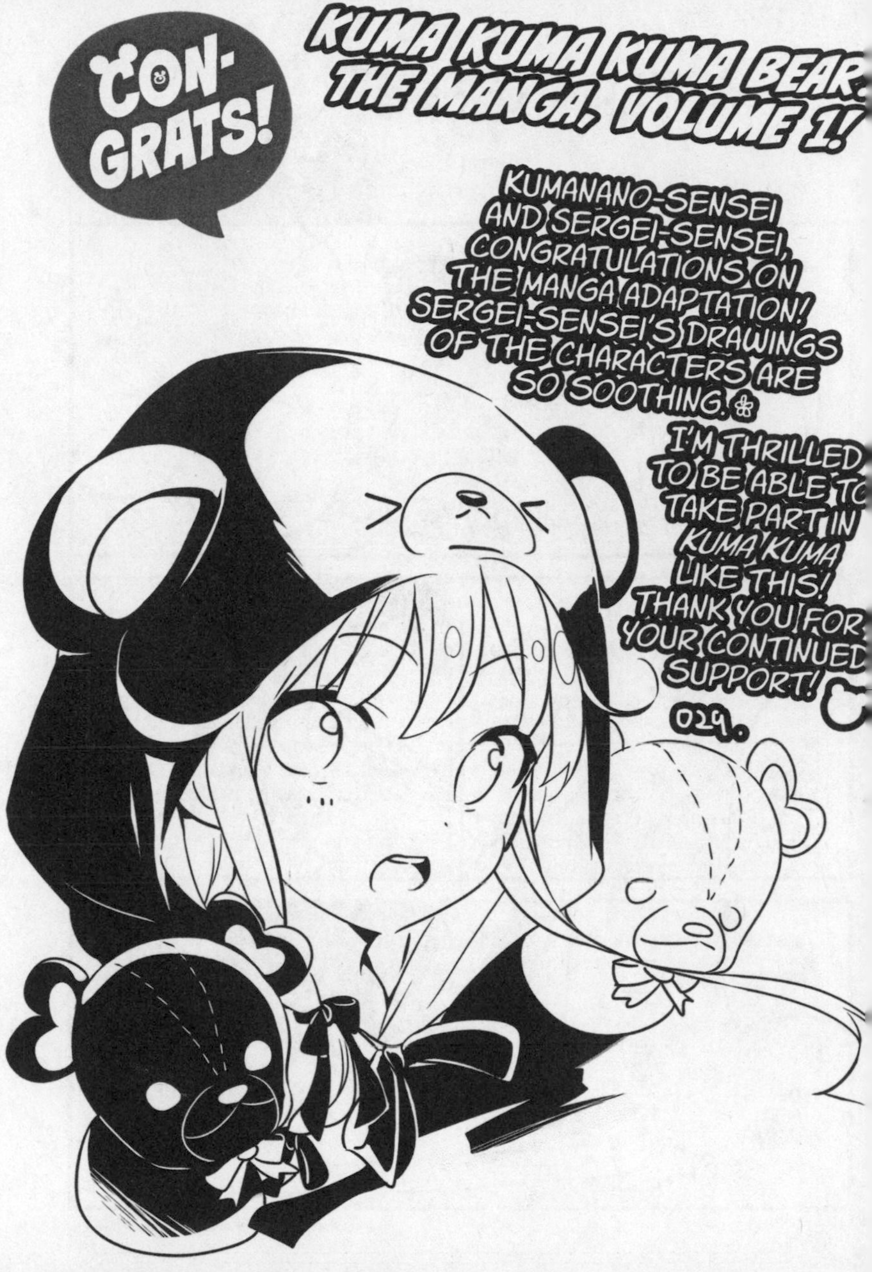
CON-GRATS!
KUMA KUMA KUMA BEAR: THE MANGA, VOLUME 1!
KUMANANO-SENSEI AND SERGEI-SENSEI, CONGRATULATIONS ON THE MANGA ADAPTATION! SERGEI-SENSEI'S DRAWINGS OF THE CHARACTERS ARE SO SOOTHING.
I'M THRILLED TO BE ABLE TO TAKE PART IN KUMA KUMA LIKE THIS! THANK YOU FOR YOUR CONTINUED SUPPORT!
029.

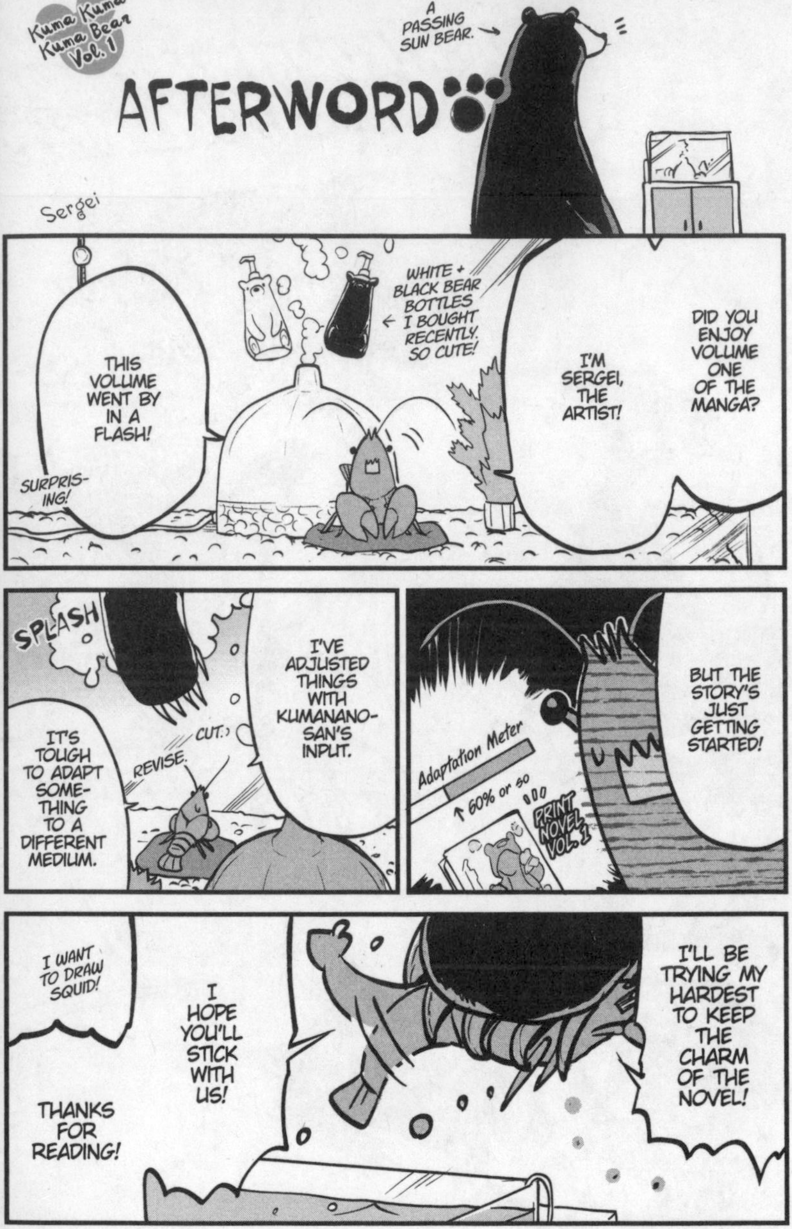
Kuma Kuma Kuma Bear Vol. 1
AFTERWORD
A PASSING SUN BEAR.
Sergei
DID YOU ENJOY VOLUME ONE OF THE MANGA?
I'M SERGEI, THE ARTIST!
WHITE + BLACK BEAR BOTTLES I BOUGHT RECENTLY. SO CUTE!
THIS VOLUME WENT BY IN A FLASH!
SURPRISING!
BUT THE STORY'S JUST GETTING STARTED!
Adaptation Meter
60% or so
PRINT NOVEL VOL. 1
SPLASH
I'VE ADJUSTED THINGS WITH KUMANANO-SAN'S INPUT.
CUT.
REVISE.
IT'S TOUGH TO ADAPT SOMETHING TO A DIFFERENT MEDIUM.
I'LL BE TRYING MY HARDEST TO KEEP THE CHARM OF THE NOVEL!
I HOPE YOU'LL STICK WITH US!
I WANT TO DRAW SQUID!
THANKS FOR READING!